J iri, ... for
his .... ord
slipped into a roar as the shaman changed, grew claws
and fangs and black-striped fur.

Jiri clutched her spear, paralyzed.

But we're winning.

Tentacles wrapped the demon, and the great tiger
Oza had become slashed its claws between them, spilling stinking gouts of blood. If Jiri stayed—

The demon threw back its head, and roared a word.

The twisted, evil power of it broke the air. It tore
through Jiri's body like poisoned hooks, filled her
lungs like filthy water. The world shuddered around
her, dimmed, and Jiri felt herself being ripped away,
sent into darkness.

No.

She held on with all that she could, straining for
light, for heat, for life, and suddenly she was back in
her body, sprawled retching in the mud. Dully, she
could see the demon, laughing as it tore limp tentacles
off its hide. The massive tiger crouched before it, his
gray-shot muzzle bent and dripping blood.

"Oza," Jiri groaned.

The cat raised his head and his eyes met Jiri's, old
and stern. Then he turned and leapt at the monster,
roaring, even as the demon wrapped its claws around
him . . .

The Pathfinder Tales Library

Firesoul

Gary Kloster

paizo

Paizo, Inc., the Paizo golem logo, Pathfinder, the Pathfinder logo, and Pathfinder Society are registered trademarks of Paizo Inc.; Pathfinder Accessories, Pathfinder Adventure Card Game, Pathfinder Adventure Path, Pathfinder Battles, Pathfinder Campaign Setting, Pathfinder Cards, Pathfinder Flip-Mat, Pathfinder Map Pack, Pathfinder Module, Pathfinder Pawns, Pathfinder Player Companion, Pathfinder Roleplaying Game, and Pathfinder Tales are trademarks of Paizo Inc.

Cover art by Bryan Sola.
Cover design by Emily Crowell.
Map by Robert Lazzaretti.

Paizo Inc.
7120 185th Ave NE, Ste 120
Redmond, WA 98052
paizo.com

ISBN 978-1-60125-741-3 (mass market paperback)
ISBN 978-1-60125-742-0 (ebook)

Publisher's Cataloging-In-Publication Data
(Prepared by The Donohue Group, Inc.)

Kloster, Gary.
    Firesoul / Gary Kloster.

    pages ; map ; cm. -- (Pathfinder tales)

    Set in the world of the role-playing game, Pathfinder and Pathfinder Online.
    Issued also as an ebook.
    ISBN: 978-1-60125-741-3 (mass market paperback)

    1. Adoptees--Fiction. 2. Druids and druidism--Fiction. 3. Mercenary troops--Fiction. 4. Jungles--Fiction. 5. Pathfinder (Game)--Fiction. 6. Fantasy fiction. 7. Adventure stories. I. Title. II. Series: Pathfinder tales library.

PS3611.L678 F57 2015
813/.6

First printing February 2015.

Printed in the United States of America.

For Brin, for everything . . .

Chapter One
Beyond the Mango Woman

Jiri crouched motionless beneath the emerald shadows of the undergrowth.

Listening.

A breeze sighed through the high canopy. Birds sang, fruit bats shrieked, and insects droned, but underneath it all came that scrap of noise again. The scuff of feet against the ground, somewhere close.

Jiri slipped the handful of bloodfern that she had gathered into her pouch. She had left Thirty Trees at dawn hunting these curly green shoots, so useful for clotting blood. Traveling a slowly widening spiral, she hadn't come that far from her village.

It's probably someone out hunting.

Probably. But Jiri's hand went from her pouch to the hilt of her knife. Being close to home, close to all that she cared about, meant she should be more cautious, not less. Hidden in brush, she drew her knife and parted her lips, ready to whisper the words that would bring the spirits and their magic to her.

Then she heard a voice.

"Boro, hold up."

Hadzi.

So, her lover had finally rolled out of his hammock to go hunting with his brother. *Or Boro tipped him out.* Letting her knife go, Jiri shook her head and started to straighten, but stopped when she heard Hadzi continue.

"I need to piss."

Maybe I won't pop up and say good morning, Jiri thought as she made sure Hadzi wasn't too close. *Maybe I'll work on my leopard impression instead.* She smiled and drew a deep breath, but held it when Boro spoke.

"It won't work."

"Again with this," Hadzi muttered, finishing his business.

"You overestimate your charms, brother," Boro continued. "Jiri may be swinging a hammock with you, but—"

"Trust me, it's more than that for her."

Really? Jiri let her breath go, listening.

"I've got Jiri like a snake with a monkey. When I tell her tonight how Father has found me a girl in Kibwe, when I tell her how much I love her, but oh no, a shaman can't marry and my family needs this alliance . . . She'll fall apart, and I'll hold her and cry, too. It will be so tragic, she'll never be able to forget me."

The undergrowth that hid her kept Jiri from seeing her lover's face, but in Hadzi's voice she could hear his smile. That stupid, cocky smile that made him so handsome.

"I promise you, Jiri will be slipping off with me less than a year after my marriage. I'll have two women, and—"

"A lot of trouble?"

"No," Hadzi snapped. "Strength. When Thirty Trees chooses a new wara, I'll be husband to the niece of the biggest fruit merchant in Kibwe, *and* the lover of the girl that old Oza claims might be greater than him someday. With those two by my side, *I* will be the new wara."

"Or dead," Boro muttered.

"Right. Better I spend my life worrying like old man Boro, too scared to . . ."

Whatever else Hadzi said was lost in the ruckus of a monkey troop swinging overhead. When the animals had passed, the men were gone.

Jiri rose and wove through the undergrowth until she came to the trail the brothers had been traveling. Hand resting on her belt knife, she stared down the narrow path.

"Like a snake. With a monkey." Jiri took one step down the trail, but a rustle of leaves and a flash of motion stopped her. A monkey dropped from the branches arcing above, landing light on the ground before her.

Jiri frowned at the animal. "How much of that did you hear?"

The monkey cocked its head then blurred, stretching up and out until it was a man. He stood taller than Jiri, and his gray braids were shorter, but like her he wore brown mud cloth patterned with black designs and a necklace. Instead of her bright beads, though,

Oza wore a menagerie of tiny animal fetishes, each carved from bone.

"Enough to know that you shouldn't be talking to Hadzi right now." Oza touched the carved monkey hanging from his necklace, a gesture of thanks. "You're a bit too hot at the moment."

"Hot?" Jiri said, proud of the levelness of her voice, the easy way she held herself.

Oza didn't say anything. He just looked down at Jiri's hand.

Jiri followed her teacher's gaze and saw the smoke slipping out between her fingers. She let go of her belt knife and stared at the black marks she had branded into the blade's leather grip.

"Well," she said, blowing on her fingertips. "Maybe a little."

The old shaman raised an eyebrow but didn't say anything.

Heaving out a sigh, Jiri brushed back her braids. "I shouldn't have trusted that dog, but I thought I knew just what he wanted from me. And that was fine, because that's what I wanted from him." Hadzi had broad shoulders, a handsome face, lovely hands and lips that . . .

Jiri shook her head, shoving those thoughts away. "I was fine with him using me for lust. That's what I was using him for. But for him to think he could use me to get power . . . Gods and crocodiles!"

"There are reasons shamans don't marry," Oza said. "And why we usually don't climb into the hammock of anyone from our own village."

"Then why'd you let me climb into Hadzi's?"

"Because." Oza sighed. "You've never truly felt a part of Thirty Trees, Jiri. You've always been uncertain here, and wary."

"That's because everyone in Thirty Trees has always seemed wary of me." *Except you.*

"I know. I thought you being with Hadzi might help." Oza looked her in the eye. "If you can't learn to trust anyone but me, the village will never trust you. And a shaman must have her people's trust."

"So you keep telling me," Jiri said. "I don't think this helped though." *Like a monkey. Hadzi, no one's that handsome.* "I wish you would have forbidden it, now."

"And how well would that have gone?"

"Do you think I would have gone against you?" Jiri's voice rose, and she pulled her anger back. This wasn't Oza's fault. This was Hadzi's, and every time she thought of his name her fingers itched with heat.

"You're a good student, Jiri. If I'd told you not to dance in front of his drum at the Orchid Dance, you would have listened to me. You wouldn't have tried to sneak into his hammock behind my back. But I think your frustration might have burned hot enough to turn our home to ash."

"I would never—"

Oza leveled a finger at her charred knife. "You were born in fire, Jiri. That bright spirit will always be too eager to serve you. I pick our battles carefully." The shaman folded his arms. "Besides, that boy might be handsome, but a sloth has quicker wits. I knew that if he did get up to anything like this, you'd figure him out before there was any real trouble."

"Another lesson."

"Life is nothing but," Oza said. "You'll have to find an answer now, for Hadzi and his schemes."

"Something that doesn't involve my friend fire," Jiri muttered.

"That would be best."

"I knew you'd say that." Jiri tapped her gathering pouch, thoughtful. "I did see some fireweed this morning."

He planned to come to me, weeping? A little of that rubbed into his loincloth, and he'll weep for a week.

"That poor, stupid boy," Oza said. "I think—"

Distracted by her thoughts of petty but satisfying revenge, it took Jiri a moment to notice her teacher's sudden silence. When she did, she found him staring into the jungle, eyes blank, face hard.

"Oza?"

The shaman's eyes snapped back into focus. "Jiri. Get my leathers and my spear and bring them to the Mango Woman. Run." Oza touched his necklace and his form twisted, shrinking down into a blur of green-and-scarlet flight.

Spear and leathers.

The words sank in and Jiri started running back to Thirty Trees, trying to move her legs as fast as the bright wings of the parrot her teacher had become.

Gasping, Jiri ran over the hard-packed red dirt that surrounded Thirty Trees' homes, the sun flashing off the blades of the spears she carried. Those blades dimmed when she reached the shadows spreading beneath the mango grove that gave her village its name. Clutching her burdens close, she dodged the children sitting beneath the trees, their slings and stones ready to drive any raiding monkey bands away from the ripening fruit. When she caught sight of the ancient statue that marked the far boundary of the grove, she finally slowed.

"Jiri, what's happening? Why do you have those spears? Why—"

Jiri whirled to glare at the chattering crowd of children that had followed her. "Go back."

"But—"

"Now, spirits take you!"

The children stared at Jiri for a moment, then ran. Muttering thanks to her ancestors, Jiri stepped out from beneath the last mango tree and set down her burdens, looking around. No parrots, no Oza, no anything but the Mango Woman.

That statue had stood here for countless years, long before the mango trees it was named for had even sprouted. Carved of dark soapstone, the beautiful woman held one hand out, and her eyes were stern. Even before Oza had taught Jiri how to decipher the runes carved into the statue's base, she had understood its purpose.

A command to go no further.

A warning.

A whirring of wings pulled Jiri's eyes away from that stone face and she spotted a green bird flashing through the trees toward her. Cursing her slowness, she reached down and began to sort through the things she had brought, jerking out the pieces she needed.

She was pulling her leathers on by the time Oza had landed and traded feathers for skin. His eyes met hers, and Jiri could see the grim fear that deepened the wrinkles of his face.

"There's trouble," she said.

"There is." Oza picked up his armor, sliding into it with practiced ease even though Jiri could count on one hand the number of times she had seen him don it. "Someone has opened the door into the Pyre."

The Pyre. Oza had only ever told her one story about the ruin that lay in the jungle beyond the Mango Woman: that the ancestors had built it to guard not a tomb or a treasure but a mistake, a piece of bad-luck magic that was meant to be forgotten.

The Pyre was forbidden, and Oza never allowed anyone to venture more than a stone's throw beyond the Mango Woman, not even Jiri. She had asked Oza, once, when he would take her there and teach her how to guard it. *Not yet* was all he had said, and for weeks after he had worked her on nothing but meditation and self-discipline.

"Who?" Jiri fumbled with the straps that pulled her leather armor tight across her chest. *No one from Thirty Trees. But who else would know of that place? Even the children know not to speak of it.*

"The spell I bought was too simple," Oza said, his straps done already. "Just an alarm, to let me know when someone came too close. They were already inside when I got there. I don't know who or what they are." He picked up his spear, the broad metal head of it flashing in a narrow sunbeam. "It doesn't matter. I mean to see that they don't come back out."

Jiri nodded and grabbed her own spear, a simple hunting weapon, not the war blade of her teacher. She began to whisper to the spirits.

"Jiri."

She met Oza's eyes and finished the spells. The air around them stirred, suddenly cooler, and the sweat that had already started to pool beneath their armor's thick leather began to dry. "I will fight with you."

"I don't doubt it. You look fiercer than the Mango Woman." The shaman shook his head. "But I don't want to fight these raiders. They opened a door they shouldn't have, and I mean to shut it. With them on the other side, more than likely. You can come with me, Jiri, but not to fight."

Oza's face went hard as stone. "If I fail—if they've left a guard or if I'm already too late and they've released something—I'll need you to run for me, not fight. I need you to protect Thirty Trees if I can't. Can you leave me and run, if I tell you to?"

Run. Jiri stared at the old man. He had found her alone in the ashes of the village she had been born in, an infant wailing beside the charred bones of her parents. She had never known any family but him. Oza stared back, understanding but unyielding.

"Tell me and I will," she whispered.

His eyes searched hers, then he nodded. "There is a man, Tirakici Kalun Kibwe. He owns an inn in Kibwe, the Red Spear. If I tell you, or if I fall, run back here and warn the village. Then go to Kalun and tell him what happened. Tell him to help you and Thirty Trees. Tell him I'm calling in his debt, all of it. You can trust him. Understand?"

Jiri nodded, mute, and Oza reached out and touched her shoulder.

"Come," he said, and they slipped into the undergrowth, leaving the Mango Woman to glare in silence at the empty space beneath the trees.

Chapter Two
The Pyre

There were no animals.

Jiri could still hear them in the jungle all around, the birds, monkeys, and bats, but their familiar cries were all distant. Even more unsettling, no insects flashed iridescent in the thin sunbeams that filtered down through the canopy, or swirled around her, eager to feast on her blood or sweat.

Ever since she was old enough to walk, Jiri had been warned never to pass the statue of the Mango Woman.

What tainted aura warned the animals to stay away?

Whatever it was, it touched the plants, too. Around her, the undergrowth grew thinner, sparser. The ground beneath the trees finally turned into empty red earth, mottled with patches of gray. Scarred ground, burned ground. The trees that arched over them looked the same: Their bark looked charred, and their leaves curled in, tattered and black. Twisted, injured, dying, they clawed at the empty sky, and the mud steamed between their roots.

"There's something here."

Jiri barely breathed the words, but Oza caught them. The old shaman nodded, but his hand touched his mouth.

Jiri locked her teeth together. They were hunting, and she should be silent, but . . . It was in the ground, in the tortured trees, in the air: a smell like smoke, a faint brush of heat. Some spirit touched the world here, something old and terrible, and Jiri burned with its presence.

With a deep, silent breath, Jiri forced the feeling back, locked it down and drifted like a shadow behind her teacher as he stalked forward. Just ahead of them, past the crumbling corpses of a few more trees, the Pyre rose.

It stood in the middle of a small, shallow lake, the black water a still mirror that refused to reflect the clouds and sun overhead. The Pyre stood like a stony splinter in the water's dark eye, a jagged rock cracked and blackened, as if touched by some ancient inferno. Ashes crowned its shattered peak, and the air over them twisted with a shimmer of heat.

Jiri stared at that warped curtain and her concentration disintegrated.

Like flames, like . . . In her head she saw fire and flame, dancing all around her. Tall and beautiful, and everything was turning to smoke and ash, burning and rising and whirling and going away, even the screams . . .

Oza's fingers pinched hard on her earlobe, and Jiri gasped into the palm of his other hand, the one he pressed against her lips. The shaman's dark eyes were inches from hers, blocking the Pyre, staring at her until she nodded. Then he slowly took his hands away. Angry at herself, Jiri looked past him at stone and ash and—

Jiri jerked her eyes away from the broken mirror of heat that hovered over those ashes. She didn't understand what it was that she had seen there, but she didn't want to see it again.

I don't.

Instead, she forced her eyes to trace over the fire-blackened cliff that the ashes rested on. Halfway up she found the door, the opening like a wound in the rock. The stone that had once covered it like a scar now lay in the water below, a slab the size of a hippo, and Jiri wondered how the intruders had moved it.

And how do we move it back?

Oza touched Jiri's hand, motioning for her to stay by the blackened trunk of the dead tree they had crept up behind. Then he stepped into the open and began to chant. Rough and low-pitched, the words scraped through the shaman's lips, a call to the bones of the earth.

They answered.

The ground shifted at the pool's edge, stone tearing through dirt skin. Oza's hands rose, and mud twisted like tendons around the rough rock, snapping it together into a crude parody of a man. An avalanche on thick legs, the elemental towered over them, staring down at the man who had called it into the world with gleaming eyes of gem. When Oza pointed, the earth spirit lurched into the water and splashed toward the Pyre, its rough hands reaching.

Stone ground against stone when the elemental grasped the great slab, and dirty water poured from its body as the rocks that formed it shifted. Slowly the earth spirit began to lift the massive boulder, scraping it against the Pyre's cliff face, until at last it raised it back into place, covering the door's dark opening. Jiri watched the stone man work, so tense with triumph that she almost missed it when the water behind the elemental began to swirl.

The thing broke the surface of the pool with a roar, sunlight flashing off slick green skin and black scales. Smaller than the elemental, but still much larger than Jiri, it looked like some hideous amalgamation of gorilla, crocodile, and toad. Lunging up, it dug great claws deep into the mud and stone flesh of the elemental. It pulled the giant back, and its teeth flashed. The sound of those great fangs scraping against stone tore the air like a shriek.

Not a beast, not a spirit—gods and ancestors, what is *that thing?* Jiri was scrambling back, her spear up, a puny, useless threat raised between her and the monster. *And how can it smell so bad?*

It reeked of stagnant water and dead things, rot and gangrene and something else, something acrid and bitter and unnatural. The smell made Jiri's stomach heave, her eyes run, and she had to wipe her tears away to see the thing snarl and attack again.

The monster's claws gouged deep into living earth as it pulled itself up, climbing the elemental. Lunging forward, it drove its fangs into the earth spirit's head. With a vicious twist of its neck, the scaly thing ripped the lumpy stone head free from the thick, muddy shoulders and spat it down into the dark water.

Terror and nausea tore through Jiri, but she held her place, not running. Forcing herself to look away from the battle, she found Oza. His eyes met hers, flashing with warning.

"They left us a demon, Jiri. Stay back, and be ready to run."

The shaman turned away from her before Jiri could answer that. His hand drew a circle over his head, and he shouted for the spirits of fire. A spark gathered in Oza's hand, grew bright and hot into a flame that shot away from him, toward the demon.

The fire twisted in the air, thickened, red flame taking the shape of a mamba racing with gaping jaws toward the demon that still had its claws deep in the elemental's stony back. As Oza's spell neared it, the stinking thing jerked its claws apart, making mud gout like black blood as it tore the earth-wrought spirit apart, roaring with triumph. Then the fire serpent slammed into it, and the roar into a howl. For a moment, the demon stood, a misshapen shadow wrapped in flame. Then it fell, vanishing beneath the dark water with a splash.

"Is it—" Jiri started, eyes watering from the sickening smell of the demon, but Oza cut her off.

"No." His hands were moving, drawing jagged lines in the air as he called the spirits again.

He hasn't told me to run yet.

That was something, wasn't it? And before it had fallen, the elemental had shoved the stone back over the gap that had been opened in the Pyre. Jiri watched the dark water shimmer, and for the first time since the demon had surfaced she felt her own power, burning like a coal beneath the dead ashes of her fear.

Stepping from her hiding place, Jiri reached for the spirits. When she felt them answer, felt life and resilience boil into her, she moved forward and brushed her hand across her teacher's back, letting the power flow into him.

"Thank you," Oza said, voice harsh with strain as he held tight to the magic the spirits had given him. "Now by all those who came before you, stand back."

For a moment Jiri didn't move, her hands hot with magic. But she couldn't disobey Oza. She took one step back, another, and then the water before them split.

The demon broke the surface roaring, claws reaching, eyes flashing hate and hunger. Oza roared back, cutting the air before him with his spear, and the water between the demon and the shaman shattered with spray. Vines exploded up, green and thick as a man's leg, twisting into knots around each other as they rose. Thorns covered the vines, long as spearpoints, and they scraped over the demon's hide as the great tangle surged over it.

Jiri felt anger and triumph burn through her, and without thinking she raised a hand. A flash of fire burst from her palm, striking the demon, barely singeing it.

"Back," Oza snapped again, and then he began to call out another summoning.

In the water, the demon tore at the vines. Thorns gouged it, but their sharp points couldn't penetrate its reeking hide. The demon ignored them, ripped one of its arms free, and lashed out.

Oza moved back, barely staying out of reach of those huge claws, and finished his call. The water behind the demon surged and swirled, roiled by the thing taking shape beneath its surface.

Rumbling something like a curse, the demon pulled itself free of the vines and lunged after Oza, claws spread. Jiri shouted and threw fire again, barely a spell, more her rage and fear flung out into the world to destroy. But her attack sizzled to nothing against the thing's slimy hide.

The demon swung its head and tiny crocodile eyes found Jiri. Its thin lips skinned back, showing its terrible teeth, and the monster hunched like a toad, ready to spring.

Jiri stared at the demon, knowing it was going to kill her, but she raised her spear and called for the spirits, determined to draw blood before she died.

Then the tentacles caught it.

Striking like snakes, they wrapped around the demon, a hundred suckers biting down. In the black water, the slimy, giant-eyed thing Oza had pulled from the spirit world clacked the beak that lay in the center of its nest of tentacles and jerked the demon back.

"Jiri, go." On the muddy bank, Oza was reaching for his necklace. "Run!" he shouted, and the word slipped into a roar as the shaman changed, grew claws and fangs and black-striped fur.

Jiri clutched her spear, paralyzed.

But we're winning.

Tentacles wrapped the demon, and the great tiger Oza had become slashed its claws between them, spilling stinking gouts of blood. If Jiri stayed—

The demon threw back its head, and roared a word.

The twisted, evil power of it broke the air. It tore through Jiri's body like poisoned hooks, filled her lungs like filthy water. The world shuddered around her, dimmed, and Jiri felt herself being ripped away, sent into darkness.

No.

She held on with all that she could, straining for light, for heat, for life, and suddenly she was back in her body, sprawled retching in the mud. Dully, she could see the demon, laughing as it tore limp tentacles off its hide. The massive tiger crouched before it, his gray-shot muzzle bent and dripping blood.

"Oza," Jiri groaned.

The cat raised his head and his eyes met Jiri's, old and stern. Then he turned and leapt at the monster, roaring, even as the demon wrapped its claws around him.

"Oza," Jiri said again, but she pulled herself up, made herself turn and stagger away, doing what those eyes had ordered her to do. Stumbling into a run, she whispered as she moved, begging the spirits to hide the tracks of her passage.

Running beneath the dead trees, Jiri tried not to listen to the booming laughter that echoed behind her, hideous and triumphant.

Chapter Three
The Red Spear

The narrow river twisted out of the trees, and Jiri finally caught sight of the walls of Kibwe.

They towered over the great clearing that had been burned out of the jungle long ago, granite bastions thick with carvings. The few times Jiri had been to the city before, she had stared with fascination at those carvings, trying to decipher the meanings of the symbols etched deep into the stone, to understand the power she could feel flowing through them like sap. Now . . .

"Faster, Hadzi."

With a grumble, Hadzi dug his oar into the water. "We've paddled for hours, Jiri. Why—"

"I told you." Told him, and the wara and all the other elders, told everyone in Thirty Trees. They had stared at her as if she were raving and asked where Oza was.

Oza.

Jiri's hands clenched, hot with anger and frustration, guilt and grief.

When the dugout's bottom scraped the mud, Jiri jumped out and splashed onto the bank. Burning to move, she made herself stop and face the men staring bewildered at her.

"I know, Hadzi. About the woman your father found, your plan to use her and me, all that. I know."

Hadzi blinked, stunned. Behind him, Boro rolled his eyes up to the sky.

"Jiri, I—" Hadzi stammered, his mind obviously churning, trying to come up with something.

"It doesn't matter, Hadzi. It's *nothing*. Someone has broken into the Pyre, and Oza . . ." Jiri took a breath, shuddering, eyes hot. He might still be alive. She had never heard him scream.

But he wouldn't.

"Go back, fast as you can. Make them move, Hadzi." Jiri watched her lover flinch away from her eyes. "You want to be wara? Then learn to lead today. Forget the mango harvest and get those people out. Something terrible is happening at the Pyre and they need to run."

"Jiri—" Hadzi started, but Boro was already moving his oar, backing their canoe carefully out around the other dugouts that filled the narrow channel of the river where it looped closest to the city.

"We'll do what we can."

Jiri nodded to Boro, then turned and began to skirt the crowd of fishmongers and porters that crowded around the bank and docks. As soon as she had enough room, she began to run toward the gates that split the walls of Kibwe.

Tirakici Kalun Kibwe, and the Red Spear. The guards standing at the gate had known both names and sent her to the western edge of the Adayenki Pavilion.

That great green space in the center of chaotic Kibwe was filled with people and banners, and Jiri could hear the thump of drums and singing, could see the whirling dancers and smell meat roasting. A feast day for the ancestors of another tribe, and crowds swirled thick around the celebration.

Some other day, Jiri would have been fascinated. Today, she snaked her way through the crowd, ignoring the constant, fluttering touch of a thousand strangers, the smell of sweat and spices, the gleam of gold and glass and steel. She hunted, and through a gap between two of the great tapestries that hung around the Adayenki she finally found what she sought. A spear, painted crimson, three times the height of a person.

The building behind the towering spear-sign was stone, with a low wall around it that echoed the city's high bastions, but its wrought-iron gates stood open. Jiri passed through them, crossed a tiny courtyard full of flowers and fountains, and stepped inside.

Wards brushed across her skin when she crossed the rune-carved threshold, invisible walls against insects, heat, and bad-luck magic. She shivered from their touch as much as she did from the sudden cool, and she stopped and stood blinking in the dim interior.

Faces turned to her, light brown or corpse pale, foreign faces, and the chatter of strange tongues stilled. The room fell silent except for the distant murmur of the crowded Adayenki. This kind of attention, from strange people in a strange place, would normally have frozen Jiri like a mouse deer before a leopard. Today, though, she managed to find just enough voice to say the name of the man she had been sent for.

"Tirakici Kalun Kibwe?"

"What of him?"

The woman popped out of nowhere, like a summoned spirit of disapproval. She wore a bright dress of red and yellow, and her hair was in the long dreadlock style of the Tirakici tribe. She stood only a little taller than Jiri, but the woman looked down her nose at the shaman as if she stood a league above her.

"I am Mosa Jiri Maju, student of Mosa Oza Thirty Trees. I—"

"Mosa Jiri Maju." The woman drew out each name, and Jiri remembered that in Kibwe many had given up traditional naming conventions, instead taking up the northern style of one or two names that told you almost nothing about a person. "I thought your tribe dressed in mud cloth, not mud." She glared at Jiri's dirty leathers, her tangled braids. "The Red Spear is no place for ragged little—"

"Feda."

The woman stopped speaking and narrowed her eyes. "You know this girl, Kalun?"

"No." Kalun stood at the back of the room, a man as old as Oza, but heavier and handsomer. He wore the loose shirt and pants common to Kibwe, but they were made of crimson silk intricately embroidered with gold thread. They were probably worth more coin than Thirty Trees altogether. "But I know her teacher." He stared at Jiri, frowning.

"Send her back. And send us some palm wine. I think we'll need it."

Kalun sat on his carved stool, holding his empty cup.

"I can't."

Jiri jerked up from her bench, almost knocking over the cup that sat untouched beside her. "You have to! Oza—" *Oza was . . .* Fear and anger flashed through Jiri like flame. "He said there was a debt."

"There is, girl." Kalun nodded, his gray dreadlocks sweeping across broad shoulders. "But I'm too old, too soft to repay it. A demon. What could I do, now, but maybe choke it with my fat gut?"

Jiri stared at the old innkeeper, then sat, numb, empty. *I deserted him for nothing.*

"Fara." Kalun looked at his daughter, playing cat's cradle behind them. The girl had brought the palm wine, then settled onto one of the other benches in Kalun's talking room. *My wife is careful,* was all Kalun had said. "Fetch Linaria, and Morvius."

The girl scampered out and the innkeeper turned back to Jiri. "I can't come. But I am a rich man now, partly thanks to Oza. I will pay my debt another way."

There was a scrape of footsteps and two foreigners entered the room. The first was a tall man, pale and dark-haired, his broad shoulders heavy with muscle beneath his strange clothes. His face was handsome enough, for a northerner, but Jiri didn't like the way his green eyes casually moved over her. A woman who stood almost as tall him followed close behind. Her skin was even paler, though, so colorless that her veins showed through, sky-blue like her eyes. Her long white hair hung loose, but her thin face was smooth, untouched by age but strangely angled, and her ears were oddly pointed, almost animal-like. Whatever she was, she wasn't human, Jiri realized. Not entirely.

"Kalun." The man smiled, his eyes shifting away from Jiri. "What can we do for you this fine sweaty day?"

"Sit and listen." Kalun nodded to Jiri. "My friend has a story for you."

"A demon." Morvius shifted on his bench, the wood creaking. "Froggy-looking? Stinking?" He looked at his companion.

"Swamp demon, probably. Nasty things." They both had accents, but while Morvius's words were rough as stone, Linaria's had a touch of something almost musical.

"A swamp demon," Morvius said. "A cursed ruin, and a group of raiders."

"The Aspis Consortium sent their people out the other day," Linaria said, thoughtful. "Amiro in the lead, but he had Patima with him. She has that charm, the one that can summon demons."

"Fantastic," Morvius said. "I feel bad for the demon, if it's working for them." The northerner's eyes slid back to Kalun. "It sounds like quite a hornet's nest. So why in five hells do you think we would want to go poking at it?"

"Because this is the kind of crap you people live for," Kalun said. The innkeeper pointed at the wine glass that hung almost empty in Morvius's hand. "And you owe me."

"What, for some drinks and a few days' lodging?" Morvius protested.

"No. For two months' lodging, and a lot of food and drink. But more than that, you owe me for your failure to finish the Ocota job."

"You sent us within pissing distance of Usaro." Morvius said. "I wouldn't call getting that close to the worst place in this whole bloody jungle and making it back a failure."

"It is when you spend a fortune on supplies, then lose them all while failing to find what I sent you out for."

"Kalun, I told you what happened with those monkeys—"

"Do this," Kalun said, cutting Morvius off, "and I will forgive all of your debts to me. Ocota included."

"Not enough," Linaria said. "Not for a demon."

Kalun frowned at her. Then he stood and stepped out of the room.

Morvius glanced at Linaria, who shook her head. He shrugged and drained his cup, waiting.

On her bench, Jiri watched them. *Thirty Trees is in danger, and they sit here and bargain.* Jiri scrubbed her hands over her eyes, wiping away tears hotter than blood. *Oza, I hope you knew what you were doing sending me here. Because if these fools won't help us, then I don't know if I can keep myself from burning this whole place down.*

The door curtain swirled and Kalun stepped back in, a long, silk-wrapped bundle in his hands.

"You want enough for a demon?" Kalun growled, and snapped the bundle open.

The spear that rolled free of the silk smelled like blood. It looked like blood, too, the metal of its blade red and gleaming as if dipped in gore.

"That's Scritch." Morvius stared at the spear. "You told me you sold it."

"I lied. But I'll sell it now."

"Done." Morvius reached for the weapon.

"Great bargaining, Mor." Linaria sighed. She whispered and spread her hands over the spear. "It's potent."

"Yes," Kalun said. The innkeeper's jaw knotted tight, watching Morvius test the spear's balance, and his empty fists clenched. "Do we have a bargain, Linaria? Slay this demon, save Oza if he still lives, and seal that ruin. For that, I grant forgiveness of all previous debts. And Scritch."

"Yes," Morvius said, slowly shifting through a series of stances with the spear.

Linaria ignored him. She folded her arms, fingers tapping on her elbows. "What if the demon's gone? The shaman dead, the ruin empty, the village destroyed?"

"Then just bring the girl back safe," Kalun said. "I'm paying back a debt myself. Poorly, perhaps, but I have to do what I can. I owe Oza that."

"Done." Linaria put out her hand, palm up, and Kalun dropped his onto it.

"Done."

Jiri jumped to her feet, barely noticing the way Morvius shifted the point of his new toy to track her movement. "We can get a dugout at the river." It would be faster this time, going downstream. The sun would have barely gone down by the time they reached Thirty Trees.

"We'll hire one tomorrow," Linaria said.

"Tomorrow!" Jiri almost shouted.

"I know you're worried about your teacher," the pale-eyed woman said. "But if we rush into this fight, that demon will take us apart. We'll leave after I've prepared my magic, and after we've gotten some help."

"Who are you thinking?" Morvius asked.

"Gavin came back into town yesterday."

"The mute archer?"

"He's not mute. He just doesn't talk to fools." Linaria ignored her partner's snort. "Sera is with him."

Morvius stopped moving the spear. "No."

"Demon, Mor. She's a paladin of Iomedae. Very useful."

"She broke my arm."

"You asked her about a threesome with her and her goddess. Then slapped her backside."

"I was drunk."

"Stay sober."

Jiri listened to their banter, not hearing.

Jiri, go!

The echo of Oza's voice trembled in her ears, the demon's laughter rumbling beneath it. She barely felt Kalun's hand on her arm, barely heard the old man's words as he led her out.

"They'll help you, Jiri. They know what they're doing, and Linaria keeps her bargains." He led her upstairs and down a hall to a room that was almost twice the size of the house where she had grown up with Oza. "You can stay here, you know. They'll be able to find that Pyre of yours themselves, if you tell them where to go."

Jiri looked up at him. You can trust him, Oza had told her. But she didn't. Not him, not his northerners, not Hadzi or Boro or . . . Her hands were hot, and she clenched them tight to keep the fire inside her. *I'm not even sure I trust myself, but Oza needs me. And if he's gone, Thirty Trees needs me even more.* "No."

Kalun looked away from her, his face etched with sadness. "I know you feel responsible, girl. But the hunt you're starting . . ." He looked down at his hands, and for the first time Jiri noticed the scars that covered them. "It's a hard one."

Her throat was thick, and her eyes were burning again, but Jiri pushed out another "No." She watched him nod, and for a moment, despite his dreadlocks and his rich clothes, he reminded her so much of Oza.

"I'll send up food and a washbasin."

He stepped out, shutting the door behind him.

Jiri stared at the blank wood panel, then slowly sank to her knees.

Oza.

In spite of her desperation, there was time now for tears, and when they fell the soft rug beneath Jiri caught them and they vanished, like blood disappearing into dark water.

Chapter Four
Ash

"You can't contain evil."

Jiri stopped, blocking the narrow trail that led from the river to Thirty Trees, and stared at the woman following her. Sera. One of the two other northerners Linaria had brought with her this morning. The other, Gavin, stood silent at the end of the line, his eyes searching the trees that surrounded them. Gavin seemed sane.

Sera?

I'm not so sure.

"This Pyre." Sera swiped a gauntlet over her scalp, scrubbing it through her short-cropped hair. Wrapped in leather and steel, the woman should have been sweating rivers, but her skin was preternaturally dry. A blessing from her goddess, and Jiri could feel the prickly touch of that great spirit when she stood close to the paladin. "It should be broken open. Cleansed."

"No." Jiri stared up into the other woman's too-bright eyes.

"What's wrong with cleaning the place out?" Morvius took a pull from his waterskin. There was no feeling of magic around him, and the broad-shouldered man was pouring sweat into his armor.

Jiri's hands tightened on her spear. "The Pyre . . ." Jiri thought of dark rock, of heat twisting the air like flames. "Something's sealed away there. I was sent . . ."

Jiri, go!

"I was sent to see it sealed again."

"Sure." Morvius gave her a smile, and for a moment he reminded Jiri of Hadzi, though the two men looked nothing alike. "But what's the harm in looking around a little?"

"For you? Not so much," Jiri said. "Maybe just death. For me? I might loose something that will destroy my home and everyone I've ever loved. This is my world, Morvius. I won't risk destroying it so you can run back north with some coin."

"Now—" Morvius started, but Linaria cut him off.

"We were paid to kill a demon and shut a door." She pushed a sweat-damp lock of hair from her face, a long strand of white that had escaped the braid she wore. "That's what we'll do."

Jiri nodded to the woman. Kalun had told her this morning that Linaria was a half-elf, while warning her about Sera.

"*Paladins.*" The old warrior had said the name like a curse. "*The northern churches take their fanatics and arm them to the teeth. Then they send them far, far away.*" Kalun had spit into one of the fountains in his inn's courtyard. "*Treat her like a spearpoint. Aim her at your enemy, and keep as far back from her as possible.*"

In the jungle, in the green dim beneath the trees, Sera's eyes never left Jiri. "The Mwangi Expanse is full of shadows. Light must touch every corner of it. Otherwise the evil of those tainted places will keep leaking out, corrupting everything it touches."

"Balls, Sera." Morvius laughed. "Isn't your family from devil-run Cheliax?"

The paladin twitched, but she didn't turn away from Jiri. The shaman returned her stare, and the wood of her spear's shaft grew hot beneath her hands.

Point her away.

Her thought, but the voice in her head could have been Kalun's. Or Oza's.

"Thirty Trees is this way," she said, and started walking.

They had almost listened to her.

Most of the village was gone. The old, the young, those with children. There was just a handful left, young men and women risking their lives for earthen-walled houses and mango trees. Jiri stared at Hadzi, facing her defiantly in front of the others, then dismissed him.

"Boro. Have you heard anything of Oza?"

"No." The young man glanced at his fuming brother, then looked back to Jiri. "The cookfires wouldn't start last night. Then they all blazed up at once, burning out in seconds. Some were burned, and we asked the ancestors for Oza, but . . ." He shook his head. "That's when they decided to go down the trail to Rough Ford."

"They were smart," Jiri snapped. She went to the tiny house she shared with Oza and stepped in. Empty. She snatched up a couple of clay pots and stepped back out.

"Ointment. For burns."

Boro took the pot from her. "You're taking those northerners to the Pyre?"

"Yes," Jiri said. Linaria and the rest stood nearby, their pale faces all flushed pink except Sera's. "Keep a close watch. Be ready to run. Understand?"

Boro nodded. "Gods, spirits, and ancestors, may they watch, protect, and guide."

Jiri nodded, then stepped to Hadzi, catching him in a sudden, fierce hug. "You're an idiot, Hadzi, but you made me happy sometimes. Listen to your brother for once."

Before Hadzi could answer, she let him go and spun away, toward the mango grove and what lay beyond.

"Medicine root. We put it in everything." Jiri broke the seal on the little clay pot, and the others stepped back as the smell hit them.

"That clears your head out, doesn't it?" Morvius muttered.

"It helps you breathe. More importantly, it's harmless and makes everything we put it in smell like good medicine." Jiri dipped her fingers into the pot and smeared the salve on her upper lip. Within seconds, her nose gave up on smelling anything. She passed the pot to Linaria.

"For the swamp demon stench," the white-haired woman said. She smeared some on, wincing. "Are you still willing to do this?"

"Yes," Jiri said.

"Being demon bait—"

"You and Sera need time to prepare your magic," Jiri said. "I'll get it for you.

"Did you know it gets hotter near you, when you get mad?" Linaria asked.

"Yes."

"Hmm." The half-elf's hands dug through her pack. "Here." She held out a small green bag.

"What is it?" Jiri asked.

"Alchemical glue. We've found that it's good for slowing things down, if they're coming at you fast."

Fast.

Jiri stood at the edge of the pool that spread beneath the Pyre. The cracked black rock towered over her, the ash that crowned it still beneath its heat shimmer. The stone door that Oza's elemental had been trying to put back lay in the water again, the narrow portal it had covered an open wound.

There was no sign of the demon.

Or Oza.

It doesn't mean—

Jiri cut off that thought.

It means it's just me. Me and those northerners hiding behind me.

Jiri took a breath, trying to calm herself the way Oza had taught her, to forget her fear, her grief, her anger. She breathed, and finally she pulled herself together enough to reach out beyond the flame that danced behind her eyes and in her hands, to find earth, cool and solid and strong.

She rasped out a call to the bones of the earth, and the muddy shore before her bubbled and heaved. It split open, and the elemental she had asked for pulled itself free from the dirt and stood before her. Wrought of stone and mud, it looked the same as her teacher's—just much smaller. With a wave of her hand, Jiri sent it toward the stone door, to see if it could even shift it.

That's when the water before her began to bubble.

The demon rose slowly out of the blank black mirror of the pool, a crude parody of a frog carved from filth. Gold eyes gleamed in scaled green pits, just above the rot-brown line of fangs that filled its wide mouth. The stench of the thing thickened the air, and Jiri could taste it like poison. The medicine root numbed her, though, and she didn't retch.

Staring up at the demon, she clenched her spear in one hand and let her other hand fill with flame. "Where is he?"

Tiny eyes blinked, hungry and amused. The demon turned for a moment to stare at her little elemental, vainly pushing on the boulder door, before looking back to her.

Words filled Jiri's head. Hideous and grating, they dragged through her mind like poisonous knives, tearing at her thoughts.

"A little morsel, but juicy. Sweeter, I think, than that old leather I chewed yesterday."

"No!" Jiri shouted. Her spear dropped and she raised both her hands, fingers curling like claws as the air erupted before her with fire.

The demon's laughter, hideous and mocking, poured from its throat as the flames danced across its wet hide.

"You have some of that old one's heat, morsel. But not nearly enough. Maybe this will make you hotter."

One claw rose and dug through the thicket of fangs that filled the demon's mouth. With a flick, it cast something out into the mud at Jiri's feet: a leather thong strung with animals, each carefully carved from bone.

"No," Jiri said again, staring down at Oza's necklace, hardly noticing as the demon raised its claws, spread them against the sky, and—

"In her light shall you burn! Iomedae!"

The battle cry snapped the demon's attention away from Jiri, and it glared past her to the figures sprinting toward it, focusing on the woman in the lead, her sword and shield raised high.

"*Godslave.*" The demon's voice rumbled through Jiri's mind, and it slammed past her to meet the paladin's charge.

Jiri hit the mud and tumbled. With trembling hands she reached out and picked up the necklace, clutched the little carvings tight. Then she raised her burning eyes to stare at the battle raging before her.

Sera crashed into the demon, punching her longsword deep into its belly. In return, the monster wrapped its claws around the paladin, plucked her up and brought her to its gnashing fangs. Twisting in the demon's grip, Sera shoved her shield into the thing's wide maw. Brown teeth grated on steel, and the paladin beat the demon's hideous face with the pommel of her sword.

Morvius danced around them both, grinning like a fiend. Scritch blurred in his hands, impossibly fast, and every time its crimson blade bit slimy hide, gore poured out like sewage. Around those streaming wounds, bright flowers bloomed, the red-fletched ends of Gavin's arrows.

Jiri could see the archer, standing calmly beyond the fight, pulling and shooting, shifting just enough to fire around Sera's thrashing form. Beside him, Linaria's face was tight with concentration, her lips moving, her empty hand lashing out at the demon. A bar of pale blue, like the sky made solid for an instant, arced from her hand and lanced into the demon's belly. A circle of white spread where it struck, and Jiri could feel the burning cold of the spell.

The demon howled, and Jiri bared her teeth at it, vicious.

Not laughing now, are you?

Her hand tightened on the necklace she held, and she threw fire at the thing, not caring if it did nothing. The demon growled something through her head, spitting words like thorns in some terrible language Jiri didn't know. Ripping the paladin away from its face, it hurled Sera at Linaria, sending half-elf and human down in a clatter of armor and curses. It roared at them, and with a crack like thunder it vanished.

Jiri heard the splash and spun, ignoring Morvius as he stood blinking alone in the churned mud. The demon was behind her, standing knee-deep in the dark water. It glared at them, its wounds streaming, and opened its mouth to speak.

That word.

Jiri remembered the terrible magic that had staggered Oza and almost torn her life away. Her hand lashed down, grabbed the pouch Linaria had given to her, and hurled it.

The demon was beginning to speak when the bag struck it straight in the teeth. The green cloth split, and thick filaments of adhesive filled the demon's mouth, wrapping around its writhing tongue. Choking, the monster raised its claws and tore at the glue that welded tongue to gums, fangs to lips.

With a whoop, Morvius charged into the water, driving Scritch deep into the pale green belly. The demon leaned forward, clutching its wound, and Sera charged.

The paladin drove her sword down, cleaving through scale and skull. The demon heaved back, trembling. Arrows hammered into its chest, and darts of energy like flashing glass flew from Linaria's hand and tore into its throat. With a strangled croak, the demon fell backward. Dark water churned as the demon convulsed, tearing at its ruined head and throat with its own claws. Then it went still and sank.

"Good work."

Jiri barely heard Linaria's words. Or Sera's prayers, or Morvius's curses as he waded back, away from the slime that slicked the water's surface over the place the demon had fallen. Her hands clutched the necklace she held, and she stared over the churning water at the little elemental she had called, still struggling uselessly to shift the stone.

"Don't worry about that." Linaria wiped at the bright blood streaming from her nose and reached into a pouch on her belt, pulling out a folded sheet of papyrus. The half-elf read the words traced over the sheet, and they faded. Below the Pyre's peak, the narrow opening scabbed over with stone, light gray against the dark rock.

"There. Sealed." Tipping her head back and pinching her nose, Linaria winced. "All in all, that actually went pretty—"

Beneath them, the ground trembled. Jiri felt a wash of heat, and something acrid burned its way through the numbness of her nose. Atop the black rock, the ashes stirred, and the heat shimmering over them rose like flames, reaching into the sky.

"Damn it, Lin, you know you shouldn't say crap like—" Morvius started, but Jiri held up her hand.

"Listen," Jiri whispered. The sound came again, faint but clear. The scrape of steel on rock, coming from the stone scab that Linaria's scroll had formed over the shuddering Pyre's entrance, then silence. "Something's trying to get out."

The air on the muddy shore beside them suddenly trembled, tore open, and then that broken, empty space was filled with people. There was a man wrapped in battered, heat-warped steel, a warhammer swinging in his hand; a pale northern woman in once-colorful silks that were now charred; a strange looking young girl; and a woman with flowing dark hair whose arms were wrapped around a bundle of wet and smoking leather.

The girl was the first one to move, and as she did Jiri realized her mistake. The woman was tiny, but her movements were too quick, too graceful for a child. The little woman flipped over the armored man, putting him between her and Sera.

"Hello there," she chirped. "Rude of you to slam that wall up right when we were trying to leave." Her hands moved, flashing fast, and Gavin and Linaria went staggering, metal blades jutting from their bellies.

The man in front of the little knife-thrower frowned and raised his hammer. "Kalun's people. Of course."

Despite his northern armor and weapon, the man looked like he belonged to the Mwangi as much as Jiri.

The woman in the silks beside him twisted her ash-smeared face into an evil smile and laughed. "Morvius! Linaria! You are the most amazing idiots!"

"What the hell are you talking about, Corrianne?" Linaria gasped, her hands clutching at the hilt of the little dagger that was growing a red flower across her stomach. Morvius had caught her, was holding her up as he stared murder at the halfling woman with the knives.

"Timing, dearest!" the silk-woman said, still smiling like poison. "Like always, yours is so, so bad. Just wait until you see what's chasing us."

"What's catching us, if you spend any more timing chatting." The woman carrying the bundle nodded back at the shaking Pyre. "Now get us out of here."

Jiri was trying to understand and react to everything happening around her, but her attention shattered when that woman moved and the leather wrapped around the thing she carried shifted. A gap opened in its wet folds, and for a moment Jiri could see something hidden beneath it. Dark carved wood, and something red, glowing like hot metal, all swimming beneath shimmers of heat. Heat that warped the air around it, twisted it like flames, climbing, consuming—

Jiri ripped her eyes away from the thing, her body blazing, her head spinning. The air around her seemed to be shivering like flames, but she forced herself to look through it and meet the woman's eyes.

"You can't," she gasped. *Can't what?* Jiri couldn't put it into words, the danger that she felt radiating out of that thing, anger and heat pounding like some monstrous heart. Couldn't force herself to speak, while an echo of that anger and heat was pounding in her own heart. *She can't take that, can't touch that, can't—*

"I'm sorry, girl," the woman said, her voice beautiful. "For the hell that follows me. It's not meant for you." There was sympathy in her words, but it was gossamer flesh over solid bones of certainty. "But if I have to drag that thing across the whole Expanse to bring it to where I need it to be, so be it." The ground trembled again, and the woman's voice cracked like a whip. "Corrianne!"

"Gods, Patima, I *know*!" Corrianne held up her hand, sketching symbols in the air that flickered and vanished before they were truly seen, and she whispered words fast and sibilant.

Jiri shook her head, tearing her eyes away from whatever the woman Patima held. Head aching with heat, she raised her hand, fire licking around her fingers. She barely noticed Morvius setting Linaria down and stalking forward, Scritch held low. Sera moved on the other side, her shield up. She didn't pay any attention to the armored man stepping out in front of Corrianne, his warhammer ready. Her only focus was on Patima.

"You can't," Jiri said again, raising her hand, her fist clenched around fire, but Corrianne was calling out—

"Lovely meeting you all, but we've people to see, riches to earn, and terribly awful things to run away from. Have fun!"

Corrianne threw her arms out, slapping one hand onto the back of the man protecting her and letting Patima grab the other. The little woman with the knives spun and leapt, grabbing nimbly onto Corrianne's skirt. Jiri's eyes remained on Patima, who cradled that smoking bundle as if it were her last child, and Jiri's arm was moving, throwing the fire she held straight at her. The woman stared back at her, dark eyes shining, reflecting the light of the flames flying at her—

And then she was gone.

Gone, her and all her companions, and the thing that they had stolen from beneath the Pyre. With a hiss, Jiri's flame hit the mud where they had been standing and fizzled out into steam and ashes.

From the ground behind Jiri, Linaria gasped. "Gods damn us. She can teleport now?"

"Of course," Morvius said, turning from the now-empty space in front of him. He frowned at the slim blade embedded in his partner. "Poisoned?"

"Of course."

"Why hasn't someone fed that halfling to a crocodile yet?" The tall man looked down at Jiri. "You're a healer, right? Lay her down and—"

"No." Jiri's eyes were back on the Pyre, staring at the stone wall Linaria's magic had made. A black spot marked its center, growing and spreading. "Something's coming."

"What?" Morvius looked over his shoulder at the door. "Balls," he said, then he went fast to Linaria, scooping her up, ignoring the white-haired woman's gasp of pain.

"What's going on?" Sera demanded.

"We're running," Morvius shouted, and started to lurch forward, away from the Pyre. "You might want to join us."

The paladin looked back at the blackening stone. She raised her sword, but cursed quietly when a streamer of blood oozed out of the cut that split her scalp and ran into her eye. "Come on," she told Jiri, backing away.

Jiri stared at the door, saw the cracks spreading across its charring surface. She thought of the thing that woman had held. A carving of wood, metal hot enough to glow. Her hand clung to the necklace she held. What had that woman stolen from beneath the Pyre? *She said she was sorry for the hell that follows her. What follows her?* Her hand ached, clutched so tight, and in her head she heard a voice, sharp and clear and sudden.

Jiri, go!

Jiri turned and started to run, but behind her rock cracked and a wall of air and heat slammed into her, smashing her off her feet. Rolling onto her back, Jiri tried to see but the air was full of smoke and ash, and her eyes were streaming, her lungs burning. Somewhere, someone was screaming, and all the ash in the air was moving, pulling in on itself, and Jiri could see wings over her. Giant wings, stretching across the sky, wings of ash that roiled the smoke as they beat, and at their center something glowed like a cinder, something shaped like a man. That thing raised its terrible, hate-twisted face of fire and ash and roared, and heat rolled over Jiri. It spun around her, an inferno that almost touched her but didn't quite, and she was howling too, her burning lungs throwing out what little air they held. Smoke swirled in and covered her eyes, and all the world was ash, and there was only darkness.

When Jiri opened her eyes and found light again, it was the red-gold light of sunset, with night coming fast. Shadows stretched thick across the clearing before her, obscuring it, though it seemed familiar. Blinking burning eyes, she coughed and sat up.

"Alive?" Linaria crouched before her, a stained rag pressed to her nose.

"Yes. You?"

The half-elf fingered the tear that marred her bloody silk shirt. "I'm fine. Mostly. Sera can be a pain in the ass, but she's useful. Now if I could just stop this nosebleed . . ."

"I've got blood fern." Jiri choked a bit on the words, coughed and spit. Her spit was black with soot. "Back in Thirty Trees."

"Ah," Linaria said, softly.

Jiri stared at her, then looked again at the clearing they sat in. Wind stirred the trees around it and scattered the ashes that filled it. Familiar, but not, because the homes that had once filled it were gone, charred to nothing.

"We never saw what came out that door." Linaria's eyes shone in the dark. "It went over us like a forest fire, all heat and smoke and ash. Then it was gone. I made Morvius go back, and we found you and Gavin back near those ruins. The archer . . ." She sighed. "The poison had slowed him down too much. That thing caught him, and there wasn't much left. You weren't far away, but other than being out cold, you were untouched. Lucky."

"Lucky," Jiri said. She could feel a weight around her neck. Someone had put Oza's necklace on her while she lay unconscious. She wouldn't have, but now she knew she couldn't take it off.

"Sera picked you up and we came back here. But whatever that thing was, it beat us. Burned a perfect circle out of the jungle, centered on your village." Linaria rested a cool hand on Jiri's arm. "I'm sorry, but there's nothing left."

Jiri stared around at what she could see of the empty clearing in the gathering shadows. The mango trees were gone. All of them? Maybe. Something burned in her eyes, and she couldn't tell if it was ashes or tears.

"That thing . . ." *Wings of ash, and something like fire, shaped like a man.*

"Gone. Who knows where?" Linaria said. "Hunting Corrianne, maybe. Hopefully."

"No. Not her." Jiri felt strangely calm, distant, despite the charred flesh scent that she could smell below the smoke and ash reek. "Patima. The one that you said could summon demons. She was holding something. That's who it wants."

"Patima. Because of what she held?" Linaria said. "Well, if it's something valuable that they stole out of that place, they'll all want their piece of it. Patima, Corrianne, Amiro, and Mikki, that poisonous goblin in halfling-skin." Linaria's hand touched the tear in her shirt again. "They're Aspis Consortium, they're always in it for the money. We . . . worked together, once." Linaria paused. "It didn't go well."

Patima. Jiri pulled herself up. *Aspis Consortium*. She stared down at the ashes that surrounded her. "Did you find anyone?"

"Just bones," Linaria said. "Sera buried them."

Buried. In the dimming light, Jiri could see a mound of earth, pitifully small, bare of offerings. She pulled her eyes away.

Lucky.

"When I was a baby, Oza found me. In a village, burned by fire. I was the only living thing he found in the ashes. He named me Jiri, after a sister he had lost. For my home name, though . . ." Jiri traced the thin trails of smoke that still rose toward the darkening sky. "He named me Maju. It means ashes. Jiri Maju, Jiri from the Ashes. Then he brought me here, to a new home. And now this place is ashes, too."

"Jiri, this isn't your fault."

"My fault," Jiri said softly, crouching down and picking up a handful of ash.

"No. Patima, or the Consortium who sent her, or that thing. They're responsible for this. Understand?"

"Understand?" Jiri's hand tightened, and she felt the smooth powder of the ash warm in her palm. "Oza is dead. Thirty Trees is ashes. I am Mosa Jiri Maju. I understand who is responsible." Her hand opened, and the fine gray ash drifted through her fingers like smoke.

"And someday, they will be ashes, too."

Chapter Five
Mosa

When the sun touched the sky over the Expanse and the black arc of stars began to fade into blue, the rhythm of the jungle changed. The roaring chorus of the night insects faltered, and the high-pitched screams of the fruit bats faded. In their place, the sounds of the dawn grew. Birds sang and squawked, monkeys chattered and squabbled, and the insects of the day began to hum.

That change in the jungle's rhythm was grooved deep into Jiri's bones. Every day of her life she had woken to it, pulled herself from the whispering spirit stories of her dreams and returned to the waking world, to the Expanse, to Thirty Trees, to her life.

My life.

The noise of daybreak surrounded Jiri, but she didn't want to open her eyes and let the coming dawn in.

She didn't want to see what her world had become.

Sleep had rolled like a flood over her last night and drowned her in senseless darkness. Part of her wanted that back so badly, that sheltering embrace of oblivion. But the currents of sleep had turned against her, and now she lay awake and the truth of what had happened wouldn't stay hidden. It sparked to life, a painful heat that burned through her, grief and anger like bright flames.

Jiri opened her eyes to the dawn of her new life, and its ashes blinded her with tears.

Everything is gone.

Jiri rubbed her hands over her face, pushing those tears out of her way. She could feel the ash mixed in with them, gritty against her skin. She could smell it too, thick in the air around her, overpowering the faint remnants of the medicine root she had smeared beneath her nose the day before to block the demon's stench.

The demon that killed Oza.

Jiri's hands fell to the necklace that lay tangled around her neck, stroked the smooth bone of the carved fetishes hanging from it. *It tore him apart. It* ate *him.* Jiri shuddered at the memory, and the flames in her grew. Their heat made her tears run faster, but that was all right. They cleared the ash from her eyes and let her see.

A smooth circle stretched around her, an empty gray death-mark branded into the tangled vibrancy of the jungle. This was all that was left of Thirty Trees. Last night, in the dim of twilight, Jiri hadn't seen how perfect the destruction was, how precise and absolute. Everything in the circle that covered where the village had been was gone, burned to ashes, gray and black and white, the shifting surface spotted only with a few shards of heat-shattered clay and the occasional gleam of a melted lump of metal.

Pots and tools, rendered down to nothing by the terrible heat of that thing, that . . .

That what?

Jiri pushed herself up, rising slowly from the gray drift of ash that had collected around her in the night. She didn't know. Some spirit of smoke and flame, nameless to her and terrible, had destroyed this place. The only home she had ever known.

Some spirit, released from its prison.

Released by those raiders. Aspis Consortium. Jiri rolled her tongue over the strange words, whispering them silently. That was what Linaria had named them. Treasure hunters seeking a fortune, they had broken into the Pyre and stolen . . . something. Jiri had seen it, cradled in the arms of that woman, Patima. It was a Bonuwat name, and Jiri thought that the woman had the look of those coastal people.

A Bonuwat woman, and the man had been from the Expanse, who knew what tribe. Then there was the halfling poisoner and the northern magician. Aspis Consortium. They were the ones who had come to Jiri's home, sneaking and stealing from the Pyre, the tainted barrow that Jiri's ancestors had warned everyone away from. They were the ones who had woken the spirit that burned Thirty Trees.

Burned and killed.

In the center of the circle, Sera had made a grave. Jiri's eyes found it and slipped away, unable to rest for long on that little mound of earth. Instead, they found Morvius and Linaria sleeping near her. They had stripped off armor and outer clothes, but for some reason they had cocooned themselves in silk sheets thin as gossamer. The silk covered them completely, including their heads, and for a moment there was almost something besides anger and grief in Jiri's head, some spark of curiosity about the northerners' madness, but the taste of ashes in her mouth killed her wondering. Instead, she searched for Sera and found the paladin standing behind her.

Sera's short hair and the pale skin of her face and neck were marked with soot, but her gleaming armor and the white tabard that she wore over it were perfectly clean, untouched by blood or mud or ash despite everything that had happened yesterday. The paladin was on watch, her dark brown eyes searching the jungle that stretched around them. For a moment those intense eyes rested on Jiri, then went back to her watch.

"I'm sorry for your dead." Sera faced away from Jiri, her words soft and hard to hear against the birdcalls. "They should never have burned. No one should."

Jiri's tongue shifted in her mouth, dry and gritty, and she stared at the paladin's back, watched her watch the jungle. Sera stood straight and tall, her head high, one hand resting on the hilt of her sword and the other on the top edge of the shield that leaned against her leg. Jiri almost asked why she only stared straight ahead. If a leopard came, it would move through the low branches, and the paladin was close enough to the singed edge of the jungle to be within reach of one of the great cats' pounces.

Not that any of those cautious cats would approach this place for days, after what had happened.

The foreigners and their strangeness didn't matter. Nothing mattered, except the thing Jiri didn't want to face.

They should never have burned.

Jiri reached up, touched the bone carvings that hung so heavy around her neck, then turned and forced herself to walk.

The grave was a lonely little thing, a small mound of charred earth. Some bones, Linaria had told her. How many, who—those were things the northern sorcerer couldn't know, couldn't tell Jiri.

Are you there, Hadzi? Did the bones of her lover lie beneath that thin crust of dirt? Did the handsome flesh that hung from those bones form some part of the ash that stung her eyes?

Maybe, Jiri thought, and her silent tears fell.

She crouched before the grave. A piece of wood, crudely carved into the shape of a sword, had been thrust point-down into it. Sera's work, probably. Jiri seemed to recall that the great spirit the paladin followed claimed the sword as a symbol. Otherwise, the mound was empty of anything but ash.

There should be more. Beads and carvings, bits of cloth brightly patterned, little dishes of food. All the traditional offerings to the spirits of the departed, the gifts that would remind them of the things they had loved in this life, that would comfort them as they prepared themselves for their journey to their new home in the spirit world. This bit of wood, this symbol of some foreign god, wouldn't help them. They needed more. They needed . . .

Their families, their friends, their village, and Oza to sing them on.

Now they had only her.

"I'm sorry," Jiri whispered, and the words grated from her mouth, came out harsh and broken by grief and ash. The sound of them made the fury and despair burn higher in Jiri. Her fists clenched, and the little wooden sword smoked, darkened, flames dancing up from it.

"No!" Jiri slapped the burning wooden sword down, smashed the flames out with her hand, each blow raising a cloud of choking ash up from the ground and making a hot flash of pain roar up from her hands. Jiri didn't care, though, didn't stop until the fire was out.

They didn't deserve this, the ones buried here. They didn't deserve any of this. Kneeling in the dirt, in the drifting remnants of the village and its dead, Jiri forced her lips to move. This was what the dead needed, now.

The fire of her rage—that was for those had brought this ruin here, and then run.

Soft, almost silent, the funeral song slipped from Jiri's lips. The last goodbye, the call to the ancestors to reach out and take the hands of those being born into a new world, to pull them through so that no part of them was left to walk unhappy among their people. It was a song she had grown up listening to Oza sing, and she clutched at the necklace that hung from her neck and forced it out of her wounded throat, into the morning air where it was lost in the sound of the monkeys and the birds and the insects and all the other sounds of life that filled the dawn.

"Three hells, why are we still here?"

Morvius wasn't yelling, but his deep voice rumbled across the clearing. Kneeling in front of the grave, hands carefully arranging the few pitiful offerings she had been able to find or make as the sun slowly pulled itself over the horizon, Jiri heard him clearly. She didn't bother to look back at him, though.

He wasn't talking to her.

"We're paying for that pig-sticker you wanted so badly, remember?"

Linaria wasn't nearly as loud, but Jiri could hear her too. She had been listening to the half-elf moving around since she had ended the funeral song. The white-haired woman had woken sometime during the song, but she had waited until it was done to pull herself out of her silken cocoon. Her strange, almost colorless eyes watched Jiri while she built a little fire and heated water over it, making coffee to share with Sera. But Linaria left her alone to gather her offerings in peace, not saying a word.

Morvius, though, had words to say the moment he stretched and groaned himself awake. "Paying? We paid. We killed the demon, and you stuffed that hole shut." The northern man was pulling at the silk wrapped around him, jerking himself free of its flimsy embrace. "That was the job. It's not our fault if something broke out after that. We're done."

"That wasn't all the job."

"What?" Morvius jerked his feet out of the silk and stood, shaking the cloth out like a bird trying to beat a snake to death. "Oh," he said, following Linaria's gaze.

Jiri sat sideways to him and the others, head bowed and eyes on her work. Ignoring them, concentrating on her task, but keeping them in sight. She twitched the last offering into place, a leaf with a mango on it, half-ripe and a little charred, but the best she could find.

"Well, go over there and talk to her. Tell her it's time to go, and she needs to stop playing house with her dead."

"Morvius—"

"Linaria, it's too damn hot already, and it's only going to get hotter. The sun is barely above the trees, and I've already got a river of sweat rolling down my ass. And that's without my armor. It's going to be like the mighty Vanji down there when I put that on."

"Morvius, will you—"

"Oh, and now I've already got a swarm of those little green bastards flying around my head. Y'know, those bugs whose only purpose in life is to try to bugger your eyeball? Those. Gods, I hate—"

"Morvius, shut up." Linaria shook her head and stood. "I'll talk to her. You, drink some coffee and get your things together. And if the bugs are so bad, wrap your mosquito cloth around your head."

"How am I supposed to drink my coffee if I do that?" Morvius waved the silk wadded in his hand in front of his face.

"Drop it over your head and ask Sera to punch a hole in it. I'm sure she'd love to help."

"I would do that," the paladin said, frowning at Morvius. The man made some strange gesture with his fingers at her, and the paladin's frown deepened.

"She's going to kill him, and I really don't care," Linaria muttered as she walked closer. When her shadow stretched beyond Jiri, the half-elf stopped. "Jiri—"

"I know." Jiri looked up from the grave. Bruises mottled the woman's pale face, and her delicate nose was crooked and smeared with ash, but in her strange blue eyes Jiri could read sympathy. "I heard. I'm ready."

"Are you sure?" Linaria asked. "Morvius is loud, but he can wait."

"I've done what I could here. My people need me."

"Your people?" Linaria tilted her head, staring down at her. "They're gone. I thought you would come back to Kibwe with us. To Kalun."

"Most of the village fled to Rough Ford yesterday," Jiri said. "If any of the ones that were still here escaped—" Jiri gestured at the burned-out scar surrounding them. "—*this*, they would have gone there. I need to find them, see if they need help, healing."

"The thing that did this," Linaria said. "It might still be out there."

"I know." Jiri stood, feet grinding in the ashes. "Which is another reason I have to find them. If it comes after them . . ." She trailed off. Across the blasted clearing, a lone mango tree still stood, the branches on one side of it badly singed. In the shadow of its remaining leaves was the Mango Woman, her warning empty now, useless. "I have to go to them. To protect them, to help them. That's what Oza taught me. I have to."

Linaria stared at her, her mouth a line, her eyes unreadable now.

"If you have to," she said finally, "then we'll take you."

A few hours of walking later, the day's rain started, a soft deluge of warm water that poured down through the branches and leaves and drenched them. Its fall altered, but didn't end, Morvius's steady stream of curses.

"What the— Oh by the crap demons that have blessed me today, hold up a minute!"

Jiri stopped in the middle of the thin trail that led to Rough Ford and stared back. The broad-shouldered northern man had just passed through a hanging curtain of vines and was now running his fingers through his dark hair, knocking out leaves and finger-long leeches. Jiri watched him a moment, then glanced at her spear. A leech squirmed across its blade, one of the few that had clung to it when Jiri had used the weapon to move the vines out of her way. It was a good trail they were on, not too muddy, not too dangerous. They should have been to the next village by now. But these foreigners . . .

They're taking me? Keeping me safe?

Jiri flicked her spear, sending the leech arcing out into the jungle. Linaria was going through her clothes now, cursing almost as much as Morvius as she peeled away layers of wet cloth searching for parasites. Sera stood still and stoic, as if she couldn't care less about such things, but Jiri could see her frown, the way her hand kept rising to brush at the back of her neck. How many leeches might have slipped down under the

64

woman's layers of metal and leather, unnoticed and unreachable? Jiri reached for a broad green leaf beside her, held it so that it caught the falling water and took a long drink.

She would never have been able to stop laughing, before.

Jiri closed her eyes. The rain had washed the ashes off her, taken the smell of them away, but she couldn't forget them.

"Come on," she said. "We're almost there."

"We better be," Morvius growled, and they trailed through the steaming jungle behind her, cursing and squelching.

"Boro!"

This close to Rough Ford, the trail opened up, linked into the network of footpaths that ran around the small river village. Looking down its green tunnel, Jiri could see the man walking toward them.

Alone.

She trotted ahead, leaving the others to trudge after her, her heart swelling. Boro had made it. Boro lived. Maybe . . . Getting closer, she could see a poultice wrapped around his left arm, could see the slump of his shoulders, the pain in his eyes. "Boro?" she said, stopping.

"Jiri." Boro stared at her, and everything about him, his expression, the way he held himself, laid a new layer of ashes in her heart. "You shouldn't have come."

They walked a little way up the trail, back toward where Thirty Trees had been, and found a spot to stand and talk.

"After you left, we waited in the village," Boro said. "For a while, nothing happened. Then our fire went out." He stared out into the jungle as he spoke, not looking at her. "Hadzi told Cava to restart it, but they argued so I said I would do it. I bent over the pit, looking for coals, when the whole thing just went up again, poom." His good hand cradled his injured one. "I was lucky. It just singed my braids and burned my hand. If I'd been closer, I would have lost my eyes."

"I can . . ." Jiri trailed off. She had not opened herself to the spirit world this morning, had not bargained with the spirits for their magic. She had no healing to give him. *Stupid. So stupid.* Oza might have forgiven her, but he wouldn't have made the same mistake. "Did you use the ointment I gave you?"

"Yes. I wanted to save it, but Hadzi used it on me. The shaman at Rough Ford said that it saved my hand." Boro cleared his throat. "Hadzi told me to go, then. Told Cava to take me here. I didn't want to, but he was right, and we started walking. We weren't that far away when it happened."

Boro stared down, his face set. "The heat hit us, a great wind of it, tumbled us down, and we heard a roar bigger than thunder. Then it was over and the air was full of ash. I went back. Cava wouldn't, but I did. I went as close as I could to the heat. I saw the emptiness, where the mango trees had been, where our houses had been. And over them, in the sky and in the smoke, I saw something with wings. Wings of fire, wings of smoke."

Boro finally turned his head and let his eyes, haunted and red, rest on hers. "What did you— What happened, Jiri?"

What did you do. Jiri stared Boro in the eyes. She had started to tremble, her eyes hot with tears, listening to Boro, knowing his story meant that Hadzi must be dead. Even though he cut it off, Jiri had heard his accusation. Heard it, and felt fear began to grow in her. And below the fear, burning through it—anger. "Do you think I did something?"

Boro looked away from her again, staring at his hands, the injured one cradled in the whole. "I— No. Not me. Whatever happened, it wasn't you. Not on purpose."

Jiri reached out and caught Boro's shoulders, turning the man to face her. "Boro, a group of raiders stole something from the Pyre, and they let something out. Something terrible that our ancestors had sealed away to die underground. They let it out, not me. Do you think I'd burn Thirty Trees?"

"Jiri," Boro said, and there was pain in his voice, and fear. He jerked himself out of her grip. "You're burning me."

Jiri felt it then, the heat in her hands, the fire that had rushed into her. On Boro's shoulders she could see the lines of little blisters, the hand-shaped print of burns on his skin. "Oh gods and crocodiles, I'm sorry." She looked down at her hands, at the faint traces of steam that rose from between her clenched fingers. "You do. You think I destroyed my home. My people."

"I don't. My father, many of the other survivors, they do." Boro spoke softly, just loud enough for Jiri to hear, but he didn't step closer to her. "Oza came from the outside, Jiri. He wasn't Mosa tribe. He never said what tribe he was. But he was kind and wise and powerful, and Thirty Trees didn't have a shaman, so the village adopted him and made him Mosa.

"When he found you, he probably thought it would be the same, that the Mosa would take you in." Boro shrugged, then winced in pain. "Me and Hadzi and the others that grew up with you, we might have. We knew you. But our parents, all the elders, they knew the village where Oza found you. They knew the people there, or at least they knew the stories about them, that they had fallen deep into the curse that surrounds Smoking Eye. That they kept to the steaming shores of that too-blue lake, away from all others, because their only true friend was fire. They told me that no one was surprised when it burned."

"I remember," Jiri said. "How the adults stared at me, when things first started to burn around me as a child. I remember how Oza always acted calm, but was so worried." Jiri forced her hands open, and the hot, humid air felt cool against her palms. "But they let me stay."

"Because Oza wanted you, and they wanted Oza," Boro said. "They never trusted you, though. You know my father didn't want Hadzi involved with you. It wasn't just because he had marriage plans for his eldest son. He worried about you, about what you were."

"What did he think I was?"

"A girl with too much magic and not enough control. Sometimes. Other times, he wondered if you were a spirit of fire dressed in stolen flesh, a demon that had beguiled Oza into caring for you, and that might be doing the same to his son."

"A demon. Beguiling Oza. And Hadzi." Jiri shook her head, and her braids whipped around her face. "Oza was too wise for that. And I didn't need to be a demon to beguile Hadzi, just a woman with a smile and a hammock I was willing to share."

"I know, Jiri," Boro said. "And I know you. You're no demon. I don't share my father's fears, but I understand them. He's lost almost everything—his home, his wealth, his son. Thirty Trees is gone, and Rough Ford fears that whatever burned our village will come for theirs next. They don't want us to stay, so we'll have to move on, scatter to the other Mosa villages and beg for food and shelter from distant relatives. That will break my father, almost as much as losing Hadzi. He needs someone to blame. So do the others. The elders have already decided. You are not Mosa anymore. "

"They cast me out?" Jiri heard her words as if they came from a vast distance. Oza, gone. Hadzi, gone. Thirty Trees, gone. Now this. Her people. Gone.

Lost in ashes, like everything else.

"I'm sorry, Jiri. I was coming to see if I could find you. To tell you not to come."

Jiri looked at him, injured and alone on the trail. "They didn't send you."

"No. They hoped you wouldn't follow. If you did . . ." He finally looked at her again. "They've set watchers, on the trail. To drive you away, before anything like what happened to Thirty Trees could happen here."

Drive me away. Would they have killed her? There were good hunters in Thirty Trees, and better ones at Rough Ford. She would have never seen them, intent as she was on getting here to warn them. If Boro hadn't come, would it have been poison darts that met her and her companions as they drew close?

Jiri could feel her anger trying to grow again, a heat in her that wanted to flash over to flame. Oza had died protecting these people, had given his life so that Jiri could warn them away. He told her to protect them. Oza—

Oza would tell her to calm herself, to breathe, and let the heat wash away. He would ask her to make the fire burn low and steady, warm and safe. Jiri could hear his voice, saying those words. He had said them to her countless times over the years, repeated them calmly as her adolescent rages had sent flames flickering to life through their home. Spoken them until she believed that she could control herself, control her fire.

She could.

Breathing deep, she forced her anger down, down with the fear and sadness and everything else. She made the fire die, and made herself cool.

"Boro," she said softly. "There was a Bonuwat woman, Patima. She belongs to some foreign group called the Aspis Consortium. She and her friends broke into the Pyre and stole something. When they did that, they released . . . whatever it was you saw."

Jiri reached into her bag, fumbled past the dirty leather of her armor and found a little clay pot. Opening it, she caught the clean smell of the burn ointment she and Oza had made. "That thing they released—it destroyed Thirty Trees, not me. You can tell them that, if you think they might believe you. What they really need to know, though, is that I think this thing might be after what Patima and her companions took, and they went back to Kibwe."

"We should avoid the city?"

"The city, and the villages around it." Jiri scooped a little ointment onto her fingers and took a step toward Boro. When he didn't back away, she moved to him and rubbed the ointment over the burns her hands had left on him. When she was done, she checked his hand.

"Thank you," she said, after she had proven to herself that the Rough Ford shaman had done a good job with Boro's burn. "For coming out here."

"Thank you for the warning." Boro looked at his hand, still held in hers, then stepped into her, wrapping his other arm around her. "Hadzi was a fool, you know. He never knew what he had."

Leaning into him, careful of his burns, Jiri held him tight. "Thank you," she said again, a whisper, then she let him go and stepped back. "Gods, spirits, and ancestors, may they watch, protect, and guide."

He stared at her, stared beyond her at the foreigners, at the trail that twisted back toward the ruin of the village they had grown up in, toward Kibwe. "And may they go with you too, Jiri Maju. With you too."

Jiri went up the trail slowly, walking to where the northerners waited.

Where else did she have to go?

Linaria stood up from the fallen tree limb she had been resting on, brushing away a thumb-sized millipede that had crawled onto her leg. Morvius, sitting beside her with his boots off, hunting ticks around his ankles, looked up.

"So are you good from here?" he asked. "Or do you need us to walk you to their doorstep?"

"Morvius." Linaria didn't raise her voice, but her warning was as clear as a naked blade. The man grumbled, but quietly. Linaria, satisfied, walked to Jiri. "We're going back to Kibwe," the pale woman said. "Come with us, and Kalun will have a place for you."

"If you heard us," Jiri said, "then you know there's no place for me. Not anymore."

"I didn't hear him. You two talked too quiet, too close, and I don't know your language nearly well enough. But I've seen the look that's in your eyes now." Linaria pushed back her hair, white as clouds even when soaked with sweat. "I'm going to tell you something, Jiri, and you're going to think it's a load of shit now, but you might find it important, later. I know what it's like to lose everything. I know that you're numb, because the hurt is too much. That's why you have to keep moving. Because when that numbness goes, when the hurt comes in, that's all you're going to have, and you're going to be useless. Fall apart in Kibwe, with Kalun. You may not know him, but he's a good man. He'll help you, and you'll need it. You've lost your world, Jiri, and you're going to have to rebuild it, one piece at a time."

Jiri stared into the woman's not-quite-human eyes. *Do you know what it's like?* The words echoed in her, in the emptiness left after everything else had gone to ash. *To have your whole world burn? Do you? I don't know that you do, and you're right, all your words sound like shit to me.*

Again, though, there was the simple question.

Where else did she have to go?

She didn't speak. Jiri just nodded, once.

"All right." Linaria turned from her, back toward Morvius, who was pulling on his boots, and Sera, who had stood silently watching, dark eyes on Jiri, like they always seemed to be. "Let's go."

"Oh, can we go now?" Morvius stood and stomped his boots into place. "Are you sure? Because if your little friend there wants to collect some more soul-crushing traumas, I suppose we can wade through another day's worth of mud and leeches."

"Morvius," Linaria said, her voice perfectly level. "I solemnly swear to Calistria that if you say one more word in the next half hour, I will freeze your balls to ice and then crush them under my heel. Understand?"

Morvius opened his mouth, then shut it. His lips tilted instead into a crooked smile, and he swept a graceful bow to the half-elf.

Sera tilted her head, waiting for them all to pass to take her place in the back. "Do you try to inspire violence from all the women you meet, Morvius, or is it just a natural talent of yours?"

Morvius flipped the same gesture at the paladin that he had made this morning, but stayed silent. Jiri stayed silent too, and dropped her eyes. She had no interest in watching these people quarrel, or in the jungle that surrounded her, or in the muddy trail at her feet. She only wanted to move, to drag herself forward, away from Boro, away from the people who weren't her people anymore, away from everything and into the nothing that was now her life.

Chapter Six
Drums

There were drums in the Adayenki.

Jiri didn't really hear them. Curled in the soft strangeness of the bed Kalun had given her, she didn't want to hear the drums, or see the whitewashed stone walls around her, or smell the rich tang of spice and perfume, animals and sweat, food and flowers that drifted through the carved latticework covering the room's windows.

She felt them, though.

Their rhythm pounded through her bones and made her tremble. She knew this music. The heart of Kibwe, the tapestry-bounded Adayenki Pavilion, was hosting an Orchid Dance. A year ago she had taken a drum and handed it to Hadzi and danced to this rhythm, her braids swinging, her heart pounding, smiling whenever she had swung near the handsome young man. So scared and proud and happy, dancing beneath the branches of Thirty Trees' mango grove in the flickering light of the fire . . .

Jiri curled tighter into herself, trying not to feel the drums.

Trying not to feel anything, and almost succeeding, until someone began to beat on her door as if it were a drum, too.

Jiri opened her eyes. Across the room, a flood of girls spilled through her door, four of them, children and adolescents. Jiri recognized Fara, Kalun's daughter, and from their looks the other three were her sisters. They wrinkled their noses and stared at her, then scattered when Kalun stomped in behind them.

"Move those screens. Get some light in here, and air this place out. Fazi, gather those food trays. Fori, you get the chamber pot."

"Eww, Papa—"

"Do it," snapped Kalun. "Or would you rather have your mother up here?"

The girls whirled into action, snapping back the lattice, picking up the dishes of food that had been brought to Jiri and ignored, hauling off the stinking pot. Jiri watched them silently, then rolled to face the wall.

"No, Jiri. Enough."

Strong hands gathered her up, lifted her out of bed and set her on her feet. She staggered and Kalun caught her, wrapping a sheet around her like a cloak.

"There's a time for mourning, girl, and it's probably longer than this, but my wife will kill us both if this room isn't cleaned. Do you want your first song in the spirit world to be about being strangled by an old Tirakici innkeeper?"

Jiri clutched the sheet and didn't answer. She just stared at the man, empty.

He sighed. "All right. Faya, take the sheets for washing. No, not the one she's wearing. Collect that from the baths. Fara, you take her there and get her clean."

"I don't want a bath," Jiri said, or tried to say. After so much crying, her voice barely worked.

"You don't want anything except for everything to be the way it was, and you can't have that," Kalun said. "I still owe your Oza a debt, and I've only paid part of it. Getting you on your feet will pay a bit more." He pushed her, gently but firmly, toward the door. "Go, or I'll carry you."

For a moment, a flicker of heat ran through Jiri, but she crushed it out before it could flare into flame. *I don't want fire. Not anymore.* She let Kalun push her, let his daughter take her hand and pull her along.

"It's all right," Fara told her in the sort of voice one used for babies. "I don't like baths either." The girl wrinkled her nose a little. "I don't usually smell as bad as you do, though."

There was hot water and stiff-bristled brushes. Then cool water, and all four of the girls were back, carefully untangling Jiri's remaining braids, pulling them apart and putting them back together. Jiri sat through it all, trying to hold on to her silence, her pain, but the feel of the water on her, the brushes across her skin, the strange smell of the soap they used in the city, the painful tugs on her hair, the sound of the drums and the chatter of the girls, pulled her unwillingly from the oblivion she had been trying to cling to.

When Jiri's bath was done and her braids were back and mostly straight, Faya tied a bright green wrap dress under her arms. Jiri moved carefully, not used to the way the long dress flapped around her ankles, and didn't realize that Faya wasn't leading her back to her room until the girl opened the door to Kalun's talking room.

"What now, innkeeper?" Jiri asked, stepping in. Linaria was there, dressed in tight-fitting breeches and a loose shirt, the pale blue cloth of both finely made. The white-haired woman's face had been healed, her black eyes gone and her broken nose back to its delicate shape. Morvius slouched beside her, staring down at a book with brightly painted illustrations of bizarre beasts, slightly more shaven than last time Jiri had seen him. His clothes were ornate but shabby, just like the ones she had first met him in.

"Well, you're talking. That's good." Kalun was dressed in silk again, a pale red embroidered with white. He caught her frown and leaned back on his carved stool. "Maybe." He pointed toward a tray by an empty bench. "There's food and drink. I don't think you've had much of either since you came back."

Jiri could smell the food, rice and goat and spices, and her stomach twisted, wanting it. She ignored her body, though, and focused on Kalun. "I'm on my feet. So what now? Do we know what those Aspis people unleashed? Has it destroyed anything since Thirty Trees?"

"Not that we know of," Linaria said. "I've asked around. No one has seen anything. Maybe it went back to its hole. Maybe it was something summoned, that didn't last."

"*You* asked around." Jiri stared at the foreigner. Her stomach growled loudly, and she gave up and went to the tray.

"She did, and I did," Kalun said. "And nothing. Rough Ford is untouched. Your people are moving on, spreading out to the other Mosa villages. The talk in the market is that Thirty Trees was destroyed by demons. Or bad-luck magic."

Jiri tore a piece of flatbread in half and dug it into a bowl of stew. *Bad-luck magic.* Yes, but not hers. "It's not gone. I don't know where it is, what it is, but I know that. That thing . . ." Dreams had come to her, in the dark valleys of sleep that she had fallen into after returning to Kibwe. Dreams of flames and screams, of ashes drifting, a great cloud of them, and behind them something bright and hungry. "It's out there, somewhere. It's going to burn again." She scooped up another portion of stew, chewed and swallowed. "What about those people?"

"You mean the Consortium?" Kalun said. "What about them?"

"Do you know where they are? Are they here? That woman, Patima. She had something, something she had stolen from the Pyre. If we get it from her, we might find out what this thing is, what we need to do to seal it back where it belongs."

"Ha!" barked Morvius, finally bothering to look up from his book. "Check the balls on this one. Steal it back. From the Aspis Consortium. That would be a good trick. Tell me, girl, who the hell do you mean when you say *we?*"

Jiri ignored the broad-shouldered man, still focused on Kalun. "They stole something dangerous, something that doesn't belong to them, and my people paid the price. Why can't we take it back, before that thing comes again, before anyone else burns?"

"Why can't we steal Leopard's teeth, so that he can't eat our children?" Kalun sighed. "Jiri, I've no love for the Consortium. Believe me. They're trying to slither their way into Kibwe the same way they've snaked themselves into the western Expanse, greasing their passage with blood and gold." The old man leaned back, frowning, and despite its lines his face showed the fierceness of the warrior he had once been. "If I could, Jiri, I'd do just what you say and more. I'd smash open that vipers' nest and stomp everything that tried to crawl away. But I can't. Nobody trusts the Aspis Consortium here, but Amiro is free with his coin and greed is as good as love among the powerful."

"Never mind the fact that his crew might be the toughest group of adventurers this side of the Shattered Range." A delicate glass half full of white wine dangled from Linaria's fingers, the almost colorless fluid moving as she swirled the cup. "Amiro is a cleric of Abadar, and he seems just as able to bargain magic away from the merchant god as he does favors from Kibwe's council. Corrianne is a spoiled brat, but a strong caster. Mikki is as vicious as she is short. Patima . . ." Linaria frowned and stilled her wine. "She's been Amiro's hound for years, digging out every hidden ruin and secret treasure barrow near this town. But I've never been able to figure her out, to understand what she wants."

"Money and power," Morvius said. "What else?"

"Yes." Linaria went back to swirling her wine. "But I feel like the why of it for her is tangled. The others, I unfortunately understand. Patima, I don't. There's something mad under that smooth facade of hers. Something dangerous."

"You know them. You know where they are. But you're not doing anything about them." For the first time since Thirty Trees, Jiri could feel something besides despair. Her fists were clenched with frustration, and Oza's necklace hung heavy on her. *What would he do? Not stand around and talk.*

No, but he had power. The spirits came to his voice, made their magic his, gave him their shapes to wear. Jiri . . .

I don't have that strength. Not yet. I'm not Oza. I'm not even as strong as these fools.

"We have to do something," Jiri said, her words almost lost beneath the distant roll of the drums.

"You will," Kalun said. He reached beneath his shirt and pulled out a small bag that clinked when he tossed it to Jiri. "You lost everything, so now you'll go shopping. Linaria and Morvius will take you to the market and help you get what you need."

"What?" The bag of coin dangled from Jiri's hand like a dead snake. "You want me to go to the market? With them?"

"He does." Morvius stood. "Here's your first lesson in the adventuring life, runt. You want to find treasure, you need treasure, and the sooner you learn to bargain like a Drumish fishmonger the better you'll do."

"I'm not a raider," Jiri said. "Not a treasure-hunting thief, like this Consortium." *Or you*, she bit back.

"'Course not. You just want to nip over to the Aspis compound and cut some throats and take their stuff." He grinned at her, his green eyes narrow with amusement and challenge. "So bring your coin, and we'll get you some pants so you can do it proper."

"Is that what you're looking for?"

Jiri stopped, trying to see the merchant that Linaria was pointing to. Kibwe's great market surged with activity, the crowd a chattering sea washing around them. Most of the people stood taller than Jiri. "There? No," she said, spotting a merchant who stood beneath a tall rack of dress cloths, their bright colors blending and clashing with the woven tapestries that spread behind him, marking the border of the Adayenki.

"No, there. Look, that ugly bird-woman statue is pointing at it with her spear."

The foreign woman pointed over the crowd, and Jiri looked up. A granite pillar stood before them, one of the dozens that dotted Kibwe. On its top stood a soapstone statue of a woman with the spreading wings of a bat and the fierce head of a hawk. The ancient warrior's spear did point down at the market, and when Jiri followed it she caught sight of bolts of black and brown cloth.

"That's mud cloth, right?"

"That's—" Jiri started to answer, but something about the statue pulled at her attention. Had it been holding its spear like that earlier? Wasn't it pointing toward the sky? When Jiri had come to Kibwe as a child, she had begged Oza for stories about these fierce statues. Even in Thirty Trees she had heard stories about them, how they moved when no one was looking, switching places with one another when the storms came at night. *They were made by the same hands that carved these walls*, he had told her, pointing to the great granite walls that ringed the city. *Our ancestor's hands were very clever, and held so many dangerous secrets.*

Dangerous secrets. Did Oza know what lay beneath the Pyre? What that thing was that had been released? Jiri touched his necklace, felt the grief and anger that seemed as firmly threaded on it as the bone animal carvings.

It's not fair. You taught me so much, but so little, and now I need you and you're gone and I don't know what I should do, and I just miss you, I miss Thirty Trees and Hadzi and everything . . .

"Jiri, is that it?"

Linaria's question barely made it through the shadows of grief that had sprung up around Jiri, but the woman's pale blue eyes cut through them, focused on her.

"Are you all right?"

"I'm fine," Jiri said. *And why do you care, anyway?* She rubbed her hands across her eyes, hating the grief that kept coming for her but helpless before it.

"Gods, is she crying again?" Morvius stood behind them, but his deep voice carried over the noise of the crowd and the sound of the drums. "What is she, four?"

"No," Linaria said, her voice cold. "She just had her entire world destroyed."

"And that's just terrible, but what's that have to do with us?" The market seethed around them, people jostling each other as they moved from vendor to vendor, but everyone dodged the broad-shouldered foreigner, giving him space. "We did the job. We killed the demon, we got paid. So what in nine hells are we doing now? I don't remember Kalun paying us to be her new best friends."

"He didn't." Linaria folded her arms and stared at the fighter, and the air around her grew cooler despite the thick heat. "*I'm* being sympathetic because I'm a decent person. And you're going to fake being polite about it because that's one of my conditions for you following me around, understand? It's been three years, Morvius. You should know by now that I do a lot of things that you wouldn't, things that aren't solely motivated by lust or greed."

"Yeah, stupid crap."

"Yes," Linaria said. "Stupid crap you don't have to deal with. You can stop following me anytime you want."

"I could," Morvius said, but his eyes gleamed and the corner of his mouth turned up. "But then I wouldn't be able to stare at your ass."

"No, you wouldn't. So just shut up and look pretty, your whining's getting on my nerves." The sorcerer turned back to Jiri, the chill around her fading away into the heat. "Let's go."

They picked their way through the crowd to the booth, dodging merchants and customers, gangs of children and revelers that had spilled away from the Orchid Dance that filled the Adayenki, draped in beads and flowers and reeking of palm wine. They stopped once to watch a group of tall Bekyar stalk by, their piercings gleaming copper and gold among their scars, their expressions fierce and disdainful. When they reached the merchant that Linaria had found, Jiri stared at the bolts of cloth that hung from the racks surrounding him. Mud cloth, just like she had worn her whole life, cotton covered with intricate designs of brown and black, yellow and white. Designs that were close to—but not the same as—the simple, angular ones she had grown up with.

Seeing them, knowing that they weren't made by her tribe—by the people who had once been her tribe—Jiri could feel her eyes grow hot, but she forced the tears away.

I am not a child, whatever that baboon Morvius might think.

Quickly, not thinking, she picked out the clothes she wanted. Loincloths and pants and long, light shirts to wear over them, done in black and brown patterns that would blend with the shadows that stretched below the jungle's canopy. Linaria argued with the merchant while Morvius loomed behind her, throwing fierce looks at anyone else who started to approach, scaring off customers until the merchant reluctantly dropped his price. Holding her new clothes, Jiri spilled out some of the coin Kalun had given her, then followed the foreigners as they moved on.

"I want to look at what scrolls they have."

"Scrolls are bloody expensive, Lin. Can't we— Oh, demon balls."

"What?"

Jiri already knew what, even as Linaria asked the question. She could see whom Morvius was glaring at over the crowd.

The paladin's armor gleamed like a mirror despite the dust. The pale skin of Sera's face wasn't quite as clean, but it was again free from sweat. The holy warrior marched through the crowd, cutting through it like a sword, but chattering children flowed behind her instead of blood. She stopped in front of Jiri's group, dark eyes flicking over each of them before stopping on the shaman.

"You've recovered."

"Gods, Sera. We've just got her up and moving." Linaria edged over, putting herself partly between the paladin and Jiri. "She doesn't want to be interrogated."

"Or converted," Morvius said cheerfully, stepping in from the other side.

Now Jiri was staring at both their backs. She reached out and touched the arms of the foreigners, her shortness making her feel like a child. "What does she want?"

Linaria stepped to the side, letting Jiri step around the unmoving Morvius. "She wants to ask you questions about the thing that came out of that ruin. She thinks—"

"She thinks it's *eeevil*," Morvius said, drawing the word out mockingly. "So she wants to go poke it with her sword. That's a thing, with her and her church."

Sera's sword hand twitched, but she otherwise ignored Morvius. "It *is* evil. It burned your village, Jiri. What was it?"

"What was it?" Jiri had no love for this woman. She could feel the condescension in her, and it made her want to spit. But Sera had killed the demon that had killed Oza.

The others helped.

I helped.

True, but Sera's sword had been the one that had carved the demon open at the end, had spilled its putrid essence out and sent its spirit back to the terrible place that was its home. Sera fought demons, and that made her a weapon, even though she was a dangerous one that might turn in Jiri's hand and cut her if she wasn't careful.

I need weapons.

"I don't know," Jiri said. "A spirit of fire, of destruction. Something trapped long ago, sealed away by my ancestors. Bound, until those raiders released it."

"Evil cannot be contained." Sera shifted in her armor, the metal shell a strange affectation inside these walls, but in the fierceness of her fanaticism she didn't look foolish. "It must be cleansed."

"Maybe," Jiri said, and the strange words of the common tongue caught in her mouth, held for a moment by uncertainty and pride until she forced them out. "Maybe you're right."

"You know she doesn't trust you," Linaria said.

Jiri carefully set aside a cluster of dried herbs, mindful of the merchant and the guards who stood so still and watchful around her and Linaria. Like crocodiles in the water, waiting for them to make the smallest wrong move. Considering the value of the magical trinkets, scrolls, and spell components spread on the tables beneath this bright awning, Jiri understood their caution, but was still unnerved by it.

Their attention made her almost as nervous as Sera's.

"I see how she watches me. She doesn't hide her suspicions well."

"She doesn't try." Linaria picked up a scroll and waved two fingers at the merchant. His face twisted into a frown, and he held up four. For a moment they flashed fingers at each other silently until Linaria spread her hand and put the scroll back down. A strange form of bargaining, just as fierce as the shouting going on in the other parts of the market, but quieter.

"Sera and Morvius have more in common than they would ever admit," Linaria said, flipping through another short stack of parchment sheets. "Neither one of them has any use for tact." She pulled her hand back and looked over her shoulder. Beyond the awning, Morvius sprawled in the shade cast by one of the Adayenki's tapestries, paging through a thin book he had found at one of the stalls they had passed. Sera stood a little away from him, her armor shining like water under the sun.

"She wants to help," Jiri said.

"Yes," Linaria said. "Herself." The half-elf looked back at Jiri. "Never forget that. She says she wants to hunt this thing because it destroyed your village, murdered your people. That's a kind of truth, but Sera doesn't care about your people. She thinks you're all savages who worship ghosts and demons, and she thinks your village was just a pile of sticks and mud. Their deaths, and the destruction of your home, were just signs for her. Like tracks for a hunter, announcing the presence of her quarry." Linaria lowered her voice a little more. "The church of Iomedae sent her here to hunt for evil, so that's what she's going to do. Hunt and hunt, until she's brought them enough trophies to buy her passage back to the north, where she thinks the real world is. She'll help you as long as it helps her, and not a moment more."

"I guessed as much," Jiri said. "Which means I understand her. Which is a kind of trust."

"A strange kind," Linaria said, looking back out again at Morvius. "But one I've used."

"It's the ones you don't understand—" Jiri began.

"—that are the hardest to trust," Linaria finished.

The women stared at each other, Jiri expressionless, Linaria smiling faintly.

"Do you need any of that?" the sorcerer finally asked, nodding toward the neat bundles of herbs.

"These things? I could gather all this within a stone's throw of Kibwe's walls. Why would I pay for them? Can we go back now?"

Linaria nodded and they walked away from the merchant, ignoring his pointed *humph*.

"Done?" Morvius said, shutting his book.

"Done," Linaria answered. "We can go back to the inn now, and you can read your dirty poetry in comfort."

Morvius grinned and shrugged. "Well, if you're tired of the heat and crying girl needs her bed, we can go back. If you want to shop more though, I don't mind waiting so much now."

"What?" Linaria asked, suspicious. She turned to look where Morvius had been staring. "Oh. Of course."

Jiri had clenched her teeth at the man's crying girl comment, but she turned to see what Morvius had found. She just saw more market, more revelers, and more workers. "What?"

"Them," Linaria said.

"Oh." Jiri could see them, a group of young women clustered around a sweets vendor. Their hair was hennaed and worked into intricate braids with glass beads, shells, and brass, and they wore bracelets on their ankles and wrists that chimed as they moved and laughed. Their clothes were bright and loose, and for a moment Jiri felt a twinge of envy. They would be beautiful when they danced, their colorful skirts swirling around them, their jewelry and beads flashing.

I never dressed so fine when I danced for Hadzi.

More memories, tearing at her, and Jiri forced them away. "It's for the Orchid Dance," she said. "They've dressed to catch the eye of a lover."

"Dressed?" Morvius said. "I wouldn't think that even you people would call that dressed."

Jiri looked to the man, not understanding, then realized that he wasn't staring at the dancers. His eyes were on a group of men and women beyond them, hauling in baskets of fish to sell. They were dirty with their work, and wore nothing but loincloths smeared with mud and sweat.

"Them? Why would you stare at them? They're not dressed for anything."

"Because," Morvius said with exaggerated patience, "they're not dressed."

"That's—" Jiri started, but Sera cut her off.

"Indecent. Just because these people don't know how to be proper doesn't mean you should stare at them."

Don't know . . . The righteous disdain in the paladin's voice made Jiri slide her eyes to her. "You come from the north."

Jiri's words came out even, but Sera must have heard something in them. The woman turned toward her, squaring off as if she were getting ready for battle. "My family is of Chelish descent. But I grew up in Andoran."

The names barely meant anything to Jiri, and she ignored them. "My teacher. Oza. He traveled in the north. He said it was so cold that the rain sometimes fell like chunks of glass and that the wind could strip all the heat from you and leave you dead in minutes. He told me the people there had to dress themselves in layer after layer just to stay warm. He told me he could barely breathe with all the cloth wrapped around him, and when he did he regretted it because all the clothes that everyone wore were never washed enough."

"What are you saying, girl?" Sera asked.

"I'm saying that you northerners drown yourself in cloth because up there, in the cold, it is *proper* to do so. You'd die without all that stinking cloth. Here, in the Mwangi, you may have noticed that things are different. There's no cold here, and the rain falls warm and often." Jiri swept her eyes over the paladin's gleaming armor. "Wearing too much clothing here makes you overheat. It gives parasites a place to hide. It holds your sweat and your scent and attracts predators. It gets wet and weighs you down, saps your strength and drowns you. It rots against your skin and helps start disease. In the jungle, dressing like you do in the north can kill you."

Jiri hugged the bolts of mud cloth she had bought close to the wrap-dress Kalun had given her. "Here, in Kibwe, I can dress like this, in something pretty, something bright. In the jungle, I wear my mud cloth. Sometimes, if necessary, I just wear a loincloth, and no one thinks anything of it." She tilted her head toward Morvius. "No one stares. Because I'm not *indecent.* I'm just dressed for the place I live in, wearing what works best in my home. I'm just dressing *proper.*"

"Ouch, Sera. She jerked you up by the short hairs there, didn't she?" Morvius laughed, looking up at Jiri. "Y'know, runt, you're not so bad when you're not crying."

Sera ignored him, frowning at Jiri. "What I mean—" she started.

"Is that the first thing you're going to teach these damned savages is how to dress themselves?" Linaria stared at Sera, and the wicked gleam in her eyes almost made her look like Morvius. "Isn't that what you told me right after you got here?"

Sera gave up trying to look reasonable. Her sword hand fell to the hilt that rode her hip, and her face went hard. "It isn't moral. It isn't right."

Linaria laughed, like bells tinkling. "Gods, woman, are you ever going to realize that people might decide to do something differently than you for good reason? That they're not just ignorant or evil?"

"Give it up, Linaria," Morvius said. "You'd have a better chance getting her into a loincloth than you would getting her to admit that, and at least the former would be entertain— Uh-oh."

Jiri had been staring at the paladin, wondering about the wisdom of trying to use her. When Morvius broke off, she looked away and saw what had caught the man's eye.

Two women, breaking out of the crowd to stop near them.

Patima and Corrianne, of the Aspis Consortium.

Chapter Seven
Fire in the Adayenki

Linaria's hand rested cool and light on Jiri's shoulder, but her grip tightened fast when Jiri started to move.

"Don't," Linaria whispered. "This isn't the place. This isn't the time."

Where then? When? Jiri didn't bother to voice her questions, but she didn't pull against Linaria's grip. Something in her had shifted. She forgot the market and the crowd, her annoyance at Sera. The dark shadows of her grief that had been so close fell away, and the bright anger that they had been covering ran through her, hot and alive. Since Boro, she had fought so hard to keep that heat down, banked and buried deep. Now she didn't care.

Patima. Corrianne. Two of the raiders who had killed Oza and destroyed Thirty Trees.

Jiri let the fire grow in her.

She wanted to burn.

"Linaria! Morvius! Sera! How *lovely* to see you all!" Corrianne flashed them a smile bright with spite. The magician was dressed in something ridiculous and fine, a black silk dress threaded with silver. Its neckline dipped low, but it had sleeves long enough to cover her hands, and her face was sweaty beneath an elaborate black hat. Behind her, Patima was dressed much more simply in a loose gray silk tunic that came down to her knees. The women were flanked by two large men who carried wooden clubs studded with brass, and a small crowd of children trailed them, carrying baskets stuffed with their purchases.

"*So* glad you made it out of that beastly jungle. Did that horrible thing trouble you much?" Corrianne's words were poisonously delighted. "I hope not. Linaria, dear! You look so much better. I can hardly tell your nose was broken. How's your belly? Mikki's knife didn't leave a scar, did it? She's so rude! Halflings, though. They're just awful."

"You stole something," Jiri said.

Corrianne glanced at her, then dismissed her. "And Morvius. I heard you're playing with a new spear. Is it long? Is it strong?" She tilted her head and looked at him with a flirty smile and hateful eyes. "Has Linaria given you a chance to try it out yet, or is she still—"

Jiri spoke again, interrupting. "You stole it from the Pyre, and my people burned."

The magician turned her eyes from Morvius and looked at Linaria. "I see you found a pet in the jungle. Is it some kind of dog, with all that yapping?"

"What was it?" Jiri had stopped paying attention to Corrianne. The magician was acting the monkey, throwing crap and howling, and just as small. Jiri looked past her and spoke to Patima. "What did you steal? What did you unleash?"

"I took what I wanted." Patima's voice cut easily through the low roar of the marketplace and the drums that still beat in the Adayenki Pavilion. She used Jiri's native language, her western accent clear. "What I needed. As for what I released. What do you think it was?"

"Something that the ancestors sealed away and warned us never to approach, for good reason. You let it go, and it destroyed my village, killed my people. And your demon—" The words caught in Jiri's throat like hot ashes. Linaria had said that this woman with the pretty voice had something that could bring her demons.

"Oh, Patima, please." Corrianne rolled her eyes. "Don't talk to it, you'll just encourage it, and I don't want it following us home."

"Corrianne," Patima said, switching smoothly back to the so-called common tongue, the trade language shared by locals and northerners alike. "I know you won't shut up, but understand that picking a fight with those three is going to end far better for you than picking one with me."

The magician rolled her eyes again and turned her back on the Bonuwat woman. "Sera! You're still doing that thing with your hair. I've always said that the servants of Iomedae were *so* brave."

Patima dismissed Corrianne and stepped away from her, getting a little closer to Jiri. Her guard moved with her, staying to the side but right there, ready to step between his employer and Jiri.

"I left the demon to guard our retreat. A good idea that worked out rather differently than expected." Patima's words came smooth, hypnotic, like a story. "I felt it, when you killed it. That's when I knew our time was up. I told the others to run and grabbed what we came for. That's when the other thing came, when it poured itself out of the air. If we hadn't been running already, those wings of fire would have closed around us and we would have been the ones to burn." Patima smiled, a slow, beautiful smile that didn't touch her hard, dark eyes. "You saved us, and I don't even have your name to give you thanks."

Saved them. Oza had given his life, and Jiri had almost lost hers, and it had all been for nothing—for worse than nothing. Dimly, Jiri knew that Linaria was cursing, that the white-haired woman had snatched her hand away from Jiri's shoulder like it was a hot coal, but all that mattered was the woman standing in front of her. "I don't want your thanks." Jiri ground out the words. "You should have burned."

"And maybe someday I will," Patima said softly. "But not today." She stepped back. "There are bigger things in the Expanse, girl, than one village. I didn't mean for your people to die, but I don't mourn them. I do what I have to."

"What you have to do is give back what you've stolen. Before anyone else dies."

Patima looked at Jiri, her eyes dark, expressionless, dead.

"No," she said. "I don't." Then she turned and started walking away.

"Well, that seems to have gone badly. I wonder what your ugly little pet said to Patima?"

Jiri barely heard Corrianne. The anger she had let warm her had flashed over to rage, and fire crackled through her. "Raider!" she shouted and raised her hand, flames springing to life around it. "You killed my father!"

"Jiri, no!" Linaria grabbed Jiri's arm, and this time her hand wasn't cool. It was cold, so cold it burned, and the flames that Jiri had been just about to throw hissed and died, swallowed by frost.

"She's getting away," Jiri shouted, uncaring that the Aspis guards had hefted their clubs and were watching her, that Morvius had moved up beside Linaria, that Corrianne was smirking. The bearer kids were scattering, and the crowd was pulling back, the merchants hastily gathering in their wares and the girls dressed for dancing fleeing in a swirl of flashing cloth. None of that mattered. Jiri's vision had narrowed down to Patima's back, disappearing into the panicked crowd.

"She's walking away, and you're going to let her." Linaria jerked her arm, using her height to pull Jiri to face her. Cold crackled around her, burning like white fire, swallowing the flames that flashed up Jiri's arm. "This isn't the place for this, Jiri. Pull yourself together, or I swear I'll have Morvius knock you out."

Jiri stared at the half-elf, and the fire in her raged. It wanted to lash out, to burn Patima, Corrianne, anyone that stood between her and the vengeance she desperately wanted. But Linaria's cold was draining that dangerous heat, and in her words Jiri could hear an echo of Oza, teaching her control.

Jiri pulled her arm from Linaria's grip. She spun, turning her back on Corrianne. On Patima. Staring at the great tapestry that separated the market and the Adayenki, she forced her anger down, out, until the fire in her had sunk to coals, burning deep.

"That's it, Jiri." Linaria's voice was steady, calming. "That's it."

"Yeah, that's great," Morvius said. "But maybe we should do something about that tapestry. It's kind of on fire."

The dancers were made of shining threads of black and gold and red, but their colors were dull beneath the heavy layer of white frost that covered them. Jiri stared at the stuff, like diamonds uncountable, covering the dancers and the charred spots that her anger had burned into the cloth, and she shook. From cold or anger or fear of what she had done, she didn't know.

Probably all of them.

"I think you got it, Linaria." Morvius ran his broad hand over the huge tapestry, one of the many that made up the Adayenki's border, the frost on it already steaming away in the sun. He stopped over the biggest burned patch, holding his hand there. "Cold as Baba Yaga's left—"

"We should go." Linaria shook her hands, scattering the droplets of water that had condensed on her fingers after she had fanned them out and poured her cold magic across the spreading flames.

"What makes you think that?" Morvius said, scooping up his book.

The drums were still beating on the other side of the tapestry, the Orchid Dance still going on in the Adayenki. Jiri's fires had gone unnoticed in the Pavilion, thanks to Linaria. Out here, though, a crowd arced in front of them, staring, pointing and talking. Jiri clenched her hands and ducked her head, shame filling her. What would Oza say?

Nothing. He'll say nothing because Patima's demon tore him apart, laughing.

Jiri pushed her fists against the dirt, shoved herself up and stood.

I will keep control. But I will keep my anger.

The crowd rippled when she rose, and Jiri felt a thread of fear growing in her as the chatter grew louder.

"Doesn't this remind you of that day in Merab?" Morvius asked.

"Yes," Linaria said, much less cheerfully. "Do you think we should start running now?"

"Nope, too late. Here comes the guard."

Jiri, not nearly as tall and trying not to look at the crowd, couldn't see them. She could hear them though, the "sa-sa-sa" that the Kibwe guard called out to clear their path, a call taken from the goat herders who drove their animals through the city. Soon they spilled through the throng, a group of big men with long clubs, short loops of rope hanging from their belts. A woman led them, older and shorter, her only weapon a little blowpipe that rested on her hip. Jiri knew that most of those darts were tipped with a poison that could drop a person into a sleep that would last hours, maybe days.

The poison on the other darts could kill a person in the time it took them to take three steps.

The woman stopped, the men flanking her, and her sharp eyes took in Jiri, her pale companions, and the charred tapestry.

"What passes here?" she asked, her voice flat and unhappy.

"Well," Morvius drawled, but before he could continue another voice cut through the low mutter of the watching crowd.

"Oh, guardswoman! I can help." From the edge of the crowd, Corrianne stepped out. One of her toughs still stood beside her, his frown and the grip on his club keeping a small zone of clear space around him and the northern mage. "I saw *everything*."

"Good gods' balls," Morvius muttered. "Of course she stuck around."

"Of course," Linaria breathed from Jiri's other side.

"How worse would it make things if we had our runt here catch her on fire?" Morvius said, his voice still low.

"Much," Linaria said. She touched Jiri's arm. "She'll try to bait you. Don't rise to it."

"—were just doing some shopping when these people accosted us." Corrianne had pitched her voice a little higher and had widened her eyes, making herself seem younger, frightened. "I know the northerners. They're raiders, and the man is notorious for making advances on anything that moves. They spoke to us, crude and insulting, but we ignored them and tried to move on. That's when the girl used magic to attack us. She pulled fire from the air and threw it at my companion. Then she began to throw it everywhere, endangering everyone around. Truly, it was a miracle that no one was killed, that the marketplace didn't burn."

"I see." The guard leader looked at Corrianne with the same expression as someone examining her feet after walking through a camel pen. Then she turned to Jiri and her companions. "Is that what happened?"

"No," said a new voice.

Morvius was just opening his mouth when that word cut him off. Jiri looked past him and saw Sera, whom she had forgotten about the moment Patima and Corrianne had appeared, stepping forward.

"I am Sera Galonnica, servant of Iomedae, goddess of truth, protector of justice. I can bear witness to what happened here."

"Oh. Well, great." The guard leader shifted her weight back. "Bear away, then."

Sera frowned at the woman, then shifted her eyes to Corrianne. "That woman and her companions are responsible for murder, attempted murder, summoning a demon, stealing an artifact, and releasing an ancient evil that destroyed my companion Jiri's village."

"All that, eh?" the guardswoman asked. "So you tried to catch her on fire?"

"No," Sera said. "My companion struck out at the other woman who was here. She did so because she was taunted by this poisonous brat."

"Poisonous brat?" Corrianne's mask of frightened innocence vanished, her snarling petulance breaking through it like a crocodile surging out of muddy water. "Listen here, you self-righteous b—"

"Let's stop that right now," the guardswoman snapped. She looked over at Corrianne. "Your companion. Was she burned?"

Corrianne glowered at the woman, considering, then shook her head.

"So no one was hurt, and nothing was harmed but this tapestry." The woman looked around, waiting for someone to object. When no one did, she turned back to Jiri. "Then the only thing that concerns me here is that burnt cloth. Which belongs to Kibwe. Do you have any coin?"

"I do," Jiri said, and handed over the purse that Kalun had given her. Beside her Morvius twitched, but he didn't stop her. The guardswoman took the purse and stared into it, then flashed her a quick smile.

"This will do fine," she said.

"More than fine," Morvius muttered.

The woman ignored him. "I want you to move along now, and no more trouble." She looked from them to Corrianne and back. "You people need to keep your quarrels outside my walls, understand?"

"But what of justice?" Corrianne had pulled the tatters of her feigned innocence back around her. "That woman is dangerous." The mage leaned forward and spoke in a voice that seemed like a whisper but was meant to carry. "I heard her whole village burned. That everyone in it died. I think you should arrest her, or cast her out of this city." Corrianne blinked, trying to look helpless. "I fear for my safety with her here."

I heard her whole village burned. Jiri's anger roared up from its coals. How long before that rumor spread about her? How long before everyone in Kibwe thought she was as cursed as the people she had grown up with? She felt the heat building in her moving toward her hand, but then she shook, cold rolling over her like a blanket.

"You should fear for your safety as long as there's anyone in this city with a sense of decency and the ability to throw a rock." Linaria eased her grip on Jiri as she spoke, and her magic stopped chilling the air around her. "There won't be any more problems, ma'am. I assure you."

"And I assure you that there will be," Corrianne said. "From her, or from me if you don't take care of her. I belong to the Aspis Consortium, you understand? The richest, most powerful trade group in the world?"

The guardswoman sighed. "Yes. And I know that these people work for Kalun, of the Tirakici. Which means I'm staying out of this. You want anything more, the Governing Council meets tonight. Bring your issues to them."

Corrianne smiled, small and vicious. "I think I will."

"I lost control of my magic." Jiri spoke slowly, balanced so carefully over the swirling storm of her emotions. "I'm sorry for that. But I don't regret it." She looked up from the glass that Kalun had handed her, full of something that burned down her throat worse than palm wine. "What else should I have done? Just let her walk away?"

"Yes," Kalun said. He had already drained his glass, and held the bottle of amber liquid as if considering another. "That is exactly what I think you should have done."

"Of course you would." Kalun's talking room was cool and quiet, but it seemed to Jiri that she could still feel the hard-packed dirt of the marketplace beneath her feet, could still feel the heat of the sun, and hear Patima's words. *No. I don't.* "That woman and her people killed Oza and destroyed my village, and you've done exactly that. Let her walk away, untouched." Jiri felt the glass growing warm in her hand, caught the scent of the drink as it began to scald and steam, and she reined in her anger. "My grief has kept me useless these past two days, but what's your excuse? Your fear?"

Kalun set the bottle down hard. "Good. Sense. Which you seem to be sorely lacking. Why did Oza decide to teach you? Did he lose a bet?"

"Oh, come on, Kalun. Runt's had a bad week." Morvius reached for the bottle Kalun had just set down and splashed his glass half full.

"And when did you start liking her?" Kalun growled.

"When she started lighting things on fire." Morvius took a swallow of his drink and smiled. "I can't stand grief and tears. That crap is boring as hell. But anger and revenge, that's interesting. Our little firebug may have been stupid this afternoon, but she was fun."

On the bench beside him, Linaria sighed, then tipped back her glass, draining it in one neat swallow.

"Stupid," Jiri said. "That's what you all think." *Though Sera hasn't said a word since we left the market.* Jiri flicked a glance back at the paladin, who sat silently on her stool behind Jiri, her drink untouched. *She just stares at me, like a crocodile waiting in the water for the bushbucks.* "I did something, though."

"What? Burned a tapestry?" Kalun shook his head. "Or do you mean wasting my coin? Or letting that poisoned-tongued magician start rumors about you?"

"I meant the meeting tonight," Jiri said. "I can tell my story to the council. Let them know what these Aspis people have done. This Corrianne, she thinks she's setting a trap for us, but really she's walking into one. When the council hears what's happened, won't they help us? Can't they force Patima to give up what she stole, and make them pay for what they did to Thirty Trees?"

Kalun looked at her for a long time. "Oh, jungle girl," he finally said. "You really think that might happen, don't you?"

"What?" Jiri demanded. "Why shouldn't I?"

"Jiri," Linaria started, then hesitated.

Morvius didn't. "Because it's stupid. But you're too backwoods to know that this isn't even about you."

"What do you mean?" Jiri looked to Kalun, but it was Morvius who kept talking.

"Corrianne may have picked this fight with you, but tonight it's going to be all about him," Morvius said, pointing at Kalun. "Our cheerful host is one of the Consortium's chief competitors in Kibwe. At least in terms of recovering some of the very valuable things that have been misplaced in this green hell over the centuries. You, girl, are just a convenient way for Amiro to try to score some points against Kalun."

Jiri looked from Morvius to Kalun, who nodded, and Jiri's hands clenched the edge of her bench. "The council. Its members. They're all from Kibwe, from the Expanse. Won't they care—"

"The Governing Council of Kibwe only cares about two things. That there is order in the city, and that the money flows." Morvius leaned back on his bench, almost tipping Linaria off it. "They're fine with us raiders, as you call us. We bring treasure to this city that they can tax. How we got it? They don't ask. What happens in the jungle, stays in the jungle. Usually under a pile of scavengers."

"But Thirty Trees—"

"Was a Mosa village," Kalun said. "And there's only a handful of people from the Mosa tribe that live in Kibwe, and none of them are on the council. There are, however, traders who deal with Aspis agents regularly, and there are quite a few tribal leaders who have received fine gifts from the Consortium. I have my own wealth, and I am of the Tirakici, the largest tribe in this city, but I don't know if that balances out the favors that the Consortium has bought itself."

"Especially when it seems that half your tribe would be happy to tear you down to take your place," Linaria said.

"There's that, too." Kalun ran a hand through his short dreads and stood. "Enough. There are many people I need to talk to before this meeting. Linaria, please make sure that everyone here is there. Morvius, stay sober or drink yourself into a stupor, whichever keeps you quieter. Sera . . ." Kalun eyed the paladin. "You mean to be there, don't you?"

"I do," Sera said.

"Of course you do." Kalun shook his head and turned toward Jiri. "And you. I probably won't have much of a chance to talk to you until after this is done. Forget what I said earlier. I know Oza, and he wouldn't choose a fool for a student. So don't let your grief or your anger take hold of you tonight. Follow Linaria's lead, and by every one of your ancestors, don't light anyone or anything on fire."

With that Kalun stalked out the door, leaving Jiri staring after him.

He wouldn't choose a fool for a student. Would he? What had Jiri done, the past few days, but be a fool? Losing herself in grief, and then in anger. *When is the last time I walked in the spirit world? What spirits can I call on for magic, besides fire?* Jiri felt her face heat, not with anger but with shame. Morvius was right, revenge was better than despair, but what revenge could she have if she were exiled from this city?

Beside her, Linaria and Morvius were squabbling.

"—but he suggested getting drunk."

"He said stay quiet, and I've never seen you in a stupor deep enough to still your tongue."

"A talent of mine that you've taken advantage of a few times." Morvius leered.

"Gods, why do I even—"

Between their words and her thoughts, Jiri didn't notice Sera until the paladin sat beside her, close on the small bench.

"You call yourself a shaman."

It was a statement, not an accusation, but still Jiri shifted warily to face the woman beside her.

"In the common tongue, it's the word that fits best. I speak to the spirits, in the air and the earth and all the parts of the world."

"Do you not follow any god, then?"

Was the woman proselytizing? "Gods are powerful spirits. I give them great respect."

"In the north, you might be called a member of the green faith. A druid." The paladin had shed her armor when she had come into the Red Spear, but losing that bulk of leather and steel didn't make her look any less dangerous. Her dark eyes still carried judgment, and her sword still hung at her hip, its worn grip never far from her hand. "I knew some of them, in my youth.

In some ways you're like them, but not in others. Fire didn't come to them the way it does to you. That's the kind of magic I would expect from a sorcerer. Or . . ."

"Or what?" *They were calling me a demon. That's what Boro said.* Jiri met Sera's gaze, unflinching. "I am a shaman, paladin—nothing more, nothing less. I don't know why the spirit of fire is so eager to serve me, but that doesn't change what I am."

"What you are." The paladin finally looked away from her, staring thoughtfully out at nothing. "I asked some questions. About what happened to your village. About that place you call the Pyre. No one knew anything about it, or would admit to it. But they did tell me about your part of the jungle. How some avoided it, because fire there could be strange. Burning too fast, too hot, going out for no reason and then flaring up again. Some call your home cursed."

"Some do." *Where is she going with this?*

"I told you, when you took us there, hunting that demon. Evil can't be contained. Chain it, bury it, and it just grows in the darkness. Spreads. Until it taints everything around it."

"You think I'm evil? That I'm somehow in league with that thing that was buried in the Pyre? Is that what you're saying?" Jiri felt herself trembling, and she didn't know if it was anger or fear, but the cool of Kalun's study was going, swallowed by a rising heat.

"No." Sera looked back at her, eyes intense, but calm shaped the pallid features of her face. "You're not evil. My goddess would tell me if you were. I think that evil has touched you, though; that the thing your ancestors buried so long ago reached out and marked you in some way. Which is why I'm with you, shaman. I think that thing is still out there, and I think you're going to help me find it."

"I actually don't like saying 'I told you so.' I'm not Morvius. But, really . . ." Linaria nodded toward Sera, striding down the street ahead of them. The paladin had changed her clothes and put her armor back on, replacing her usual tabard with a gleaming white cape. Night had fallen over Kibwe, and Sera shone in the light of the lanterns that lined the way to where the Governing Council met.

"She wants to hunt that thing. So do I." Jiri adjusted the flowing wrap dress that Kalun's daughter Fara had brought to her, insisting that Jiri must wear it for the meeting. The folds of its orange silk felt strange against her skin. "But gods and crocodiles, you were right. She cares nothing about me or Thirty Trees. She just sees a snake, and I'm the closest stone. The thing is, she could say the same about me."

"And what are we?" Morvius said. He had dressed up, again in the strange layers of his northern clothes, but these fine fabrics still had a bit of luster left to them, and he barely smelled of alcohol.

Linaria had changed, too, into a simple dress that looked a bit like Jiri's borrowed one, but its silk was white, and around her waist she wore a thin belt of linked silver rings. "We're here," she said, answering him and not answering.

Jiri glanced at the white-haired half-elf. What were they? Tools to be used, like Sera, but Jiri didn't understand them. *Well, I don't understand Linaria*. Morvius followed her, that was obvious enough, but Linaria's interest in Jiri seemed to go beyond Kalun's coin.

She keeps acting . . . friendly. That thought made Jiri worried, fascinated, and suspicious, but she pushed it away. They were here, and it was time to focus on this meeting.

They had walked across the Adayenki, silent and empty now with the night, the successful couples from the Orchid Dance gone to whatever hammocks they could find, taking their drums and leaving silence. The hall of the Governing Council lay just on the other side of the pavilion, a great, round building without walls. The thick thatch of the high roof was held up by great pillars of teak and mahogany beams carved with intricate vines, from which hung lanterns of brass and colored glass. Beneath those bright blooms, colored carpets had been spread, and each one held a chattering group of people. Mostly Zenj—jungle residents like Jiri—but she saw scattered among them the colorful clothes of Bonuwat traders, tall and ritually scarred Bekyar, the pale faces of northerners, and a few things that she was unsure of. Busy trying to stare covertly at a group of broad, impossibly hairy man-things that she thought might be dwarves, she almost walked past the carpet where Sera had already taken a seat. Fara was there though, too, and Kalun's daughter clicked her tongue at Jiri and caught her attention.

"Here." The girl patted the carpet. "Father sent me ahead to hold your place. It's going to start soon. Do you want anything? There's coffee, and tea, and sweets, and palm—"

"No," Linaria said firmly, cutting off Morvius before he could speak. She handed Fara a coin as she folded herself gracefully onto the carpet. "Get yourself something, though, with my thanks."

The girl grinned and bounced away, heading for one of the vendors circulating through the hall. Jiri dropped into her place, with Linaria between her and Sera, and Morvius groaned and sat behind them.

"Haven't these people heard of chairs?"

"They've heard of stools," Linaria said. In the center of the pavilion, a ring of stools waited, empty. "You just have to be on the council to get one."

"It hurts my scars to sit like this," Morvius grumbled.

"Good. Maybe the pain will remind you why taking a wererat to bed is a bad idea."

"He didn't look like a wererat when I took him to bed," Morvius grumbled.

A week ago, Jiri would have begged to hear that story. Tonight, after all that had happened, she could focus only on searching the crowd. "Where are they?"

"Aspis?" Linaria said. "There." She pointed across the hall to a broad carpet spread a few rows away from the council's circle of stools.

Jiri saw Amiro first. The man was dressed in a blue silk suit trimmed in gold, and rings flashed on his fingers as he whispered to a group of men who clustered around him holding slate tablets and slivers of chalk. On the other side of the carpet Corrianne sat sulking on a thick pillow, waving a bright pink fan that matched her dress. Patima sat behind her, dressed in the same clothes she had been wearing in the market. The Bonuwat woman's eyes were searching the crowd, and when they found Jiri she nodded at her, not mocking, simply acknowledging her and then moving on.

This was the story Jiri needed to hear, now. "What can you tell me about them?" she asked Linaria.

"Amiro is a local. He apparently started working for the Consortium as a child, running messages. He worked his way up, imitating his Aspis bosses to the point of converting to the worship of Abadar. He became a cleric of the merchant god, and a few years later he was given a brass badge and made an official agent of the Aspis Consortium. His boss started him relic hunting, and assigned him Corrianne, Mikki, and Patima to help." Linaria shook her head. "I think the man considered Amiro a threat, and wanted to get rid of him. But somehow Amiro made those vipers work together, and they've done well. So well that when his boss died of the red drip, Amiro took his job. It's surprising that he was out in the jungle, really. He's been here in the city for months, trying to make his promotion permanent.

"Corrianne is from Taldor," Linaria continued, "by her name and her accent and her dress. And by her attitude, though I wouldn't say that in front of any other Taldans. She can't stand the Expanse, but she's here for traditional reasons."

"Traditional reasons?" Jiri asked.

"She's on the run. According to a bounty hunter I once met, she had a bit of fight with her family back in Taldor. The few that survived put a nice price on her head."

"Was that the bounty hunter that got eaten by a giant eel in the baths?" Morvius asked.

"Yes."

"One of the many reasons you should be damn careful about picking fights with wizards," Morvius said, staring at Jiri.

He said he liked me better when I started lighting things on fire. Jiri shoved the thought aside and made herself ignore Morvius. "I don't see the little one that stabbed you."

"Mikki?" Linaria rubbed her hand across her belly. "You won't. She's wanted too, but by the locals. Mikki got into a fight over a dancing monkey with the favorite grandson of a Tirakici elder a few months ago and knifed him. He lived, but the poison she used destroyed his mind. The council has ordered her capture and execution if she's found in the city."

"So she's not in Kibwe?"

"No, she's here," Linaria said. "Amiro and the Consortium find that halfling assassin far too useful and too dangerous to let out of their sight. You just won't see her outside their compound."

A compound. I wonder where that is? It wasn't a question that Jiri thought she should ask Linaria. "What about Patima?"

"Patima." Linaria said the name carefully. "Patima is strange. She's the quiet one of that group. All I knew about her was that she was a bard, and a gold hound. She was good at finding the forgotten places, the secret ones where things were hidden. With Corrianne and Mikki around, I never paid much attention to her. These last couple of days, though, I've asked about her.

"She was found in the jungle five or six years ago, alone and raving. The merchants who found her brought her here and left her. She lived as a beggar for a while, telling tales and singing for coin, until she pulled herself together and started working for the Consortium. Since then, she's done very well for herself.

The woman I talked to . . ." Linaria paused, remembering. "She said it was hard to connect them, that calm, quiet woman in the nice clothes and the beggar that she used to warn the children away from, because her stories always gave them nightmares."

"What kind of stor—" Jiri's question was broken with a crash of cymbals, followed by a cacophony of bells and chimes and more cymbals as a group of children ran through the hall, all of them ringing bells and beating drums. To frighten away bad-luck spirits, Jiri knew, but it also did a fine job of breaking up all the gossip and trading going on beneath the flower lanterns, and when the children ran out and the council marched in, the hall was impressively silent.

A tall man with a carved staff marched in with them, and he stood and waited until all the old men and women had taken seats on their stools, all facing in toward each other. "Kibwe," he called out, in a voice deep and strong enough to easily reach the edges of the hall. "I am the Voice of the Hall. I tell you, your elders have assembled, and the Governing Council is now in session. I call on the spirits of our ancestors to watch, and lend us their wisdom." He raised the staff and knocked it against a rafter, in a spot worn smooth by previous blows, and Jiri, impressed despite her nerves by the panoply, settled in to watch the show.

Two hours later, Jiri had very much had enough of the show.

"How much longer will this go on?" she whispered, and beside her, Linaria surreptitiously slipped the slim book she had been reading beneath a fold of her skirt.

It looked suspiciously like the book that Morvius had been reading at the marketplace, the one that Sera had called an insult to poetry, decency, and anatomy.

"Are they still arguing over whether the tax on cotton bales should be raised by a copper?"

"No. Now the old man with the hat is arguing that roosters should be banned in the city, because they wake him up."

"Well, they're into civil matters then. They should open the circle soon. That's when Corrianne will make her complaint."

"Shouldn't Kalun be here?" Jiri looked around for the man. He was still nowhere in sight.

"Don't worry, he'll show." Linaria's sharp features shifted to grumpy. "He's important enough to come in as late as he wants." Behind them, a soft snore rumbled, and without looking Linaria jabbed her elbow back. It didn't wake Morvius, but it made him shift, cutting off the snore.

Jiri sighed. All this time wasted, listening to these fools ramble about scraps of coin, while Patima and her friends sat so close to her. *Where is the thing she stole?* Not here, so had they left it in their compound? *Or have they sent it out of the city already in one of their caravans?* The thought shook Jiri, but she didn't believe it. *That thing. Patima wants it for something.* What, Jiri didn't know, but she wanted to wring that answer from the woman too.

Lost in her thoughts, she didn't notice the shift in the council's talk until the Voice of the Hall took his staff and knocked it again against the rafters. Paying attention again, Jiri saw that all the old men and women were turning on their stools to face out at the people sitting around them.

"The Governing Council of Kibwe is now open to its citizens. Are there any here who would seek their wisdom?" The Voice gripped his staff like a weapon, and the way his eyes flashed seemed designed to make any petitioner think twice. Still, the hall rustled with motion as people began to get up and make their way forward.

"Citizens," Jiri said. "Corrianne isn't a citizen, though, is she?"

"Of course not." Kalun carefully stepped from the broad aisle running through the hall to their carpet, seating himself with a grunt. "Kibwe seems like it might be going to hell, lately, but it's not so far gone as to allow someone like *that* to join its ranks. Corrianne has no citizenship, no standing, and no tribe, so Amiro will bring her case."

"Nice you could make it," Morvius said, yawning and stretching. "How did the bribery and intimidation go?"

"As well as could be expected." Kalun watched the flurry of activity as various children and clerks ran scraps of parchment up to the council members or bent to whisper in their ears. "I'll know for sure when they pick the council member to judge Amiro's case. At least he went right up. We won't have to wait."

Amiro was first in the line of petitioners who now stood in front of the Voice. Unlike most of the others, he looked perfectly at ease before the looming man. This close, Jiri could make out the darker gold pattern of keys woven into the shining borders of his shirt.

"You know what to do?" Kalun said, tilting his head toward Jiri.

"Shut up unless I'm questioned, then just tell the truth," Jiri said grimly. "And don't light anything on fire."

"That's it." Kalun turned to face the center of the hall as the man with the staff called out in his booming voice.

"Amiro Kibwe has come to the Governing Council, and he wishes to speak! What say you, wise ones?"

The elders on their stools waved away the messengers around them, settled their mugs of coffee and tea and wine, and nodded.

Amiro bowed and walked forward.

Chapter Eight
Judgment

"They've chosen Simla to judge this."

Jiri heard the tension in Kalun's whisper. "Is that bad?"

Amiro had given a long speech to start out with that said nothing but managed to compliment the council and its wisdom in a dozen ways before his breath ran out. The Aspis man didn't have a voice like, well, the Voice, but his words still carried through the hall, level and assured. When he was done, the council members had turned inward and whispered to one another until one of them finally rose. An old woman, but not ancient, her hair gone gray, not white, and she stood tall and straight.

"She's known for honesty, impartiality and fairness," said Kalun.

"So it's a good thing, then," Jiri said.

Kalun frowned without looking at her. "Impartiality is the last thing we want from a judge. I wanted the old man whose grandson Mikki knifed. The whole trial would have been about Amiro working with her then."

"At least Amiro didn't get his favored judge," Linaria said. "His influence isn't greater than yours."

"No. But when the hell did it grow to be equal to mine?" growled Kalun.

In front of them, Amiro had started speaking. "—and it was there that Corrianne ran into Linaria, a foreign adventurer in the employ of Kalun of the Red Spear. She attempted to exchange pleasantries, but she was rudely interrupted by a young woman that was with these northern mercenaries, someone they had brought in with them from the jungle. This girl accused my good employee of . . ." Amiro spread his hands and shrugged. "Something. When my other employee, a Bonuwat woman called Patima who has lived respect-ably in this great city for years, tried to calm her, she was unsuccessful. So Patima wisely decided to leave, and at that point the girl attacked. Using magic, she pulled fire from the air and tried to strike Patima with it. When that failed, she apparently went a bit mad and lashed out with her flames. Thankfully no one was hurt, which I'm sure was due to the prompt arrival of a squad of your fine guards, but I do believe city property was damaged." Amiro ran his fingers over the smooth gold silk of his cuffs. "I don't have to tell you, I'm sure, how upset my employees were. They stopped their shop-ping, as I'm sure many others did, and hurried back to our compound. I come to you tonight, as a citizen of Kibwe, to speak for them, to ask you to exile this dan-gerous young woman from the city so that they, and all others, can feel safe in our marketplace once again.

And further, I ask that you might lend your wisdom to those who would bring such an unreliable person into the heart of our city. Thank you."

Simla didn't thank him back. She simply looked at him, and Jiri thought her hard dark eyes were unsettlingly reminiscent of Sera's.

"Is this young woman here?" Simla said. "Does she have a citizen that can stand and speak for her and defend her actions?"

"She is and she does," Kalun said, rising smoothly to his feet, looking strong for his age. A buzz of conversation rippled across the hall, but it fell silent when the Voice cleared his throat and glared out at the crowd.

"We have just heard Amiro's complaint, and we have all heard that something troubled the marketplace today." Simla turned her eyes on Kalun. "What is your account of what happened?"

"The same, and different," Kalun said. "My employees, all non-citizens of Kibwe but good, tax-paying inhabitants of this city, did meet Amiro's this afternoon. It was their second meeting this week."

"Councilwoman Simla—" Amiro started, but Kalun kept speaking.

"Their first was near the village of Thirty Trees, home to the shaman Jiri Maju." Kalun waved his hand at Jiri. "I sent my people there to help her deal with a team of Aspis Consortium raiders who were stripping a ruin that lay close to their village, raiders who had killed her teacher, the shaman Mosa Oza Thirty Trees."

"Councilwoman—" Amiro interjected, to no avail.

"Amiro, Corrianne, Patima. They were the raiders, along with a halfling called Mikki—"

"What? You were with that murderous little—"

This time the interruption came from an old man in an orange robe, sitting on a stool halfway around the circle. *The grandfather that Kalun wanted as a judge.* Jiri watched the man jump up to shout obscenities at Amiro, who had folded his hands and was staring up into the shadows gathered over the lanterns. *Yes, he would have been more partial to our case.*

It couldn't matter now, though, Jiri thought. *They can't ignore this. Amiro with a criminal, killing a shaman. And when we tell them of what happened to Thirty Trees, of the danger that is still out there . . .*

The Voice stepped forward and cracked his staff against the rafters until the hall quieted and a small knot of council members pulled the old man in orange back down to his stool. When he was settled, Simla spoke.

"This encounter you speak of. It happened beyond the bounds of Kibwe, yes?"

"It did," Kalun said.

"Then it has no bearing on this council, and is immaterial to this case."

What? The word was on Jiri's lips and she was starting to stand, ready to shout it out when a hand grabbed the back of her dress and jerked her down, hard.

"You told Kalun that you knew what to do, girl," Morvius rumbled. "Do you? Or should I go get a bucket of water?"

Jiri didn't say anything, didn't look back at him. She settled back down and adjusted the wrap of her dress with a low growl. Before her, Kalun was trying to argue.

"—believe it does have bearing, because—"

"Your *belief* does not matter here, Kalun." Simla leaned forward on her stool. "The law is clear. The council rules Kibwe. What happens beyond a spear's throw from our walls is none of our concern. You may object to that law, and you may have good reason, but it is the law and we will follow it. Now. Do you have anything to say about what happened at the market today?"

Kalun considered her, and when he spoke again his voice held no trace of anger. "Yes, Councilwoman. Amiro has given his version. Mine differs mostly in who struck first in this little skirmish. That woman," Kalun pointed back at Corrianne without bothering to look at her, "did not greet my employees, or my guest. She attacked them with words as sharp and poisoned as darts. She did it with every intention of provoking a scene like the one that occurred. I believe the council has ruled before on the concept of fighting words, and has spoken against them."

"We have," Simla said. She looked from Kalun to Amiro and back. "You have both brought the parties involved. Bring them up, and tell them that I would ask them questions, and they are to answer."

"Right, that's us," Linaria said. She rose and Jiri followed. Beside them, Sera and Morvius stood too. All of them moved out into the corridor, and a little ways from them Patima and Corrianne did the same. "You're doing well, Jiri. Just keep yourself in control," Linaria whispered as they walked forward.

Walking up the aisle beneath colored lights, Jiri didn't answer. She couldn't even if she had something to say. All her anger, all the powerful heat of it, had been shoved suddenly into a distant corner of her mind, forced away by fear.

When they rose, hundreds of eyes had turned on them. Turned on her. Strange eyes, watching, focused, waiting. *So many eyes.* Jiri clenched her hands to keep them from shaking. The last time she had felt like this was when she had danced the Orchid Dance in Thirty Trees, and that had been with a dozen other girls, in front of people she had known all her life, people who . . . *Wouldn't fill a quarter of this hall.* The thought shook her, and now her whole body trembled. The crowds of Kibwe had always made her feel strange, nervous, but excited too. This being watched, by all these strangers . . .

It was terrifying.

She barely heard Simla when she began to speak. "I've heard from our citizens. Now I wish to hear from you others. You first, Corrianne." The old woman rolled the foreign name off her tongue as if it were distasteful.

Corrianne's mouth twisted, but the mage forced it back into a little pout of worry. "Oh, noble Councilwoman, I would be happy—"

"You would be silent," Simla snapped. "Until I've asked my question."

Corrianne did a worse job of hiding her annoyance this time, but at a look from Amiro she pulled her features back to a sort of wounded innocence.

"How did you speak to these people?" Simla waved at Jiri and her companions. "Did you greet them, or insult them?"

"Insult?" Corrianne gasped. "Why, I would never! Discourtesy is the gravest of sins in Taldor, my noble birthplace, and I would never allow an insult to pass my lips, no matter how deserved. I merely greeted my old friends, Morvius and Linaria, and congratulated them on their recent success, surviving another trip into the dangerous reaches of the Expanse, despite all the odds that fate had stacked against them. The woman wrapped in all that dull steel, I barely know her, and the young woman I know not at all, so I ignored her until she attacked. It was terrible—"

"Enough. I don't need your opinions," Simla said. "Though they do seem to drip from your words. You, Patima. Do you believe your companion was being friendly, or was she trying to incite these others to violence?"

Patima looked up, her face open, serene. "Corrianne?"

With everyone's attention focused on Simla and the other women, Jiri had relaxed enough to get a little angry at Corrianne's words, but they had mostly relieved her. The sweetness the magician had tried to put on them hadn't hidden her venom. When Patima spoke, though, a new fear touched the shaman. Patima's voice was clear and perfect, a beautiful instrument. *She's a singer, a storyteller. They'll listen to her.*

Believe her.

"She spoke to them as she speaks to everyone," Patima said. "And while I don't believe Corrianne had any wish to be attacked, I don't believe she was surprised by it."

Both Corrianne and Amiro shot Patima looks, Corrianne's annoyed, Amiro's exasperated. Simla watched them and then spoke. "Jiri Maju attacked you. Did you provoke her?"

"I told her truths she didn't want to hear," Patima said.

"And did you feel threatened by her?" Simla asked.

"No."

"Even after she attacked you?"

"I didn't really notice when she attacked me." Patima's eyes turned toward Jiri.

For that moment, Jiri's rage almost pushed back against her fear of the crowd, but then she realized that many other eyes had swung to stare at her, too. Her fear smashed her anger back again and froze her, far more so than Linaria's cool hand on her arm.

Simla turned her attention away from Patima and to Linaria. "What do you say, Lan— Len— white-hair?"

"I say Corrianne's reputation is well known," Linaria said smoothly.

Simla didn't even try Morvius's name. "And you?"

The northern man seemed to consider a few things while Linaria frowned at him, then simply said, "Corrianne's a bloody bowl of awful. And that's the best I can say about her without getting into those fighting words you're talking about."

"And you, *holy* warrior?" Simla asked.

"By my *holy* vows," Sera said calmly, "I must keep as close as possible to the truth. So I would ask, is calling someone a yapping dog an insult in this city?"

"Yes, it is," Simla said, and there seemed to be a certain amount of amused respect now in her voice.

"Then Corrianne insulted my companion Jiri, with that and with most of the rest of her *fighting* words."

"This woman is—" Corrianne started, but was cut off by a thunderous boom as the Voice raised his staff and knocked it against the rafters.

"Speak out of turn again, woman, and that stick won't be knocking against wood," Simla said. Her eyes turned to Jiri.

Jiri, who had been beginning to feel better as each of her companions spoke, felt those sharp old eyes on her, and behind them the crushing weight of everyone else in the hall.

"Jiri Maju. What do you say?"

Say? Jiri stood, trying to breathe, and was desperately afraid that the answer would be nothing. She clenched her hands and felt the moment stretching, time pouring past as she stood motionless, silent. *I was ready to stand and shout earlier. I had to promise Kalun not to speak. Speak!*

"Jiri?" Kalun whispered, and Linaria touched her shoulder, her hand for once not cold as ice.

Jiri forced her eyes up, staring away from the crowd. Into the shadows that lay beyond the colored lamps and the rafters, into the dark that gathered beneath the heavy thatch of the hall's roof. Were the ancestors' eyes on her too, staring down at her, waiting? Her hands were starting to shake, no matter how tight she made her fists.

"Jiri Maju. Will you answer me?"

Angry or patient, Jiri had no idea what emotion ran behind Simla's words. Too busy trying to make her tongue move, to make breath leave her lungs, to make the room stop shifting, she stared up and prayed. *Ancestors, help me.*

Jiri tore her eyes away from the shadows and tried to face Simla. But that old woman's eyes were on her, waiting, and she had to look away. Kalun and Linaria, they were no help either, concerned, expectant. Her gaze jumped, and there was Patima, serene, and Corrianne beside her, a vicious little smile on her face.

She smiles like a mamba, but I bet the snake is friendlier.

The thought rolled through Jiri's head, but it didn't feel like hers.

It seemed more like something Hadzi would say.

"Well," Simla said. "If you—"

"They stole something, I don't know what, from the place outside our village, where the ancestors told us not to go, and something was released, some spirit of fire that destroyed Thirty Trees, and it's loose somewhere out there and I think it's not done, I think as long as they have what they stole it might burn again."

The words came out fast, a solid line of sound that Jiri shoved out, and then her lungs were empty and she was trying to breathe and everyone was still staring at her. In her head, though, Hadzi was laughing, laughing like the time she had tried to roll over to kiss him and had flipped herself out of his hammock. That laughter, fading away in her head, made her straighten, open her hands and hold up her head, even as she kept her eyes down.

"So," Simla said. "That is what happened to Thirty Trees."

Jiri, not wanting to try to speak again, nodded.

"That is not what happened," Amiro snapped. "And it—"

"Doesn't matter," Simla said, breaking in. "Whatever happened there, it is beyond our bounds. Our marketplace is well within our bounds, though." The old woman considered them all, then leaned back. "We've wasted enough time with this. The woman Patima was not harmed, nor did she feel threatened. One tapestry was damaged and paid for. This is a minor matter. But. We cannot allow this sort of thing to disrupt trade. Tirakici Kalun, I order you to compensate the city of Kibwe a ten weight of gold for the actions of your guest. See to it that she knows that Kibwe is an orderly city, and her temper must be held in check."

"Yes, Councilwoman," Kalun said.

"As for you, Amiro." Simla frowned at the Aspis man. "I want the same from you, in compensation to the city for the provocative words of your guest. Order requires good manners, and the council has no use for those who would try to hide daggers behind sweet words. Done."

Jiri blinked, unsure, but Linaria was pulling on her arm and Kalun had turned and was ushering them down the aisle. Behind them, the Voice was booming out the name of the next citizen of Kibwe, and suddenly Jiri realized that it was over. Her feet began to move, and soon Linaria's hold on her arm had shifted from a gentle tug to get her moving to a white-knuckled grip to keep her from bolting out of the crowded hall.

In the dim outside, beneath the spread of stars, Jiri breathed and felt the paralyzing fear of the crowd going away.

"Well, that could have been better, but it could have been much, much worse," Kalun said.

"Could have been better?" With the last of her fear fraying away, Jiri's anger was crowding back in, running its heat through her. "They'll do nothing about that thing that Patima released! They wouldn't even discuss it!"

"But you managed to slip it in," Kalun said. "Very nicely. Were you really that terrified?"

"I . . ." Jiri didn't want to admit it, but what was the point of denying it? They were standing right next to her when it had happened. "I've never had so many people staring at me."

"Sure you have," said Morvius. "There were more staring at you in the market today."

"They weren't expecting me to speak."

"True," he said. "They were expecting you to catch Corrianne's hair on fire. And if that had only cost us ten coins, it would have been well worth it."

"Enough. You all did well, now go back to my inn before you stir some new trouble. Sera, your drinks are free tonight, with my thanks." Kalun adjusted his clothes and looked around. The open circle around the Governing Council's hall was lined with stands selling coffee, tea, and other drinks. Many people sat drinking and talking, staring at the council hall. "Now I need to go back to work. The rumors of this will spread, and I need to see that the proper weight is put on the proper words. Especially those that you said, shaman." He clapped Jiri on the shoulder and started toward one of the coffee vendors. "Next time, though, try to speak a little more slowly."

Next time. Jiri thought of all those eyes, gleaming in the colored lights, and shuddered. *I'd rather face another of Patima's demons.*

"Well," Morvius said. "Shall we? Sera?" He gave a little bow and gestured for the woman to precede him. She frowned at him and stayed still.

"Just because Kalun is giving her free drinks, I don't think that means she's buying for you, Morvius," Linaria said.

"Well," Morvius said again, but he paused when a girl came scampering up to them. When she drew close enough, Jiri recognized Kalun's daughter, Fara.

"I have news for Father!" the girl gasped. "Where is he?"

"There," Linaria said, but she snagged the girl's hand before she could start moving again. "What news?"

"A caravan was attacked at the first camp of the Ndele Gap Trail," Fara said. "They say whoever did it killed everyone and burned the whole thing to ash!"

Chapter Nine
Two Burnings

"How far is it from the city?" Jiri asked. They were walking fast toward the Red Spear, and around them she could hear the people chattering in the street, could see the children racing through the dark bearing messages. "And where?"

"To the northeast," Linaria said. "And it's only a few hours' walk. It's closer to the city than it really should be, but it's the only dry place in the swamp that's over there."

"White Crocodile Wallow," Jiri said. That swamp stretched to the north and east of where Thirty Trees had once stood. Its edges stretched around the Pyre. "If it's only a few hours' walk, we can be there by moonrise if we move fast."

"We?" Morvius said. "We *are* moving fast. To the inn, and a drink, and a good night's sleep in a good bed. Which is what we do when we're waiting to line up our next job." Morvius stopped in the circle of light cast by a group of lanterns that hung from a granite column.

On its top, the soapstone statue of a leopard-headed warrior seemed to snarl down at him in the flickering light, but the northern man paid no attention to its stone hostility. "You're not so bad, runt, when you're not all weepy, but you assume too much. We helped you before because we were hired to, but that contract is done. You want to run off into the jungle in the dark so that you can stare at a bunch of charred camels, feel free. Enjoy the mosquitoes and the vampire bats and all the other things out there that think they have a better use for your blood than you. We're staying here."

Jiri bounced where she stood, her body flush with adrenaline, impatient to move. "You'll just sit here and let that thing stalk around out there, killing people?"

"Until I'm paid to do something about it, yes." Morvius folded his arms, looking down at her. "Gods, girl, you're looking at me like I'm Corrianne, but I'm just telling you the truth. Adventurers are a kind of mercenary. We get paid to do this kind of thing, and since you gave your only bag of coin to that guard in the market today, I don't think you can afford our rates. You'll probably be hauling drinks for Kalun for months just to pay him back for that fine the council gave him."

Jiri looked over to Linaria. The half-elf was staring at Morvius, her strange blue eyes hard to read. "Kalun is paying us to watch her."

"Here in the city," Morvius said. "Not out there."

"We can talk to him," Linaria said. "New terms can be negotiated."

And how long will that take? "Forget it, don't bother," Jiri said. "I'll just do it myself." With that she started walking again, toward the crimson spear that rose a little way ahead, and the stone building that sprawled below it. *It's not like I need them. They'd just slow me down in the jungle.* It was the truth, but these people . . . Whatever else, they were strong.

I'm strong, too. Oza taught me to be.

Good words, but that swamp demon would have destroyed her, alone, and this thing was bigger than that demon.

I'll do what I can. I have to.

"Is this just about coin? I have that."

Sera's voice stopped Jiri and made her look back.

"I thought you sent all your coin to your church," Morvius said.

"When I have a reliable way to send my tithes on, I do," Sera said. "It's been a while since that's happened. I'm sure I have enough to pay you for a few days."

"To do what?" Morvius asked.

"To help me find the thing that destroyed this girl's village."

Jiri walked slowly back, pulling herself up a little taller as she did. *I think I've heard myself referred to as 'girl' quite often enough these last few days.*

"You don't know that this is the same thing," Morvius said. "We just heard a rumor passed along by an eleven-year-old. Maybe something else happened to this caravan. Maybe it was fire-happy bandits, or a dragon, or a cooking accident."

"Maybe," said Sera. "We can find that out by looking."

"You really want this thing," Jiri said.

The paladin turned toward her. "I told you I did, and that I would use you to find it. Do you still want to find it?"

By every spirit, yes. But . . . A moment before, Jiri had been wishing for their strength. Having Sera around, though, paying for things . . . She would think she was in charge.

And that's the cost I'll have to pay.

"I do," Jiri said, and started again toward the Red Spear.

The others followed, Linaria and Sera dickering over terms, Morvius trailing behind, muttering something about the gods and their anatomy.

Jiri was ready first, of course.

Off with the borrowed wrap dress, on with her new clothes. She scooped up the bag with her few supplies, grabbed her spear, and then rushed to the common room where she anxiously waited near the front door while the inn's mostly foreign customers chattered to each other in a dozen languages and glanced at her curiously with their strangely colored eyes. Finally, Morvius stomped in wearing his battered armor, the spear Scritch gleaming like fresh blood in his hands and a pack slung over his back.

"Where's your gear?" he asked, looking her over.

Jiri tapped her bag and touched the spear that leaned against the wall behind her.

"I liked the way you told off Sera this afternoon," Morvius said. "But you do realize that armor is more effective when you wear it, not carry it in a sack."

"I'll put it on if I need it."

"You seem to think that you'll be informed of when you'll need it." Morvius set down his pack and leaned

Scritch against the wall. "That's not how it works. What's this?"

"My spear," Jiri said.

"That's not a spear." Morvius stared at her weapon with contempt. "That's a stick with a spoon tied to it. Watch my pack, and if someone tries to touch Scritch, bite them. Your teeth will do more damage than your spear." The tall man turned and walked back toward the room he shared with Linaria, passing the half-elf and Sera as he went.

"What's he doing?" Linaria asked. She had wrapped her hair into a thick braid and changed into tunic and leggings, light for the heat but durable enough to resist thorns.

"I don't know. Criticizing my things, mostly."

"He's like that. Most adventurers are. Obsessed with their gear." Linaria sighed. "I used to worry that hanging around places like this, I would be forced to hear nothing but brag after brag about who had slain the most monsters, won the most treasure, or earned the most carnal gratitude from grateful princes or princesses. Instead, I get to listen to people argue for hours over what kind of grease waterproofs a boot best, or the proper way to strip and clean a crossbow."

"Good equipment can mean the difference between life and death," Sera said. Despite the time she'd taken to get ready, the paladin seemed to have only swapped the white cape for her usual tabard.

"So I've been told. Many times." Linaria shifted her own small pack. "Still, I think I'd really rather hear about the grateful princes."

Morvius came striding back from his room, another spear in his hand. It was shorter than Scritch, and its point shone with the normal gray of steel, but its edges glittered wickedly in the candlelight. "Here. It's my second-best thrower, but it's not an embarrassment."

"And what am I to do with my embarrassment?" Four years ago, Jiri had spent her entire share of the profits from Thirty Trees' mango harvest to buy her spear from a trader. It was more for hunting, yes, but . . .

"Leave it. Maybe somebody can use it for a toothpick."

Jiri bristled, but Morvius was handing her the new spear and she could feel its lightness, its balance, the way it felt in her hands. "Fine," she snapped, then paused, entirely certain in that moment just how Oza would be looking at her. "Thank you."

"What are you lot up to? No good?" Near them, a Keleshite man in long robes leaned back in his chair, a wine glass dangling from his hand.

"Just chasing smoke, Basan," Linaria answered.

"Ah. Checking out the fire, eh?" The man finished his wine and set down the cup. "I don't know why you're bothering. Sounds like a classic goblin raid."

Morvius swung his pack onto his back and grabbed Scritch. "There's no goblins living near the Ndele Gap Trail, Basan."

"The Ndele Gap Trail?" The man cocked an eyebrow, puzzled. "I thought you were talking about that village that got burned out tonight. What happened on the trail?"

"Pakala is a Tirakici village, a bit south of Kibwe. Not far from Thirty Trees." The spear in Jiri's hand glowed, its tip shining as if she had somehow pierced the dark canopy that spread over them and snagged a star down. In its light, she scanned the branches of the trees that grew beside the eastern trail, looking for the green flash of leopard eyes.

"So, not close to the caravan site." Linaria looked like a wraith in the light that Jiri had gathered with her magic and hung on her spear tip. "These two burnings may only have bad luck linking them."

Bad-luck magic, Jiri thought. "That thing could fly."

"We'll check the caravan first," Sera said. "Then we'll go to the village that Basan heard about. It might have attacked both."

"Or neither," Morvius said from behind them.

No. Jiri kept the thought to herself, but she was sure of it. That thing that had been unleashed . . . Her last moments before the Pyre spun through Jiri's head—the stone wall burning, the ash gathering in the air into gray-white wings, and something glowing, like the sun burning through clouds . . .

Then she had fallen, and everything had gone black until she woke again in Thirty Trees. Alive, spared for some reason by that thing. Why had it done that, let her live while it burned that northern archer, then Thirty Trees and Hadzi and the others who had waited with him? It had let her escape, and then come back when her anger had kindled once again to flame.

No. Jiri wanted to shout the word, but she clenched it between her teeth. Hadzi's father and all the others were wrong. *It's not me. I'm not bad-luck magic. I'm not.*

That woman is dangerous, I heard her whole village burned. Corrianne's mocking voice echoed in her head.

No.

I think evil has touched you. Sera's voice, Sera who was following her now, convinced that Jiri could lead her straight to this thing, this evil that Patima and her friends had unleashed.

They did it. She did it. Not me. They freed this thing, this curse.

Not me.

Moving down the trail, Jiri shoved that fear down, away, and in the empty place it left behind the coals of her anger glowed bright.

They reached the caravan camp just past midnight. The half-moon had risen and was shedding its pale light onto the low hill that rose from the surrounding swamp. It was light enough to confirm Jiri's fears.

"It's the same as Thirty Trees."

She stood in the center of the clearing and stared at the destruction. The packed dirt of the hilltop was charred black, and ash had settled across it, gray and white and dead. Mixed in here and there were bones, twisted and broken with heat. Camel bones, mostly. The human bones were few and scattered, mostly femurs and pelvises and skulls, bigger bones that hadn't fully melted or burned in the heat.

"There's metal here," Morvius said, stirring the ashes with his boot. "Melted iron, mostly, armor or weapons or cooking pans, who knows. Some copper." He bent and touched a chunk of the dark metal. "It's still hot, but not burning hot."

"Are there any tracks?" Sera asked. The paladin stood in the center of the clearing, looking around, frowning. "Can you lead me to the monster that did this?"

"No." A breeze sighed through the trees, stirred the ash, and Jiri closed her eyes. She had no use for tears.

Not now.

"The caravan came in, set up, and this thing burned them. Charred a perfect circle that took the whole camp." Jiri opened her eyes and stared at the blasted ground. "It flew in and killed them all before they had a chance to run. Then it went on. Same as Thirty Trees."

They spent a few more minutes searching the ashes, but there was nothing more but those blackened remnants of the dead and swirling clouds of mosquitoes.

"We've found what we can here." Sera stepped around the twisted remains of a camel skull, walking toward the path. "Let's find this village that burned. There might be something there."

"Because we found so much here," Morvius said.

"We found out something," Jiri said.

"What?"

"That I was right. That thing is still out here." Jiri shouldered her bag and started walking after the paladin.

Jiri studied the branching of the narrow trail they were on. "This one."

"You're sure that leads to Pakala?" Linaria asked.

"Yes."

"You've been on it before?" Morvius asked, then stifled a yawn. They'd been walking most of the night, back almost to Kibwe, then out along the winding network of foot trails that ran through the jungle around

Kibwe like a crazed spider web, linking the smaller villages to the ancient walled city.

"No. I've never been to Pakala before. But it's the right direction."

Morvius stared at the narrow footpaths that twisted through the giant trees and hanging vines. "Right. How much are we getting out of Sera, Linaria?"

"Our usual rate of not quite enough." Linaria yawned and stretched. "C'mon, lets go. It's almost dawn."

"Yeah, it would be a shame to try to walk around here when we could see where we're going."

Jiri ignored Morvius and led them down the trail, sure that it was the right one. It had to be; nothing else ran the right direction. Soon, her confidence was rewarded. Drifting through the jungle, almost lost in the scent of water and orchids and rot, came the smell of smoke.

Basan hadn't known much. He had been visiting a friend in the Kibwe guard who was standing watch on the wall while Jiri and her friends had been trapped in the council hall. They had seen the glow of sparks and flame rising from the dark blanket of trees to the south of the city.

"He thought it might be coming from Pakala," Basan had told them. "He was worried about it. Said he had a cousin that had married a boy and moved out there."

The guard might worry, but Kibwe won't.

The trail bent around a thick grove of redmark trees, their branches bristling with thorns, and the canopy opened a little, showing a sky gone gray with the approaching dawn. In that thin light, smoke drifted from the broken homes of Pakala like blood flowing from a wound.

Jiri stopped, then slipped back a little. With a thought she extinguished the light that clung to the tip of her spear and crouched, staring out at the shadows of the village. Behind her, the others drew up, silent as she was.

She didn't see any dead. No bodies lay on the earth between the ruined houses. The vague shadows scattered across the ground all slowly resolved into broken pots, spilled baskets of fruit, piles of tangled cloths, and torn hammocks. Nothing more, except . . . Jiri stayed still, breathing silently, watching, waiting, until she saw that flicker of motion again. A shadow shifted beside one of the baskets, and Jiri heard a tiny sound, a liquid, tearing noise. The thing shifted again, rippled like one of the cloths had come to life, then lifted its head.

Breathing out, Jiri relaxed and stepped back onto the trail. Whispering to the spirits, she circled her hand through the empty air, fingers leaving a wake of shadows as she scooped starlight and moonlight into a tiny globe of white light that she fixed again to the tip of her spear.

"Are you sure it's clear?" Linaria asked.

"The fruit bats think so." The shadow Jiri had been watching blinked in the light she had made, a long red tongue running out to swipe at the banana pulp that covered its snout. When Linaria and the rest stepped out, the bat spread its wide wings and flapped off into the trees. Its flight kicked off a screeching retreat as all the other bats that had gathered to feast on abandoned fruit took off after it, leaving the village.

"Well, whatever did this knows we're here now," Morvius said, watching as the last bats vanished into the trees, their cries waking a troop of monkeys to screeching complaint.

"Whatever did this is gone," Jiri said, looking around. "And whatever it was, it wasn't the same thing that destroyed Thirty Trees."

There had been fire here, that was obvious. Most of the small houses were burned down to the dirt, but there was no circle of devastation. The ground between them hadn't burned, and the food and belongings scattered around the still-smoking ashes were mostly untouched by flame. No brand of heat had been pressed against the earth here. Something had destroyed Pakala in the night, but it wasn't the thing from the Pyre.

"Bandits?" Linaria asked as they walked into the ruined village and looked around.

"Stealing what?" Morvius said.

"People." Sera went to one of the few homes that hadn't burned and peered in, then shook her head. "No one, no bodies. I would bet slavers."

"This close to Kibwe?" Linaria shook her head. "The council may talk about isolation, but I don't think they would allow this. They'd squeeze the Bekyar quarter until those scarred flesh dealers squealed."

"I think you put too much faith in those greedy old cowards." Morvius shifted some debris with the butt of his spear, then bent over and picked something up. "But I think you're right about it not being slavers. I found a few coins dropped here. And some of this cloth was decent before it got trampled into the dirt. Slavers would have taken everything of value, along with all the people."

"They didn't get them all."

Jiri looked up from the ground, where she had been studying a set of strange tracks printed into the dirt, and looked at Sera. The paladin's face was even paler than usual, and her eyes for once weren't full of judgment or ambition.

"That hut." Sera pointed back at the crumpled, half-burned mess she had been peering into. "There are bodies there. A person and . . . some children. I think they barricaded themselves in. The hut burned around them. They're all together, charred together." The paladin's voice grew softer as she spoke, her eyes distant, haunted. She stood silent, her hand on the hilt of her sword, staring at nothing. Then she shook, once, like a water buffalo shedding flies, and the hard polish slipped back into her eyes, armoring them like the steel that wrapped around her body.

"Slavers wouldn't burn their profit," she said, words crisp. "What do you see in the dirt, girl?"

That *girl* drove the curious sympathy that Jiri had begun to feel for the paladin away. I'm not your hunting dog, she thought.

Not exactly.

"There was something here." Jiri started walking, moving around the village, looking for places where the dirt was softer, where marks had been left. "Not human. Smaller, with clawed feet. Not charau-ka." *Thank the spirits.* Things were bad enough now. They didn't need to involve those demon-worshiping ape-creatures.

"Are you sure about that?" Sera asked. "Usaro has a long reach in this jungle."

"As if Jiri doesn't know that from growing up here. Anyway, even I can tell it can't be charau-ka. There's not enough crap thrown around." Morvius pocketed the coins he found, bent over and picked up a banana and began to peel it. "Goblins?" he asked, words slurred by the fruit he was chewing. "They like to burn things."

"Kibwe pays a bounty on them. I've not heard of any this close to the city my whole life." Jiri found another track and crouched over it. Something about it worried her, but she couldn't place it. She moved to the edge of the village, then started to walk around it. The light was growing around her, dawn fast approaching, and the trail when she found it was obvious. "They came in from all directions, it looks like. An ambush from all sides. But they left all together. Going this way." She pointed down a narrow track that twisted into the jungle.

"Do we follow?" Linaria's eyes shifted between Jiri and Sera. "Whatever did this, it's not the beast we're looking for."

"No. But . . ." Jiri stared at the scuffs in the packed dirt. *Two fires in the same night. Does something tie them together?*

"We'll follow for a while," Sera said. The paladin looked back at the village, to where she had found the bodies. "It may not be what we're looking for, but it's not anything that deserves to live."

They were in a grove of yellowwoods, the tall trees all webbed together by the spreading trunks of strangler fig, and beneath all those leaves dawn was just a rumor of heat. Jiri crouched low to the trail, making sure of the tracks that still ran along it, and saw a flash of muted color in the shadows. Stepping off the trail, she found the bracelet, a string of little brass bells. She searched the ground around it and found some of the small, clawed footprints that she had been following. Beside one of them, she found another print, one that had been lost before among the clawed ones. A human print.

Holding her hand up to the others, she glided forward. The thick undergrowth seemed to bend around her as she moved, and she gave thanks to their green spirits for letting her pass. Moving as silently as she could, she followed the marks on the ground toward the tower of vines that rose in front of her. An empty tree—a strangler fig had grown over some great tree long ago, wrapped it like a python in its embrace and killed it. That tree had rotted away, and now the fig stood in its place, a twisted mass of huge vines that wrapped around nothing. In that void, Jiri saw a flash of red, and that color sent a shock through her. Her memory unlocked, and she felt her stomach clench with fear and disgust.

She knew what they were trailing.

Rising slowly, she moved back to where the others could see her and waved to them, beckoning. Watching them push and hack their way through the undergrowth to reach her, she whispered an apology to those plant spirits she had just thanked. When they finally reached her, she pointed toward the empty tree.

"One of the things that attacked Pakala is there. With one of the women from the village."

"What is it? What's it doing?" Morvius asked.

"It's a biloko," Jiri said, and saw their blank stares. "They're always hungry. It's eating her."

"Can we surround it?" Sera was pulling her shield free from her back. "Keep it from running?"

"We won't have to. Not with the way they feed." Jiri took a breath, gathering herself. "Come on."

They trailed behind her, struggling to keep up even here where the leaves overhead blocked almost all the sun and undergrowth was thin, but they caught up with her at the base of the empty tree. A large opening lay between the strangler fig's trunks, and through that gap the great hollow space where the dead tree once stood could be seen. Dappled light fell in it from far above, where the strangler fig pierced the canopy, and in those tiny spots of sunlight, the biloko crouched.

The creature was the size of a child, maybe three and a half feet tall, and shaped something like a child, with a large head and thin limbs. But it was no child. Its skin was red as blood and hairless, thatched instead with green growths like vines. Its hands and feet were clawed, and its face . . .

It was gaunt, and the crimson skin wrinkled and drooped like an old man's around its huge eyes. Those eyes were yellow and lidless, with tiny black pupils, and its ears swept up into points. Its mouth was a nightmare. Jiri remembered Oza's stories to the children, how he warned them to run if they ever heard music, beautiful and strange, whistled to them from the dark places in the forest. He had warned them about the biloko's terrible, hungry mouth, the thin lips that spread ear to ear, the teeth in rows like neat daggers. He'd told them how that mouth could stretch wider than any snake's, to swallow them whole.

Like this one's mouth was stretching now.

Jiri thanked the spirits that at least the creature had started with the poor woman's head first, and prayed that her death had come quick and that her spirit had not looked back when it fled her body. No one needed an image like this following them into the next world.

The biloko lay on the ground like an animal, its scrawny arms and legs sprawled limp in the dirt. Its belly was huge, swollen from some earlier victim. Its mouth stretched far too wide, wrapping around the body of the woman it was slowly, slowly swallowing. Its teeth worked methodically, grinding at arms and ribs, pulling in flesh and bone, and its yellow eyes were filmy with some sort of ecstatic satisfaction as it filled itself.

Beside her, Jiri heard Linaria curse, and when she looked at her the half-elf was somehow even paler, her hand over her mouth.

"Don't, Linaria," Morvius said, and his slightly darker face had taken a greenish cast. "You puke and I'll puke, and damn it, I need to get my balance back so I can kill that thing."

"Don't bother," Sera said, and the paladin moved forward, pulling a dagger from her belt, long and thin and sharp.

"Wait," Jiri shouted, Sera's movement snapping her out of the horror of the scene, but too late.

Sera stepped forward, pulled back her arm, and the biloko finally saw her. Those hazy yellow eyes suddenly went sharp, shining with rage and, despite the thing's grotesque feasting, with hunger. Somehow, through the absolute fullness of its mouth and throat, it began to whistle, a bizarre, haunting tune that drove itself deep into Jiri's brain. She felt a drifting weakness sweep through her, a feeling of strangely listless desire, as if the only thing that mattered now was to move toward that music and lie down, rest . . .

Jiri dug her fingernails into her palms and clenched her jaw, throwing the compulsion away.

Sera, meanwhile, slowed not at all. The strange melody wrapped around the armored woman, but she smashed through it, her eyes gleaming like the steel of the blade in her hand. Then she punched her dagger forward, slamming it hilt-deep into the wide yellow eye of the biloko.

The creature shuddered, a massive convulsion running down its body from the gaping jaw, through its swollen neck and belly, making its scrawny limbs flail. A gout of clear fluid splashed out around the dagger, followed by a jet of blood. The gore splashed across Sera's armor, dimming the polished metal, soaking the white tabard, marking her face, but the paladin didn't step back. She leaned forward instead, pressing her blade deeper until Jiri heard the ugly grate of its tip breaking through the back of the biloko's skull. The creature gave one last, massive jerk, its limbs stretching out, clawed fingers and toes digging furrows into the tangled roots that made up the floor of the empty tree, then relaxed.

Sera stood still for a moment, staring down at the dead thing, then raised one booted foot. Bracing it against one of the biloko's teeth, carefully avoiding the legs of its last victim, she jerked her dagger out. She stepped back, away from the pooling blood, and wiped the weapon her tabard. "Wait?"

Jiri stared at the woman. The dark blood splashed across her armor was running off—unable, it seemed, to cling to the metal. It dripped and fell from her tabard, too, a steady shower of gore that left the paladin standing shining, clean, except for the spots of blood that marked her face.

I forget. Jiri watched the woman wipe those spots away with her tabard. *Arguing with her, being annoyed by her, deciding how I can use her. I can't let myself forget how dangerous she is.*

"We might have questioned it."

"We can question one of the others," Sera said. She sheathed her dagger and touched her palm to the golden sword embroidered on her tabard. "Honor this woman with a prayer that she will recognize, but do it quickly. I don't want that trail to go cold."

An hour later, the thin trail broke out of the jungle into the sun.

In front of them stretched a wall of grass, its base rooted in water. A curtain of green, glowing with the sunlight that spilled down from overhead, it stretched who knew how far before them, the sloppy edge of a lake or a great, slow-moving river.

"No," Morvius said, slapping at the cloud of bugs that had whirled up from the water and now whined around them. "This is not a good idea."

Sera didn't look at him. "Can you still track them?"

Jiri crouched at the muddy edge, looking at the prints that sank into the thick muck, the broken stems. "Maybe. But I shouldn't." She straightened up. "Morvius is right. It's all mud and water in there, and we'll have no idea how deep. One of us, probably one of you in armor, will step in a hole and drown. Unless we get pulled under by a crocodile or bled out by giant leeches first."

"Yep, not a good idea." Morvius yawned again. "Well, this isn't the worst wild-goose chase I've ever been on, but it's up there. Can we go back now?"

Jiri watched Sera tap her fingers on her sword hilt, considering what she wanted. These biloko . . . Jiri had spent this morning following their tracks, and the knowledge that each clawed mark had been driven into the dirt partially by the weight of some swallowed victim made her gut twist. They worried her, too. Banding together like this wasn't like them. Usually, they feared each other's hunger too much to work together. Whatever was driving them to do this made them dangerous, unpredictable, like a leopard gone rabid. They had taken that village so easily, and that bothered her too, and the burning, and . . .

And, and, and. Jiri shoved her braids back away from her face. She had no idea if this attack was related to the thing that had destroyed Thirty Trees. This all might be a wild whatever-it-was chase, and she might be wasting her time while that thing found another caravan, another village.

A city.

"I think we should." Jiri straightened up. "They could have gone anywhere in there."

Sera glowered at the grass before her, clearly unhappy about giving up the hunt, and Jiri thought carefully about how she would argue with her if she wanted to keep going, but that argument never had time to happen.

The spears were crude, sticks sharpened and fire-hardened, and small, but they hammered down from the trees behind them in a sudden, deadly rain. Jiri heard the clinking ring of them as they bounced off Sera's armor; the more muted clatter as they struck and fell from the overlapping metal scales of Morvius's armor; the thin, ripping sound as one tore through one of Linaria's sleeves.

She didn't hear the one that hit her leg.

That one she felt, not as pain at first but as a hard shove to her thigh, making her stumble and fall. The grass whipped around her, long leaves slashing across her skin, then she hit the shallow water. She saw the spear then, a branch barely stripped of its bark, the point of it buried deep in the muscle of her leg a hand-span above her knee. With a grunt she slapped it, and it fell easily away, but blood flowed fast from the wound and the pain hit her, sudden and sickening.

"You hit?" Linaria had flung herself behind the vine-covered corpse of a tree that had fallen out of the forest into the grass, pressing into the mud to keep the rotting trunk between her and their ambushers.

"Leg," Jiri said, clamping her hand over the wound. "It's not—" *Not bad,* she wanted to say, and she had seen so much worse in the years she had spent helping Oza treat the villagers of Thirty Trees, but she had never been stabbed before, and she had no experience with the pain, the shock of it.

"Watch out!" Morvius shouted. The man had dropped his pack and now crouched beside Linaria, but he was staring back at the jungle and the next wave of spears arcing down at them.

Jiri forgot her pain and rolled, twisting in the grass to hide from the falling spears. The bone fetishes of Oza's necklace dug into her chest as she flattened herself into the mud and water, and Jiri wished desperately that she had her teacher's power to bend her shape, to become a bird and fly, a fish and swim, to be anything but stuck bleeding and hurting in this muck while the spears splashed down around her.

"It's those bilo-things." Sera still stood in the open, but she had her shield out. "They're in the trees."

"Really?" Morvius rolled his eyes at her. "I hadn't noticed. Why don't you invite them down?"

"Why don't I?" Sera said and started forward, spears crashing like hail off the steel of her shield.

In the grass and water, Jiri took her eyes off the paladin. *She can distract them.* Murmuring to the spirits, she laid her hands over the wound in her leg, pushing away the flies and mosquitoes that had swarmed in, attracted by the scent of blood. She felt the warm touch of the spirits' magic flowing through her as they answered her, and the pain in her leg faded to nothing. When she moved her hands she found her skin whole, marked only by a little blood and a few wriggling leeches. Ignoring them, free of the pain's distraction, she searched the trees for their attackers.

They clung to the low branches like red monkeys, thirty of them at least, their yellow eyes flashing, their bellies swollen from their hideous feast. They had run out of spears, except for the ones they kept in hand, so now they tried another weapon. Their mouths, too wide and crowded with teeth, opened. Thin lips pursed, and they began to whistle.

The sound cut through the low roar of the insects that had been stirred into motion by the fight and the distant rumble of thunder. The high piping, so weird and beautiful, drilled into Jiri's head and tore at her reason. She half rose out of the cover of the long grass, ready to start stumbling forward, to go to the trees and lie down and shut her eyes and wait, wait patiently for . . .

Clear and sickening, the image came to her of that woman's body being slowly drawn into the maw of the biloko Sera had killed. Nauseous and furious, Jiri snapped out of the spell that the biloko were whistling around her, not even noticing that the cloud of insects around her had pulled back, driven away by the waves of heat that crackled from her.

Under the trees, Sera stood, glaring up at the creatures, unaffected by their song. Linaria had stood, but she hadn't moved forward, and the sorcerer's hands were clapped over her ears as she fought the magic woven into the biloko's whistled music.

Morvius was up and moving, his eyes glassy, spear dangling uselessly from his hand.

"Gods and crocodiles," Jiri swore. Bending, she scooped two handfuls of mud from the muck below her and charged out of the grass. She sprinted through tangles of vines and low brush, the plants bending out of her way. When she reached Morvius she dodged around him and stopped, blocking his path. Seeing her but paying no attention to her, he tried to step around, but she stepped with him and slapped him with both hands, driving a handful of mud into each of his ears.

"Ow!" Morvius stumbled back, his spear snapping up. "What the—" he blinked at Jiri, then at the trees stretching over them, their branches heavy with biloko. "Shit. Where's that throwing spear I gave you?"

Jiri blinked. "I must have left it by the water."

"What?" Morvius yelled, deaf, and Jiri just shook her head.

Over them, she could see a biloko give up on its whistling and pull back its spear. Not again, Jiri thought angrily, and flames flashed from her hand. The fire hit the biloko, wrapping around it and ruining its throw. With a high-pitched shriek it fell from the branch, the tangles of vines and moss that grew from its skin instead of hair smoking, and crunched into the ground near them. It made a croaking noise, beating at the little flames that still crept across it, until Morvius slammed Scritch into its chest.

That crunching blow silenced the biloko—silenced them all. The mad, piping notes of their voices stopped and the air went empty, the sound of the approaching storm, the roar of insects, the squawk and chatter of birds all unable to fill the air the way that mad whistling had. In that strange hush-not-hush, pinned beneath the glaring yellow gaze of all the hanging biloko, Jiri almost missed the question.

"You feel it too, don't you? His fire flows in us both. Like wine, like acid, like magic." On the branches above, one of the biloko shifted. Leaves wrapped its body, covering some of its crimson skin, but on its face, its hands, everywhere the red still showed, there were marks. Burns, long broken blisters that wept dark fluid. Brands that twisted into the rough approximation of symbols, marks that teased Jiri with their almost-familiarity. "He marked you. Like me." The branded biloko's lips twisted, making the words, and its voice was shrill and weird, inhuman. But the words were Jiri's language, if strangely accented. "Marked you inside. That's where he starts, at the center, then he burns out. Out, out, and you go to ash there first, ash in your center." The thing's skin began to glow, sparks dancing across the marks burned into the too-big mask of its face. "Burns your soul, wherever it is, sealed in wood or iron or flesh. He burns you!"

The biloko's words rose and became a shriek, a clashing chain of noise that Jiri recognized as a spell. The branded biloko hurled something small at them, something that gleamed like a bright ember in the dark shadows of the trees. Jiri stared at it, time seeming to slow around her so that she could see that ember flying toward her; see Morvius trying to throw himself to the side, his curse drawn out long; see Sera trying to move, trying to get in front of her with her shield up, but not moving fast enough. Then, behind her, she heard the whisper of another spell complete.

Linaria's spell whipped by Jiri's ear, a piece of light the color of stars, and suddenly Jiri's perception slammed back to normal and she could barely make out the rest. Red ember and white smashed into each other and burst in front of her. Two spheres blew outward, one red and gold, one white and blue. The colors rolled over each other, clashing and warring, mixing and devouring one another. Jiri felt heat, then cold, felt them both and then felt nothing but wet as fire and ice smashed together and became an explosion of water, dropping out of the air in a sudden deluge.

Jiri slapped the water from her eyes and looked up. The biloko snarled down at her, the crude symbols branded in its skin pulsing with heat, steam rolling off them. "No," it growled. "Your magic won't take me. I won't let you seal me in that carved prison again, chained by spells, buried with that thing. Burning. Burning. I won't!" It raised its claw and hissed out the same incantation, and Jiri moved this time, sliding behind Sera's metal-wrapped back, but her eyes were on the biloko, caught by the thing she could see clutched in its other hand, the hand not hurling fire and flame at her. Linaria spoke again, and blue-white red-gold smashed through the air, deadly heat and killing cold dancing across Jiri's skin and then gone, leaving only warm water to splash down over her once more as the elements canceled each other out.

The biloko shrieked, a shrill spike of angry noise that echoed off the trees. Jiri could see the creature, hazy through the steam, waving its thin arms, could almost see the thing it held. Then the other biloko were moving, leaping from their branches, swinging down toward the adventurers like a troop of giant-mouthed monkeys, teeth flashing and spears clutched tight.

Jiri reached for the spirits, pulling their magic to her without thinking, calling to the same green souls that had let her slip so easily through stem and branch and vine. Asking that the boon they granted her be twisted into a curse for her enemies.

The spirits heard, and answered.

Vines twisted like serpents, lashing around the clawed red hands that held them, grabbing wrists and legs, spears and necks. Branches shifted, caught, and great broad leaves wrapped around falling biloko like green mockeries of the always-hungry creatures' hideous mouths. Only a handful of biloko made it through the writhing screen of clutching vegetation to land on the jungle floor.

The second their claws hit, Morvius was moving. The fighter had been crouched, half behind a tree, but now he hurled himself out, racing into the fray. He punched his spear into the chest of one of the creatures, picking it up and shoving it back. Its whistling shriek ended in a crunch as it slammed into the trunk of a tree. Like water pouring through rocks, Morvius kept moving. He spun away from the biloko he had just pinned to the tree, using the momentum of his whole body to pull Scritch out and sweeping it in a great killing arc, the blood-colored blade tearing across the face of another biloko, biting through flesh, breaking bone, tearing out an eye.

Only a little slower, Sera charged forward the moment she could reach her attackers. Her shining shield smashed one of the biloko's spears and crashed into the creature's face, breaking its teeth and sending it sprawling. The paladin kept moving, boots stomping across her fallen foe as she engaged another, her sword rising. Her shout of "Iomedae!" blended with the tearing-gristle crunch of her sword through the next biloko's shoulder and into its chest.

Over their battle, bright darts tore through the air, streaking from Linaria's hands. They curved through the air like white wasps, each one finding one of the tangled biloko. Where they struck and stung, the creatures screamed, or else stopped their frantic, thrashing attempts at escape and hung limp.

Everything was chaos and violence, pulling Jiri's attention in a thousand directions, but she forced herself to focus, to stare up through the writhing, gnashing forms of the biloko above her and find the branded one, the one that had shrieked at her. There—no, there. She could see it, the long grass that grew behind its pointed ears brown and charred, the symbols glowing dull in its flesh. The biloko was on the run, throwing itself from branch to branch, fleeing. Shouting at Linaria, trying to get her to throw her magic at it, Jiri reached out to the spirits and—

Wham!

Jiri hit the ground, ribs bouncing painfully off the ridge of a raised root. She flipped herself over and saw the biloko that had fallen onto her. A chunk of vine still writhed around its leg, its end cut by the heavy blade of the machete that the hideously grinning creature held. *Stolen from the village.* The thought was strangely calm as the biloko raised the weapon, preparing to throw itself at her. Jiri's fear slapped out, desperate to keep the thing away, and fire leapt from her hand. The flames flew past the biloko, though, singeing the vines that covered its head but not slowing it, not stopping it, as the machete fell.

Jiri's fire had missed, but the heat of those flames had made the biloko flinch. The cutting blade slammed down beside Jiri's ankle, digging into the dirt. She could see the thin muscles of the biloko bunch beneath its crimson skin as it jerked the machete back up, see it moving forward at her, teeth gleaming as its mouth stretched open, wider and wider. Jiri, weaponless, scrambled back. She shoved her foot into the biloko's chin, trying to keep that gaping maw away from her, and from her mouth poured a gasping prayer for help.

The spirits answered.

Jiri saw it flash by, a blur of green and white leaping over her. It hit the biloko and sent it sprawling, then crouched before her: a frog almost as big as Morvius. It rumbled, gold eyes watching as the biloko pushed itself up and screeched. Then its tongue flicked out. Like a great red vine it whipped around the biloko, catching it and jerking it off its feet. One pull, and the biloko was almost gone, just one clawed foot projecting from the frog's wide mouth, and the amphibian raised the long toes of its forefoot and tucked that last bit in. It blinked once, spat out the machete, and gave another low rumble.

"See how you like it," Jiri said as she pulled herself up and grabbed the slimy machete handle, looking around. The biloko were breaking, the ones that could running into the trees or the tall grass. The ones still caught in vines or leaves were thrashing desperately, trying to escape. There was no sign of the branded biloko.

Jiri looked at the giant frog beside her, saw her muddy face reflected in its great, hungry eyes. "My thanks," she said. "Now eat while you can."

The frog blinked at her, then turned and leapt into the air, catching a tangled biloko in its mouth. It leapt again and caught another, landed, swallowed loudly, and leapt. And in mid-leap faded, the vibrant green of its skin blending in with the leaves, vanishing, gone.

"Aww," Morvius said, wiping his spear blade clean with a wide leaf. "I could have watched that all day."

Chapter Ten
Return to the Pyre

I take your point, girl, about the armor. I don't wear it when I don't have to." Morvius had his armor off now and sat clad only in his sweaty smallclothes on the edge of the ruined village of Pakala. He was working at the steel, fixing one of the overlapping scales that had been driven almost off by a biloko spear. "But I'd like to think my point about usually not having time to put it on when you need it has been made." He pointed to where the spear had dug into Jiri's leg.

That spot was unmarked now, but Jiri could feel the ghost of the pain that had been there. Yes, it would have been better to have had something between her skin and that fire-hardened point. But. "When I fell in the water it might not have helped so much."

"Shallow water," Morvius said. He finished his repair, and without even looking at her cut off her reply. "And yes, the water's not always shallow. I said I saw your point. Anyway." He set down his armor and looked up at her. "You should be doing push-ups."

"Push-ups?" Jiri finally looked over at him. She had been watching the survivors of Pakala, the ones who had fled the raid last night and hidden in the trees. When they had come back, these people were wandering the town, dumb with grief and shock. Jiri and Linaria had talked to them, told them that the biloko were gone, that many of them had been killed, that they would probably not return.

Probably.

The villagers' raw grief tore at the thin scab of anger and purpose that lay over Jiri's spirit, separating her from despair. Talking about stupid things with Morvius eased her, strangely. His ridiculousness was distracting.

"Push-ups." Morvius dropped face-first to the ground, then pushed himself up, using only his arms. He did a few, big muscles shifting in his arms and broad shoulders, rippling under the surprising amount of hair that grew on his chest and belly.

"Why would I do those?"

Morvius stood up, his skin marked with the mud his sweat had made from the dirt. "When I was a child, training, if I dropped my spear, my grandfather would make me do a thousand of those. Then we would spar, and he would always knock my spear from my hands again. Then he'd make me do more push-ups, until I couldn't move. Then he'd piss on me. Oh, Gramps. Uglier than a dwarven succubus, and twice as mean."

"Gods, you're not telling her stories about your family, are you? Hasn't she been through enough?" Linaria walked over to them, Sera trailing behind. The paladin had stripped out of her armor and the undercoat beneath and wore just a thin cotton shirt and the tight pants that the northerners called hose. Unlike her armor, these clothes didn't shed dirt, and the white of them was filthy.

When they had gotten back to the village, the paladin had found a digging stick and made a grave for the burned bodies she had found. While she worked, Jiri had gone back for the body of the woman they had found in the empty tree and brought it back, wrapped in cloth. Sera had nodded and dug the grave wider.

Jiri had watched her, wondering what went on behind those dark eyes.

"The burial's done, and the shaman from the village down the trail has gathered all the survivors up. She says she'll take them there, give them shelter."

Linaria watched Morvius pull on the worn leather of his pants as she spoke, but Jiri knew those words were meant for her. The white-haired woman hadn't questioned her when Jiri had said that she didn't want to be there when that other shaman spoke.

"So what do we do now?" Linaria said.

"Back to Kibwe, right?" Morvius jerked the sweat-stained cotton of his shirt over his head. "By Asmodeus's balls, I could use a drink."

"No." Sera had stepped behind the rough log walls of a goat pen, and Jiri could see her arms raising and lowering as the paladin changed her underclothes. When she stepped back out, she was pulling her heavy undercoat into place, the strange cords and hooks that held her armor to it rattling against each other. "If we start now, we should reach the girl's old village only a little after sundown."

"What?" Morvius had his arms in his scale armor, ready to pull it over his head, but he stopped to stare at the short-haired woman. "Why by all the good-looking gods would we go back there?"

"Because we haven't found what I hunt, spearman. Which is what I'm paying you to do." Sera began to pull the metal plates of her armor into place. "So we'll go back to where we saw it last and we see if we can find it again. It, or its track, or some other clue as to where this fire demon might have gone to ground."

Some other clue.

There had been no sign of the branded biloko after the fight. It had vanished into the jungle with the others, taking its mysteries with it. The symbols branded in its skin, the same kind of symbols Jiri had seen carved into Kibwe's great walls and the Mango Woman's base. The words the red-skinned creature had spoken, words of Jiri's language, if strangely accented.

The thing it had held.

That thing.

A carving, Jiri thought. Dark wood and something that had glittered like metal. She had barely seen it. But something about it . . .

It was like the thing Patima stole from the Pyre.

It was a feeling, something that twisted in Jiri's guts. There was nothing certain about it, but it wouldn't leave her. That biloko had been carrying something like what Patima had stolen. Its skin had been branded with the marks that were sacred to the ancients who had built the Pyre long ago. And the things it had said to Jiri . . .

His fire flows in us both.

Jiri didn't know how yet, but that biloko was caught up in this too. Whatever Patima had released from the Pyre, its influence was spreading.

"Sera's right," Jiri said. "We have to go back to the Pyre." To the place where the ancients had tried to bury their nightmares, the place where Oza had died. "We need answers. We need to know what this thing is, what it wants, and what we need to do to stop it."

"Answers." Linaria picked up her pack, pulled the long braid of her hair out of the way and settled it into place. "That biloko with the magic. Did it give you any, when it spoke to you?"

Jiri looked at Linaria, wondering how much of the creature's speech she had understood. "No. Only more questions."

The half-elf stared at her, her strange blue eyes unreadable. "Well," she said. "As long as we're taking Sera's coin, we go where she tells us."

"And how long are we selling our pretty little asses to Mistress Holy Terror?" Morvius settled his armor on with a jingling clank.

"Until she runs out of coin, this stops being interesting, or we burn," Linaria said. "Whichever comes first."

Exhaustion was a gift sometimes.

When they had stumbled again into the clearing that had once held Thirty Trees, Jiri's grief had come roaring back. She had stared at the empty dirt, the last mango tree, the Mango Woman, and felt the tears coming, silent but unstoppable. Linaria had seen them too, and had helped Jiri wordlessly into her blankets.

There, thank all the spirits, sleep had gripped Jiri tighter than grief.

Blinking awake, the grief wasn't gone. But Jiri's eyes were dry, and she had cast aside the thin cotton of her blanket, her skin blazing with heat.

Her dreams had started with memories of Thirty Trees, so aching, but they had ended with demons, biloko, and flames, and her anger burned in her.

Rage was a gift, too, sometimes.

She sat up. Linaria was sitting in the shade of the scorched mango tree, rebraiding her hair while she kept watch. Sera was up, too, but she knelt silent in her armor, head bowed before her sword, praying to her goddess. Morvius still slept, wrapped snoring in his silk.

"Good morning," Linaria said, and it sounded like a question.

"Good enough," Jiri answered, rising to her feet. Linaria watched her, her hair shining in the flecks of sun that shone through the mango leaves.

"Sera is hunting," Jiri said, keeping her words soft, not wanting to wake the man or break the paladin's meditations. "She wants that thing's hide, for her goddess. Morvius is here because she's paying him to be— and Kalun, I suppose—and because he follows you. But why are you here?"

"I'm getting paid, twice, like Morvius." Linaria smiled, just a little. "Three times, really, since I get to watch him be annoyed. And this thing, whatever it is, seems to deserve having its hide nailed to someone's wall. Don't those reasons suffice for me?"

"They might," Jiri said. "But it doesn't explain why you're trying to be my friend."

"And that is such a rare thing, it surprises you."

Jiri shifted uncomfortably. "I—" Her voice faltered. Oza hadn't been a friend. He had been her teacher—her father, really—but that was different. Hadzi had been her lover, but had he been her friend? She'd thought so, before hearing his schemes. Boro? Maybe. Had anyone else in Thirty Trees ever been her friend, after fire had become so close to her?

They respected me. They needed my magic. But they feared me.

"We're different, in that way," Linaria said. "I used to have friends, lots of them. But then I lost them." She tied off her braid and dropped it behind her shoulder, her movements crisp like her words. "I lost my friends, my home, my family. Everything, all in one day. Like you."

"Were they killed?" Jiri asked.

Linaria looked away from her, the strange blue of her eyes cloudy. "No. They betrayed me. All of them, all at once, and suddenly I was alone, and everything I had once had was gone. I would have been lost, probably would have died. But someone helped me. Saved me."

"Morvius?" Jiri looked at the snoring man.

Linaria snorted, and her eyes swung back, sharp again. "No. It was someone else. Someone I can't repay, except by trying to help someone else, someone who lost all their world all at once, the way she helped me."

Now it was Jiri's turn to look away, to stare at the jungle around them with a tight throat and burning hands.

I have no interest in being someone's charity. But gods and crocodiles, I need her help.

I think I'm going to need every bit of help I can get.

They were going back to the Pyre today. Turning away from Linaria and the others, Jiri walked toward the center of the burn, somewhere she could be alone, to speak to the spirits.

At least she was used to asking them for help.

"I'll come out when this bloody cloud of itching death goes away."

Jiri looked up from the slightly underripe mango she was peeling. Morvius still lay on the ground, wrapped in his silk covering, with Linaria standing over him.

"It's just a few mosquitoes," the half-elf said, waving her hand at the cloud of insects. "They're not even biting."

"*You.* Between that sickly sweet elven blood mixed in your veins and that ice in your skin, they never bite you. Me, with my delicious, lusty warm-bloodedness, they bite."

"You're such a baby, you know that?" Linaria sighed.

"Baby?" Morvius muttered. He rolled in his blanket, cursing as he bumped over roots until he was in the sun. Then he unwrapped himself, stood and shook his cloth through the air, trying to scatter the cloud of bugs that had followed him.

Linaria snorted with laughter, then slapped at her arm. "They do bite me sometimes," she said.

Jiri put down her mango and dug through her bag, pulling out a little clay pot, tightly stoppered. "Fever grass oil," she said, working out the stopper. She poured a little of the pungent stuff into her palm.

"We bought some of that in the market once," Linaria said. "It only worked a little."

"Did you take it to a shaman?"

The white-haired woman shook her head.

"Hmm." *How long have they been here, and they don't know even that?* Jiri bent her head over her palm, whispering to the spirits, and wove their little blessing into the oil. She dabbed a little on her wrists, ankles, and neck, then held out her palm to the half-elf.

Linaria watched the cloud of bugs that had been gathering around Jiri drift away and smeared some of the oil on her fingers, applying it the same way Jiri had. "How long does this last?

"All day, usually. Do you want to give some to Morvius?"

Linaria looked over at him. "I don't know. I kind of like watching him dance around in his smallclothes. He has such a nice back."

"Is that why you took him for a lover?"

Linaria shook her head, reaching out and swiping her fingers through the oil on Jiri's palm. "No. It's because he's the only person I've met who's never lied to me." She smiled sadly at Jiri, then turned away. "Mor. Come here. Our shaman has found a way to keep you from smelling so bad."

Jiri stood, hand still held out. *I didn't lie to her. I just didn't tell her everything.* Because she didn't want Sera to hear what that biloko had said. *No. I didn't want anyone to hear. I'm not tainted.* In Jiri's hand, the oil began to steam a little, hot in her palm. Clenching her teeth, Jiri reined in her anger and turned, heading toward where Sera was getting into her armor. If she wanted to prove that, to believe it, she needed to keep her control, and to keep in mind what she was.

Shaman. Healer and protector.

"Sera," she said. "You might want some of this."

When they went beyond the Mango Woman, Jiri took the lead.

She walked slow and silent, even though the leather of her armor made her feel awkward. Watching. Listening. Noting all the differences.

A beetle buzzed past her, landed on one of the stunted trees and closed its iridescent armor over its wings. A tangled line of butterflies drifted past, and in a sunbeam a swarm of gnats danced. Somewhere above, birds flapped and chattered through the branches of the trees that were shedding their crumpled, dark leaves and sprouting better ones. Below their branches, the mud of the ground no longer steamed, and Jiri could see green shoots sprouting. The shallow pools around them were turning green, too, the dark water filling with algae.

Just a few days ago, that thing had flown free from the Pyre, and already the jungle was pouring into the land it had claimed.

I should feel happy.

This was the triumph of the jungle, green and beautiful, over destruction and death. It filled this terrible place with life, but Jiri could only think about what it meant. That thing was gone from the Pyre, free, and the destruction it spread would no longer be limited to just this small, hidden corner of the jungle. It could spread, wider and wider, until . . .

Until someone finally stopped it.

Jiri gripped her spear tighter and kept moving forward until she could see the top of the Pyre rising over
the tortured trees that surrounded them.

"What is that?"

Morvius breathed the words, staring at the pool that
surrounded the Pyre's charred stone tower.

The black mirror of the water had clouded since
they were last here. Something drifted on the surface
like a rough, dark carpet. It wasn't foam, like Jiri had
seen collect in the still pools beneath rapids. It was too
low and dark for that. It looked something like a mat
of waterweeds, but it was too dark for that, too, and
nothing like that could have grown here in just a few
days. Remembering the stench of the demon, and the
slime that had risen from its body after it had fallen,
she would be surprised if anything good grew here for
a long time.

"I don't know," Jiri said.

"I can hit it with some ice. See what it does."

"Save that, Linaria," Sera whispered. "We don't want
to attract attention too soon if we don't have to."

*This from the person in the shiny armor who isn't both-
ering to hide behind a tree.* Jiri shook her head, but she
reached out to pick up a chunk of broken wood that lay
beside the tree she crouched behind. Looking at the
paladin, she held it up.

The woman settled her shield and nodded. Morvius
lifted Scritch before him and Linaria flexed her fingers,
staring intently at the stain that spread across the
water. Taking a breath, Jiri stepped out and tossed the
branch into the water.

The wood hit right before the mass. It splashed the water up and sent ripples across the black mirror. Those ripples stirred the carpet, and the mass began to move. It bristled as thousands of legs shifted. It went hazy, as thousands of clear wings spread. Then it roared.

Not like the roar of a beast challenged. This was a high, grating whine of wings beating, pulling a thousand bodies up into the air, gray and red and black, where they churned like a thunderhead brought to earth.

"Bloodhaze mosquitoes," Jiri said. They could be nothing else, but these were the size of small birds.

"I don't suppose your oil will drive these things off?" Morvius asked.

"I wouldn't count on it," Jiri said, just as the swarm shattered, roaring toward them. "Linaria?" Jiri shouted and raised her hands.

Fire burst from them, a swath of flames that cut through the swarm, sending smoking corpses crunching down, but the little gap her flames made filled in an instant.

"Too close for the good stuff," Linaria shouted over the roar. Her hands moved, and a white fan burst from them. Giant insects shattered from the cold of it, but not nearly enough, and then the cloud was on them.

Jiri felt clawed legs scrabbling over the skin of her neck and hands and face, wings tangling in her braids, the sharp sting of a bite, then another, and another. She gritted her teeth, intensely aware that she must not open her mouth, and made herself concentrate on reaching out to the spirits. She could feel the magic flow, feel the call go out, but she could barely see anything but the jostling, hideous bodies that surrounded her. Morvius was a grunting shadow, swinging his spear in cutting arcs, the weapon little better than a blanket. The bright steel of Sera's shield flashed through the gaps between the bugs when she swung it, smashing insects back while her other hand pulled away the ones that were wriggling against her neck, trying to shove their way under her armor. Linaria was snapping out an incantation, and Jiri could see her weaving her hands through the cloud of swollen insects surrounding her. Then the sorcerer became much more visible. Flames whirled around her, blue and white, and the swollen insects that had been trying to land on her to feed dodged away. The ones that were too slow fell to the ground and shattered.

Then the air grew even more crowded.

They fell from the sky, brown furry bodies and black wings, needle teeth flashing in red mouths. The cloud of bats smashed into the mosquito swarm, biting and tearing with all the simple fury that the spirits Jiri had called could push into them. Their leathery wings whipped around Jiri, driving the mosquitoes back, but only a little. There were simply too many of the insects, and each of them was almost as big as the bats that were attacking them.

We can't fight these things. Cupping a hand over her mouth, Jiri shouted, "Through the water! Into the Pyre!"

Charging forward, she crashed into the dark water. It washed around her, warmer than her blood, the mud beneath it pulling at her feet. She shoved her way deeper, feeling the water rise, pouring into her armor, catching her and slowing her as the swarm pursued, swirling around her head. She took a breath and ducked beneath the surface, almost dropping her spear as she reached up to jerk away the parasites that still clung to her head and neck. Her legs thrashed, half running, half swimming. Praying to all the spirits that she was wasn't just spinning in circles beneath the murky water, she pulled herself forward until her shin slammed painfully into something hard.

Lungs burning, Jiri shoved her feet down onto stone and muck and pushed herself up. Out of the water, and the Pyre was there, rearing up right in front of her. Morvius already stood on the stones, breathing hard as he snatched bugs out of the air, crushed them and flung them down. There weren't so many here, and when Jiri turned she could see that main part of the swarm still buzzing over the water behind her. Through the head-aching whine of their wings she could hear splashing, could see the water moving where Sera dragged her armor through it. The paladin must have been tall enough to keep her head above the water, because she was moving steadily forward, but Jiri couldn't see her. All she could see was Sera's shield, raised like a steel roof over her head to ward the vicious insects away. Not far from her, the water seemed to smoke, white vapor pouring up from it. Through it and the swarm Jiri could glimpse the shadows of arms moving, and she heard a brittle crunching noise and Linaria's voice, cursing.

"Linaria?" Jiri felt a mosquito latch onto the back of her neck and slapped it away, swung her spear and cut it out of the air. It fell, spilling her stolen blood across the Pyre's black rock.

"Stay back," Linaria warned.

The swirling not-smoke came closer and Jiri could see Linaria standing up, her hands pulling clear shards of ice out of her white hair. The pale flames still surrounded her, and Jiri could feel a chill even though the half-elf stood well over a spear length away. The swarm wasn't trying to feed from her.

"Come," Jiri said. She crossed the slab of stone that had sealed the Pyre for so long, then began to climb the rough stones, heading for the rock wound that was the Pyre's door. She moved, but the swarm didn't follow. By the time she reached the spot where Linaria's spell-wrought stone wall had once stood, all of the insects had circled away, leaving Jiri alone but covered in huge welts, a painful dimple in the center of each one weeping a trickle of blood. Morvius was behind her, then Sera. Linaria came last, keeping her white flames between them and the swarm.

While they made their way up the stones, the swarm pulled in, circling over the water until it had calmed. Then it landed, thousands of the insects resting lightly on the surface of the water, waiting.

"I should freeze them all," Linaria said. The half-elf had the fewest bites on her of any of them, but one sat next to her left eye, swelling it shut.

"Save it," Morvius said. He had sat to pull off his boots, dumping out water and the broken corpse of one of the bugs. "They're not chasing after us, and we might need that magic later."

Jiri eyed the settled insects, then forced herself to turn her back on them and face the Pyre. The stones around them were covered in soot, and a dull heat radiated off them, as if they had been in the sun all day, even though they were in the shade. *Life may be coming back to the area around this place, but it will be a long time before it comes near these stones. Even life warped by feeding on what was left of that demon.*

"We have to take care of these bites," Jiri said. Or tried to say. She had bites near her lips and on her cheek, and her face was so swollen she had trouble shaping the words. "The bloodhaze carry the sleeping sickness," she slurred.

Sera understood her, though, or at least understood why Jiri was digging through her bag, hunting for a salve that would help clean the wounds.

"We don't have the time for that now," the paladin said. Setting down her shield, she slid the steel and leather gauntlet off her hand.

Jiri stared at her, wary, but didn't duck when Sera reached out and pressed her palm against Jiri's forehead.

The paladin's goddess hit her like a thunderclap.

The immensity of the spirit staggered her, a vast force that burned out everything else around her, left her alone in a world of golden light. For a moment, or an eternity, Jiri stood balanced on a sword blade that stretched from one end of the sky to the other, and there were eyes on her. Eyes like Sera's, judging eyes, but so much more, eyes filled with knowledge and courage and wisdom and pain, eyes that flicked across Jiri and knew her, from the depths of her soul up. Those eyes touched her, and Jiri wavered on the thin blade, trying to find her balance, her purpose. Then they were gone, the light whirling away, and in its diminishment Jiri could see something tiny in the center of the goddess's power, something plain and small and ordinary in all that brilliant light. The soul of the human that goddess had once been, buried beneath all that divine power. She saw that, and she could breathe again.

Jiri opened her eyes. She was sprawled on her back, the stones of the Pyre hot against her palms, Sera staring down at her.

"What did you do to her?" Linaria stepped forward, putting herself between Jiri and Sera.

"I asked my goddess to heal her wounds, and to cleanse her of the vermin's disease," Sera said, still watching Jiri. "And she did."

She did. Jiri could feel it, the burning itch that had been starting in her face gone, the skin of her face and neck back to normal, unswollen. "I'm fine, Linaria. I just . . . Gods and crocodiles." Jiri smiled slightly as she realized what she'd just said. "Two things you don't want to surprise you."

Jiri scrambled up, ignoring Sera's staring. *Does she have any idea what she's sworn herself to?* It didn't matter. She needed this woman, and the vast spirit of righteous justice that pressed its power through her. "Heal the others, if you can. I'll see what I can find here."

Sera watched her a little longer, than reached her hand out to Linaria. Jiri, watching surreptitiously as she moved around the opening melted into the stone wall they had tried to seal the Pyre with, saw the others flinch when Sera touched them, but they didn't react like she had. *Do they just not feel her power, or did Iomedae pay some special attention to me?* That thought didn't help anything, and Jiri pushed it away and focused on her search.

Past its rough exterior, the Pyre was obviously a made thing. The walls of the passage that started here were marked with thin lines, the almost invisible joints between huge stones. These stones formed the corridor that ran down into the stone. Unlike the outside, the stone in here was gray, not marked by char except for right at the end, where that thing had melted through Linaria's stone wall.

Jiri stepped back to the entrance and called to the spirits. When she felt their regard, so small and familiar, so different from the goddess's, she reached out and scooped a little bit of sunlight out of the air and fixed it to the tip of her spear. Its light was weak with the sun flashing off the water outside, but the stone throat of the passage stretched into darkness. The others were healed now, skin unmarked, unswollen, including Sera.

"Well," Morvius said. "Shall we see what's up for the rest of the day?"

Sooty ghosts of small clawed feet marked the stone just beyond the entrance, humanlike but inhuman, and so familiar.

"A biloko." Jiri knelt on the smooth stone floor, tracing one of the smudged marks.

"How old?" Sera asked.

"I don't know." Jiri looked at the tracks, dark near the door but rapidly getting lighter. "Sometime in the last few days, obviously."

"Did it leave?"

Jiri stood. "I can't tell. It's just dust on stone here, and Patima and her friends stirred all that up. But I'm betting it did."

"You think it might be the one we fought yesterday?" Sera said. "The one that threw fire at us?"

"I think so. When it spoke to me . . ." Jiri trailed off. She stared down the stone passage, so dark and silent, its stones still warm. She didn't look at Sera, or Linaria. "I thought I saw it holding something, something that reminded me of the thing I saw Patima holding when she ran out of here."

"That thing you can't describe, because you barely saw it? This other thing, that you think you maybe saw, it looked just like that?" Morvius snorted. "Are you holding out on us, runt, or are you an idiot?"

"I didn't see either clearly, but I had a feeling from both. A sense of power, of something dangerous, something . . . alive. Call it idiocy if you want, but that's what I felt. And that's what I feel coming from down there." Jiri pointed her spear down the passage that slanted away in front of them.

"Good. It's better if these evils share the same roots. It makes them easier to tear out." Sera settled her shield, dropped her hand to her hilt. "I'll take the lead now."

Jiri stared into the darkness. All her life, she had been warned to stay away from here, that disturbing whatever mistakes the ancestors had chosen to seal away was dangerous, to herself and all she loved. Warnings that had proven themselves true. But her ancestors' mistakes had already been released, hadn't they? Taken and carried away by Patima and the Consortium so they could be traded for gold.

"You can, but I should. There's something here, but it isn't the thing that destroyed Thirty Trees. Whatever

that was, it's moved on, and we're here to find its track."
Jiri looked at the paladin. "I'm your tracker, aren't I?"

"You are." Sera pulled her sword, the scrape of its steel loud in the stone passage. "So you can lead. But I can fight, so you should be ready to get out of the way. Morvius, you watch our rear."

"Don't say it," Linaria said, falling in behind the paladin. In a line they started down, boots and sandals scraping against the dust and stone, obliterating the last few faded marks of the biloko.

The passage curved more and more as it dropped, circling in on itself. Jiri thought they must be below the level of the pool outside, but the walls stayed dry, the almost invisible seams between the great blocks free of moisture. There were symbols carved into each block, line after line of charms chiseled into the stone. They were echoes of the symbols that Jiri had run her fingers over on the walls of Kibwe, the marks of her ancestors' lost arcane alphabet, and she could feel the magic that they had once spelled out into these stones. Spells of strength, of confinement, of concealment, ancient charms that had once kept this place secret and sealed.

Charms whose magic had long ago fallen apart into dust and ash.

Age and heat had broken them. Centuries had rolled over these stones, and entropy had taken its bite, breaking the careful pattern of charm and spell. That, Jiri could understand. But the heat—it was in every stone, like the last ghost of a conflagration, and somehow it had consumed most of the magic that had been woven into the stones, left it gray and broken.

The heat was breaking her companions, too.

"All the gods damn me," Morvius cursed. "This isn't a ruin, it's an oven." The fighter had stopped, leaning over. His face had turned red, and sweat ran like rivers through his dark hair.

Jiri wiped her own damp braids out of her face and set down her spear. Stepping past Sera, whose prayers kept her cool as ever beneath her metal and leather, and Linaria, sweaty too but not so red, Jiri went to Morvius.

"I was saving this for myself, in case I needed it, but since biloko red isn't a normal color for you, I think you need it more." Jiri whispered to her spirits and felt a breath of coolness gather in her hand. Then it was gone, wrapping itself around the tall man. Morvius immediately heaved a great sigh of relief and straightened.

"Now that's useful magic," he said. "Why can't you do that, Linaria?"

"I can. The cool comes all at once, though, and you'll have pieces breaking off after." The half-elf raised her hand and held it close to the warm stone. "This heat isn't volcanic. It's not natural. Are you sure that thing isn't down there?"

Sure? How am I supposed to be sure about any of this? Jiri didn't let her doubts into her answer.

"It's not. But it smoldered here a long time, and the stones remember."

Down the corridor, Sera started moving forward again. "Let's see if they remember anything else besides heat."

Jiri rubbed the sweat from her eyes, cursed the chafing heat of her armor, and hurried after, pausing only long enough to scoop up her spear. By the time she slipped past the paladin the corridor had taken its last curve. Beyond it, Jiri's pale light revealed two statues of dark soapstone, a man and a woman standing before a wall of stone. Their hands were raised, and Jiri saw the same command carved into them that the Mango Woman had. *Stop. Go no further.*

Forbidden.

Between the statues, the stone wall had been broken, large blocks shifted out of place, leaving a low, narrow gap to what lay beyond. Jiri stared at that gap for a long time, her ears straining to hear anything.

Silence and nothing, nothing and silence. When Sera shifted behind her, impatient to move, the creak of her armor sounded like a shriek. Jiri held up her hand and crept forward. From the sound of it, Sera waited only a moment before following.

The gap was just three blocks, broken and hauled out of the wall, but Jiri could see the cracks running through the stones that still made up the wall, wide black veins that disappeared into the ceiling. The Consortium team had smashed something low into this wall until they had broken one block enough to haul it out, then taken two more. This close to the gap, Jiri thought she could feel the last weak remnants of the old magic of the symbols still crackling, broken with the stone carvings that had channeled it. Ignoring the antlike tickle of its touch, she pushed her spear forward through the gap.

A room stretched beyond, large and circular, an empty pocket beneath a shallow domed ceiling. Sliding carefully through the gap, Jiri held up her spear, throwing light across it.

The stone walls here were not covered with symbols. They were a jungle, and a city.

Stone trees stretched up the walls, their branches and leaves tangling over the dome. Behind their trunks were the carved walls of a city. Symbols were etched into those walls, tiny and intricate, and over them rose towers and rooftops. The walls pulled at Jiri's attention, but she forced herself to stare out across the room at the debris that littered the polished granite of the floor.

Stone carnage covered everything. Pieces of onyx, granite, and soapstone lay everywhere, some the size of her head, others chips of gravel. The bigger pieces still held onto the shapes of their carvings. There was a hand, fingers and thumb curled around a piece of a spear. The smooth lines of a man's chest and part of his belly. The lower part of a leg and a foot, missing its toes. The feathered edge of a wing. A snarling, tooth-lined jaw. A snake's head, mouth gaping, fangs and forked tongue broken.

Statues, Jiri thought. What's left of them. There were four short plinths standing over the debris, empty low pillars that reminded Jiri of the taller ones that held the statues high in Kibwe. Each of them stood before an arch that had been carved into the wall, a stylized city gate like the one Jiri had come through, and which her companions were slipping through.

"Looks like Corrianne and company didn't like the art," Morvius said, rolling a broken head over. It had a man's face, but instead of a nose and mouth it bore a hooked beak.

"I think the art didn't like them," Linaria said.

"Golems?" Morvius stared around the room, as if expecting the stone fragments to begin moving.

"Lots of them," Linaria said.

Besides the four plinths, there were empty spaces in the carved walls. Among the tree branches and vines that rose up the walls and covered the ceilings, there were gaps, niches of smooth stone shaped like the shadows of the animals that had been carved there once. Monkeys and parrots, jaguars and eagles, a crowd of empty spaces.

Linaria bent and picked up a broken piece of stone, an eye and part of an ear, and whispered a spell over it, wrapping light around it. That cool blue light blended with the gold of Jiri's and brightened the room. Now Jiri could read the marks of the fight that had happened here. Dark scorches marred the walls and ceiling, and in one spot the stone floor was pitted and etched, as if with acid. Sliding aside a stone leopard paw, Jiri found a dagger, small and wickedly sharp, its point bent as if it had been thrown into a stone wall—or stone body. Nearby, there were dark spots on the floor, rust-brown spots that led to a wide, dry stain. Jiri found a hand-print smeared beside it, small as a child's.

"I think Mikki got hurt here," she said.

"Too bad she wasn't killed." Morvius said. "Even Amiro wouldn't resurrect her scrawny ass."

"She should have been killed, though. They all should have." Sera kicked one of the stone chunks across the room. It hit the wall with a crunch and shattered into dust and gravel. "One of my instructors told me of a fight he had with a stone golem. It almost killed him, and did kill two clerics and another paladin. He described the thing as deadly, not brittle."

"It's the heat." Jiri touched one of the trees on the wall, and the stone powdered beneath her fingertips, like ash. "All the enchantments woven through the walls, in what's left of these statues. They're crumbling like the stone."

"I feel it, too," Linaria said. "Layers of spells. This place should be impossible to find, much less get into. But the magic has faded."

"Not faded." Jiri rubbed her fingers against her armor, trying to clean them. "The magic's been consumed from the inside, turned into nothing but heat and ash. Something here, something that *was* here, burned it all."

"So we learn a little, but not enough. Let's keep moving." Sera cut across the room, the broken pieces of the golems crunching like pumice beneath her boot heels. "Bring some light," she ordered, standing in the dark arch to the right of the one they had came through.

Jiri frowned but went over to her, bringing her light-tipped spear.

"It's blocked," Sera said. A wall of stone rose in front of them, filling the passage. There were marks on it and around it, scrapes and scratches in the symbol-etched stone, but they were shallow.

"They didn't get through here." Morvius stepped up to the wall with them, giving it an experimental and ineffective shove. "So if there was anything they didn't clean out—"

"Treasure hunt on your own time, Morvius," Sera said. "I want to see what they did get into." The paladin turned and headed for the archway that lay opposite the one they had entered the room through. Jiri paused, not happy that she was following, and not exactly sure how she felt about agreeing with Sera. She gave up and followed, wanting to see what was in the next room, even though the idea that there was something down here, something alive in the heat with them, kept pulling at her thoughts.

"They broke through this one."

Sera's good at speaking the obvious. Through the archway beyond the paladin, Jiri could see a hole in the wall where one of the tightly fitted stones had been broken and pulled out. It left a gap just large enough for someone to crawl through. Jiri crouched down to look through the hole and Sera knelt beside her, her armored presence both reassuring and unnerving.

"Do you see anything?" Sera asked.

"Shadows, stone, and something that might be metal." Jiri squinted at the gleaming reflection, but she couldn't tell what the thing was, other than shiny.

"Give me your spear. I'll push it through, then go in. You'll follow."

Jiri felt her grip on her spear tighten, felt the heat around her grow a little, but she reined in her anger. *If I'm going to use this woman, then I might as well use her.* She handed her spear over and Sera slid it through the hole, sending its light into the other room. The paladin then slung her shield onto her back and started to crawl through the hole, her sword in front of her.

Jiri watched her go, her empty hands ready to flash with fire.

"Ten gold if you goose her," Morvius whispered behind her, and Jiri's whole body flinched.

She didn't bother to look back, though. She could hear Linaria growl softly and the jingle as the half-elf hit the man's armor, hear Morvius's muttered protest. In front of her, Sera was through, and the light shifted in the other room as the paladin picked up Jiri's spear.

"Jiri," she called, and this time Jiri didn't care that she was being summoned. She crawled through the hole and found herself in a broad, square room, its sides arranged like terraces, marching up in a series of ledges to the high ceiling. A long stone block filled most of the floor, its top smooth as a table.

That table, and all the terraces that climbed like shelves around it, were crowded with figures. Men, women, animals, plants, spirits, each carved in exquisite detail in ebony and mahogany, ironwood and teak, the wood inlaid with ivory and turquoise and obsidian. Every one was different, but the little figures shared one thing. Each had a spike of iron through it, the dull gray metal gleaming without rust in the light from Jiri's spear.

"Oh ancestors," Jiri breathed, staring at the carvings. Her skin and soul shivered, and she felt that touch, that sense of something alive, aware, watching her.

"They're kindi."

Chapter Eleven
Kindi

"Don't touch them," Jiri breathed. *Why didn't I think of this? I should have guessed.* She stared at the carvings, still beneath their thin coating of dust, and their eyes all seemed to stare back. "Don't move." Tearing herself away from the kindi, Jiri examined the floor. The dust was scuffed with tracks, too disturbed to decipher.

"Kindi." Sera held the spear up, raising the light. "What does that mean?"

Jiri bit her lip. *I should never have named them.* She shouldn't have, but the shock of realizing what these things must be had unnerved her. Years ago, she had made that promise to Oza, when the stories he taught her had touched on these dangerous little carvings. Promised him to never speak of them to the other children of the village. Promised him to never even breathe their name in Kibwe, where foreign ears might hear it. Jiri didn't answer Sera, taking a careful step forward instead, moving around the table. She kept to the center of the aisle, as far as possible from the figures that surrounded her. The way the shadows shifted when the paladin moved the light behind her made Jiri's skin crawl. It was far too easy to imagine that the carvings were moving, turning their heads to track her as she walked by.

"What's what mean?" Linaria slipped through the hole and stood, looking around. There was a sound behind her, and she called back, "It's not treasure, it's just a bunch of little wooden carvings. No, stay there and watch our backs. I don't want anything trying to seal us in here."

Just little wooden carvings. Jiri kept moving around the table. How many? A thousand? *So many pieces of so many souls. Oza never said they made so many.*

He said they destroyed them.

"Don't touch anything," she said to Linaria. Then she saw it: A gap in the neat rows of figures along the edge of the great stone table. Just a little space of disturbed dust. On one side was a carved ebony woman clutching a malachite child and an iron arrow. On the other, a mahogany lion curled around itself, an iron thorn piercing its paw. Jiri bent over, careful to keep her distance from those figures and all the others, and examined the empty spot. In its center she could see a mark that resembled a few links of chain carved into the stone. The carving must have stood on that symbol. Holding her breath so that she didn't disturb the dust, Jiri found something else. The mark of fingers on the table edge, as if something had rested its hand here. Something small as a child, but with claws. "The biloko took this one," she said, barely aware that she was speaking out loud.

"Jiri. What are these things?" Sera's question was a command, and Jiri straightened.

"Dangerous," she said. "Step out of here, and I'll tell you why."

"They were magic, I could feel that. Some mix of divination and necromancy, illusion and enchantment." In the domed room of broken statues, Linaria folded her arms, staring at Jiri. "Strong magic."

"Necromancy." Sera said the word with disgust. "I didn't have nearly enough time to examine them all, but none of them felt evil to me."

"Evil? I don't know what you or your goddess think evil is, but kindi . . ." Jiri could think better out here, without all those eyes on her, staring at her, but her mouth still felt dry, her throat tight with fear. "From what little I know, they're not evil. But they can be dangerous."

"Jiri." Linaria's voice cut her off. "*What. Are. They.*"

Jiri took a breath and pulled her thoughts together. "They're a kind of fetish. A made thing that has had a spirit bound to it." Her hand rose and touched the bone carvings that hung from the chain around her neck. "Like this. Each of these charms is carved from the bone of the animal that it represents. Each has a little piece of that animal's spirit attached. Kindi are like that."

Like that. Jiri couldn't look at Linaria. She stared at the carved walls around her, guilt and anger rolling through her. *You made me promise, Oza. Not to talk about them. Too dangerous, you said. But you also said they were all gone.*

They're not.

And I think Patima has one.

"Fetishes. Kindi." Sera's mouth twisted around the words as if they left a bad taste. "How are they dangerous? What can they do?"

"Nothing, if you don't touch them," Jiri said. "If you do, if you call out their spirits, then—" Jiri shook her head. "Then I don't know. Many different things could happen, good or bad, depending on what's bound inside. You could get pulled into the spirit's dreams and be lost. Or it might take you over. Or escape, and turn on you."

"Is that what happened?" Sera asked. "Did Patima or Corrianne or one of those others touch one of these kindi and set that fire-thing free?"

"I think—" Jiri cut herself off. *I've said too much already, and not enough.* "I think we shouldn't stand around in here, guessing."

"Really? Seems like that's mostly what we do, now," Morvius said.

Jiri ignored him and took her spear over to the last arch. The stone blocks that had once filled it were broken, shattered into gravel. Only the ragged edge of one remained, sitting on one side of the archway. When Jiri touched it with the butt of her spear, it crumbled into dust.

"The stone here is falling apart," Linaria said. The half-elf stepped back, staring up at the ceiling. "There are cracks spreading from this, across the walls and up the dome."

Jiri looked down the dark hall, which twisted and dropped, just like the passage that had led them to this room. Another dark throat, and it breathed, a current of air flowing up it, hotter than the stones around them. "That was where they kept it sealed away. I have to go down there. I have to—" For a moment, the room swam in front of Jiri, the trees in the jungle shifting, the distant carved buildings moving, as if seen through shining curtains of heat. "I need to get out of this armor."

Her hands moved, and she jerked the leather off, breathed deep as it came free and the hot, dry wind blew across the sweat-soaked cotton of her mud cloth. She dropped the leather, not bothering to pack it. "I'm going down there."

"You're having trouble standing," Linaria said. "And that tunnel looks like it might collapse."

"I'll be fine." Jiri pulled out her waterskin and took a long drink. "I need to see what's down there."

"So do I," Sera said. She eyed the ceiling. "Linaria, you and Morvius stay here. If there's a collapse, you can dig us out."

Linaria folded her arms, thinking about it, but she eventually nodded, her long white hair dripping sweat. "I don't like splitting up. But if that ceiling does fall, you'll need someone to save you."

"Save them?" Morvius asked. "Those rocks fall, they're likely dead."

"You'll pull us out," Sera said. "Dead or alive. Because Linaria has said she will, and because you have some idea of the value of my armor." The paladin looked to Jiri. "Let's go."

There's no way you would let me do this alone, is there? Jiri took one last long pull of water, then picked up her spear. Before her, the passage breathed out its heat like a sleeping dragon. *Right now, though, I can live with that.*

"Let's go," she said, and started down the tunnel.

The tunnel made three full circles, getting gradually steeper. Notches were carved into the floor like crude steps, and they were the only things that kept Jiri and Sera from sliding down like morsels of meat bound for some hellish gullet. By the end they were both struggling, Jiri climbing down cautiously with sweat-slick fingers and toes, Sera clumsier in her armor and boots. Finally the steep slant of the floor evened out, the stone hall opening into a small alcove. There was another opening here, where one last wall had once cut this place off from the outside world. That wall was just a pile of dust on the floor now, and as Jiri wiped the stinging sweat away from her eyes she wondered if it had been like that when the Consortium raiders had broken in, or if had still been standing, a seemingly mighty wall of stone that had broken into dust at a touch.

Doesn't matter, she thought, watching as the wind pulled the dust up into the air like gray flames. "Doesn't . . ." she trailed off. "Hot," she mumbled, and a hand touched her shoulder, pressed a waterskin against her lips. She drank. When it went away, she blinked, and there was Sera, her sharp eyes staring at her.

"You don't know anything about me," Jiri breathed over heat-cracked lips. "About Oza, or Hadzi, or my village, or all those that died. You just want a dog to lead your hunt."

"Does it matter?" Sera asked.

"No. Yes." Jiri reached out and took the paladin's waterskin, lifted it and drained it. "Does it matter to you, if your goddess thinks the same of you?"

"No," said Sera. Then, "Yes."

Jiri handed back the skin and shook her head. The world wavered around her, but she pulled it back together, piece by piece. She was buried in the Pyre, almost in the heart of it, surrounded by heat. She couldn't, she wouldn't fall. Turning her back on Sera, Jiri entered the final room.

Beyond the dust, another passage stretched. It was different from the ones they had traveled before, narrow and tight, and her light gleamed off the dark stone. This wasn't carefully cut granite. It was obsidian, and the images cut into those black slabs had edges sharp as knives. Jiri walked between those walls, razor edges looming like threats on either side of her, and stared at the carvings.

It was a city again, and a jungle, like before but different. This city's towers burned, spires wrapped in ebony flames. Its walls were broken, and through them Jiri could see figures running. They were tiny and dark, but their maker had somehow gifted them with such a sense of terror that Jiri had to look away.

The jungle offered no comfort, though. In the twisting stone branches, things were hidden, not quite human, not quite animal. Clawed, thick-fingered hands clutched at the branches, and through broad leaves Jiri glimpsed faces that might have been apes, but their black eyes blazed with a focused hate that no animal could contain. Jiri tore her eyes away from those snarling faces and made herself keep moving, until the narrow walls pulled back and she stood staring into the Pyre's burning heart.

The heat here was immense, a crackling, blazing beast that ate Jiri's breath, made her choke and dried her eyes. It came from the floor, a circle of black and gray soapstone intricately carved with symbols. Blinking and half-stupid with the heat, Jiri couldn't understand them, but she felt the prickly touch of broken magic sizzling in the heat.

Around her, the obsidian walls rose up and up, until they came together, making a point somewhere high above. Up there, set in that dark, glossy stone, diamonds sparkled like stars. Closer to the floor, the carved city still covered the walls. It was truly lost in its burning now, its buildings bursting, its towers falling, the ground itself opening up to spill fire through its black streets. The carvings told a story of smoke and flame, of a city collapsing more and more as it marched around the wall. By the time it reached the other side, opposite the arch where Jiri stood, there was nothing left but smoke and ash, rising up, and those swirling clouds twisted together to make a sculpture, an obsidian statue that stretched high up the wall. It was a man with great black wings of smoke and flame, his face twisted into something horrible, an expression that might be agony or delight, suffering or triumph. Jiri looked up at those clenched teeth, the narrow eyes, and the wings of the statue seemed to flicker and swirl. It was terrible and beautiful, and Jiri felt fire curling through her, felt the magic of it, so rich, so potent, so destructive—

"That's it, isn't it?" Sera's voice, harsh with heat, cut through the rippling air. "That's the thing that destroyed your village."

Thirty Trees. The name felt meaningless, but there were sensations buried in its syllables, love and shame, and Jiri took a gasping breath of the hot air and wrenched her eyes away from that terrible face.

She slipped a little as she did, stepped forward and caught herself, her toes touching the soapstone floor, and she felt pain jolt through her as the calluses on them began to burn. She jerked her foot back, the hurt clearing her head.

"It is," Jiri rasped. She looked at the statue, avoiding its dark eyes, and found the hands, cupped before its belly. As if it had held something once. *That's where it was. The kindi that Patima stole.*

Did she know what she was unleashing?

Jiri blinked at the room around her, her eyes too dry. *She had to guess. It's not like the ancestors were being subtle here.*

"Step aside." The paladin was moving forward, her sword raised. "I want a closer look, and I have boots."

Jiri hesitated. Patima might have stolen the kindi from this place, but it still felt dangerous, crackling with heat and magic. But Sera was moving past her and Jiri had to step carefully, trying not to touch the burning floor before her or the sharp walls beside her.

Sera stepped out into the room.

Her boots began to smoke, and for the first time Jiri saw sweat appear on the paladin's face, tiny drops rolling from her short hair down beneath the metal collar of her armor. The magic that had been bound into the stone of the floor and the walls sputtered and sparked against Jiri's soul, but nothing came together, nothing *did* anything. Age and heat had stripped the purpose away from these carved curses and charms. Still, Jiri stared at them, watching, and that was how she spotted it: A kindi the size of her hand, standing in a little niche in the wall not far from the door, its dark wood blending in with the stone. A man, holding a spear and standing in a gate, one of the few pieces of the carved city depicted as still whole. Like some last guardian, standing alone against the wings of destruction that were closing around it.

Jiri glanced at Sera. The paladin stood before the statue, staring up at it as if memorizing its features. Moving quickly and quietly, Jiri slipped her pack from her back and set the leather bag on the hot soapstone. Taking a deep breath, she stepped out into the room. Jiri felt the heat of the floor through her bag, but she wasn't burning, not yet, and she scooped up the little carving. And almost dropped it when pain seared across her palm.

Locking her teeth against a startled cry, Jiri shifted her grip but held on to the kindi and stepped back. Off the burning floor, she made herself pull her pack back before looking down at the little figure.

The spear. That had been the thing that burned her when she picked it up, that spike of hot metal. *I almost cut myself on it, almost did what I was warning Sera and Linaria not to do.* But she hadn't, and now she held the little wooden man and stared at him, wondering why he was here, sealed in with this thing. *Who are you?* she asked the little carving. *Why did they leave you alone with this monster? And why do you look so familiar?*

"I feel it."

Sera's growl interrupted the spiral of Jiri's thoughts. The paladin was still staring at the obsidian carving that towered over her, its wings stretching across the walls and around her like the promise of conflagration.

"I can feel the taint this thing has left behind. I feel its evil." Sera spun to face Jiri, her boot heels smoking and her eyes shining. "I will find it and send it back to whatever hell claims it, and I will prove myself again. To Iomedae, and all those who serve her with doubt in their hearts."

"We should go," Jiri said, the hand that held the kindi hidden in her pack. "We push our luck, staying . . ." She trailed off, her eyes rising. The obsidian above them was shifting. Not like heat shimmers, not wavering, but moving, and the diamonds that gleamed up there were moving, too. Moving in pairs, two of them together at all times, like—

"Sera," Jiri warned, and she slung her pack over one shoulder, holding her spear. Above, stone hissed against stone, and a black shape fell from its spot high on one of the walls. It spread wings and dove at them, Jiri's light flashing across it. Something like a person, something like a bat, a swooping piece of obsidian with diamond eyes, whose hands carried sharp splinters of stone.

"I see it," Sera said, and her sword swung through the air.

The obsidian creature twisted in its dive, but not quite enough. Sera's sword edge crashed against a wingtip and sparks and stone fragments flew. The creature shrieked, a sound like grating stone, and hit the floor. Its wings scrabbled loudly over the symbols scribed there, then it flipped itself over and drove both of its blades into Sera's boot. The paladin didn't make a sound, just pulled back her foot and kicked the obsidian face, crushing it. The stone carving dropped its weapons, pulled in its wings, and exploded.

Fire bloomed out of it, red and gold, and jagged fragments of obsidian clattered against the walls. Jiri felt a sting across her calf, looked down to see a line of blood drawn by one of the stone chips.

"Shit," Sera said, her voice almost thoughtful. Her boot was shredded, and beneath its torn and charred leather Jiri could see blood. Over them, the movement increased, more and more of the things above waking, spreading wings, staring down with jewel-bright eyes.

"Move," Jiri said, backing up. She hissed as her shoulder hit a wall carving and the sharp stone bit her, but she didn't take her eyes off the chamber in front of her, off Sera limping backward, her shield up, her armor scraping the carved walls. When she was clear of the obsidian walls of that narrow hall, Jiri stepped to the side. When Sera got within reach, Jiri reached out and caught the paladin's white tabard. Then she ducked the armored elbow that the woman threw back.

"Careful girl," the paladin warned. "Don't touch me in battle."

I don't want to be anywhere near you in battle, Jiri thought. "Start up. I can slow them down."

Sera's eyes narrowed, but she sheathed her sword and slung her shield with only an instant of hesitation. "I hope you can."

Jiri stepped in front of the obsidian passage and squared her shoulders. She reached out for the spirits, feeling the ones she wanted tangled in the hot wind that pushed at her. Behind her, she heard Sera whisper a prayer, the same words she had used when she had healed Jiri earlier. Then the paladin moved, the sound of her boots scraping against the stone as she scrambled up. Jiri listened, praying that the woman's ancestors were watching her and willing to help.

Whether or not this works, I might need her healing again.

The sounds of Sera's escape were drowned out by the clicking and grating of stone wings moving. Jiri could see the dark cloud of bat-winged creatures swirling at the end of the narrow tunnel, spinning around the circular chamber, faster, faster.

And then, like a storm, they broke. They poured down the passage, wings clinking off each other and the walls, their tiny knives glinting in Jiri's light. Jiri felt the magic in her and wanted to let it out, to throw it at these creatures before they could get too close, but she held it. Held it until they had almost reached the end of the tunnel, then let it go, along with her breath.

That little bit of air, released from her lungs, hit the wind that pushed its way out of the heart of the Pyre and mixed with it. Mixed and grew, swelling, quickening, taking over, and a new wind roared down the corridor, away from Jiri. The gale caught the little flying creatures, shoved them tumbling backward, colliding with one another and the walls, and then it started. First one, then another and another, a cascade of fire and deadly fragments filling the hall as the stone creatures shattered and burst. Jiri spun away, running, but she felt the fragments hit her, cutting her back, her legs, her scalp. She could still run, though, and deaf from the sound of their deaths, half-blind from sweat and heat and blood, she turned and began to scramble up the steep stone ramp that led back to her companions. Up and around the first curve, waiting for tiny hands to catch her, for little wings to smash around her as black stone knives rose and fell. That fear crushed everything else away, and she was halfway up the passage before she noticed the shaking.

The trembling ran through the stone, up her hands and her feet. Jiri pulled herself up, the tunnel flat enough now to let her run, and she could see the haze of dust sifting down from the ceiling, the chunks of rock that were beginning to fall.

The force of the explosions below had run ahead of her, and the Pyre was falling apart.

Chapter Twelve
Little Knowledge, Hard-Won

Jiri ran.

Her bare feet pounded over the shaking stone, through dust and gravel, the pain from her burned toes and cuts drowned beneath adrenaline. She tore down the corridor, away from the wings that were following her, away from death beneath tired, uncaring stone. She ran, and only slowed when she reached Sera.

"Keep going," The paladin might have been trying to shout, but dust and heat and exertion had left her voice a dull croak. "Warn the others."

Jiri didn't answer, just sped up and raced around the last bend. In front of her she could see Linaria through the arch of the door, her hand wreathed in a smoking white nimbus of light. The half-elf called out, "Jiri!" but didn't move, didn't release the cold magic she had caught in her fist. Jiri pelted past her and brought herself to a skittering stop on the stone fragments that covered the floor, the smashed chunks of statue now mixed with pieces of the wall and ceiling.

"Sera. Coming!" Jiri flung the words out, fighting for air. She could see Morvius now, standing on the other side of the tunnel's entrance, Scritch held tight in his hand. Ready to skewer any foe that came out of the tunnel for Linaria. "Things. Following!"

"Expand on 'things'!" Morvius shouted, then cursed when a fist-sized chunk of stone fell from the cracked ceiling and bounced off his arm.

Jiri moved back, away from the possibly collapsing tunnel, trying to raise her voice enough to be heard over the groaning stone. "Little flying statues. They shatter into fire when you break them!"

Now it was Linaria's turn to curse. The sorcerer backed up and joined Jiri in the center of the room, where the cracks in the ceiling were thinner and only dust seeped down. Morvius moved with her, his spearpoint leveled at the door.

"Should we keep going?"

"We wait for Sera," Linaria snapped.

"Just thought I'd ask," Morvius said. "I know how you hate being buried alive."

"We're not—"

Two *cracks*, sharp explosive pops that almost overlapped, rang out from the tunnel that Sera was in , and with a groan the roof of that passage began to give way. Rocks rattled and dust bloomed, hiding everything and making it impossible to breathe. Jiri squinted, trying to make her dry eyes yield a few tears to wash away the dust, and stepped forward. There came a sharp rattle of stone against steel, and in front of her dust swirled around polished metal.

Sera ducked through the archway, boots sliding on the loose pile of rubble that half filled it. The paladin's armor and tabard were as clean as ever, bright as the shield she held over her head. The grandeur of her image, the warrior striding through disaster, was only diminished by the ragged ruin of her left boot and the dust that caked her face. That dust turned to mud on her right cheek, where a slash spilled blood down to her chin.

"There are more—" Sera cut off as a chunk of rock half the size of her head pulled loose from the ceiling and smashed off her shield with a dull boom. The shield caught the impact, but Sera couldn't keep the steel from collapsing under the blow and cracking into her head. "—coming," she finished, the word edged with anger and pain. "Why aren't you running?"

"It was suggested," Morvius said. "Shall— Oh, Rovagug love me tonight."

In the dusty air behind Sera a shadow moved, pulling itself through the dust: a small, black shape, stone wings flexing. Jiri raised her hand, and fire ran down it, flashing away to wrap around the obsidian monster. An instant later a bolt of white struck it, and with a sharp crack superheated stone suddenly froze. Shedding pieces of itself, the thing struck, swinging stone razors at Sera. The impact of Jiri's fire and Linaria's ice had slowed it, though, and its knives only scored the back of the paladin's neck, cutting skin but not driving in through muscle and veins.

Sera snarled and spun, sword arm moving like a snake, but at the last moment she pulled her blow, made her sword miss and struck the thing instead with her shield. It shattered against the steel, blowing apart in a hail of stone and flames, staggering Sera. Her shield, though, caught most of the biting fragments.

The little explosion shook the room, and Jiri could see the cracks in the ceiling widen and stretch.

"Go!" she shouted, and it was all of them shouting at once. Then they were pelting through the dust. Linaria was in the lead, but she was heading the wrong way, turned around in the dust, and Jiri had to howl and point toward the door they had taken in. The half-elf stopped, confused, then turned to race the way Jiri was going, Morvius and Sera hard on her heels. Then the white-haired woman stopped, her strange blue eyes widening.

Jiri risked a look over her shoulder and saw it. The arch Sera had just run through was almost totally gone, with only a narrow gap at the top still open to the passageway beyond. That gap was full now, though, crowded with black shining bodies, a sliding tide of stone wings and claws pulling themselves through, ready to leap into the air and follow.

Too many. Oh Oza, I'm sorry, I tried but I couldn't. May you and all our ancestors forgive . . .

Whatever Linaria said was lost in the sound of crumbling stone, but her hand moved and a handful of flashing darts leapt from it and slammed into the carved face of the first obsidian creature, smashing away Jiri's despair.

Jiri whipped her eyes forward and ran as fast as she could. From behind her came the first pop. Then another and another, a rising cascade of explosions, their sharp snaps being drowned out by a steadily building roar as the ceiling gave way and began to fall, crunching down.

She raced up the passage's curving path, the whole Pyre shaking beneath her. The stones here weren't falling, but they groaned with the stress of the collapse. Jiri could feel magic all around her, hissing over her skin like a million insect wings, itching and burning. All those charms, gutted by heat and time but still trying to hold the stone together, were finally breaking. Jiri staggered, trying to run but failing. The broken magic rolled over her like a scourge of fireweed and she stumbled, started to fall.

A hand hit her, smashed into her belly and knocked her air out, folded her over an arm wrapped in leather and steel. Burning, gasping, Jiri barely noticed being jerked up over an armored shoulder, barely felt the bruising, jolting impact of the metal against her belly until she was surrounded by light, bright sunlight, and the hundred-thousand tiny knives of all those shattered spells stopped scratching across her.

"Linaria!"

Jiri could hear Morvius's voice, and picking up her head she saw him staggering out of the door that opened to the Pyre. Dust like smoke spewed out of that rough opening, and she could see that the rocky peak above had changed shape, broken and slid, the whole stone pile of the Pyre collapsing in on itself. Tearing her eyes away from that destruction, Jiri looked at Linaria, shaking in Morvius's arms.

"Get her. Away," Jiri told him, voice shaking. "Farther better."

Sera. She picked me up and carried me out.

"Put me down," she said, and Sera let her go. Jiri slipped off her and splashed down into the water that surrounded the Pyre. It had been warm as her blood when they swam through it before, but it felt cool now against her overheated skin. She dipped her hands in it and splashed it across her face, washing dust out of her eyes. Something distracted her, though, some other distant worry. Watching a trickle of blood roll down her arm, she remembered.

The swarm.

Lifting her head, she could see it rising from the water, a buzzing cloud of wings and hunger.

"Gods and crocodiles," she groaned, and tried to find her magic.

Morvius had stopped beside her, Linaria still awkwardly cradled in his arms with his spear, and he cursed too. Linaria, still trembling from the shock of racing through all those breaking spells, opened one eye.

"No," the sorcerer said, then raised her hand and spoke. The air chilled around her, and a flash of white flew from her hand and into the gathering swarm. It bloomed out into a great, seething ball of blue and white, and a cold wind rushed by. The ball faded, falling apart into water and steam, and most of the swarm now lay trapped in the circle of ice that coated the water's surface. A few buzzed weakly, trying to pull themselves free, until Linaria spoke again.

Another flash of blue-white, and all the swarm was swallowed by cold, their corpses embedded in a steaming circle of ice.

"We could have stayed in town, y'know, and earned as much coin chilling drinks as doing this," Morvius said.

Linaria didn't say anything. She just pointed at the shore, and Morvius started to splash toward it, still carrying her.

"Hold still," Sera muttered, and Jiri gritted her teeth and tried. It was hard, though, since it felt like the northern woman was trying to dig all the way through her shoulder blade.

Jiri lay on the packed dirt where Thirty Trees once stood, her thin blanket under her, stripped down to her loincloth. Sera was going over her back, digging out the tiny fragments of obsidian embedded in her skin.

"How deep are you going?" Jiri asked, trying to look over her shoulder to see the sharp little knife that Sera had taken out of her healing kit.

"No further than you went into the back of my neck." Sera flicked away another chip of obsidian. "Hold on. This last one is a bit deeper."

"How deep?" Jiri asked before her teeth clenched shut. It felt like Sera was trying to carve out her kidney. Jiri's fingers and toes curled but she held still until Sera finally stopped digging and pulled something out of her back.

"Huh. Lucky you." The paladin dropped something on the blanket in front of Jiri's face.

Slowly recovering, Jiri stared at the bloody little lump without recognizing it. One part of it, not covered in her blood, flashed in the sunlight, and she understood.

"One of the diamond eyes."

"Diamond?" Morvius wandered over. "Not huge, but worth some coin."

"Jiri's coin," Linaria said from the shade beneath the mango tree. "Your rule, as I recall, was that any treasure stabbed into someone belongs to them."

"Hey, I earned that dagger," Morvius said. "And that was stabbed. Not exploded."

"Don't quibble."

Morvius muttered and walked away, though he took the time to look over Jiri's backside first.

Jiri rolled her eyes, and barely noticed Sera putting her palm on her back. Then light rushed through her, white and gold, sweeping away the pain in her back and in her feet, healing her and stunning her with the force of the great spirit that was its source.

"Gods and . . . Gods," Jiri croaked. "Warn me before you do that."

Something like a smile touched Sera's lips. "Here's your shirt," she said, dropping the tattered, bloody piece of mud cloth on Jiri.

Jiri rolled over and pulled it on, moving easy. However else she felt about it, Sera's healing worked.

And do I like feeling indebted to her and her goddess for it? No, I do not.

"Kibwe?" she said, rising.

"Is that where the trail lies?" Sera picked up her pack and shield.

"The trail is . . ." *Cold? Lost?* "Scattered. We know more now, but not enough to find this thing. And there's nothing else for us to learn here."

"And you think Kibwe will hold answers?" Sera asked.

It holds Patima. And the thing she stole from the hands of that thing in the heart of the Pyre.

"I think so."

Linaria was looking at her, blue eyes sharp, but she didn't say anything. Not before Morvius spoke.

"It holds wine, food, and a decent gods-damned bed at least." The fighter slung the bag holding Jiri's armor at her, then picked up his own pack. "Let's go."

Sera tapped her fingers across her sword hilt. "All right."

Jiri stuffed her blanket into the bag with her armor, then carefully cleaned the diamond with her shirt and dropped it into the little pack with her healing things, her water, and the little kindi she had taken from the pyre. "All right," she whispered, staring down at the little carved man. Then she closed the bag.

"What in seven hells is going on?" Morvius said, staring at Kibwe.

They had stopped where the narrow trail opened onto the wide plain that circled Kibwe, a clearing burned regularly to keep the jungle at bay. From here they could see the city's high walls, a black bulk against the night. Light spilled over them, and through the gate that stood open ahead. Open, but crowded with guards.

"Another attack," Jiri said. *A caravan? A village?* She could see it, a charred black circle in the jungle, empty except for the ash drifting in the moonlight . . .

"We'll find out," Sera said, and walked into the open.

The moon shone down bright, and they were spotted fast. Before they were halfway across the clearing the guards had broken out of their loose huddles of talk and arranged themselves to meet them, a few in front with spears, the rest behind them holding short bows, throwing spears, slings, and blowguns. The weapons weren't pointed at them, but their threat was clear.

"Who approaches the walls of great Kibwe?" the guard in the lead called out when Sera reached the edge of the city's light.

"I am Sera Galonnica, servant of Iomedae, goddess of truth, protector of justice."

"A brave, bright goddess," the guard said. "So why is her servant slinking around in the dark?" He was a young man, heavy with muscle, and acted as if he were staring down at Sera even though they were close to the same height.

Jiri didn't have to look at Sera to know that the paladin was doing her best to look down at him.

"I am *not* slinking. I—"

"Why do you think we're out in the dark, Taba?" Morvius's question trampled Sera's answer, but he ignored her glare and stepped forward. "The bloody sun went down. Now can we go in? I haven't had a drink in days and my boots smell like crocodile piss."

"Morvius." The man's arrogance had turned into something more complicated. "Every time I hear you've left, I expect to never see you again."

"Well, the gods crap on everyone's dreams, don't they?"

Taba stared at Morvius, brown eyes unreadable; then he laughed and slapped him on the arm.

"Come on. I'll give you a drink before I turn you loose on the city." His voice went low, and Jiri barely heard the rest of his words. "You need to hear what's going on before you go in there."

"How do they know each other?" Jiri sat on a short bench in the guard house that stood on the other side of the gate, sipping at a cup of watered palm wine. Linaria sat beside her, watching Morvius show off Scritch to Taba, a large cup of unwatered wine in his hand.

"They got into a fight once, over a woman." Linaria shifted on the bench beside her, edging a little farther away from the granite wall beside them. The guard house was built directly against the great granite blocks of Kibwe's wall, and Jiri could feel them too, all the charms that flowed through that stone, bound by the symbols carved deep into those blocks. It hadn't been that long since they had both felt charms just like those being pulled apart, their magic breaking loose and blowing across them like sparks.

Jiri edged over a little too, and they were pressed tight together at one end of the bench, but she didn't care and Linaria seemed to welcome the contact, a buffer against the magic's touch.

"They seem to get along now," Sera said. The paladin hadn't sat down, hadn't taken the drink offered her, only stood, looking vaguely annoyed in her perfect armor and tabard. In the lantern light, Jiri could see a smudge of dirt on her pale nose, and for the first time in a long while she had to fight not to smile.

"The woman got disgusted and left with another man while they were fighting. So they went home with each other," Linaria said. The sorcerer noticed Jiri watching her and shrugged. "I've never cared how many other lovers he has, or even tried to keep track. I've just told him that he better be ready whenever I am. He seems to take that as a challenge." Linaria smoothed back her hair. "Sometimes, I make it one."

This time, Jiri did smile. But Taba had stopped admiring Morvius's weapon, and his words grabbed at her.

"There have been at least two more burnings, maybe three." Taba had poured himself a drink of wine, too, unwatered but only a small splash. He drank it down in one gulp. "Last night, Zawao village went. No one saw anything, but some traders were passing through there on the way to here. They said there was nothing, not a person, not a basket, not a goat. Just a circle of ash. No one saw what happened, and that place is a half-day's walk from these gates. The marketplace was buzzing with that all day, along with talk of the caravan and Pakala and Thirty Trees." Taba's eyes went to the bench, touched Jiri and then went away. "A lot of talk about curses, and bad-luck magic."

"What about biloko?"

Taba's attention snapped back to Morvius. "What about them?"

"There were biloko at Pakala."

"So we've heard," Taba said. "Some of the survivors showed up in the city, asking for help. They were followed by another group, from Green Spring. Their village had been hit by a band of biloko this afternoon. Luckily for them, they had hunters out. They saw the biloko coming and fought them off, but half the village burned, and they spoke of many dead and missing."

"That's two," Jiri said. She pushed the words out through a throat tight with nerves, but she had to know everything she could. "You said three. Maybe."

"There were some hunters. When everyone started talking about the burnings, they said they had seen something like that. In the jungle they found a charau-ka, dead, covered in burns. They tracked it backward and found a circle of ash, a burned place in the jungle. This was before the caravan was lost."

It did attack, then, that night I lay useless with grief. Jiri didn't mourn the charau-ka. When she was six, one of her playmates had vanished from the edge of Thirty Trees, swallowed by the jungle. Oza had gone hunting and returned with the hands of the boy's killers, long-fingered like an ape's, but clawed. One of them still clutched a stone dagger. Oza wouldn't tell Jiri what had happened to her friend, not until she was sixteen.

She'd had nightmares for weeks.

Jiri didn't care that the charau-ka had died, but she cared deeply about how they died. *This thing. This thing I don't even have a name for. It kills humans and charau-ka. After Thirty Trees, it's only attacked at night. It burns a circle of destruction, killing everything in it, and then vanishes. What is it? What does it want?*

How do we stop it?

"So what's being done?"

Sera's words broke Jiri's thoughts.

"By who?" Taba said. "The villages are setting up guards or running here to hide behind the walls, depending on how brave they're feeling. The traders are staying in place, complaining to the council and bidding with each other over guards. The council . . ."

"The council doesn't care what happens beyond these walls," Jiri said softly.

"That's a convenient thing for them to say, when the trade is flowing," Taba said. "But when something slows or stops that trade, then even their eyes might turn beyond the circle of these walls." The guardsman took the jug of palm wine and poured himself another, much more generous than his first. "I've been hearing tales lately, of what happened at the last council meeting. A girl came there, claiming to be a shaman, saying that some people from the Aspis Consortium had released a fire demon on her village."

"What do you think of that story?" Linaria asked.

"It's one of many. There's another going around that the girl is a demon herself, bought by Kalun to curse his enemies."

"Really?" said Linaria.

"Yeah." Taba said. "That's not one I believe. All the ones telling it seem to have northern silver in their palms. The kind the Consortium pays out. But I'm not everyone." Taba raised his cup and drank deep. "I'm just a poor, unappreciated sergeant of the guard."

Morvius tapped his fingers on his belt, next to the pouch that held his coin. "And if you weren't so unappreciated?"

"I might tell my friends that the council may be about to order the guard to round up all the foreign rabble that's accumulated behind these walls lately. So that they can be sent out into the jungle, and not let back in without a bag of biloko heads."

"Your friends might appreciate that." Morvius's hand dipped into his pouch and came back down on the table with a solid click. "Well. Looks like we might want to get back to the Red Spear. We wouldn't want to be forced out into the jungle again before we've even had a drink." Morvius looked down at his empty cup. "Or another drink."

"That sounds smart," Taba said, fingers reaching out to cover Morvius'. He gripped the taller man's hand for a moment, and leaned toward him, whispering some-thing in his ear. Then he pulled back, and his hand went to the beaded pouch that hung from his belt, dropping something in it with a soft clink. "May all your good-luck ancestors be watching."

"I think they already are," Morvius said, slapping the man on the back and heading toward the door.

Jiri followed Linaria and Morvius out into the night, Sera not far behind.

"Do you really think the council will issue that order?" Sera asked.

"They already did," Morvius said, long legs stretch-ing as he walked fast. "Taba told me that a messenger brought it to him a few minutes before we showed up. He hadn't told anyone else about it yet, though. Lucky us."

"Lucky that he liked you enough to let us go," Linaria said.

"That's not luck," Morvius said. "That's a little coin, and being the best damned lover in this city."

The carved stools in Kalun's talking room were more comfortable than the guards' benches, and the Red Spear was cool. But the old innkeeper wasn't offering them palm wine tonight.

"You didn't even think to send me a message about where you were going? What you were doing?" Kalun sat on his bench, his frown carving deep lines in his face. "You just take off without telling me anything?"

"We told Fara," Morvius said. "And Basan."

"You told a child and a drunk that you were going to check a burned-out caravan. Then you were gone for a day and a half." Kalun's frown lines got deeper. "What were you doing out there?"

"Working for her," Morvius said, pointing to Sera. "Apparently. Though she hasn't come across with any coin yet, I've noticed."

"Working for—" Kalun cut off, turning his glare on Linaria. "I can't talk to him. You. Tell me what happened."

"Well," Linaria said carefully. "We have a contract with Sera. Any information we found would—"

"Oh, so you *are* working for her now? Not me?" Kalun leaned back. "Fara!" he snapped, and the girl appeared so quickly that she must have been lurking in the hall. "Go find some guards. I have some of those foreigners that they're looking for and—"

"Kalun," Linaria said. "Now listen—"

"Stop!" Jiri almost shouted. "What are you doing now? Arguing? Dickering?" The words snapped out of her, and she found herself standing, heat blazing through her. "Is that all you people do? I came here asking for help for my teacher, and you bargained while a demon picked its teeth with his bones. When I confront his killers, the people who let loose that *thing* that destroyed my village, I get told how wrong I am because now there are fines to be paid. When we hear about the caravan, about fire and death falling from the sky and destroying it, just like Thirty Trees, we can't go out and try to help until coin is passed. Now this?"

Jiri glared at them all, her fury making the room hot. "That thing is out there, burning men, women, and children alive and leaving nothing but ash. We know so little else, but we know that. And what are you doing? Sitting in here bargaining like fruit merchants, trying to decide how much coin it will take before you lift your fingers to help save them."

"Jiri," Linaria started, her voice tired and angry at the same time. "We—"

"No, Linaria." Morvius stretched his long legs out and leaned back, staring at Jiri. "Let her talk. I want to hear how selfish we are, for killing her demon. For keeping Corrianne from slapping her down like a bug in the market. For keeping the council from kicking her out of this city. For killing those biloko before they swallowed her down. For pulling her alive out of that cursed ruin." He leaned forward, smiling without a bit of humor. "Don't pretend to be noble and good, runt. You don't do half as good a job at it as Sera, and your real motivation is even more obvious. She wants her glory, even more than we want our coin. And you? You want blood." His smile faded. "And you won't get it without our help. Which costs."

Jiri picked her bag up from the floor, and there was a sound, a faint hiss as the cloth singed beneath her fingers. Her hands were clumsy with anger, and the leather thong that held the bag shut resisted her until it finally broke, half burned through.

"What about this?" Jiri pulled the diamond out of her bag, the one that Sera had cut out of her back, and threw it at Morvius. The man caught it, then dropped it with a curse. Jiri watched him wet his fingers and pick it up, blowing on it. Her hands were making her bag smoke, and she slung it over her shoulder before the smoke became fire. "Is that enough?"

"This and Sera's coin will get you a few more days." Morvius rolled the gem in his palm. He looked up at her, and this time his smile did hold humor, of a dark, evil sort. "So you better figure out how to find that thing, or you might never get a chance to save your villagers. Or to burn Patima down, just like that thing did to your Thirty Trees."

"I'm sorry," Fara said. The girl led Jiri around one last tight turn of stairs and into a hall at the top of the Red Spear. "Mama said— Well, she thought it might be better to give you one of the smaller rooms."

"I don't care, Fara," Jiri said. She felt exhausted. So much had happened these last few days, and then that argument downstairs. When she had let go of her anger, she had nothing left. It had been easy enough to leave, to let Linaria and Sera explain what had happened to Kalun while Morvius made his snide comments.

Let them waste their time with talk. Jiri's hands clutched her bag close. *I'll try to keep this hunt alive.*

"Here." Fara opened a narrow door at the end of the long hall. Beyond it was a tiny closet of a room, bare but for a stool, a candle, and a sleeping mat. One small bundle sat on the stool—the rest of Jiri's clothes from the market.

"Do you want me to bring you things for washing up?" Fara asked.

"No," Jiri said. "Maybe in the morning."

"All right," the girl said. She fidgeted with the wrap of her dress. "He's not a bad man," she said in a sudden rush. "Morvius. He tells stories that make us laugh and make Mama mad. And he gets us treats from the market. And Linaria, she's always nice. She makes ice for us, sometimes, when it's hot."

"Sweets and ice." Jiri thought of a monster, crouched stinking in the water before the Pyre, roaring as a bolt of white struck it and slicked its slimy hide with ice. *Morvius was right. Without them, that demon would have crunched my bones, too, and no one would know what Patima has done.* "What about Sera?"

"She's too picky about how well we clean her room," Fara said. "But she kills spiders if you ask, no matter how big."

"I'll keep that in mind," Jiri said. "Goodnight, Fara."

"Ancestors watch your dreams," the child responded.

"And yours." Jiri left the door open, letting in the thin light of the single lantern in the hall. When Fara's footsteps had gone, she could hear almost nothing but the sounds of the city outside and the distant racket of Kalun's guests downstairs. Strange noises, compared to the jungle, but soft.

Kalun's wife might think she's slighting me, putting me up here. But this is a better place.

With a whisper, Jiri gathered a handful of light from the air and rolled it into a little ball. She put it on the dead wick of her candle and shut her door. Staring at it, Jiri realized that the little wooden thing on the back of the door was a latch, a way to keep people out. She slid it into place, then rolled out the sleeping mat and settled on it.

Then she opened her bag.

Chapter Thirteen
Lost Things

Nestled in the bag, the kindi stared up at her with brown agate eyes. Its face was small but exquisitely detailed. Not stylized, but realistic, so realistic that Jiri almost expected the little lips to curl up into a smile.

A smile. Jiri could picture it, a cocky little smile that would make this face so handsome. Make it look just like—

Hadzi. It looks like Hadzi. Jiri picked up the carving. The ebony wood was warm to the touch, but not hot. The iron spear, free from rust despite the passage of centuries, didn't burn her when she ran her thumb lightly over it.

She didn't touch the face.

It wasn't exact. The nose wasn't quite right, and there were lines lightly carved in the wood. This was an image of an older man. But it was close.

Our ancestors made this. Long ago. When they made the walls of Kibwe, when they made many things.

Many dangerous things.

Who are you? What do you know? What can you tell me? Jiri felt the questions crowding around her. What was this carving doing in the heart of the Pyre? Did that mean something? Was it related somehow to the kindi that Patima had stolen from that terrible place?

"Or were you just lost?" Jiri whispered. She tilted the carving, watching the sharp edge of the spear sparkle in the light. Oza had warned her about the kindi. *But he told me how to use them, too.* Why would he do that, if he hadn't suspected that some still existed? If he hadn't expected that, someday, Jiri might have to use one?

Before she could think more about it, Jiri pressed her thumb down on the sharp point of the kindi's spear. The pain was instant, a small sting, and she raised her hand. Her blood tipped the spear now, and a fat drop of red sat on the pad of her thumb. Jiri took a deep breath and brushed her fingers across the necklace that hung so heavy around her neck.

Watch over me, Oza. If you can.

She pressed her bloody thumb to the carved lips of the kindi.

"Speak, and I will listen," she said, and darkness rushed in, boiling over everything like smoke, and took the world away.

The stars were bright.

They hung over Jiri, brilliant white dancers turning in the sky. Jiri blinked at them, then let her gaze fall.

She was in a city.

A city like Kibwe, but not. In places she could see the walls, high and dark against the sky, but mostly they were cut off by the buildings that stood around her. Buildings of hard granite and soft limestone, buildings solid but graceful, their walls crowded with carvings. Beautiful stone inlays made those walls glow with color beneath the too-bright stars, gorgeous as butterfly wings.

Jiri turned slowly, staring at them all. She stood in a vast open space, a great circle of smooth stone bounded by those buildings. On its edges, high pillars rose, each one topped by a statue. Men and women carved in stone, their features mixed with those of the animals that filled the jungle beyond the city's walls. Men with leopard jaws and women with bat wings, all holding weapons and shields, all looking in. At Jiri, and at the round building that rose beside her in the center of the circle, the city's heart. It was something like the council hall of Kibwe, but instead of carved wood the pillars were malachite and lapis lazuli. They supported a dome of onyx, black stone threaded with thick veins of shimmering white. The floor beneath that dome was granite, so polished that it looked like water.

"What is this place?" Jiri said, and her soft words echoed in the silence.

That echo grew. Multiplied. Bounced from wall to wall and filled the air, first with whispers, then words, then laughter, then shouts. It grew into thousands of voices, all talking and clamoring around her, and the city came alive.

There were lanterns, strung between the pillars and dangling from the tents that now filled the circle, tents of bright silk and painted canvas, gaudy in the oil and mage light. People crowded the tents and the aisles between them, laughing and talking and arguing and dancing. They looked like the people of Kibwe, just more richly dressed, with more gold and copper in their ears and around their wrists and necks.

"This is the Yeniki, dear one. The festival circle of Lozo, the stone flower of Garund. Have you never seen it?"

Jiri heard the words and understood them, even though they were strangely accented. Turning, she found a man behind her, leaning against the carved mahogany post of a tent. He smiled, and by that smile Jiri knew him.

That smile does make him look like Hadzi.

The man from the carving stepped forward and touched his hand to his lips. He seemed younger than the face carved in ebony—Jiri's age, and alive. Very much alive and real, and Jiri tried to remember the city as she had seen it just moments before, empty and silent.

It's all a vision, the memory of a man long dead. I must remember that, and not get lost in it.

"I am Shani, and this is my city. Do you want to see it?" His smile faded a little and his face shifted, aged decades in minutes. "It feels like a long time since I've been able to show it to anyone."

"It has been," Jiri said. How long ago had the Pyre been raised? How long had those kindi been there, hidden in the dark and the dust while the rocks grew warm around them? "A very long time."

"Well." Shani's eyes seemed haunted for a moment, worried, and the city around Jiri flickered, becoming something else, something dark and frightening. Then the light was back, and Shani was young and smiling again. "It's good you've come, then. I have so many things to show you."

Shani led her around the circle, through tents giant and small. There were markets, with jewelry and clothes and books bound in ivory and darkwood. There were places where you could lie on thick mats and listen to music, and other places where you could dance. There were storytellers, telling tales with masked figures or clever dolls that danced on sticks and strings or sometimes all by themselves. There were magicians weaving illusions in the air, menageries of trained animals, brothels and poets and wrestlers and philosophers. Jiri and her guide wound past them all, and Shani knew everyone. They all waved and smiled, offered him hands to grasp and lips to kiss, palm wine and little glasses of aga. He took all that was offered, and encouraged Jiri to do the same.

She trailed him, uncomfortable when any attention was turned on her, and set the drinks given to her aside untouched. It felt so real, so true, like walking through the market in Kibwe, but Jiri found the things that marked it as unreal. There was the temperature—perfectly comfortable, not hot, not cold. There were the smells—so many smells, of food and perfumed oil and spice and flowers, but no hint of sweat, no musky animal smells, no faint reek of excrement, animal and human, that was ever-present in Kibwe. This was an idealized memory of a place, a beautiful lie woven out of truth. Eventually she tired of it, and steered Shani to the center where the great pavilion stood. A low stone bench ran around its edge, and they sat on it in the relative quiet.

"There's more," Shani said. He set a basket of dates between them, two delicate porcelain cups and a small jug of palm wine. He had pulled them from the air, apparently, but when Jiri took a date it tasted sweet in her mouth. "So much more."

"I believe you," Jiri said. His face was young again, like it had been for most of their walk, quick to smile and flirt. A handsome face, but she wanted to see him old again. He was more serious when he was old.

"But what is this place?" she asked.

"The Yeniki. The heart of Lozo. Like I told you." He splashed the wine into the cups. "When the great festivals come—the birth date of the queen, the turning of the year, or the Orchid Dance—then the tents are cleared and all this space is dedicated to them. But most times, it is like this, wild and beautiful." He took a long drink from his cup, then cocked a sly eyebrow at her. "I could show you the Orchid Dance if you want. All the young couples dress in petals and feathers and bells, and they dance until they fall. Usually on top of each other."

"No thank you," Jiri said, and she felt an almost smile touch her lips just as a stab of pain went through her heart. *He looks like Hadzi, and he acts like him, too.*

"What I meant," she said quickly, before the clouds of grief that she felt inside could gather into a rain of tears, "is what is this whole place, this kindi, supposed to be?"

"This kindi," he said, slowly.

Jiri got her wish then, and almost wished she hadn't. Shani's face shifted in front of her, aging in an instant. His dark hair threaded with gray and lines grew around his mouth and eyes. Scars came with those lines, a long thin mark over his right eye, and a twisting, furrowed path along the side of his neck, close to the blood vessels whose severing would have cost him his life.

"They did a good job on the likeness. They paid me well. Though I wish they had made me look younger. When I was in my prime." He set down his cup. "Shani the Strong. Shani the Slayer. Oh, the names I accumulated. I loved them all. Tell me, did you hear those stories? Is that why you came to visit me?"

"I'm sorry. No."

"No?" Shani frowned, aging a little more. "I would have thought . . ." He looked down at his hands, and Jiri could see the scars on them, too, and she thought of Kalun's hands with all his old battle wounds. Then Shani looked up at her, years sliding away from his face. "I can tell them to you. Do want to hear about the time I defeated Mother Shade and her great slugs? Or the days I spent in the belly of the great western crocodile?"

"Shani," Jiri said. "I do want a story. About a spirit of fire, a thing that burns and destroys. Did you ever hear about anything like that?"

"All-in-Ashes." Shani said the words all at once. Not a statement, but a name, and when he spoke it, the little bit of youth that his face had regained fell away. "So you want to know about the war."

"The war?" Jiri said gently, trying to lead him on.

"I don't . . ." Shani looked away, and the city went quiet around them. The circle stood suddenly empty, all the tents and people gone, the lanterns and laughter and the smells of spice and perfume swallowed by the night. Jiri sat in an empty city with Shani, and she was suddenly acutely aware that this city of Lozo was long gone, and that Shani was surely long dead.

"I don't like talking about the war." The city flickered around them for an instant. Jiri caught something—some great light, the sound of drums, the smell of smoke and blood. Then the city was back like it was, beautiful and empty. But the stars overhead had dimmed.

"We were expanding, making a new empire on the ruins of the old," Shani said. "We didn't have the flying cities of the Shory, but we could shape stone and wood better than anyone, making carvings so perfect that they could trap a piece of a soul inside them. We were getting strong. This." He raised his hand, gesturing at the city. "Lozo, a living jewel, constantly changing and growing, was our pride. We were making others, too, carving other jewels in the jungle, raising walls and building roads, making trade with all the nations far around. We grew fast and strong. But not fast enough. Not strong enough. We caught the attention of our enemy, and he came for us."

"This spirit. This All-in-Ashes?"

"No." Shani stood. His eyes were red with anger and tears held barely in check. "You want this story, then listen. They came for us from Ocota, the great lake to the north. Bands of charau-ka, raiding our villages, burning our fields, taking our people. Like they've always done, and we fought back, like we've always done. I fought back." There was a spear in Shani's hand—not there, and then there—a tall weapon with a blackwood shaft and a blade of steel that shimmered like water. "I killed many, drove more away, but they kept coming back. Nothing we did kept them from returning."

The old warrior stared up at the sky, where the stars were half-hidden by dark, curling clouds. "There was something driving them at us. Something they feared more than us. So they kept coming, attacking here, there, bleeding us, terrifying our people. The new cities we were starting were abandoned, their stone walls left empty. Everyone fled back to here, back to Lozo. We rounded ourselves up, ran like goats into the slaughterhouse, and the Gorilla King laughed on his throne."

"Usaro," Jiri said.

"So you know that name." Shani looked at her, his eyes angry, tired, despairing. "You don't know mine. You don't know Lozo. But Usaro, the city of demons and apes, that festering abomination—that you know." Overhead, darkness swallowed the stars, a flowing, twisting curtain of black. The smell of smoke was back, heavy in the air. Somewhere far away, a drum began to beat, a deep steady thud, like a fist into flesh. "They won, didn't they?"

"I don't know," Jiri said, and she didn't but she did. In all his stories, Oza had never spoken of Lozo. Only of cities that had risen briefly, then fallen, their towers pulled down by the jungle and the things that lived there.

"You know!" Shani shouted at her, his eyes blazing, tears coursing down his cheeks. The air filled with the sound of drums, crashing and booming, like thunder that would never stop, but it didn't drown out the screams. The screams of men and women, terrified, agonized, horrified. "You know them, but you don't know us." He spun away, staring out at the dark, distant walls.

"We couldn't fight them in the jungle, so we pulled back here. We thought we would hold them, but they poured like ants out of the trees, a flood of demon-ridden apes. We would have broken that first night, but our mages woke the city, brought the statues to life to fight for us. Still, we almost fell. My son—" Shani cut off, his whole body trembling. Beyond him, the stone pillars that ringed the circle stood empty, all the statues gone. In the distance, the sound of drums and screams mixed with the clang of steel on steel, of steel on stone, and the bellowing roars of demon-worshiping apes.

"My son died." Shani's cheeks were wet, his eyes red, but he cried no longer. "Not far from me. One of those great four-armed apes caught him and tore his arm off, then threw his body off the wall. I killed it for that. I put my spear through its heart, killed it and killed all the others who tried to gain the wall behind it. I am old, but I am Shani. The slayer. I killed so many, and when the dawn came they vanished into the trees. But I never saw my son again."

Jiri had nothing to say. The smell of smoke wrapped around her, and the sound of battle faded, like a storm rolling away. But not gone.

"They were coming back." Shani leaned on his spear, his voice thick with despair. "My daughter had survived the night. She stood on the wall with me, covered in blood, but I knew that when they came again I would see her die, like my son. I couldn't let that happen. I had to save her. My daughter. My wife. My city. My people. I was Shani the Strong.

"I had to save them all."

"How?" Jiri's question was a whisper. She didn't want to speak, but this, she sensed, was the center of the story she needed.

"All-in-Ashes," Shani said, and over them the smoke began to glow. Red and gold, beautiful and terrible.

"It had always been here. Chained in a cavern deep beneath the city. A spirit of fire, not a demon, not an elemental, but something else, something old, something that existed only to destroy." Shani stared up at the glowing sky, the glowing, twisting clouds of smoke. "Some greater spirit had bound it long ago. But when we made Lozo, we dug deep for our stone and we found it. Found it, and sealed it back up. But we remembered. And when Usaro came, the mages— Well. Maybe they went mad. Like me."

"What did they do?" Jiri breathed.

"What?" Shani threw back his head and laughed, a wild laugh tangled with madness. "I don't know. I forced them to make this kindi before I gave myself to them. I wanted to leave something of me behind, my memory of this place in its days of glory. My memory of *myself* in my days of glory." Shani shifted, becoming young, old, scarred, handsome, smiling, furious, despairing. "I can't tell you what they did after that, in the stink of the blood and the smoke of our broken city. I can just tell you what they planned."

His face settled—old, scarred, and angry—and his eyes flashed with the red light of the hell that blazed in the sky overhead.

"Revenge."

Chapter Fourteen
Other Coins

Revenge.

The word rolled over Jiri like crashing drums, and the burning sky fell, covering the city and swallowing Shani. It wrapped around Jiri, fire and smoke, burning her hair, her clothes, her skin, tearing her apart until there was nothing left but ash, ash in the wind, scattering—

Then cold hit her like scalding water, a chill that clung and burned, and Jiri felt her whole body clench.

I can't breathe, can't breathe, can't . . .

The words ran through her head, but she held onto them. Breathe. She needed to breathe, because she had a mouth, a body.

I'm not ash. I'm alive. I just have to breathe!

With one last, twisting bolt of pain her body unclenched and Jiri took a gasping breath, pulling air deep into her. There was light around her, she realized, bright sunlight spilling in through a narrow window, and she was lying on the floor, sprawled across a thin sleeping mat, and there were people.

Morvius stood above her, holding a dripping hide bucket. Flanking him were Kalun and Linaria. Behind them, in the doorway of the tiny sleeping room, Sera stood watching. Behind her, Jiri caught a flash of something. Fara's head, popping into view when the girl jumped, trying to see into the room.

"What's going on?" Jiri asked. She sat up and realized that she was soaking, her braids and skin and clothes dripping cold water. "What are you doing?"

"What are we doing?" Kalun shoved past Morvius and reached down, picking the little kindi up out of the puddle beside Jiri. "By all the bad-luck spirits, what are *you* doing?"

"Careful," Jiri said reaching for the kindi, but Kalun glared down at her and she stilled her hand.

"I know what this is, girl." Kalun's thumb wiped across the carved wooden lips, taking away the last traces of Jiri's blood. "You, though, don't seem to know anything at all."

"I know the name of the thing that destroyed Thirty Trees." Jiri scrambled to her feet, facing them, still shivering and dripping. She was angry and terrified, but she only let the first show. "And I was learning more, until you broke me out of my vision."

"You mean when we saved your life?" Morvius growled.

"What are you talking about?" Jiri snapped, and the man pointed down.

Jiri looked at the floor. The water was slowly disappearing, sinking down into the floorboards' narrow cracks, and she could see the marks on the boards now. The outline of a foot, a hand. Across her sleeping mat, the dark mark was charred deep, the curled curve of her body. For the first time, Jiri realized that her long shirt felt wrong, the cloth of it rough and tattered in the back, and when she reached back with her hand she felt the material give, falling apart to cinders in her hands.

"I—" she said, staring at the warm gray dust that coated her fingertips.

"You almost choked to death on smoke. If I hadn't sent Fara up here to fetch you down for breakfast, you might have caught this whole place on fire." Kalun glanced back at the door. "Fara. Stop hopping like a mouse deer and check the room under this one. Clean up any water you find, and apologize to the guests."

"Oh, Papa," the girl whined.

"Go," he said. "And knock first." His brown eyes came back to Jiri. "Why?" he asked, his fingers tapping on the kindi in his hand.

"I found it in the heart of the Pyre," Jiri said. She didn't like Kalun's scowl, but she *really* didn't like the disappointment that shone in Linaria's eyes. "I thought it might have information in it, something about All-in-Ashes. And it did. That's the name of the spirit that destroyed Thirty Trees. The one that's been attacking villages. That's why."

"That's why you did it," Linaria said. "But why did you hide it from us? Why didn't you tell us that you found this thing, and why didn't you tell us you were going to use it? Why didn't you tell us what these things really were?"

The half-elf's voice was steady, her tone free of any accusation, but Jiri knew it was there anyway.

"I couldn't," Jiri said. "I made a promise. Not to tell anyone about them."

"Oza," Kalun said.

"Oza." They had sat on their mats, on the hard-packed dirt of their little house's floor, Oza's light glowing down on them, and he had whispered to her the stories, of the ancestors and the kindi. "Did he tell you?"

"A little. Enough to recognize a kindi when I see it."

"Did he tell you to keep it secret too?" Jiri stared at the older man.

"He did, and I agreed. I could see the danger of speaking of them easily enough. " Kalun wiped a bead of water off the carving he held, careful to keep his fingers away from the sharp blade of its spear. "That time has passed. Oza was afraid that if the old stories got out, that if people knew about these things, they would hunt them. Well, that jug's been broken, and we'll never get the water back in. I don't know if Patima knew about the kindi before she led Amiro and the rest to your Pyre, but she knows now."

"Maybe," Jiri said. *Did she?* Did Patima go to the Pyre by chance, or was she seeking this thing, this All-in-Ashes? If so, why did she let it go? If it was trapped in the kindi she found and stole, why free it? She had run from it the moment she let it go. *What is she doing? What does she want? I know more, and I still don't know anything!*

"We have to get it away from her," Jiri said. "We have to get it back. That kindi Patima stole, it's the key to all of this."

"So you keep saying." Linaria tilted her head, her strange eyes like ice. "And I think you might be right. But we can't get to her, or what she stole."

"We haven't even tried!" Jiri shouted. She looked at Sera, standing silent in the door. "You want me to find this thing for you, so you can claim its heart as a trophy? Then help me do this." Jiri looked to Morvius. "You want to earn that jewel? This is what I need." Kalun was next. "You want all your debt paid to Oza? Help me get his killer, and stop her." Finally she turned to Linaria. "And you. You want to earn my trust, be my friend, help me so that you can feel good about how someone else once helped you? Then do this. Help me get to Patima, and help me get that kindi back from her. If I had that, we could stop this All-in-Ashes, I'm sure of it. Help me stop it, because if we don't, I think more villages will burn. I think Kibwe itself might burn."

Linaria looked back at her, her so-pale face smooth, expressionless. "I've fought for you, and with you. I almost died for you. I thought I had earned your trust."

Jiri stared up at the tall woman. She burned inside, angry and ashamed and frustrated. "I made a promise."

"To a dead man," Morvius said. "A man who tried to keep that secret and failed and died because of it." Morvius dropped the bucket and dug a hand into his shirt. "You talk a lot, runt. About what people should do, and why they should do it. You miss out on the how, though. And the how, that's the sticking point. The hard part. Figuring out the how is why greedy, hard-hearted bastards like me survive and get shit done, while people like you, the ones obsessed with telling people the what and the whys, need us to haul your asses out of the fire."

Morvius pulled his hand out of his shirt and tossed something at her. It bounced off her chest and landed at her feet, glittering in the sun. The diamond she had given him.

"I think I'm done doing that."

"But—" Jiri started, but Morvius cut her off.

"But that All-in-Asses thing is going to keep killing people? Yeah, probably. Maybe you should have thought of that when you were keeping secrets. When you were flailing around, getting yourself into trouble that we had to haul you out of. Just like your dead teacher."

Jiri clenched her fists, her anger blazing, and she could feel the heat running through her, so eager to burn that look off of the broad-shouldered man's face.

"Go ahead," Morvius said, smiling down at her. "Do another stupid thing. How many can you get away with, before you finally get burned?"

"Enough, Morvius," Linaria said.

"Almost." Morvius's eyes never left Jiri. "You want Patima, runt? You want what she stole? Stop trying to make us solve your problems, and figure it out yourself." He turned from her and pushed his way out of the room. At the door, waiting for Sera to step out of his way, he spoke one more time. "My bet is you'll just try something stupid on your own again. When you do, try not to feel too surprised if we don't come and haul your little butt out of the flames."

The room smelled like charred wood, water, and smoke.

Jiri sat in the corner, in one of the few not-damp spots, and stared at the little kindi with the spear, standing rigid and silent on the stool where Kalun had left it.

"What am I supposed to do?"

When Oza had spoken, people had listened. He was a shaman, the most powerful shaman in all the jungle around Kibwe. They had done what he said, because he had proven he knew what to do.

What have I proven? That I can run for help?

Kalun had said that he would try to find information. Sera and Linaria had said nothing. And outside Kibwe chattered and the sun rolled overhead, slowly moving toward night, when All-in-Ashes would rise again, and fall.

Is Patima doing this? Jiri stared at Shani's face, carved into the dark wood, and wondered. *Can she control that spirit with the kindi she has? Can they work like that?*

Questions. That's all she had, and no answers.

How do I get answers?

How. The word burned her. How would Oza have done it? *He would have gone to the council. They would have listened to him, and forced those Aspis people to give Patima up.*

Or he would just get her himself.

Jiri raised her fingers to touch the necklace around her neck. The bones were warm under her fingers, their carved lines smooth and polished. Oza could take the shape of a bird and fly into that place. Find that kindi, and become a monkey and steal it. Or become a tiger, and take Patima, too. Jiri's fingers tightened on the bones. She thought of wings, of feathers, of scaled feet and claws and beak.

Hear me, spirits. I need you. Give me your wings.

The carved bones rested against her skin, skin that stayed stubbornly her own, not sprouting feathers, not shrinking in and becoming small.

Jiri snatched her hand away, jerked herself up, all her helpless frustration turning to fury. "I served you! All my life, I did what Oza told me. I gave you my respect, gave you my belief, honored you. And now, when I need you most, you give me nothing! Is that all I can expect from everyone?" No spirits, no northerners, no Kalun. No Oza. No Hadzi.

No one.

Just her, against Patima and a spirit made of fire and rage.

Hands aching with heat, Jiri pulled on her last set of new clothes, picked up the kindi and her spear, and slipped out of the room.

Finding the Aspis Consortium was easy enough.

Kibwe still seemed like chaos to Jiri, its streets rolling rivers of people, all crashing and moving and noisy, but she swam through them, hunting. When she found a likely target—a child playing, a group of women chattering, an old man carving on a bench—she would ask directions. They helped, somewhat, though they were still confusing, the landmarks of streets and statues and buildings nothing like the tangled trails and jungle that she was used to. But Kibwe was not so large after all, and by the time most people were settling in to rest through the afternoon's high heat she had found the compound.

It stood near the western gate, in a neighborhood of stables, warehouses, and markets, a place where caravans were put together and taken apart. The streets here were full of animals: horses, mules, and camels, most packed high with goods. Crowds flowed along them, children playing or running messages, laborers hauling bundles of goods or looking for work, guards watching everyone with suspicious or drunken eyes. Through them all, the traders moved, arguing, laughing, bargaining, ordering and threatening, louder than the bawling of the camels.

Jiri slipped through it all, grateful for the noise and the confusion. She could work her way around the compound, looking it over, and no one would notice her. Which was good, because she needed the time to stare.

The Aspis Consortium holdings had been built for strength. Unlike the thatched roofs and wattle and daub walls of most of the buildings surrounding it, the compound had been built of stone. There were six structures that stood in a rough rectangle, three large warehouses and two smaller ones, each windowless and squat with one wide door leading into it. Each door was either gated tight or open and well guarded. The last building stood taller, with many windows, the lower ones all barred with iron. More guards stood by the single door. They didn't stop the steady flow of people in and out, but they kept a careful eye on all of them.

Between each building, granite walls ran, separating the inside of the compound from the rest of the city. Jiri could see the peaks of a few orange tile roofs over those walls. Which meant that the compound contained several more shorter buildings, full of guards and workers, all surrounded by stone walls and closely watched doors.

"My ancestors curse me," Jiri said to herself, staring at the little fortress. Morvius had been right. To get into that place and search it would require powerful magic or an army.

Neither of which she had.

Jiri leaned against a wall, clutching her spear tight. She was in a narrow space between a warehouse and a tavern, a dark twisting passage empty of everything but garbage, mud, and the stench of piss. From here she could see the door to the not-warehouse, the building where traders and other well-dressed people kept going. Amiro's house, probably, the place where he did his business. If Patima were to come and go from this place, this is where she would do it.

And what would I do if I saw her? Follow, and then what?

For a moment, Jiri allowed herself the luxury of imaging the Bonuwat woman coming out alone, walking away oblivious as Jiri stalked behind her, and . . .

Even in her fantasy, Jiri couldn't imagine how she could capture the woman. Or force her to give her the kindi she had stolen.

I don't think she's going to bring it out with her.

With a groan, Jiri set her spear against the rough wall beside her. Her fingers reached up and touched Oza's necklace.

Feathers and talon. Wings and beak.

Please.

Her only answer was the buzzing of flies around her, trying to drink her sweat.

The day was starting to fade.

The street was crowded, packed with bearers hauling bundles of goods now that the cruelest heat of the day was behind them. Jiri stared over them, still watching the door that led into the Aspis compound. A door that had opened just a little, enough so that a small figure in a feathered, hooded cloak could slip out. Jiri tensed, but the figure was joined by a dozen more, and even from across the street Jiri could see that none of them was Mikki.

Not unless the halfling had grown scales and a sharp-toothed muzzle.

Kobolds. Those things were probably the strangest creatures Jiri had seen passing through that door, but only by a little. Merchants and traders of all nationalities and a few different species had gone in and out of that building all day.

Patima had never been among them.

"This is useless," Jiri muttered. She had spent hours watching, thinking, and still had no idea of how she could get into that place unnoticed, much less how she could find the stolen kindi.

"Oh, don't say that."

The voice, high-pitched and full of sly humor, came from behind her. Jiri whipped around, her fist tightening, growing hot. Behind her, the narrow alley lay empty of everything but shadows. Her eyes hunted through those dark places, while her ears strained to hear anything more. She saw nothing but mud and darkness, and heard too much— the sound of music and voices through the tavern wall, and from the street behind her the bawling of camels and shouting of their drivers, the low roar of people talking and moving things and laughing and arguing.

"So glad you came to find us."

The voice came from . . . Jiri raised one hand, shimmering with heat, while she reached out for her spear with the other. She couldn't find the source of that mocking voice, but she recognized it now. Like a child's, but not.

Mikki. Linaria called her an assassin.

That thought made Jiri turn her head, and she saw them: a group of men standing where the narrow alley opened into the street. The two in front held the corners of a thick cloth blanket between them. Like a net.

"Gods and—" Jiri gasped, whirling around. She raised her hand, ready to throw fire, and then something crashed down on her.

It smashed her into the stinking mud, knocking the breath out of her. Jiri felt it clinging to her, digging at the back of her head and neck. She thought of a leopard, leaping down from a tree and biting at the back of its prey's skull, and panicked. She brought her hands in and shoved herself up, and whatever the thing was grabbed the back of her head.

Little fingers knotted in her braids, and that piping voice rang out merrily just behind her ear.

"You coming here made this *so* much easier."

A hand slapped over Jiri's mouth, cutting off her shout, and she went to bite it, but there was something in it. A cloth, wet and reeking, smelling of . . . of . . .

And then the darkness came, sudden and absolute, and Jiri knew no more.

Chapter Fifteen
Behind the Walls

The drums of the Orchid Dance pounded, their rhythm infectious, insistent, and Jiri danced beneath the stars. A fire blazed in the center of Thirty Trees, its light shining off skin and eyes, brass and glass beads, the dancers whirling and spinning. Jiri spun with them, spun and spun as the drums got faster, their music building. Jiri tried to keep up, but her feet faltered, stumbling on the hard-packed earth, and she couldn't breathe.

The air had gone hot and smoky, and Jiri choked. Around her, the light grew and the drums bellowed, and the fire wasn't in the center of the village anymore, it *was* the village, every house blazing, and the drums were the sound of dried thatch and wood being eaten by hungry flame. Jiri staggered, eyes hurting, lungs desperate, but all the other dancers were stuck in place, dark shadows against the fire's terrible light. They had to run, to get away, and Jiri stumbled toward one of them, a girl posed delicately on her toes, arms raised. Jiri reached out to grab one of those arms and her hand touched something soft and hot.

Ash. The girl was ash, and her arm fell apart when Jiri touched her, crumpled down as all the rest of her went, her face and breasts and belly and legs, all crumbling into white and gray, riding the hot wind upward, while the fire roared like drums—

No!

Jiri tried to shout, but she had no voice. Not here, where the darkness spun.

"Spin her again!"

A voice, a woman's voice, horrible and accented, and it drilled through Jiri's head. Big hands were on her shoulders, and she recognized Morvius looming over her, grinning. Behind him, Corrianne screamed with laughter and shouted again, "Spin her!"

No, you have to listen! The words echoed through Jiri's head, but they couldn't get out. Not while Morvius was grabbing her shoulders and spinning her in place. Around her, the Council Hall of Kibwe spun, and she could see all the people. Linaria and Sera and Kalun and Fara and all her sisters, Patima and Amir and Mikki, all in a ring around her, and behind them everyone else, *everyone*, staring and pointing and laughing as Morvius shoved her and sent her lurching away, barely able to keep her feet. Over her head the jewel-colored lanterns spun, and behind them her ancestors laughed, and the spirits too, Monkey and Crocodile and Iomedae and . . .

Oza.

Oza! Jiri tried to call, but she couldn't speak, couldn't say anything as Patima caught her.

"Spin her. Spin her!" This time it was Linaria, or Mikki, or Sera—Jiri didn't know. She just knew they had to stop, had to listen, but she couldn't talk. Jiri tore her eyes away from the crowd, turned her head, hunting for any place without eyes, and found Hadzi behind her.

Help me! Jiri silently pleaded, but Hadzi wasn't looking at her. He was looking up, through the rafters and the spirits, up at something beyond the darkness of the roof. His hair was going gray, his hands on his spear growing scars as his handsome face shifted, grew lines and became Shani's face.

"He's coming," Shani said, and his eyes boiled.

"No," said Jiri, but the word barely forced its way past her teeth, and in front of her Patima gave her a smile, small and full of pity. Then she took Jiri's shoulders and started to spin her.

Jiri's belly cramped, and there was a taste in her mouth of something horrible. Jiri spun, and this was like the time when she was twelve and someone— *Hadzi*—had dared her to kiss the bright-colored back of a dreamdealer frog.

Frogs.

Giant, brightly colored amphibians surrounded her, leaping all around her, trying to catch Mikki. The halfling was swinging through the trees over them, dressed in red, her mouth stretching impossibly wide as she laughed and spit fire at the frogs.

No. Dreams. Fever dreams. This spinning world felt like that. Like when she had bonecrusher fever, and had dreamed such terrible things until Oza—

Oza.

The world swung again, and Oza stood before her, hip-deep in dark water. Behind him the Pyre rose toward the sky, crowned in flames. "You worry too much about the how of it, Jiri," he said. "You already have that. I taught you how. You can become whatever you need to become, when you need to become it."

Standing in the mud before him, Jiri tried to open her mouth but couldn't. Her lips were gone, melted into something like a crude beak. Feathers sprouted around it and in scraggly bunches down her arms. The skin of her chest and belly was rough with crocodile scales. On her legs, fur grew, orange and black.

But I can't! You never taught me this!

That was what she wanted to say, but all that spilled out of her was some terrible noise, painful and sad and angry. She beat her hands against her legs in frustration, and the feathers that grew out of her skin flowed together and became sheets of skin that hung like bat wings from her arms.

I don't know anything! Memories flashed through her mind, of fire and smoke, kindi, and faces so strange. *I barely know what's happening, and I don't know why!*

"The what is hard, Jiri." As Oza spoke, the water behind him began to bulge, stretching its dark surface toward the smoke-covered sky, shaping itself into something terrible. "And the why is hardest of all. You'll find those answers, though. I know you will. You must."

The water rising behind Oza had become a great, crouching beast. In its rough head, currents spun, forming two whirlpools. They stared down at Jiri— mad, malevolent eyes. Below their hungry spin, the water pulled open into a gaping mouth.

"Must?" the thing hissed in a wet, sucking voice.

Oza never turned to look at it. He just kept his eyes on Jiri, patient and calm.

"There are very few musts, old man." The stinking mass of water fell. It roared down onto Oza, swallowing him, and then it surged forward, a great tide of filthy water that caught Jiri and smashed her down.

Jiri flung her arms over her head and wrapped them tight over her face, trying to block that dark water out, but she felt it wrenching her arms apart, pushing through her lips and teeth, shoving open her eyes, pouring into her ears.

"There are only two musts for you, girl," that voice came, gurgling and terrible. "Fear and failure."

Jiri lashed out, flailing against the killing tide, trying to pull herself free. Deep inside her, something sparked, that anger that had always been there to serve her. She felt it spring to life and she welcomed it, needed it. She let it flare through her, let it go and go and felt the joy of its destruction as it flashed the water to steam.

Fire boiled all that terrible murk away, and Jiri opened her eyes and saw the darkness of it twisting in on itself. Pulling back and changing . . .

Changing. The dark water became a shifting, roiling cloud of smoke, shot through with light. Light red and gold, light so hot, and now Jiri felt the heat building in her again, swelling until it tore out of her, breaking her body into flames, and when she screamed she heard a new voice crackling through her, filling her.

"There is only one thing that all must do."

Jiri could see her hands in front of her go white as the moon and then break apart, each piece of her hot and dead and drifting, and before she could scream her mouth was gone too, and all she could hear was that terrible voice.

"Burn, and join the ashes of everything."

Jiri tried to groan but couldn't. Something rough and bumpy filled her mouth, and her jaw ached fiercely, wanting to close. That wasn't the only pain, though.

Like a flood, all her other agonies rushed through her. Her hands were numb from lack of blood. Something was wrapped tight around her wrists, forcing them together behind her. Those same bonds pulled her shoulders back, and her joints felt like they were packed with broken glass. The rest of her body ached too, though much less. That was from having been dropped naked onto a rough floor made of cold, uneven stone. With a jerk, Jiri was able to move her head, turning it so that her right cheek pressed against the ground instead of her left.

That one tiny pain eased, but none of the rest. The movement also made her aware of two other things.

The first was that someone had tied a cloth over her eyes. She could feel her eyelids scrape against it when she blinked, could see the faintest trace of light coming up from below her left eye.

The second was a sound. A soft tap, then another. The noise stopped beside her head.

"I think she's coming around."

Mikki's voice.

Something nudged Jiri's shoulder, and the touch made agony flare through her. She twitched.

"Yeah. Go get the others."

There were more sounds of feet on stone, the groan of a door, and then Jiri was too distracted to listen anymore.

Something had touched her throat, something small and thin and sharp. It moved lightly over her skin, tracing the path of her pulse.

"Is this what you wanted?" The halfling's lips tickled against Jiri's ear, like a little girl telling her a secret. "To be in our house? I brought you here. It's fine, I know you can't thank me now." The blade against Jiri's throat stopped moving, its point pricking her skin right beneath her jaw. "We'll save that for later."

Jiri felt a little hand pat her cheek, while the pressure of the knife point increased one subtle fraction and then vanished.

Biting into her gag, Jiri barely kept herself from shaking.

"Spellcasters," Amiro said, "are problematic."

Amiro sat before her, his shaved head smooth and immaculate in the lamplight. He held himself very still, posed almost, his spine perfectly in line with the back of his northern-style chair. His hands were folded, long fingers pressed together, and his eyes were cold and calculating as a crocodile.

Jiri didn't feel problematic.

The guards that had come with Amiro had jerked her up by the arms, making her scream into her gag. Then they had dumped her into one of these hard-backed chairs and cut the rope that bound her wrists. That relief had almost instantly been overwhelmed by the pain of the blood rushing back into her hands.

While she groaned about that, the men had buckled her ankles, wrists, and waist to the chair with heavy leather straps that scraped across Jiri's skin. Then they had jerked off her blindfold. Jiri barely noticed them stepping out of the room, too caught up in her pain and the sight of Amiro sitting before her.

Corrianne stood behind him, looking at Jiri like a cruel child regarding a spider, wondering which leg to pull off first. Mikki stood on the other side of Amiro's chair, eating candied dates and playing with a scarab beetle tied to a string.

There was nothing else in the windowless stone vault. Its only features were a battered bucket that sat in one corner and the heavy wooden door that stood open behind Amiro.

There was no sign of Patima.

"Magic is unpredictable," Amiro continued. He was dressed in northern garb, a white linen tunic and hose with a gold half-cloak and a necklace of heavy gold links, from which dangled a golden key. Strangely formal garb for these surroundings. "Those who wield it—"

"No matter how pitiful and useless," Corrianne said.

"—must be respected," Amiro continued, as if unaware of the interruption. "I just want you to understand why we've taken these precautions, and to let you know that we respect your abilities." Amiro ignored Corrianne's snort. "If I had the proper resources here in Kibwe, we could have done this more comfortably, with a cell properly charmed. Since I don't, I'm forced to use the methods we have at hand. I apologize for that, and whatever inconvenience they've caused you."

Jiri, bound naked, gagged, and aching to the chair, just stared at him.

"That being said, we're going to have to remove your gag. You may be tempted to try casting when we do. I would recommend against it. Let me tell you why."

Amiro opened his hands, his first motion since Jiri's blindfold had been removed.

"I am a cleric of Abadar, the Master of the First Vault." Amiro's hand tilted toward Corrianne. "Corrianne is a wizard, trained by one of the finest—"

"*The* finest," Corrianne interrupted again, huffy.

"The finest academy of magic in all of Taldor," Amiro said. "We are both familiar with magic—divine, arcane, and spirit. We both have more knowledge and more power than you. So. Should you decide to do something, we'll know it, and we'll give Mikki a signal. Mikki?"

The little woman caught her beetle and pushed it into a pouch on her belt. She drew something else out of the pouch: a short, wickedly sharp little spike. On small, bare feet she walked over to Jiri and stood on her right side. Jiri tried to keep her eyes on Amiro, but her head twitched when she felt the prick of that spike against her ear.

"If Mikki sees our signal, she will drive that spike straight into your ear," Amiro said, his voice still detached. "It's just long enough to rupture your eardrum, which Mikki assures me causes a vast and unique kind of pain."

"I can only go by how people scream, but I'm confident of that statement," Mikki said cheerfully.

"Pain like that should disrupt any spell you might attempt. The resulting deafness would only affect one ear, and after a short rest we would be ready to begin speaking again." Amiro folded his hands again. "Of course, if you tried it again we would have to puncture one of your eyes. But I doubt things will go that far. You are young, but you are a shaman, are you not? I'm sure your judgment is sound." He smiled at her, a banal twist of the lips that didn't touch his crocodile eyes. "Mikki," he snapped.

Despite herself, Jiri twitched, and she felt the point of that spike dig into her ear, a quick sting of pain, and the dread gathering in her wound tighter.

Amiro's dead-eyed smile was still aimed at Jiri, but he kept speaking to the halfling. "Let's try to avoid any accidents this time. You're a professional."

Mikki shrugged. "I just get so *bored* sometimes, when these things go on and on."

"Well, I'm sure this one won't." Amiro snapped his fingers, a sudden sharp pop that made Jiri almost twitch again, and Mikki jerked Jiri's gag off. "Will it, Jiri Maju?" Amiro paused just a moment before her name, as if emphasizing the space where her tribal name had been.

Bound to that chair, Jiri's stomach clenched, and her skin streamed with cold sweat. Somehow she managed to keep her voice calm. "It depends on what you ask."

"I'll start easy," Amiro said. "Why were you and the others trying to seal us in that ruin?'

How much do I fight them? Jiri wondered.

Not at all. Not until it matters.

"That place was under my teacher's protection." Jiri said. "He felt it when you broke in, and we went there to seal it up again. To trap you inside, so that nothing evil would be released. But when he was trying to do that, he was attacked by a demon."

"Well, I'm glad Patima's little playmate did something useful," Corrianne sniffed. "She summoned that stinking thing too close to me, and it slimed my outfit. I had to burn it, and that bitch refuses to pay me back."

"The demon killed your teacher?" Amiro asked.

"Yes." *I can't let them know how much his death hurt me. Amiro will use the pain against me, and Corrianne will use it just to amuse herself.*

"He told me to get help," Jiri said, to drag the questions away from Oza. "To run to Kibwe, and find Kalun."

"They knew each other?"

"Apparently," Jiri said. "My teacher never spoke of Kalun before. He told me to go to the Red Spear, so I did. I told Kalun what happened, and he sent the others back with me to deal with the demon and seal the Pyre."

"That must have taken some time." Amiro's eyes slid sideways to the tiny woman who stood beside Jiri.

"Do you want fast, Amiro, or do you want alive?" Mikki asked. "Those are your choices when you're dealing with traps."

Amiro waved his hand at the assassin. "So you brought them back to the place you call 'the Pyre.'" Amiro made a face. "Did they know it was us in there?"

"They guessed it might be. But they were doing what I asked, what my teacher asked me to do. They came to kill the demon and seal the Pyre, not attack you."

"I'm surprised Kalun thought he could seal us in there with just stone," Amiro said. "He underestimated us. Or he wanted us to get out."

He thought about that for a minute, and Jiri thought too. *Did Kalun know how easy it would be for them to get past that stone wall?*

"It doesn't matter," Amiro said. "I know what happened when we came out. What happened after we left?"

"That thing you released came out, and it went to my village and burned everything and everyone in it to ash."

"How unfortunate," Amiro said.

"Everything? Everyone?" Corrianne asked. "Ah, what a dark day for lice and goats."

Anger flickered through Jiri, warming her chilled skin, but she forced her breathing to stay steady, in the calming pattern Oza had taught her. She couldn't let the fire in her go today. That spike would drive into her ear long before she could burn through her bonds.

"Corrianne," Amiro chided. "I'm asking questions. Now, Jiri—did you see what this thing looked like?"

"Like living fire and smoke. Like fury and destruction," Jiri said. "And it's out there. It burned Thirty Trees, and that caravan, and Zawao village. Will it burn another village tonight, or will it come here to Kibwe? You set that thing free, Amiro. You let Patima steal that k—" Jiri broke off, trying to turn the sound into a cough. "—that thing, and you released that terrible spirit into the world. How many have died because of your greed? How many have to die before you start to try to make things right?" Jiri looked him in the eyes, desperate to see doubt, guilt, uncertainty. Desperately hoping that he didn't notice her slip.

Of course he did.

"What was that? I let Patima steal a what? A k—?" Amiro pronounced the consonant like a cough.

Jiri gripped the rough wood of the chair arms tight in her hands and shifted her eyes away from him, studying the stains of water and mildew on the granite blocks of the walls.

"So here it is, so soon. The sticking point." Amiro unfolded his hands and reached out, catching Jiri's chin. He tipped her head toward him, and Jiri was painfully aware of Mikki's spike shifting with her head, but just a shade more slowly, its tip digging a little deeper into her ear. "This, girl, is why you're here, talking to me, instead of in a sack at the bottom of some swamp, a gift to the crocodiles. You know something about that thing Patima found. Something that might be useful. Now here's my question: Are you going to be smart and tell us what you know, and survive this? Perhaps even profit from it? Or are you going to be foolish and drag this out, making it unpleasant for everyone involved?"

"Except me," Mikki whispered beside her, then giggled.

Jiri kept herself from cringing away from Mikki, just barely. Kept herself from jerking her chin out of Amiro's long-fingered hand and impaling herself on that thin spike. "You have an accent when you speak Taldane." Jiri spoke in her native tongue, shaping the words like they were most often used around Kibwe. "You sound like a northerner."

Amiro's fingers tightened on her chin. "Is that your plan?" he said. "Appeal to our common culture and try to shame me for abandoning the ways of my people and joining up with these foreigners?" Amiro had switched to the same language, his Kibwe accent thick enough that Jiri had trouble making out all the words. "An interesting tactic, much better than bravado or seduction. Your true emotions are too obvious for those. But it has one great flaw."

"Which is?" Jiri said.

"I hate our common culture." Amiro tapped a finger against her jaw. "Let me tell you something about my life, girl. I was born in Kibwe to a woman without a tribe. I grew up without a tribe, and I was picked on, despised, mistreated, because the other children knew they could get away with it. I had no one to help me, no one to defend me. Neither did my mother. She was murdered when I was seven, knifed by someone who thought the couple of coppers she carried were worth more to them than her life was to her. Her body was left in the streets, until the street cleaners threw it into the city midden, meat for the rats and the vultures.

"Since she had no tribe, no one cared about her death. Since she had no tribe, no one cared about her child." Amiro dropped his hand from Jiri's chin and folded his long fingers back together again. "I was left to die on the streets, and I would have. But a man—a northern man—decided to hire me to run messages for him. He was the head of the Aspis Consortium. I worked for him, and he fed me, gave me a place to sleep. When I impressed him with my service, he began to educate me. He saw potential in me, and he used it. You see, the

Consortium doesn't care where you come from. Who your parents were. How rich you are. What tribe you belong to. It cares about only one thing: Can you feed it? Can you grow it? Can you bring the money and power that the Consortium needs to survive and thrive, here in the Mwangi Expanse and in all the rest of the world?"

Amiro gave Jiri a tight smile. "The Consortium is a hard master, Jiri, but it's a fair one. When I understood that, I did my best to bring it everything I could, and it gave back. The Consortium shared the wealth I brought it, and I have prospered.

"Do you understand then, girl, why I've learned to speak the common tongue of the north so well? Why I've dedicated myself to one of their gods? Kibwe never offered a place for me. I had to find one for myself." Amiro tilted his bald head, shifting just a fraction, as if he were contemplating an ambush. "And what about you, Jiri Maju? Girl with no tribe, no place? Where do you fit, now?"

"I . . ." Jiri stopped. *I don't know. But I know I don't fit with you.* "I belong to this place. Not this city, but this land, and all things that live here. Especially the people. The people that are dying, right now, because of what you did."

"Because of what *we* did," Amiro said, switching back to Taldane. "What do you think would have happened if your new friends Linaria and Morvius would have found out about your secret Pyre before we did?"

"I think Kalun would have told them to leave it alone," Jiri said. "And if they didn't, I think Oza would have sealed them into that stone, and All-in-Ashes wouldn't be killing its way toward this city."

"It wouldn't be destroying those villages if we controlled it. If we knew how to leash it. Which you could help us with. All-in-Ashes," Amiro echoed back to her. "You know its name and more, don't you?"

Every spirit sees my stupidity. Jiri kept her mouth shut, not saying anything more.

"Jiri. Listen to me." Amiro switched back to their shared tongue, and he spoke to her like a teacher, like a parent to a child. "I can't bring back your dead. We've harmed you. I've harmed you. But I have no interest in harming you again. Tell us what we need to know, and we'll call All-in-Ashes in, control it. No one more will die, and I will reward you. You've lost your tribe, but you can have something else, something better. You can join us. In the name of my god, I make you that offer."

Jiri studied the bald man in his strange clothes and her stomach twisted. "I understand that you offer that as a gift," Jiri said. Her eyes shifted from Amiro to Corrianne, staring bored at her nails, and then to Mikki, bouncing lightly on her toes beside Jiri, still holding that sharp spike to Jiri's ear. "But I would rather share a hammock with a mamba."

Amiro stared at her, unblinking, unsurprised. "I understand. But remember that offer. I will hold it out to you for as long as I can. I see potential in you, Jiri Maju, and while my people might have their issues, I would not let them call you 'runt.'" He tilted his head a fraction when Jiri blinked. "I have my ears in the Red Spear. Kalun has too many daughters to buy them all beads. I know what Morvius said, and I know that you came here on your own. You're all alone, girl. Think on that."

Amiro moved, sudden and smooth, rising from his chair. "You don't have to be," he said, then switched back to Taldane for the others' benefit. "All you have to do to get out of here is tell us how to stop that thing from killing, which is what you want. Tell us, and you'll be free, to make whatever choices you want about your future. This will all be done, just as soon as you speak."

"You don't want to stop All-in-Ashes," Jiri said. "You want to control it. Nothing good can come of wanting to control that."

Amiro sighed. "So be it, for now. I'll speak to you about this again later. After more have died, and after Mikki and Corrianne have had their chance to persuade you." He gave the women a hard look. "Go gentle, tonight. And don't forget the dreamless."

"Oh, we won't forget anything, love." Corrianne walked forward, the heels of her boots clicking on the uneven stone. She had dressed in black again, a silk skirt and a long leather vest, and she pulled a pair of leather gloves from the wide belt that ran around her waist. She wiggled her fingers into them, then reached out to rap Jiri on the bridge of the nose, just hard enough to make spots dance in front of Jiri's eyes. "And we'll be as gentle as lambs."

They spent a little while rearranging the cell.

The guards came back after Amiro left and dragged Jiri in her chair to the back of the cell. Then they brought in a table and another chair to match Amiro's empty one, and filled that table with platters of food and bottles of wine. The northern women had sat down and started to eat, chatting as they did.

"I saw Orvin in the market today." Corrianne took a bite of bread, smeared with butter and some kind of lurid red stuff that smelled of fruit and sugar. "He had both his eyes again."

Jiri looked away, keenly aware of how long it had been since she had eaten.

"He must have paid a healer quite a lot to grow back the one I took," Mikki said, putting her glass of wine down beside her beetle, which was feasting on a slice of melon. "I suppose I'll have to take his other one."

Worse than Jiri's hunger, though, was her thirst.

"Would that be his right or left?"

And worse than that was the humiliating, painful pressure building in her bladder.

"Y'know, I'm not sure." Mikki began to neatly slice apart a fish. "I guess I'll just have to take both."

"Seems safest."

"Here, what do you think of these?"

Jiri couldn't stop herself from looking up. There was nothing else in here but these terrible women and their terrible talk. Nothing but them and the pain in Jiri's body and limbs, tied too long to this chair.

"Where did you get those?" Corrianne was studying the earrings that Mikki was holding up, rounds of opal surrounded by silver.

"Stole them from a Garundi trader that came through today. You don't like them?"

"Garundi jewelry is gaudy. Besides, they're made for a darker complexion then yours."

"More like hers?" Mikki looked at Jiri.

"Maybe," Corrianne said. "Try them."

Mikki rose and came over to Jiri, the earrings dangling from one hand. With her other she caught Jiri's chin, turning her head. "Your ears aren't pierced."

"The Mosa don't do that," Jiri growled, her skin crawling beneath Mikki's fingers.

"That's all right," Mikki said, smiling. "I do." The little woman set the earrings down on Jiri's thighs, then reached into a pouch that hung from her hip. She pulled two acacia thorns from it, long and sharp. The halfling stuck one in her mouth, picking at her teeth with its rough tip as she considered Jiri's right ear. "Well, I've done things *like* that. Put holes in people, I mean." Mikki caught Jiri's ear. "I think holding still would make this easier for us both."

Jiri gritted her teeth and said nothing, kept gritting them when she felt the thorn biting into her skin, then pushing deeper, carving a slow, agonizing path through her lobe.

When it was through, Mikki twisted the thorn a few times, grinding its rough sides into Jiri's torn flesh. "Half done," she said brightly, holding up the other thorn. "Oops. This one's lost its tip. Might take a bit longer."

It did, but again Jiri didn't say anything, just clenched her teeth against the pain as the little assassin bored through her flesh with the blunt thorn.

"There," Mikki said, finally, giving the thorn one last twist. "All done. Now let's try those earrings." With two jerks, Mikki pulled the thorns out, leaving pain and slivers behind. Then she picked up the earrings and pressed their hooks through Jiri's torn lobes.

Having the earrings put in barely hurt, compared to the piercings, but their weight was a burning agony. Jiri clamped her teeth against it, trying to breathe in the steady rhythm Oza had taught her. It helped, not easing the pain exactly, but making her accept it.

It did almost nothing to push back against the mixture of shame and fear that filled Jiri now, body and spirit.

"See?" Corrianne was saying. "They look terrible on her. On you, they'd look ridiculous."

Mikki grabbed Jiri's braids and twisted her head back and forth, staring at the jewelry that dangled from Jiri's bloody ears.

"You're probably right. I'll have someone take them to the market tomorrow. I need a new chameleon anyway. I lost my last one." She pulled at the earrings, and for a moment Jiri was sure she was going to rip them out, but Mikki plucked them carefully free. Then she shoved the thorns back in. "You don't want those holes to close up." Her finger slid across Jiri's face, tracing her cheek, eyebrow, nose and lips. "Those Bekyar pierce themselves all over. Face and body." Mikki's hand glided down Jiri's neck. "Including some places that seem like they would be *very* uncomfortable. I've always wondered how much that hurt, but I've never asked one." Mikki pulled back her fingers and looked at the blood that tipped them. "Maybe you could tell me. I have a lot more thorns."

Jiri looked at her, unblinking, all of her concentration focused on not lashing out and wreathing this woman in flames.

I couldn't kill her before Corrianne stopped me. I have to control my anger, save my strength. Jiri kept repeating that thought to herself, over and over.

It was the only kind of hope she had.

"It's hot over here," Mikki said. "I think that means she's angry."

"Angry? About what? We've barely started to do anything." Corrianne dabbed at her mouth with a napkin. "That reminds me, though: she hasn't used her bucket yet, and probably needs to. How are we supposed to trust her out of her chair if she's so upset?"

"We can just leave her there until she calms herself," Mikki said. "Or pisses herself."

"Like I want to smell *that*."

"I won't do anything." The moment the words were out of Jiri's mouth, she hated having said them. They felt too much like the first small steps toward surrender.

"You promise?" Corrianne's voice was both acid and sickly sweet.

Jiri didn't want to say anything else, desperate not to slip any closer to obedience. But her bladder throbbed like a knife in her, and she couldn't stand the idea of voiding herself in this chair, certain that these women would leave her tied down in her own waste. She let her head tip into a tiny nod.

"Good girl. Unbuckle her, Mikki."

The halfling rolled her eyes and reached out for the buckle on Jiri's wrist, popping it free. She worked her way through all the others until she crouched before the chair, undoing the ankle ones.

"Better hope she doesn't piss now," Corrianne said.

"I'll put those thorns through her eyelids if she does," Mikki said. She finished with the buckles and stepped away.

"Well?" Corrianne lifted a jug of wine and splashed her glass full. "Do you have to go or not?"

Jiri ignored her, ignored her screaming bladder and concentrated on her legs. They were knotted and trembling, and she wasn't sure they would hold her. *I'm not crawling in front of them.* Using her arms, Jiri pushed herself up, every joint groaning. Wavering, unsteady, she took a shuffling step toward the bucket. Just hearing Corrianne speak again almost toppled her.

"Look at that, Mikki. Look how tough she is. Moving so well after being stuck in that chair for so long. You know, maybe we should have some sort of guard on her. Just to be safe." Corrianne spoke again, a quick spill of words in some harsh tongue, and her fingers flickered over the candle that sat on the table beside her, casting a long shadow on the stone ceiling.

That shadow twisted, pulled in on itself, and fell. It landed on Jiri like a thick rope, heavy and hot. Its weight slammed Jiri down, and her knees and palms hit the floor. Skin scraped away and blood flowed, but Jiri didn't feel these new hurts. All her attention was on the thing wrapping around her, loop after loop, a coiling, grasping thing that caught her tight. On the floor, on her belly, Jiri fought. Without thinking, fire flickered out of her, burning along the length of the thing, but it didn't let her go. It flexed instead, pulling tighter, and Jiri lost all of her breath.

"I wouldn't do that," Corrianne said. "That thing isn't impressed by fire."

Jiri felt the thing shifting, and then its head was in front of her face. A wide, blunt head, mailed in scales black and crimson, with two great slitted eyes that stared at her with predatory disdain. A forked tongue flickered out of the mouth and touched her face, tasting her, and the slime covering that tongue stung her skin. A snake, or the bad-luck spirit of a snake, given temporary flesh by Corrianne's magic.

"Are you just going to lie there?" The northern woman's voice was full of cruel amusement. "We let you go for a reason. Attend to it."

Jiri watched the snake's tongue flicker, saw its jaws part to show lines of hooked white teeth. But it relaxed its coils around her, drew its head back. Jiri moved on her belly, getting one arm under her and pulling on her other, trying to work it free from the hot scales that pinned it to her chest. When she got it free she pushed herself up to her hands and knees, the heaviness of the snake dragging at her, and when she tried to rise she fell, dragged down by pain and exhaustion and the weight of scales. She pitched forward, turning her head barely in time to keep from smashing her nose into the stone. Instead her ear hit, and the thorn still stuck in her earlobe drove its point deep into the soft skin at the base of her skull.

Jiri would have cried out, but the snake had shifted when she fell, tightening around her again with crushing force. It drove the air out of her, made her ribs creak, made the world start to go dark.

"Careful, my legless one. I don't want you to squeeze her eyes out."

The snake relaxed its coils, and Jiri breathed, panting air in and out while her ribs groaned with pain.

"She still has her eyes," Mikki said, "but I think your pet squeezed something else out."

"Oh, that *is* disgusting, isn't it?"

Jiri could hear them moving over her long, gasping breaths, could see them as they came and stood above her. Corrianne looked down at her, her nose wrinkled. "Where's your sense of decency, girl? You've pissed yourself, and all you can do is lie there and wheeze. What did they teach you out in that jungle?"

"Nothing about how to use a bucket, apparently," Mikki said. "Are we done here? She stinks, the food's gone, and I think my beetle's drowned in the wine jug."

"I suppose we are." Corrianne waved her hand, and the black-scaled snake faded, dissolving away into shadow. "We need to put the dreamless on, though."

Mikki pulled something from the pouch at her belt, a black band three fingers wide and edged on both sides with silver. "Here. I'm not getting close to her now."

"Fine," Corrianne said. She spoke softly to herself and pointed at the thing. It rose from the halfling's hand and drifted over to Jiri. When it neared her, Corrianne pulled her hands apart, and the band stretched open. It went around Jiri's head, over her ears and down to her throat. There it settled, snugging tight to her skin. It felt like soft leather, but that silver fringe had an edge to it, as if it were made of tiny claws.

"There. A little something for your dreams." Corrianne moved her hand, opening it as if letting go, then made a pinching motion. The thorn in the ear that Jiri hadn't fallen on twisted. "We're done for tonight, girl, but I want you to know something. Tonight was just a little teasing." The thorn twisted a little more, making Jiri raise her head. "Just a way to illustrate our roles in the little drama we've got going. Tomorrow, we'll start this for real. Think about that tonight, and think about whatever deal Amiro offers you in the morning. Because I can guarantee you, if you make me come back down here again and sit in this cell and breathe in your reek, I will make you remember tonight with great longing for how sweet and gentle I was with you. Understand?"

Jiri said nothing, but when the thorn in her ear twisted again she hissed out in pain, and Corrianne was satisfied with that. The black-clad magician opened her hand, and the pain in Jiri's ear returned to a dull ache, lost among all the other complaints of her body.

"*I* don't mind coming down here," Mikki said. "It's cooler, and I've got a whole basketful of thorns I can bring to keep us busy. So if you want to fight Amiro, go ahead. It might smell down here, but the smell of blood is stronger. It'll cover that right up."

The guards came, after Corrianne and Mikki left.

They dumped a bucket of water over Jiri, rinsing her off before they dragged her to the other side of the cell. With brutal, practiced efficiency they gagged her, blindfolded her, then shoved her hands together into some kind of bag that they laced shut around her wrists.

When they let her go after that, Jiri lay on the rough stone, so grateful they hadn't tied her hands behind her back again, or belted her to that chair, that she almost cried.

The door closed, and the thin bit of light trying to press in under the blindfold vanished.

Alone in the dark, Jiri forced the tears away. What use would they be?

Instead, Jiri made herself breathe, in and out, slow through her nose and around her gag, trying not to choke. She had to be calm. She had to think.

How do I get out of here?

The question circled in her head, over and over, and no answer came. Nothing came but fear and anger and a monstrous sense of failure.

They're going to torture me. For as long as it takes, until I either break or All-in-Ashes burns this city down around us. And there's nothing I can do.

Jiri bit into her gag. She tried to feel for the magic that lay in her, the gifts she had brought back in her dreams from the spirit world, but she couldn't focus on them, couldn't touch them. Wrapped in anger and fear, the only gift she could feel was fire, and that gift was useless now.

Unless she wanted to burn.

No. Jiri twisted in the darkness, rolling herself up onto her knees, then stood. *I am more than fire. I can do this. I can be like Oza. He told me I was strong. I can make the spirits come to me. I can become—*

Something. A monkey, a rat, a bird—anything that could slip these bonds.

They took Oza's necklace. Those smooth bones were gone, and the only thing around her throat now was the thing Amiro had called a dreamless, smooth and scratchy.

It doesn't matter. I have to do it.

Jiri reached for the magic, reached for the change, teeth clamped tight on the rag in her mouth, hands knotted into fists, her whole body tight, shaking—

Then she smelled the charring leather and felt the heat growing around her hands. Swelling from warmth to pain as the bag around her hands began to smolder. With a grunt she fell to her knees, slapping her hands against the floor, trying to keep the bonds that held her hands from flashing into flames. Pain rolled up her arms, from heat and from her hands slamming against the stone, but the heat began to fade. Jiri stopped, half-choking on her gag, wishing desperately for sight, for the ability to see if the flames she had started were out. All she had was time, though, slowly passing, and the gradual realization that her hands were burned but not burning.

Jiri slumped over. Her hands throbbed, her greatest pain now. When she was a child, when the fire had first started coming to her, she had burned herself a lot. This pain had been so familiar, yet so shocking each time.

Oza had always healed her, then.

He can't now. It's just me. Jiri thought about trying to reach for her healing, and her stomach clenched. *I can't. The only spirit I can feel right now is fire, and I don't want to burn.*

Jiri lay on the stone, hands throbbing but still bound. She had started her bonds on fire, but she had slapped out the flames before they freed her. That last realization unhinged something in Jiri, and through her gag she started to laugh. At some point the laughter turned to tears, and finally they stopped, too.

Sleep came for her like death, and Jiri welcomed it.

Until she started choking.

Something had her by the throat, tight around it, cutting off her air. At the same time, something bit into the skin of her neck, like a thousand tiny claws. Jiri thrashed, flailed uselessly at her neck with her burned, bound hands, then felt it ease.

The strange necklace that Amiro had told Corrianne to put on her relaxed. The band stopped choking her, and the fringe of tiny silver hooks stopped digging into her skin.

So this is why Amiro called it a "dreamless."

Jiri was sure she would have no dreams tonight. This dreamless would come alive every time she started to fall asleep and wake her with pain and suffocation.

She would not walk the spirit world tonight, could not bargain with the spirits for their magic. She would lie awake, aching, thirsty, hungry, exhausted. Knowing that she had failed, that she was useless. Knowing that they were coming for her, tomorrow.

Knowing that tomorrow was so far away.

Chapter Sixteen
Horror Stories

"Oh, gods, Jiri. What did they do to you?"

Jiri lifted her head, but behind her blindfold there was nothing but darkness. Were her eyes open? She blinked, and wasn't sure.

It was hard to be sure of anything.

Hands touched her, and she flinched, but they were firm and strong. They found her gag and pulled it out, and for the first time in an eternity Jiri could shut her mouth. The pleasure in that was so much that she ignored the hands, barely felt them as they pulled the bag from her own hands.

"Did they do this?" Fingers touched her burns, light as a butterfly, but Jiri still twitched. "Or was it you?"

It was a woman, speaking to her, her voice familiar, but Jiri couldn't pull her thoughts together enough to recognize her.

"It doesn't matter, I suppose." The woman touched the side of Jiri's head. "I'm going to take your blindfold off now. There's not much light in here, but it will probably seem bright. You might want to close your eyes."

Maybe they are closed, Jiri thought. How can I know?

That question was answered when the cloth was pulled from her head and light crashed in on her, blazing like the sun. Jiri's lids slammed shut, even though she wanted light, was desperate for it. As soon as she could, she made her eyes open and drank it in. One small candle burned on the table that Corrianne and Mikki had left in the cell. That was all, but its flame seemed so great after all that darkness.

In its glow, Patima leaned over her, brown eyes soft with sympathy.

Jiri jerked backward. Her hands rose, to ward the woman away or attack, she wasn't sure, but through them she could see Patima watching, calm and patient. Jiri stared at her through burned fingers, then let her hands drop.

"You." The word came out a croak, barely recognizable, but Patima nodded.

"Me. Hold still."

Jiri sat still as the Bonuwat woman reached out, even though the feel of Patima's hands made her skin crawl. Patima took hold of the evil necklace that Corrianne had put on her. The dreamless clung to Jiri's neck as if reluctant to let go, but Patima worked at it until the dark band stretched over Jiri's head. When it was off, Jiri sighed. She had lost count of how many times that thing had dug into her neck, stealing her breath and clawing at her skin.

"Amiro got this from a Nidalese trader." Patima folded the horrible thing in her hand and tucked it into a pocket of the embroidered vest that she wore over her tunic. "They've invented many kinds of torture in Nidal."

"I'm not going to tell you anything," Jiri said. The words tore at her throat, aching from lack of water. "No matter what you do."

The woman nodded. "All right." She straightened up and edged something toward Jiri with her foot. "Here's a bucket, if you need it. I'll be back in a few minutes."

Jiri watched Patima walk out of the cell, leaving the door open behind her. She pushed herself up off the floor, her whole body groaning with pain.

She left. I should run.

Can I run?

Jiri stood there, legs shaking, body trembling. Breathing in and out, she pulled herself together. Stopped the trembling, made her legs steady. Took a step.

I can do this.

Do what?

Run out naked into the hall, and get past Patima and whatever guards were out there? Or locked doors? Find her way out of this building and out of this compound?

One open door isn't freedom. It's just a test to see how stupid I am.

At least she left the bucket.

Patima wasn't gone long. When she came back, she was carrying a tray. One of the guards trailed behind her, holding another bucket and a pile of cloth.

Patima set the tray down on the table, and the smell of it hit Jiri. Curried goat and rice, flatbread and fruit, a jug of watered palm wine and a pot of tea. Despite herself, Jiri found her eyes focusing on that tray.

"Put those down and take the other bucket out," Patima told the guard. He silently did as he was told, and Patima and Jiri were alone again.

"I know you're hungry and thirsty, but we should take care of a few things first."

Jiri waited, staring at the woman. She could guess the next part of the game. The food and drink would be hers, if she talked. Part of her wanted to rush the tray, to drink and eat as much as she could before Patima could snatch them away, but she still had her pride.

For now.

"What?" she grated.

"Your hands and your neck need tending. And your ears. Unless you like them pierced?"

Jiri could feel the thorns, hard spikes grinding into her swollen ears. "No. No I do not."

"Then let's get those thorns out."

Patima started to move toward her, but Jiri shook her head. She raised a burned hand and grasped one thorn, yanked it out, then the other. The pain of them going was like a coal against Jiri's ears, and a rush of blood followed each one out, but she didn't cry, didn't fall. She stood, holding the thorns in her hand, and breathed between clenched teeth.

"Here," Patima said, reaching for Jiri.

"What are you doing?" Jiri said, staring at Patima as the woman's hand closed around hers, pressing lightly against her burns, and against the thorns.

"Helping you," Patima said, and she spoke a soft ripple of words, like music.

Jiri recognized the healing magic as it flowed from Patima's hand into her. She almost refused its solace, but she was already weak enough. She let the magic run into her, and the pain in her hand, her neck, her ears, and her body was washed away. On the back of her hand she could see the burns closing, knitting together, flesh red, then pink, then dark and whole.

Jiri let Patima go, and the thorns fell from between their hands to the floor, sticky with blood.

"There's water and soap and a cloth," Patima said, nodding toward the new bucket the guard had brought. "And clothes."

"Helping me." Jiri went to the bucket, picked up the soap and the cloth and began to wash. "Where were you last night, when your friends were helping me?"

"Out," Patima said. "Otherwise that wouldn't have happened." She paused as Jiri sniffed at the soap. "Sorry, it's northern and horrible. They make it with something called lye. It won't poison you, but it'll dry your skin out something terrible."

Jiri rubbed a little onto her cloth and scrubbed it over her skin. "So you have no interest in interrogating me." Despite Patima's healing, faint bruises still mottled her skin, patterned like snake scales. A reminder of Corrianne's serpent, and the marks ached whenever Jiri ran the cloth over them. "Am I free to go, when I'm done washing up?"

"No, of course not." Patima sat and poured out two cups of the tea. "I need to know about these kindi, and about this All-in-Ashes. Very badly. Torture, though, is an awful way to get questions answered. It's repugnant, it takes too long, and the quality of the information it produces is terrible."

Jiri put down the washcloth. She wasn't clean—not even close—but the worst of the blood and dirt were gone and she needed to eat and drink. She rinsed and dried herself, then slid into the loincloth and light robe that Patima had brought her. Dressed, she went to the table, taking the other stool. "Your friends seem to like it."

"My *companions* are simple people," Patima said. "And they use torture for the same reasons most people do: not for information, but as a punishment for anyone who doesn't do what they say, a way to demonstrate their power, or entertainment." Patima stared at her tea, her eyes distant. "I've seen enough suffering, and I don't like lying to myself. Hurting those who are weaker than me doesn't make me any stronger, it just wastes time." She looked at Jiri. "Chagu village burned last night, less than a mile from our walls. The guards on the wall claim a spark fell from the sky, then rose with the smoke."

Jiri's stomach clenched. *How many more are dead, now?* She picked up her teacup, and though it trembled in her hand she made herself drink. When it was drained, she put it down. "All-in-Ashes."

"Yes." Patima refilled her cup. "The council has decided to ignore the guard's story. They claim it's the biloko, because that's a threat they know how to face. They're forming militia groups and sending them out."

"They'll die out there, too. Unless All-in-Ashes comes for Kibwe." Jiri stared the other woman in the eyes. "It has to be stopped. You have to give back what you stole."

"So you can do what?" Patima asked.

Jiri's healed hands made fists on the table, and she felt the heat in them. "Stop it," she said.

"Mmm," Patima said. "I'm guessing you don't know how."

"At least I would try!"

"You think I wouldn't? You think I took that kindi so that innocents could burn?" Patima shook her head. "Calm yourself, Jiri, before you burn your food. We don't have to be enemies."

"You broke into the Pyre. You set that thing free. You destroyed my village, killed my people. You got me cast out of my tribe." A wisp of smoke drifted up from the table under Jiri's hands. "You killed Oza, my teacher. My father. Because of all that, and more, I think we do have to be enemies."

Patima sighed. "Fine. I've wronged you, and you are, it seems, burning for revenge. But you also need to eat, and I need to tell you a story. So why don't we spend a little time on that, and then I can ask you my questions and you can spit in my face."

A story. Something like Amiro's, probably, something that this smooth-voiced woman thought she could manipulate Jiri with. *I should just spit in her face now. But I need all the strength I can gather.* Jiri tore a piece off the flatbread and dug it into the bowl of curried goat. "Talk fast," she said. "We're wasting time."

Patima shifted in her seat and straightened her back, reminding Jiri of the storytellers who would come through Thirty Trees. When she spoke, her words spilled sweet from her tongue, beautiful and compelling.

"I come from the city of Bloodcove, on the shore of the Fever Sea. My family owned a boat, but I wanted to do more with my life than sew sails and gut fish. So I apprenticed myself to Marisan the Magical, the finest entertainer in the city. A singer, dancer, storyteller, illusionist, joker—she could do it all. Except hold on to her coin, or knife fight when she was drunk.

"I was four years into my apprenticeship when those faults became abundantly clear to me. Marisan got into a fight over some pretty elf boy with the first mate of a pirate ship out of the Shackles, and she ended up falling on her own knife. Losing my teacher was bad enough. Finding out that she was up to her eyes in debt to the meanest moneylender in Bloodcove was worse. That old bastard wanted his coin, and if he couldn't get it from Marisan, he figured he would get it from me."

Patima took a sip of her tea. "He sent some of his bully boys over, and I spent a night just about as fun as the one you just had while they laid out the terms of my new contract. Which, in short, was that he owned me. I countered his offer by throwing myself out a window into the bay.

"I probably would have drowned, or died in the jungle, or been caught again, but as luck would have it I was picked up by a boat owned by the Apsis Consortium. They were starting an expedition into the Expanse, looking for trade. I had no interest in the jungle, but they were getting out of the city, and that was all I cared about. It didn't take me long to convince them that they could use another translator.

"We traveled and traded. Those northern fools thought that since they knew one dialect of Polyglot— that's what they call the jungle languages—they knew them all. They learned their error soon enough, and I started earning my keep." A smile flickered across

Patima's face. "It was funny. I liked it. Everyone on that expedition loved me. I entertained the guards and workers, and I translated, and when even I couldn't speak the local's dialect I could usually make everyone understand what was going on. Because of me, that expedition went deep into the Expanse, and the riverboats were full of rare things. We were all going to be rich, and the head of the expedition promised me that I would have a valuable place with the Aspis Consortium, and that I wouldn't have to worry about that old bastard back in Bloodcove."

Patima put down her teacup and reached for a porcelain cup and the palm wine.

"We were just about to turn back. We finally had enough, the boats were riding low in the water. Then we heard the drums." She took a long swallow of wine. "They came from ahead of us, deep and dull. When they heard them, every Mwangi member of the crew went still, as if they were already dead. The northerners had no idea. They questioned and cursed until someone finally explained it to them. We had gone too far. We had heard the drums of Usaro.

"I won't bother with describing our useless flight, or our capture. I won't go into details about the lucky ones who were torn apart right away, or who slit their own throats. I won't talk . . ." Patima stopped, staring down at nothing, her eyes turned in, her body seeming to shrink. "I won't talk about what happened after those demon-worshiping apes brought us back to Usaro. I will just tell you that in Usaro, torture is an art and an entertainment, and they could spend weeks in its appreciation.

"The apes found out early that I was a translator. That saved my life." Patima smiled, a terrible, bitter expression. "They found that useful. Not because they pretended that they wanted information. No, those monsters were honest about their torture. They wanted me because they wanted to know what their playthings were shrieking, what terrible blasphemies they could force from them. What awful promises they could extract. They broke minds as avidly as they broke bodies. So my body was left alone, while they made me watch what they did to every other member of that expedition.

"This went on for months. Until the last one died, his flesh neatly sliced from his bones, teased delicately away from every vein and artery so that he would last. When they finished, they looked at me, smiled, and led me back to my cage."

"But you escaped," Jiri said, then shut her mouth. It was rude to interrupt a storyteller, and despite everything else, Jiri had to admit that Patima was just that. Jiri had finished her food, and she barely remembered eating.

"Escaped," Patima said. "I got away. There was a coup attempt, I think. Some member of the Court of Hateful Smiles moved against the Gorilla King. Ape battled ape, and blood and chaos were thick in the streets of Usaro. My cage was broken, and I ran. There were other humans running too, slaves and prisoners screaming their way toward the jungle, and I saw them get cut down. That would have been my fate, but my luck, oh my cursed luck, blessed me again. At my feet was a body. A huge silverback gorilla, wrapped in armor. I made myself go to it, rubbed its blood on me, stole its cloak and the amulet around its neck.

"The cloak and blood scent got me out of the city. But it wasn't long before I heard the sounds of charau-ka pursuing me. That's when I learned how to use the amulet." Patima pulled at a fine silver chain that ran around her throat. From beneath her shirt came an amulet, blackened silver set with a lump of polished sardonyx. "I touched its magic, and one of the demons bound to it answered.

"It came, and tested me. It should have bested me, but my terror gave me strength. I mastered it, and it killed the charau-ka. I could hear it, tearing them apart while I ran, and I laughed at their screams, laughed and cried, and for a long time I didn't know anything else.

"Somehow I survived the jungle. Moving, always moving, away from Usaro. Until I was found and brought here." Patima took a sip of her wine and nodded toward the bottle. "Have some. It's well watered. I'm not trying to get you drunk."

Jiri frowned, but she took the jug and poured herself a glass. "I heard about you. How you lived as a beggar, telling stories in the market."

"It took me a while to put my mind back together. Mostly." She set down her cup. "I can go days now, not thinking about it, not remembering. Then I'll hear a monkey call from the trees, see a butcher cutting meat, hear drums from the Adayenki, and it all comes back. And the nightmares. They never stop."

"I'm sorry for your pain," Jiri said, and it was unsettling how true that was. Patima's story had dug into her. Usaro was the Expanse's nightmare, the place where all the bad-luck shadows pooled. "But what does this have to do with the Pyre, and All-in-Ashes?"

"Everything." Patima looked at Jiri. "Usaro taught me many terrible things, but the most important is this: The strong can hurt the weak, and I was weak. So very, very weak.

"That was what made me pull myself together. Why I went to the Consortium and told them that I used to work for them, that I wanted to work for them again. This place, these people, have money and power. They were strong, so I joined them and made myself stronger. I learned everything I could about magic, about how to fight, about . . . everything. Ever since Usaro, getting stronger—getting *smarter*—is all I've done. And you know what? It's not enough. It will never be enough. I'm human. Weakness is written in my flesh. No matter how well I fight, I can bleed. No matter how much I know, I can still be outmaneuvered. No matter how strong I get, I'm still just meat for the beast.

"I am still Usaro's prisoner. It just has to claim me."

Jiri set down her cup. There was something in Patima's voice, some strange certainty that curdled the little bit of sympathy Jiri had been feeling for her and made her want to edge away. "All flesh is mortal. It's a vessel for our spirits, which will go on. Usaro can't touch your spirit."

Patima looked up at Jiri, her eyes gleaming. "You're so young and stupid. Usaro has already drawn scars across my soul, and I will never be free. Unless I destroy it."

"All-in-Ashes," Jiri said.

"Yes." Patima stood. "A spirit to save my spirit. I found hints of it in the books and scrolls Amiro had collected, things that were meant to lead him to ancient treasures and relics. A thing of fire and destruction. A weapon meant to destroy a city—Usaro. I spent years hunting for it, and where do I find it? Right on my doorstep."

"It's not a weapon," Jiri said, staring up at her, but she remembered Shani. *Ancestors, what did you do?* "It's a disaster."

"All weapons are disasters," Patima said. "And I mean to use this one on that cursed city." She looked down at Jiri. "I found All-in-Ashes' prison. I freed it from that kindi when I touched it. But I cannot control it, and so it turns its wrath on the innocent. That's why I need you. Tell me how to use that kindi. Tell me what I need to do to control that spirit, and no more villages will die. Tell me, and I will burn the evil of Usaro out of the Expanse. Tell me."

Patima's voice filled the chamber, pounding Jiri down, making her small. She was still weak from the night before, exhausted and frightened. But she was angry, too, and she clung to that heat. "You're a raider. You treat with demons, and you killed my teacher."

"I am. I do. I did." Patima said the words slowly and quietly. She seemed to pull in on herself, no longer a force towering over Jiri. Now she was a woman again, tired and sad. "I've done so much wrong, trying to do this one right." She knelt down on the stone before Jiri, looking up at her. "I never wanted to hurt anyone, Jiri, believe that. I just did what I had to. What I must.

Believe me. I'm trying so hard to do this good. Believe me." She reached out her hand to Jiri.

"Believe you?" Jiri said, her anger flaring. But there was something in Patima's voice, in her eyes, that shook Jiri. The fire in her faltered, and all she had left was despair and the overwhelming truth that she was all alone—alone, except for this woman, kneeling before her, hand stretched out, her eyes so wide and beautiful and trusting. The anger in Jiri sputtered and went out.

"I . . ." she started, and stopped, confused, uncertain without her anger, but Patima's words were echoing in her head, *believe me, believe me,* and suddenly Jiri wanted to, as much as she wanted Oza back, and Hadzi and Thirty Trees and her life. "I do," she said, and took Patima's hand.

"Thank you." Patima rose, pulling Jiri up into an embrace, then let her go. "Thank you. What do I need to do?"

"Simple," Jiri said. "There should be a sharp piece of iron somewhere on the kindi. Draw a little of your blood with that, and smear it on its lips. That will pull you into its dream."

"That's it?" Patima said. "I was trying . . . everything. And that's all I had to do?"

"That's all," Jiri said. "But you must be careful. Kindi are dangerous. That's why they were sealed away."

"Then tell me about them." Patima sat back down and poured them both more wine. "Tell me everything."

Jiri took a deep breath, and did.

"I should be there, when you try this," Jiri said. "That kindi. I never heard of them trapping a spirit as powerful as All-in-Ashes in one."

"I'll think about it," Patima said. "But you should rest. You need your strength back before trying anything like that." She was bent over the floor, spreading out a pallet that the guards had brought. "Sleep, and I'll talk to Amiro about getting you out of here. Tonight."

"Tonight?" Jiri stood, and felt the world waver around her. She didn't want to sleep, she wanted to help Patima, but the woman said she had other preparations to make, and Jiri was exhausted. "Tonight."

Patima patted the pallet and Jiri stretched herself out on it.

"We'll stop it," Jiri said. "We will. And you'll have your chance for revenge."

"I hope so," Patima said, her eyes distant.

"We will." Jiri watched the woman get up and walk toward the door. "Patima?" she called out.

"What?" The woman paused, a dark silhouette.

"Let me help. I know you hurt, but . . ." Jiri shook her head, feeling foolish, but she had to say it. She cared too much. "All I wanted, these past few days, was to punish you for what you had done, because I didn't understand. I know it's nothing like that with Usaro, but still. Revenge and rage and despair warp your thoughts. Be careful."

"Thank you, Jiri. I will." Patima swung the door shut, and darkness swallowed the cell.

In her blankets, Jiri closed her eyes, sleep rushing for her, despite her worries.

By all who came before, it's good to have someone I can trust.

Jiri opened her eyes and blinked in the darkness.

She had been dreaming of curling in a hammock, Hadzi warm behind her, the familiar sounds of the jungle all around. Lying there, rocking gently, watching as the stars faded outside and the sky began to glow, crimson and gold, bright and beautiful with sunrise.

Except it hadn't been the sun, and when the tops of the mango trees had caught, Jiri couldn't wake Hadzi, couldn't get out of the hammock, couldn't cry out. All she could do was lie there and watch the flames roll out over the village, spreading like water, brilliant and beautiful, the ash dancing in their wake.

All-in-Ashes.

Patima.

The two names hung in her head, then intertwined.

I told her everything.

In the darkness, Jiri shoved herself up to her feet, her heart hammering.

"I told her how to use it. I told her *everything*. Why?"

Believe me.

Jiri remembered those words, so clear, remembered the way the world had twisted just a little when Patima had said them.

"Gods and crocodiles. She charmed me." They had caught her, questioned her, tortured her, then Patima had come, with her story and her sweet voice. She had used her magic to pull the information out of Jiri as easily as a honeyguide pulled bee grubs out of broken honeycomb.

Charmed me.

The door was thin lines of light, glowing in the darkness in front of her. Jiri was pounding on it before she could think.

Chapter Seventeen
New Skins

W hat?"
    The voice was deep and male, speaking with a Kibwe accent. Maybe one of the guards that had dragged her around this cell yesterday.

"I want to speak to Patima!"

"You already did. Now stop beating on that door or I'll beat on you."

Jiri pulled back her fist, but stopped. That bit of defiance would be worse than useless. She wanted this guard gone. She made herself move instead, walking around the perimeter of her cell, hand brushing against the stone walls.

How long have I been asleep?

There was no way of knowing, but the answer was obvious.

Too long. She's used the kindi, or is using it now.

Jiri walked and turned, moving around the small space, crowded now with table and chairs and pallet. Thinking and moving and trying to keep her anger in her in check. *I don't know what it will do. Neither does Patima. Maybe it can't control All-in-Ashes. Maybe it will kill her.*

Maybe she'll succeed.

Jiri stopped moving. The rough wood of the door lay beneath her hand, solid and unyielding. A barrier between her and the woman who had stolen everything from her. Her village. Her life. Oza. Her secrets.

Jiri felt the fire moving in her, rushing through her blood, making her want to burn.

I could burn this, she thought, and the wood was hot beneath her hand.

And choke to death on smoke before I got out.

Locking her teeth against her anger, Jiri made herself look at the door. Burn it? She could do so much more, with the help of the spirits. She could turn these stone walls to mud or sand. She could make the wood of this door twist itself out of her way. She could pull a spirit animal into the world with her, and have it tear down the door and drive the guards away.

I could. But I can't.

That knowledge didn't help Jiri keep her anger in check. She had no magic, not now. The pacts she had made with the lesser spirits had all frayed away, undone by time and the shifting of the planet, the sun and moon and stars. To do anything now, she would have to still herself and sink into the waking dream of the spirit world, where she could bargain for magic again.

And that would take time.

Time I don't have. Jiri faced the door, both hands fists, and ground her knuckles into the uncaring wood. Her eyes were shut against the darkness, and behind her lids she could see fire dancing, so bright and eager. The only spirit that still clung to her.

It would never leave her.

"I can't," Jiri groaned. "I'll burn, too."

But I want to.

Jiri forced her eyes open, staring at the darkness and the bright lines of light that marked the edges of the door. There were lines at the bottom of the door, too—thin seams of light that edged a smaller rectangle. Crouching, she examined them.

There was a slot cut into the door where it met the floor, wide but short, probably a way to slide trays of food in to a prisoner. She hadn't noticed it before because the slot had its own little door, which swung up into the cell. She could feel two simple hinges but no handle. Still, it would be easy enough to get her fingers under it and pull it up.

Why? I could barely slide my arm out it.

But she could see. Dropping to the floor, Jiri wormed her fingers beneath the bottom of the door and pulled up on the little wood panel that covered the slot. It swung open, and she blinked, blinded for a moment by the light in the hall outside. When she could see again—

Jiri jerked back, letting the little door fall shut, her heart hammering. *Eyes. Someone staring at me. Little eyes.*

Like a child.

Gritting her teeth, she carefully lifted the flap again and stared out into the hall. Just a few inches away, on the other side of the door, Mikki sprawled comfortably on a folded blanket, looking back at her.

"It was worth lying here, just to see that," the halfling said, smiling.

"What are you doing?" Jiri said. There was nothing else out there that Jiri could see except a stone floor and walls.

"I told you, I come down here sometimes. It's cooler. When I heard you yelling at the guard, I thought I'd come visit."

"Where's Patima?"

Mikki rolled onto her back and stretched like a cat. "She's busy with her new toy." Mikki pulled an orange from the pouch on her belt and drew a long acacia thorn out of it. "She magicked all your secrets away, didn't she?" When Jiri didn't say anything, Mikki shrugged and started picking at the orange with the thorn, tearing open the fruit's skin. "That's so unfair. Here you were, all ready to fight me and Corrianne and Amiro, to bravely stand against us while we did our worst, and she just waltzes in and sugar-talks it out of you with a story and a spell." Mikki dropped the orange peel. "It's like when you're getting ready to take on some big fellow, and you're all worked up for a long, hard go, and then they only last a second. So disappointing. And *you* don't even get to slit a throat after as consolation."

Jiri had no idea if the halfling was talking about sex or battle, and didn't want to. "You can't let her do this."

"Why not?" Mikki chewed on a wedge of orange.

"That kindi might kill her."

"Yeah, we'd both cry. You have anything better than that?"

"Better?" Jiri said. "I have something worse. Patima might succeed, might get control of that thing. What do you think she would do with it? Do you think her destruction would stop with Usaro? Do you think that spirit would let her? How much of the world would she burn?"

In the hall outside, Mikki chewed her last piece of orange, staring up at the ceiling. Then her eyes slid over to Jiri's. "Not enough."

"Well." The halfling sat up. "I suppose I should get your toys. The ropes and mitt and gag and dreamless. Can't have you casting your way into trouble down here. Patima and Amiro both want you alive, for now." Mikki stopped gathering up her blanket and bent enough to look through the slot at her again. "Don't worry, though, me and Corrianne will keep you company. They said that's all right, as long as we didn't do anything too permanent to you. I'll go get her and your things now."

The halfling stood, but Jiri could still hear her just fine. "Use your bucket, if you need to. We might be here awhile, and you wouldn't want to shame yourself like you did last time, would you?"

Jiri let the little door fall, cutting off the light from the hall and plunging her into darkness.

Patima is using the kindi, and I'm trapped with these poisonous spiders. And I don't even have the magic to make a light.

Jiri's hands were fists, pushing hard against her thighs, the angry heat pulsing through her and gathering in them.

No.

Forcing her hand open, Jiri pulled at the sleeve of her robe. On the skin of her arm, she could still feel the outline of Corrianne's serpent's scales, pressed into her bruised flesh. Jiri traced her finger over those marks and settled back on the floor. A bruise was nothing like the bone fetishes from Oza's necklace. But it was something to focus on. Hand on her arm, Jiri thought of snakes: The thick black one that Corrianne had conjured up came first, but that thought brought fear, hate, anger. Heat. *No.* Jiri focused instead on the memory of a boa, curled in a knot in a tree, eyes open but dreaming. Jiri could see the snake clearly, and she pressed her hand against her bruised skin and tried to *be* it, to call its spirit to her so she could borrow its shape, could slip away, could escape.

Could do something, anything.

She felt it. A feeling in her arm, like the ghost of scales pressed to her skin, into her skin, and she fought to connect that feeling with the image she held in her mind, to string them together with a thread of magic and weave that feeling through her and change— Jiri fought for it, the fingers of her mind clutching again and again at that cobweb-thin strand of magic, but it kept slipping away like smoke. Crowding close to that faint slip of magic was Jiri's fire. It danced, eager to be held, wanting to be used. Jiri tried to ignore it, but its light and heat were distracting, overwhelming, and she felt her concentration burning in the flames, and that thread of change was gone.

"No!" The anger Jiri had been trying to hold was loose now, set free by her frustration, and she shouted again. "No!" She lunged up off the floor, and her hip cracked against the side of the table, flipping it over. Dishes and glasses, the remnants of the meal Patima had brought her before she betrayed her, shattered on the stone.

Jiri shoved the table away; her hands caught one of the stools and she spun, throwing it at the bright lines that marked where the door stood. Wood hit wood, a solid boom, and from somewhere beyond she thought she heard something, something like laughter, high-pitched and merry.

That sound made Jiri hotter. She found the other stool and threw it, tangled her feet in the blankets of her pallet and kicked them away, spun to face the door as glass bit into the bottom of her foot. She barely noticed the pain, because there was light in her cell now. Bright, golden light, running up her arm and dancing in her palm, and Jiri threw the fire as hard as she could at the door. It burst and fell, leaving a black mark that glowed with a few embers, but the wood didn't catch. She threw another, and another, the light flashing through her cell, blinding her to everything but the sparks and the flames. Another, and she stood, chest heaving, streaming sweat, and now there were flames. They flickered on the door, small ones, and on the floor beside it. One of the thin blankets from her pallet had caught, the little flames running fast over to the tangled remains of her bed, all of them quickly catching.

"Oh, ancestors weep," Jiri breathed, watching the blankets go up. In the light of the growing fire, the door stood, charred but still solid.

The smoke rose, twisting, filling the top of the room, and Jiri dropped below it. The fire was growing fast, hot and bright in this tiny space, and Jiri shoved herself away from it, pressed herself to the wall.

I don't want to die like this.

"I don't want to burn," she said, dropping to her belly beneath the smoke.

Then don't. The words echoed in her head, but not in her voice. Over her, the smoke twisted, and Jiri thought she saw something through the stinging tears that poured from her eyes, something like a face. Like Oza's face.

You know how to escape this, Jiri. You just need to understand what's stopping you, and why.

How.

The snake.

"I tried that," she choked out, and started coughing. *I can't.* She couldn't draw enough air to speak. Over her, the smoke swirled, Oza's face forming and falling apart, his eyes staring down at her, waiting for her to find the answer.

Or join him in the spirit world.

The how is the snake. The what, the why . . . What's stopping me? Why can't I do this? Jiri clutched her fingers around her bruised arm again, tried to picture the snake, but all she could think of was fire, the flames in her and around her.

It's the fire. It's what stops this. She shut her eyes against the heat. *And why does the fire fill me?*

Because of my anger.

She felt that anger tighten in her. What was she supposed to do? Stay helpless, trapped? Her anger, her fire, were the only things that she had.

They are tools. Her voice, but Oza's words, repeated to her so many times over her childhood. *But all tools have their place. Your anger and your friend fire must learn theirs. You must learn to put them down as easily as you pick them up.*

Put them down. Jiri rolled, lay belly-down on the cool stone floor, breathed in the clear breeze that was flowing from under the door. *My anger is my tool, and I don't need it now.* In her head, she pictured a snake slipping along a branch. She held the picture and breathed, steady, in and out, ignoring the heat, ignoring the pain in her feet and back as the table caught fire. *Fire is my tool, and I don't need it now. I put it down.* She breathed, and pushed away the panic fueling her rage, breathed and searched for the thin, almost invisible thread of magic connecting the memory of scales on her skin to the image in her head. For a moment, she saw it, then it flashed away, vanishing into flames. Her anger sparked, tried to spread. *I put it down.* A whisper in her mind— not a shout of defiance, not a bellow of command. *I put it down.*

In her head, spinning with smoke, she saw it, the thread of change, so slim but there. She reached her hands for it, physical and spiritual, and caught it.

The change slammed through her. Not pain, but a twisting kind of vertigo. Jiri's body went horribly, sickeningly wrong for a moment, then that feeling was gone. She was herself again, scales and tongue and long, looping body. A body that she quickly tightened up and pulled away from the flames that crackled behind her. In front of her loomed the door, stretching high overhead. At its base was the slot. Her way out.

Shut now, of course.

With a low hiss, Jiri wrapped her tail forward and pushed the end beneath the door flap. She jerked her tail and the flap popped up, letting her jam her head underneath. Flattening herself to the ground as much as possible, she slid her length out into the passage.

The cool stone beneath her sucked away the heat, and she curled in the hall for a moment. It was empty, just three closed doors on one side and two more closed doors at either end. Jiri flicked out her tongue, tasting the air, but all she could taste was the smoke that poured out of the top of the door behind her, pooling at the vaulted top of the hall. But she heard something. Voices, hollow and strange, as if the speakers were underwater. She could barely make them out—a high one, Mikki, and a low one, chattering about something.

The voices were coming from the door to Jiri's right. She glided the other way. There was nothing but silence behind this door, and at its base she found a hole gnawed in the wood. Her tongue flickered, and through the smoke she faintly tasted rats.

It might be large enough.

Behind her, the voices stopped, then Jiri heard Mikki. "Do you smell smoke?"

Turning her head, Jiri shoved her way into the hole, pushing until she had poured her whole body through. The room beyond was nothing but a closet, stuffed with junk and empty of any other exit. She considered it. The smoke taste hadn't filled this room yet, and the rat taste was strong. And good. She slithered between empty barrels and broken stools, following it, and found a broken stone in the wall. Beyond it lay darkness.

Jiri poked her blunt head in. The hollow beyond the stone was narrow—a handspan wide, maybe—but it was wide open above her and to both sides. Nothing but darkness filled her eyes, but she could taste mildew, stone, rats, roaches, water, and a tiny portion of fresh air.

Ignoring the sounds of shouts behind her, people yelling for buckets and water, Jiri flowed into the hole and began to climb.

The hollow was a space between the walls. A way for them to breathe, to keep the inner stone from sweating in the heat and damp.

Jiri puzzled that out as she worked her way up. The gap stretched on and on—around the whole building, she supposed—blocked only by support buttresses and broken stones. Getting around those was easy enough. She just followed the rat trails.

She climbed, pushing herself up, going for height. It was dark, except for the occasional bright crack, but she didn't care. Sight was not nearly so useful as taste. Voices came through the stone occasionally, but she heard no more shouts, no cries of alarm.

They'll probably get the fire out fast. That room was all stone. It will take longer to clear the smoke and let it cool enough for them to go in, though, and find out I'm not there.

The thought should have been amusing, but Jiri was figuring out that a snake was not a particularly emotional beast. Her fear had guttered with her change, and she found herself considering her situation with a detached, thoughtful manner. Only her anger still flickered, and even that was only a few fitful coals.

So I know how to control my anger at last: turn into a snake.

Which I can only do after I control my anger.

Coiling around a stone that had tilted in, Jiri blinked.
There was light above her—not bright, but steady—and
she shifted her direction and slid toward it. Now she
could see that she was almost to the top of whatever
wall she was climbing. The narrow space she was in
ended just a little above her. The light she saw was a
gap in that space, a piece of stone that had broken out
of its mortar and fallen. Stopping just before that gap,
she flicked her tongue out.

She tasted fresh air, and people, rats, stone, and
rain. Carefully, Jiri pushed her head out of the hole and
looked around.

A lattice of wooden beams surrounded her, angling
up into shadows. They supported a roof of tiles, and she
could hear rain pattering against the other side. Below
that roof, the rafters ran over the rooms that split up
this long building. None of them had ceilings, so that
the heat could rise out of them and collect up here,
where it would slip out the vents to the outside. From
where she was right now, Jiri could see one of those
vents. It would be a simple thing to crawl over the rafters and slip out into the rain.

She flicked her tongue at the vent, then turned her
blunt head away. *Not yet.*

It was a risk. Patima and her kindi might not even
be in this building. But she had to check. Jiri slithered
out of the wall and on to the nearest rafter. She made
for a thick beam that ran through the center of the
building, looking down as she went. Storerooms and
offices passed by below, nothing useful, the few people inside bent over ledgers. Jiri reached the beam at
the center and started to flow along it, startling a few

rats into scurrying, panicked climbs away from her. She forced herself to ignore them, and stared down at the rooms passing below her. Nothing yet, just an empty library and a cluttered office, but she was only halfway down the building. Then she heard a clatter below.

Coiling on her beam, she stared down. She was over a hallway, and against one wall a flight of stairs opened in the floor, heading down. A man and a woman were lying before the stairs, a spilled bucket spreading water beside them.

"—idiot, why are you running—"

"—a fire, and you're in the way!" The man pulled himself up, and Jiri thought she recognized him as one of the guards from her cell. "Get others, get some buckets, and start running them down these stairs."

"Buckets?" The woman was pulling herself up, wringing water out of her clothes. "Of water?"

"By all your stupid ancestors, what else?" The man snatched up his bucket and rushed back out to refill it.

The woman turned and ran into another room, calling, "Fire!" as she did. The cry was picked up, and Jiri could hear it echoing through the building.

I have a little time, while they're confused. But only a little. This place would soon be crawling with clerks and guards. If she wanted to get away . . .

Jiri stared ahead. She still had half the building to search. She hesitated, her tongue flicking, tasting the air.

Tasting something faint, buried in all the other scents rising around her, but sharp.

Blood, burning.

Jiri dropped her head and slithered toward that taste as fast as she could.

Patima lay in her room alone, sprawled across the stone of her floor like a broken doll.

Jiri lowered herself silently from the rafters, watching the woman. She twitched sometimes, body jerking, head turning. Her dark hair was tangled over her face, black strands covering her eyes. Her lips moved, as if she were trying to talk, parting, going still, then moving again. Her chest rose and fell, breathing, but sometimes she would stop, then start again with a gasp or a muttered, broken word. Her left hand was clutched over her heart, and Jiri could see blood, wet on Patima's skin.

She's caught in the dream.

Jiri twisted her body and looked at the low table beside Patima. On one side, Jiri could see the little kindi she had taken from the Pyre, Oza's necklace of carved animals beside it. On the other side, a slim journal lay open, its smooth pages covered in tiny, neat writing. A quill lay dripping on those pages, and a pool of ink lapped at the book, its jar tipped beside it.

In the middle of the table stood the kindi Patima had stolen.

Jiri moved slightly, made sure she was over Patima's pallet, then let herself drop. Her body thumped into the tangle of sheets, and she reared up. Patima, lost in the vision that filled her head, just twitched and muttered. Jiri made herself ignore her, and stared at the kindi.

It looked like the statue that had held it in the Pyre, something like a man with wings of smoke and flame.

Carved from ebony, with obsidian inlays, the carving's darkness was broken only by the veins of iron that ran through its wings like sharp metal pinions and the iron spike that jutted from its chest. It was as if the statue had been impaled on that spike, a spike that glowed a dull red. The wounded wood around that metal was charred and smoking.

The face, carved with exquisite detail into the black wood, was Shani's.

Slowly, wary of those gleaming, obsidian eyes, Jiri crawled off the pallet and toward the kindi. The smell of burned blood and scorched flesh was thick here, and she could see the marks of Patima's blood on the kindi's lips.

How long ago did she start this? Jiri tilted her head and stared at the woman twitching on the floor beside her. *Will she survive this?*

Will I let her?

That was a thought that would have to wait for a moment. Jiri pushed herself up, crawling on the table, carefully avoiding touching that dark kindi. She looked at the things arranged on it and hissed.

I miss my hands.

Jiri could turn back. That would be easy. But she wouldn't be able to become the snake again—not until she rested, until she walked the spirit world in her dreams again. Oza had taught her that much. And she had no hope of escaping this place in her real form. She would have to do without hands for this.

She examined the things on the table, and realized that she had one thing going for her at least: the kindi shaped like All-in-Ashes stood in the middle of a pile of shining metal links, a bag made of metal loops all hooked together. Patima must have put it in there to keep the kindi's hot iron from burning whatever it touched, and when she used it, she hadn't taken it completely out of the bag, just dropped the sides around it and left it exposed. All Jiri had to do was put the other kindi she had found beside it, with Oza's necklace, and then pull the bag up around them all.

All while making sure that she didn't touch that sharp, scorching spike that jutted out of that kindi.

This should be easy.

It wasn't. Long minutes passed as Jiri pushed and nudged, picking things up with her mouth, wishing for her thumbs. Outside, she kept hearing voices, people yelling about fire, feet pounding past the room, someone yelling about a prisoner, calling for Amiro, for Patima. Jiri ignored it all, and kept moving.

She had finally pulled the bag up and closed, cursing those sharp iron-tipped wings the whole time, when someone pounded at the door of Patima's room.

"Patima! Amiro needs you! There's been a fire, and he told me to—" The door rattled, and Jiri lunged for the bag, grabbing its drawstrings in her mouth, ready to try to climb up and out. The door stayed shut, though, latched from the inside. "Patima?" The man cursed, and Jiri heard feet running away.

Someone will be back. Soon.

Jiri had what she had come for. She just had to get it out of here. But on the floor, Patima still muttered.

Helpless. Alone.

Like I was.

Anger stirred in Jiri, and a faint echo of heat passed through her scaled body. It was enough. Jiri poured herself off the table, down to Patima. She hesitated, her tongue dancing over the woman's face. Tasting her scent, tasting burned blood, soap, and fear sweat.

She only had one way to do this in this form.

So do it.

Moving fast, she snaked herself around Patima's neck. The woman shifted and groaned, but didn't raise her hands, didn't open her eyes. Jiri stared down at Patima's face, body wrapped tight around her neck, and began to clench her muscles. Below her, the woman went rigid, mouth opening, trying to breathe. But her eyes didn't open, her fingers didn't tear at Jiri's scales. Jiri was choking the life from Patima, but the woman was unable to fight, dying while wrapped in whatever nightmare that kindi had trapped her in. Jiri stared down at her, watching her choke.

She's helpless, alone, like I was, and I'm killing her. Images flickered through Jiri's head: Oza dead and Thirty Trees burning. A terrified woman in a cage surrounded by apes. A city ablaze. Jiri's coils eased for a second and she heard Patima wheezing for air, trying to live, and she started to—

Someone pounded on the door behind her. "Patima. Are you in there?"

Mikki's voice was easy to recognize. Moving fast, Jiri released Patima, slithering up to the table to grab the metal ring bag by its leather drawstrings. Behind her, she heard Patima cough and groan.

"I hear something," Mikki muttered, and the door rattled. "Break this down. You're twice my size."

There was a thud from the hall, and a curse. The sounds goaded Jiri, made her climb faster even though the heavy bag pulled her down. It was almost impossible, but the thought of being caught, of being taken back to that cell, kept her moving. Looping a coil over a rafter, she dropped her head down and snagged the bag, lifting it out as the door shuddered again.

"Damn, you're useless. Give me a boost and I'll go over the top."

Gods and crocodiles. The curse came out as a hiss through Jiri's clenched jaws, and she moved, sliding along the rafter to the edge of the roof, the bag fighting her the whole way. In the shadows where the rafters met, she looked back. There was a flash of a small hand clutching the edge of one of the rafters, then another, and Mikki pulled herself up. Jiri tensed in the shadows, terrified for a moment that the halfling would taste her, but she stayed still and watched as the assassin jumped nimbly down into Patima's room. A tinkling laugh came up a moment later.

Jiri didn't want to listen anymore. She wanted out. Looking around, she tried to find another vent. She didn't see any, and started crawling forward, pulling the bag with her, until she felt a drop of water tap on her snout. There, a little ahead and above, was a broken tile and a hole to the outside. She shoved herself toward it as fast as she could. Behind her, Mikki was shouting.

"Patima's been attacked! Somebody tried to kill her, or she's getting hickeys from snakes."

There was another voice, maybe Amiro's, but Jiri couldn't tell as she shoved her way into the rain, breaking more tiles with her coils to force the hole wide enough for the bag. Mikki's answer covered the noise.

"Fine! I'll look for her. But that means you get to deal with those idiots in the east warehouse!"

Outside, it was darkness, rain, and confusion.

Jiri coiled on the roof, trying to sort it out. She could taste rain, bird droppings, rats, the distant reek of latrines, and the smoke of a thousand cooking fires. The rain blinded her, and she could barely see over the compound stretched around her. She was in the middle, surrounded by buildings, and there were people rushing with lanterns through the darkness below. They were shouting at one another, a confusion of voices mixed with the storm. To Jiri's flat, serpent ears, their voices blended together, and she could barely pick out the occasional word, a shouted "Fire!", a howl of pain. Those shouts blended with another noise, something that sounded like distant thunder, long and low, but didn't stop. It just kept going, rising and falling.

It wasn't All-in-Ashes. That fear passed quickly. No flames rose from the city, no terrible wings spread across the sky. Jiri didn't know what was happening. What she did know was that she was getting sluggish, tired, her cold-blooded body chilled by the rain.

Enough.

After all the difficulty she had taking this shape, changing back was as easy as taking a breath. She closed her eyes and remembered her hands, and she felt the change. It spun through her, dizzying then gone, and she was herself again. Herself, with arms and legs and good eyes and a tongue that stayed in her mouth. Herself, dressed in the light robe Patima had given her, her teeth clenched on the drawstring of the chain-metal bag.

Jiri grabbed the bag and spat out the string. The movement shifted her, and she suddenly became very aware of her position, standing on a steep, rain-slick roof high over the wet brick of the courtyard below. She quickly lowered herself to all fours, grabbing at the tiles with her free hand. This perch had seemed so secure when she was a snake.

I should have climbed down first.

But she had wanted to see.

Jiri took time for that now. The dark and the rain still made it hard, but her eyes were much sharper now, and so were her ears. She could watch the people moving below, clerks and laborers heading in, toward the center of the compound, while the guards were heading out toward the low walls, the warehouses, and the big house that she had been watching before she got caught.

Are they under attack?

They were acting like it, moving like termites whose mound had been kicked open.

Mixed in with their shouts was that low rumble Jiri had heard, the one that sounded like thunder. The sound of voices, hundreds of voices, raised into the rain from the city. Beyond the walls of the Aspis compound, she could see lanterns and torches moving, could see that the Adayenki Pavilion was filled with their flickering light.

Lightning flashed, and real thunder boomed. The light and noise stopped Jiri's staring and got her moving. Whatever was happening in the compound and in the city beyond, she could use its confusion to get out. Scrambling over the wet tile, she crawled across the roof to a tree that rose beside the building. A mango tree, Jiri realized when she got there and saw the shape of the leaves, and she decided to take that as a good omen. She slid along the edge of the roof and found the thickest branch she could, hanging just out of reach. She slung the metal bag around her neck, then cautiously rose, balanced on bare feet, and jumped.

She was in the air for only a second, but that second stretched, until she was sure it would never end. Then she crashed into the branch, and everything was moving too fast, the wet bark sliding away from her clutching fingers, and her hands were lashing until somehow she was clutching desperately at the branch, unsure of how she got there and not caring. Heart hammering, she worked her way to the trunk and down the tree.

On the ground she crouched, deciding where to go. People were still running around, shouting and pointing and going in circles, and their confusion frustrated her. *How can I avoid you if you don't know where you're going?* She watched a couple of guards dash back and forth in front of her. Someone shouted at the men, and they both charged toward one of the warehouses, the eastern one. Jiri stared at the building and the crowd of guards that were clustered around its door. Mikki had said something about the east warehouse, and as Jiri watched she saw something flicker through the door. A splash of light, not fire or lightning—something blue-white, like when Linaria—

"No," she whispered, starting toward the warehouse. It was all open courtyard, and she gave up on the pretense of trying to hide, moving quickly instead, trying to look like she had purpose, like she belonged. Halfway to the building, she saw a group of guards spill out the door, some of them rushing toward her. Jiri's heart skipped, but she kept herself moving forward. The guards reached her and swept by, heading somewhere else, a Zenj man and a northern woman. In the man's long dreadlocks Jiri saw something gleaming. Ice, a long band of it, steaming in the rain.

Yes, Jiri thought, and kept moving.

In front of the warehouse, a northerner was snapping orders at guards. "—somewhere in the northwest corner, behind the crates of cocoa. You three go up the center aisle and help the others keep them pinned there. The rest of you will come with me. We'll sweep—" He cut off, seeing Jiri. "What?" he shouted over the rain and the city's roar.

Jiri started to open her mouth, but all the others had swung to look at her, and suddenly she felt her throat closing.

Don't do this. Not now!

"Gods, girl, use your tongue before I knock it out! What does Amiro want now?"

Her throat was locked, but Jiri made herself move. She shoved through the guards, put herself right in front of the northerner. Focused on him, ignored the others. *Amiro. What does Amiro want? Speak!*

"Amiro." The word barely squeaked out, and the man growled, leaned over and grabbed Jiri by the collar of her robe.

"Amiro what? I don't have time for —" He was shaking her as he spoke, his pale face dark with blood, and Jiri focused on that, on him, and her tongue finally moved.

"The prisoner escaped. Amiro needs men to hunt for her."

"What prisoner?" The man snapped.

"A . . . halfling woman. That's all he told me. 'Tell them to find the halfling woman, she escaped.'"

The man let out a stream of curses, shaking her with each word. But then he let her go. "Tell Amiro I have my hands full trying to catch these idiots *and* keep those rioters at bay. If I see any halflings, I'll kick them his way."

Jiri nodded, stepped back the moment he let her go. When he turned back to his guards, barking orders again, it only took one step backward to get into the warehouse.

There they were, trapped in the northwest corner, just like the man had said. Jiri edged her way along the wall, watching the fight. Sera was obvious, wrapped in her shining steel, only half-hidden by a crate. Morvius and Linaria were better concealed, but Jiri could see the marks of Linaria's magic, slick patches of melting ice, dripping spears of it hanging from the boxes and barrels that half-filled the warehouse.

In front of them, a group of guards crouched behind a line of crates, holding crossbows. They took the occasional shot, but seemed content to stay under cover and keep their targets pinned in their corner.

I have to do something, before those other guards get in here.

The large outside door to the warehouse stood half open, the path to it clear, and that was the problem. If they made a break for it, they would be shot full of quarrels before they covered half the distance. *If I had any spells ready . . .*

But I don't. So what do I have?

Jiri looked at the crates, the barrels, then scanned the rafters the same way she would check trees for leopards. And up there she saw it: a great net stuffed with bales of cotton, roped up out of the way. Behind her, Jiri heard the other guards coming in, and she raised her hand.

Fire came to her, easy as always, but she welcomed it now.

It flashed from her hand and struck true. Flames wrapped around the top of the net, right where it pulled together. The thick strands of hemp caught and parted.

It wasn't perfect. The whole net didn't give way and plummet onto the guards, but it was good enough. All the ropes on one side parted, and the net sagged, spilling cotton bales down onto the floor. They hit the stone and burst, each one exploding into a thick cloud of drifting white strands, filling the warehouse like a fog bank.

When the avalanche of bales began, Jiri started running. She charged through the drifting cotton, dodging crates, heading toward the door, hoping that Linaria and the others were doing the same. At the gap she threw herself outside, then looked back.

Morvius was out and running, Linaria hard on his heels, Sera not far behind. They crossed the street and stopped, looking back at the compound, and Jiri started toward them.

"We can't, not that way," Morvius was saying. "We need to circle around, hit them from a different spot."

"We've lost the cover of your diversion," Sera said. "How can we get in to find her now?"

"I don't bloody know," Morvius snapped. "But—" He cut off when Linaria hit him, turned to see what she was pointing at. He stared at Jiri, then nodded. "Right, we rescued her. Good on us. Shall we go?"

A crossbow quarrel buzzed out of the warehouse, smashing into Sera's shield.

"Time to go," Jiri agreed, and they started to run.

Chapter Eighteen
Leaving Kibwe

"What's happening?" Jiri gasped.

They were in a narrow lane well away from the Consortium compound, leaning against a warehouse's rough brick wall as they caught their breath. In front of them stretched a neighborhood of small houses, their thick earthen walls and thatched roofs dark shadows in the rainy night. The houses were quiet, but beyond them Jiri could hear voices shouting.

"There were more attacks while you were in there," Linaria said. "And the city was on the tipping point. People were getting scared, and there were stories. Of a woman summoning demons"—the white-haired woman glanced at Jiri, then away—"and that the Aspis Consortium was behind it. Among other stories. But then one of the hunting groups the Governing Council had organized showed up this afternoon with a bag full of biloko heads."

"They found the ones that attacked Pakala?"

Linaria nodded at Jiri. "Sounds like. At least a lot of them came back with burns. But they won, killed most of the biloko and drove the rest away. The council told everyone that the danger was past, and the whole city started celebrating."

"Too soon," Jiri said.

"Too soon." Linaria paused, staring at Morvius, who had just raised his hand. He was peering around the corner of the warehouse, and Jiri could hear footsteps: the slap of bare feet, and the heavier sound of boots. They all stood silent, even Sera, and watched a group of shadows move by. Consortium guards, or just caravaners, it was impossible to tell. When they were past, Linaria started whispering again.

"Another group of hunters was coming back to the city this evening. They were passing a sugarcane plantation when your All-in-Ashes fell out of the sky. At least that's what I assume it was. They described something like a man, with great wings of fire and smoke. When he landed, a circle of flames spread, destroying everything."

Did Patima do that? Does she control that thing now? The metal bag tucked beneath Jiri's arm felt heavier, the rings of it warmer against her side.

"The hunters ran back here, arriving in the middle of the celebration, telling everyone what they saw until the council got their guard to shut them up. Too late. The news started a fresh panic. Now the city is completely confused, some of it still celebrating, some panicking, and the rest either taking advantage or lying low."

"And we get to wade through it," Morvius said. "We're heading to the Red Spear, right?"

Linaria looked at Jiri, who nodded. She needed time to examine this kindi. Kalun's place would work well enough.

"Then we should move." Morvius shifted Scritch in his hands, looking at Jiri. "You're all right?"

"I'm all right," Jiri said.

"Good. You need to keep up." He started to turn away but stopped when Jiri put a hand on his arm. "What?"

"You came here to haul me out of the fire," she said. "Thank you."

Morvius looked down at her. "You're a pain in the ass, sometimes. So am I, sometimes. But no one deserves to be Corrianne's prisoner. Besides, Sera paid us to do it, and you did most of the work."

"Blessings rain down," Sera said, the first time Jiri had heard her speak since they left the warehouse. Her armor gleamed, flashing back a stroke of lightning. "Did you get what you went in there for?" The paladin nodded at the bag Jiri carried.

"I did," Jiri said. She didn't feel like saying anything else about what had happened in the Aspis compound, or how she had ended up inside it.

"Good. This hunt needs to start again." Sera's eyes flashed like her armor.

Jiri made herself meet those eyes and nod. Sera didn't intimidate her now. Maybe because of what had happened to her, maybe because she had gotten away, or maybe because Sera had come to help her.

Or it could have been all the sodden strands of cotton that were plastered into the tall woman's short hair.

They moved through the mud and the rain, sticking to the narrow lanes between the quiet houses. It was late, but lights still glowed behind many of the shuttered or mosquito net–covered windows. No one had sought their mats or hammocks yet.

Not when that rumble of voices still filled the night, a counterpoint to the rain.

The crowd was in the Adayenki and in the market, so Jiri and her companions avoided those places, taking the long road to the Red Spear. "What are they doing?" Jiri asked, as they walked between tall mud-brick boarding houses that bulged and grew together like termite mounds. The Adayenki lay just beyond them, and she could hear arguments and shouts.

"Being confused. And afraid, and angry." Morvius stopped where the lane turned abruptly out into an open square, looking it over carefully. "Waiting for daylight, mainly, so they can be less afraid and more angry. At least they're not rioting."

"No thanks to you," Sera said.

"I didn't hear any ideas from you on how to distract the Consortium guards back there," Morvius said. "Besides, all I did was convince a bunch of drunken kobolds that the Consortium had cheated them. No one else in this city was going to join them in doing anything. Which is too bad. If they had kept throwing rocks at the Aspis offices, we might have been able to sneak through that warehouse."

"How did you know I was there?" Jiri asked Linaria.

"Kalun has connections," the half-elf said. Then she reached out and touched Morvius's shoulder. "There's someone on the other side of the square. Behind the well."

Jiri squinted into the dark and the rain, but couldn't see anyone. Not until lightning flashed and she caught sight of a shadow moving around the edge of the communal well. She tightened up when she saw how small it was. "Mikki," she whispered, hands clamping down on the bag she held. She had no weapon, no magic . . .

"No. It's Fara." Linaria stepped away from the wall and waved at the girl. A few moments later the girl was gasping in the mud before them, her dreadlocks dripping.

"Father sent me . . . to find . . . you." Fara took a breath and shoved her wet hair out of her face. "Amiro is at the inn. With some of his people, and council guards. Says you attacked their compound and stole something."

Morvius glanced at Jiri and the bag she held. "Does he? What message did your father have for us?"

"Get out of the city and lie low," Fara said. "She thinks Amiro is calling in all his favors. He isn't sure he can protect you now."

Jiri stared at the girl, listening, thinking. She touched Linaria's shoulder, and whispered into the woman's pointed ear. "Amiro told me that he had spies in Kalun's house. His daughters."

Linaria turned her head, staring at Jiri with her strange eyes. "Amiro told you," she said.

Jiri paused, then felt her face heat in the rain. "He lied."

"Feda, Kalun's wife, has been taking money from Amiro for years. She splits it with Kalun, sometimes evenly. Kalun and Amiro, they play deep games with each other. But I trust Fara."

"Why?" Jiri asked.

"Because I know her. And I know Amiro."

Deep games. These men make Hadzi's lies so small. Jiri didn't say anything more.

Their politics were too complicated for Jiri to deal with now. She concentrated instead on what all their plotting likely meant: that the Consortium wasn't going to let her take this kindi out of Kibwe without a fight.

They were almost in the shadow of Kibwe's great wall when Jiri saw the ambush take shape. The rain in front of her shifted, splattering as if it were ricocheting off something that wasn't there. Then something was, furred and toothed, like a dog but much bigger, its eyes shining with a dull red light like coals about to die. The thing attacked, and Jiri didn't have time to shout. She just shoved her hands into Linaria's back and the half-elf stumbled forward, lurching into Sera, just out of reach of those snapping jaws.

The beast growled and lunged at Sera, teeth tearing at her armored leg, sending her sprawling. It went for her throat, then yelped as Morvius slammed Scritch into its flank.

Jiri's hand rose, growing hot, but she ripped her eyes away from the fight. That thing had been summoned, and that meant there must be a summoner. Spinning, Jiri searched the rain and the dark, and behind her—

Patima was there, just out of reach, her dark hair plastered to her shoulders, her eyes blazing. "Come with me."

Magic ran through her words, tangled around Jiri's soul like vines, and when she tried to pull away Jiri felt the bite of its power like thorns. Without thinking, she moved, walking away from the fight that raged behind her.

They ended up in a tiny square behind a shuttered coffeehouse.

"Close." Patima stopped, so Jiri jerked to a stop too, watching her, waiting, while inside her skull her thoughts screeched and leapt like a troop of monkeys, never resting, never going anywhere.

"So close." Patima's voice had lost its beauty sometime in the night. Her words were full of certainty, triumph, but they rasped out of her throat as if she had spent hours screaming. "Do you understand that? Do you know what it means?"

Patima turned, and her wide brown eyes danced with lightning. "It means I forgive you for trying to stop me. Come here."

Jiri stepped forward, even as her teeth clenched and her lips pulled back, baring her teeth.

Patima reached out and cupped Jiri's chin. She tipped Jiri's head back and stared down into her eyes. "You don't understand. No one understands. This world is wounded, and it bleeds nightmares. Nightmares that spread, that *infect*." Patima's fingers tightened on Jiri. "They infect me, but I know how to get rid of them now. I can burn them out." She smiled, a baring of teeth. "I will become the fire, and I will burn away all my nightmares. I will cauterize the wound that is Usaro. I will become All-in-Ashes, and I will *burn*."

"No." The word whispered between Jiri's teeth—a plea, a command, a prayer, all tangled together, all useless.

"You are marked by its flames," Patima said in her broken voice. "You are its herald, and you told me what I must do. You saved me, girl. You saved the world." Patima's hand fell from Jiri's chin and hovered, empty between them. "Now give me what's mine."

"N—" Jiri tried to speak, but that short syllable of resistance was too much. Her hands were moving, lifting the bag, but their smooth motion faltered. *Give me what is mine.*

Jiri's hands flew over the bindings that held the bag shut, wrenching it open. Her hand reached in, found Oza's necklace, and jerked it out. She reached in again, and this time she felt the searing heat of the All-in-Ashes kindi press against her palm, but she kept her hand from jerking back. Searching, she found the smooth wood of Shani's kindi and pulled it out. Then she handed the bag over.

Patima took it, holding it close as if desperate for its warmth. Her eyes were on Jiri, though, and the little kindi she held. "What—" she began, then stopped. The sound of puddles splashing beneath feet echoed up the narrow alley that led into this square, and moments later Mikki, Amiro, and Corrianne appeared, pelting through the rain.

"You have it?" Amiro held his warhammer in one hand, and the steel of his armor dripped with melting frost. "They're right behind us."

"I have it," Patima said.

"And you know where to go?" Amiro looked over at Corrianne, who was hunched over, gasping for breath, her ornate dress soaked with rain, her white skin livid with the red marks of Linaria's cold.

"No. I never heard of this damn place. But I can get us out of here and closer."

Amiro nodded, then pointed his warhammer at Jiri. "This one?"

"I'm done with her," Patima said. She turned to Jiri. "Tell them I'm going to burn all the darkness away. Tell them I'm going to save the world."

"They're coming," Mikki said, staring down the alley, a knife spinning in her hand. She launched it into the darkness, then skipped back, grinning.

"Let's go," Amiro said, and they moved together, linking hands.

Corrianne spoke, and the rain splashed down, plunging through the space where they had stood a moment before. Jiri stared at that empty gap, clutching necklace and kindi, and Patima's last words echoed in her ears.

When Sera pounded up behind her, pale face streaked with mud, armor and tabard gleaming, Jiri felt her lips move.

"She . . . will . . . save . . ." *No.* With a wrenching, sickening pain, Jiri tore at the thorny vine of Patima's magic, finally ripping it free from her soul.

"Save what?"

Jiri looked at the paladin, at Morvius and Linaria and Fara running up behind her.

"Nothing. She will save nothing. Least of all herself."

They slipped over the walls of Kibwe and into the night, moving until they found a village built not far from the edge of the great burn scar that surrounded the city. It was empty, the population fled to hide behind Kibwe's granite bastions. In its center was a crude echo of Kibwe's Governing Council's hall, and in the dry beneath its thatched roof, they stopped.

"Jiri," Linaria said, pushing back the frayed remains of her braid. "Come here."

"What is it?" Jiri hung back, seeing the careful way Linaria was watching her.

"Patima dominated you," Linaria said. "That kind of magic has a way of . . . clinging. I want to make sure it's gone."

"It's gone," Jiri said, angry and ashamed at the memory of the spell's violation, but Linaria just stared at her until she took a breath and nodded. "No, you're right. We need to be sure."

Linaria reached out, rested her hands lightly on Jiri's forehead, her lips whispering her magic.

Jiri felt the magic sweep through her, a cold wind that made her shudder, but left her clean, scoured, pure. "Thank you," she said, and Linaria nodded and stepped back.

"So." Sera stood in the center of the villagers' meeting space, the carved rafters meeting just above her head. The rain had washed the mud and blood from her face. "What now?"

"Patima took the kindi." Thoughts whirled through Jiri's head, jumbling together with what she had just heard from Patima and the others. "She thinks she can use it to make All-in-Ashes hers. To become it, somehow. But she has to take it somewhere first."

"Where?" Sera asked.

"I don't know," Jiri said. "But I know who to ask." She held up the little kindi she had carried out of the city with her.

"That thing?" Morvius said. "The thing that almost made you burn down the Red Spear last time you used it?"

Jiri glared at him, ready to retort, but she heard Linaria speak first.

"The thing you felt you had to keep secret from us?"

Jiri stared down at the little carving, its dark eyes staring blankly back at her.

I made my promise to Oza.

But Oza is dead, and all I have left are these people.

"I told you about fetishes."

"Yes," Linaria said. "Items that have a spirit bound to them, to give them magic."

"I said kindi were like fetishes. They are, but instead of spirits they hold a piece of someone's soul."

"A soul?" Sera frowned at the carving. "But it's not evil."

"No. They capture just a fragment of a freely given soul. Usually. My ancestors made them to hold knowledge, memories, stories, so they could be passed down. Using this one—" Jiri turned the kindi in her hand, careful of its sharp spearpoint. "I can speak to the little preserved ghost of a man who died long ago. I can see his home, listen to his stories, and it seems as real as us speaking now."

"Any memory?" Morvius said. "Sexy memories?"

"I suppose," Jiri said. She thought of all the kindi lining that room in the Pyre. "Someone must have done it."

"See, that's useful magic." Morvius tapped his fingers on Scritch's shaft. "So why did they stop?"

"There were dangers," Jiri said. "Sometimes people gave too much. Or too much was taken from them. The kindi became dangerous."

"Undead?" Sera asked.

"Maybe. Maybe something else. It was long ago, and the stories Oza knew were half lost." Jiri remembered huddling in the dark, listening to Oza whisper those story fragments that had been passed down, generation by generation. A kindi could have preserved them forever.

But magic always had a price.

"The kindi themselves could get dangerous, too. Those little ghosts in them sometimes went mad. Or they were mad from the start. They would try to take over whoever used them, pass from the kindi into the person's soul and possess them." Jiri made herself stop turning the kindi in her hands. "That was what Oza knew. What else they might have done, I don't know. I just know that the kindi were dangerous enough that my ancestors gave them up long ago."

Out in the night, sounds echoed up from behind Kibwe's towering walls. "They built many great things, but the kindi were their greatest. But Oza told me that their shamans came to understand that the magic of the kindi was something that would destroy them, so they gave them up." Jiri stared at those dark walls, a distant, angry heat kindling deep in her. "He said they destroyed them. Burned them, and buried their remains beneath the Pyre to be guarded, so that no one would learn how to make them again. That was the story he knew. But the real story was that they couldn't." *Did Oza suspect as much? I think he did. I think that's why he kept such a careful watch over them.* "They buried them, sealed them off, warned everyone away, but they couldn't give them up. So the kindi survived, until someone dug them up again."

"The Aspis Consortium," Sera said. "But what was the one that they stole? What is All-in-Ashes?"

"I don't know." Jiri met Linaria's eye. "I don't. I know from using this kindi that All-in-Ashes is a powerful, dangerous spirit. I know my ancestors feared it, but I also know that they were desperate. They were under attack from Usaro, and they wanted a weapon."

"A weapon," Morvius said. "Something that could wipe out a village in one strike. No wonder Amiro wants it. He could charge dear for that."

"It's not Amiro I fear," Jiri said. "It's Patima. She thinks she can control All-in-Ashes and turn it on Usaro."

"Usaro?" Morvius said. "Why?"

"She was there," Jiri said. "And they hurt her. Badly. All she can think of is revenge."

"Well." Morvius looked over at Linaria. "Why are we trying to stop her, then? I mean, I know Sera wants this thing's head for her trophy case, and Jiri is looking for her own revenge, but if Patima is doing all this to destroy one of the worst places in this whole rotten world, should we really be interfering?"

"If Jiri's right," Linaria said, "someone has already tried to destroy Usaro with this thing. And as I recall, Usaro still stands."

"My ancestors had a city. Much greater than Kibwe. I saw it in this." Jiri held up the carving of the spearman. "But I'd never heard of it before I used this. I've never seen its ruins. All that's left of my ancestors' works are the walls and statues of Kibwe, and the Pyre, where they buried their weapon. A weapon that I think turned on them."

Morvius grunted, but he didn't argue.

"Evil cannot be used against evil." Sera nodded at the kindi in Jiri's hands. "If you think using that will let us find All-in-Ashes, then use it. Let's finish this hunt."

Finish it. Not very long ago, Jiri had stood outside Thirty Trees with Oza, talking about Hadzi. In the time between then and now, her life had fallen away, piece by piece, like petals from a flower. Now this was all that was left. Finding Patima, finding All-in-Ashes, finding . . . *What? That my life is gone? That Mosa Jiri Maju is as dead as Oza and Hadzi?*

I will find their killers, and I will face them, and I will find an end.

Morvius set a stool out for her in the open.

"Better out here, than under all that dry thatch."

Jiri sat down on the stool and it sank deeper into the mud. The rain had passed, but water dripped from every branch and leaf in the jungle beside them, and wide puddles reflected the stars that peered through the broken clouds. Morvius was right, but Jiri still felt terribly exposed out here, knowing that soon she would be lost in the dream of the kindi that she held.

Linaria picked up on Jiri's hesitation. "We won't let anything happen to you."

Jiri nodded. "I know. I trust you."

"Do you?"

"I do," Jiri said. "You've earned it." *And I have to.* Jiri raised her hand, held her finger over the sharp point of the kindi's spear. She could feel their eyes on her, watching, and her hand hesitated. *Why? What does it matter now? Patima already made me break my promise, in the worst possible way.* Quick as she could, Jiri brought a finger down on that iron point. The pain flashed through her, quick and sharp, and she raised her finger. Blood ran from it, darker than her skin and darker than the wooden, ebony lips of the carving that Jiri spread it across.

"Speak," she said, "and I will listen."

"Be quick," she heard Sera say, but the words stretched out, became long and faint, and Jiri was falling into another night, into a city that had died long ago.

"Shani!"

The name echoed through the empty square, off the ornate buildings that towered over Jiri, the tall pillars topped with their soapstone statues. She moved, bare feet padding across the polished stone circle that surrounded the heart of long-dead Lozo.

"What's this? A woman calling for me?" Shani stepped out from behind one of the pillars, smiling. He was young, dressed in white cotton so fine it edged toward transparency. So handsome, so much like Hadzi, and Jiri's heart twisted, the pain sudden and unexpected. Behind him, the city began to come alive, lights springing up, whirls of color that hinted at moving crowds, the sound of music and laughter, the rich scents of curries and sweets. "And who are you, my lovely?"

"I'm Jiri, and I've been here before, Shani. Do you remember?"

Shani walked closer, Lozo waking around him. There were lanterns and people moving past, insubstantial but beautiful, gathering light and color and presence with every moment. "I remember many beautiful things, Jiri." Shani plucked a glass of palm wine from the hands of a woman wrapped in thin silk and stopped in front of Jiri, holding it out. "Lozo is a city of beauty. Come, I will show you, and tell you my stories."

Jiri took the glass from his hand. She could feel its weight, the hard edges of its facets. When she threw it down, she heard it shatter, felt the splatter of cool wine against her muddy feet.

"I don't want your dreams of your city, Shani. I don't have time for them."

"No time for Lozo?" Shani still smiled, but the city had stopped coming to life behind him, the music and the smell of good things fading from the air.

"Lozo is dead, Shani. Usaro destroyed it centuries ago."

"No." In a moment, Shani aged decades. His face split with lines, and his bright eyes went dim with age and grief. His clothes changed, became armor, leather brightly dyed and studded with iron, each piece of metal etched with a symbol of protection and warding. But that armor was torn, rent by claws, its colors half-covered with the dark stains of blood. In his hands he clutched a spear, its shaft rough with nicks, the tassels hanging below its blade clotted with gore. "My city."

Behind Shani, Lozo changed. The buildings went dark beneath a sky full of smoke, and the music became the sound of drums, pounding like a terrified heart.

Their thunder almost covered the noise coming from the high walls, the roaring and the screams that came from throats human and inhuman.

"No." Shani stared at the distant walls, holding his spear tight. "Lozo can't fall. The walls will hold, and my family . . ." Shani stopped, and overhead the smoke began to glow crimson and gold. "My son."

Shani spun, his eyes flashing with the light of the fire that flickered over the city. "They told me I could save it. Me. Shani the Strong. Those mages said we could do it. They promised me this would work!"

"What?" Jiri said. "What would work? What did they do to you and All-in-Ashes?"

"All-in-Ashes." Shani's face twisted. "They took me to see it. Bound in its prison, deep beneath our city. I saw it writhing in its chains, burning. The rock around it baked with heat, and the water, the blood of the earth, boiled. It was a monster, and they would make me part of it."

"How?" Jiri had to shout the words over the sound of drums and the wind that roared around them, reeking of smoke and blood.

"They had a kindi. They would put me in it. All of me, all my soul, and then they would bind All-in-Ashes to it, like a fetish. They would mix our spirits, make us one, so that I could control that thing. When they freed it, I would destroy the armies of Usaro." Shani dropped his spear caught Jiri's shoulders, pulling her close. "Do you understand? I will kill every demon-touched ape of that cursed place. I will burn them to ash, and I will avenge my son and save my city. My people. My wife. My daughter." He stared down at Jiri, his hands tight on her shoulders. "You look like her, a little. My daughter. What happened to her? Did I save her?"

"I don't know," Jiri said, almost a whisper. "Someone survived. The kindi were saved. The descendants of your people still live. Usaro doesn't rule this part of the Expanse. Shani, I need to know how the binding was done. Where it must be done."

He let her go, stepping back and staring up at the burning sky with shining eyes. "I don't know what they plan to do. I'm no mage. I just know they would put all of me in a kindi. Except this little piece, this part of me that I made them split off, so that some portion of me could remain untainted. So people could remember me." Shani bent and picked up his spear. "Did I fail? Did I lose control of All-in-Ashes? Was I not strong enough? Was it because I made them split this piece off?" Shani looked at Jiri. "No one remembers me, do they?"

"No," Jiri said softly. "Except me. Now. Please, tell me where this happened. I need to know."

"You remember," Shani said, then stood, silent.

Jiri waited, torn between a burning need to shake him from his reverie so that she could go, and the wish to take him in her arms and share his grief, so much like her own.

Finally, he spoke again. "They were going to take me to where All-in-Ashes was chained. The binding had to be done where that thing was weakest, in its ancient prison in the caverns below Lozo."

"And where is Lozo?"

"You don't know. It's gone, then."

"The city is gone," Jiri said. "But its descendants live. You saved them, but they're in danger. You have to tell me where Lozo was."

"How?" Shani asked. "If you've never heard of my city, what landmarks would you know? The Golden Road? The Clearing of An? The Steaming Eye?"

"No," Jiri said, fear curling through her. "No, I don't know— Wait. The Steaming Eye?"

"A small lake, just outside our walls. Its waters are blue, dark in the middle and lighter on the edges. The water is hot near the shore, and it boils and steams near the center. I told you how All-in-Ashes heated the springs."

"It steams," Jiri said. "It smokes." *Smoking Eye. The lake beside the village where I was born.*

The lake where the jungle's curse of fire was supposed to be strongest.

"It smokes," Shani said, and a curl of darkness drifted down from the sky, rolling over them.

Jiri felt its heat around her, and she coughed, but she still heard Shani.

"Do you know it?"

"I do," she gasped out. She coughed again, stared with burning eyes at Shani, a dim figure in the dark smoke, the sky crimson behind him.

"The Steaming Eye lay just before the gates of Lozo. Go there, and do what I wanted to do. Save our people."

Jiri nodded, her throat too tight to speak. *Go. How? Go!* She concentrated, and the city around her began to fade, to lose itself in the smoke. But before it could vanish, she saw Shani again. A man of smoke, and now—oh, by every spirit, she could recognize him now. She could see how that handsome face was the same as the twisted, monstrous mask of the thing that had flown over her when it escaped the Pyre.

"Remember me, Jiri," she heard his voice, faint and tearing apart. "Remember me, and my family, and my city. Remember that we fought. Remember that we were beautiful . . ." and the rest was lost.

Chapter Nineteen
Smoking Eye

Jiri opened her eyes, shivering and gasping.

Water soaked the robe she wore, dripped down her arms and braids. Morvius stood in front of her, an empty clay pot hanging from one of his hands.

"Did you just throw water at me?" Jiri's throat still felt raw, as if she had been breathing smoke again, and her shoulders ached from Shani's grip.

"I did. You were getting a bit smoky."

"Oh." Jiri could smell the smoke, like an echo from the kindi's vision, and see the dark marks on the cuffs of her robe. "Thank you."

"Do you know where All-in-Ashes is now?" Sera stood nearby, a little mud on one ear, but her tabard shone with the coming dawn's light.

"I do." Jiri pushed herself up, wavering on unsteady legs. Sera reached out and caught her, holding her up easily with one hand. "I can take you there."

"You will," Linaria said, "once you've rested."

Jiri and Sera spoke at the same time, their words tangling together. "We don't have time!" They broke off, frowning at each other, and Sera let go of Jiri's arm.

"You can barely stand, Jiri," Linaria said. "And when's the last time you meditated, or whatever it is that you do? Do you have any magic that you can do, now?"

"Patima hasn't stopped," Jiri said.

"Like you know," Linaria said. "Considering the spells Corrianne and Amiro threw at us last night, I damn well guarantee you they have. They won't want to walk unarmed into wherever Patima's taking them. Now. This place—where is it?"

"It's past Thirty Trees, in the jungles to the southeast. There's a hot spring, called the Steaming—Smoking Eye. It should be near there. It will take us all day, even if we go now."

"It will take us all day after resting for a bit." Morvius looked her over. "You have no magic, no weapon, and you're wet. We can lose by missing them, but we can also lose by showing up unprepared. Understand?"

Jiri stared at the broad-shouldered man, burning to move, to stop Patima. But with what? She was useless at the moment, helpless. "I'll walk with the spirits, and get my magic."

"Good," Linaria said. "I will meditate, and Sera will pray."

"And I'll stand here and play with my—" Morvius began.

"You'll keep watch," Linaria said, walking toward the shelter of the little pavilion at the center of the village. "And make us breakfast. And find Jiri a weapon."

"Anything else?" he called after her.

"Could you find me some better clothes?" Jiri asked.

Morvius rolled his eyes. "Sure. Shall I braid ribbons into everyone's hair too, while I'm at it?"

"No thank you," Jiri and Linaria said, echoing each other, but Sera stared soberly at the broad-shouldered man as she walked to the pavilion.

"Only if they match my armor," she said, running her fingers through her short-cropped hair.

By the time the song of the jungle had changed from night to day, they were on the trail.

Jiri had a belly full of food, a boy's rough shirt and pants, a long and wickedly sharp bush knife, and a head full of spirit magic. No sleep, but she didn't feel tired, and whether that was the tension running through her over the coming confrontation or the bitter sludge of coffee that Morvius had made her drink, she didn't care. She moved down the muddy path through the jungle, fast as she could while keeping an eye out, and still had to stop to let her northern companions catch up.

"How are we doing?" Linaria asked as they stopped beside a winding stream, swollen with the night's rain.

"Better than I thought," Jiri said, eyeing the thick curtain of vegetation on the other side of the water. "We should make Smoking Eye by nightfall, if we keep this pace."

"Easy enough," Morvius said, taking a drink from his waterskin, breathing easy. Jiri had touched him this morning, spending a little of the magic she had borrowed, and now he looked as cool in his armor as Sera. He had been quite happy about that, and had actually stopped calling Jiri 'runt' briefly. Right up until she insisted he leave coin to pay for the things they had taken from the empty village.

"This place," Sera asked. "Smoking Eye. You said you were born near it?"

"Yes. There used to be a village near the hot spring. Oza found me there."

"You told me that placed burned," Linaria said, carefully. "Why wasn't it rebuilt?"

"It had a bad reputation. Like the Pyre. Fire was always too eager in that place." *Like it is in me. I should have guessed that Lozo's ruins and the cavern that once held All-in-Ashes lay near there.*

"Your tribe. The Mosa. Did they fear you because you were from there?" Linaria asked.

Jiri looked at her sidelong, wondering what the woman was reaching for. *Will she wonder if I'm tainted, like Sera?* "Yes. All except Oza."

Linaria wiped the sweat from her pale face. "I grew up in a place called Irrisen. I left it, by trick and then by choice, but almost everyone who knows judges me for being born there, and they fear me, and refuse me their trust."

"I don't know that place," Jiri said.

"Few people do, in the Expanse. That's why I like it here. That and the flowers."

"Aw, you're making up. Sweet." Morvius tucked his waterskin back into his belt. "But aren't we supposed to be running headlong toward our fiery deaths?"

"Yes," Jiri said. "But lets deal with one possible death at a time." She bent and pulled a rock out of the mud, stared carefully at the patterns of leaves and vines on the other side of the stream, and then threw the rock, shouting, "Sa!" as she did.

The rock hit the leaves and something squawked, the noise like a bird call but deeper. Vines shifted and something stepped out onto the path across from them, an animal scaled and feathered, a birdlike thing the size of a man that stood on its hind legs, huge sickle claws twitching on its feet. Yellow eyes gleamed at them, and it opened its mouth and squawked again, showing sharp teeth.

"What in six hells is that?" Morvius settled into a fighting stance with his spear pointed at the creature.

"Makumo," Jiri said. "Dangerous, but much less brave when they know you've spotted them." She picked up another rock and threw it at a different spot in the trees. There was no squawk this time, but the leaves shivered as something moved behind them. "All of them."

The raptor on the trail in front of them twisted its head, listening to the retreat of its companion. Its bright eyes glittered as it faced them again, and the great claws on its feet twitched, as if eager to slash. Jiri stepped back, putting her smaller target behind Morvius's bulk, and Linaria slid in beside her. Sera stepped around them both, her sword hissing as she pulled it from her sheath.

Across the stream, the makumo pulled back scaled lips to show a thicket of hooked teeth, still glaring. But as Sera settled in beside Morvius, her shield up, it gave a disgusted-sounding grunt and darted after its companion, the green-and-black feathers of its back blending in rapidly with the undergrowth.

"That's what I love about this bloody jungle," Morvius muttered. "It's so full of nasty things."

"It's full of hunters," Jiri said, scanning the leaves on the opposite bank again before splashing across the stream. On the other side, the trail stretched on, empty of everything but the clawed footprints of those graceful, deadly beasts. "Let's go," she said, heading down the trail, searching the jungle around her for more hunters, and for her prey.

The trail narrowed, almost disappearing before it reached Smoking Eye. No human foot had trodden it, it seemed, since Oza had brought her here on her twelfth birthday. Jiri had wanted to see where she was born, and she found nothing but a tangle of growth, the jungle having swallowed the place where the village had once stood.

It would have swallowed this trail, too, but for the animals that used it. Jiri looked up from the tracks in the dirt, frowning into the dying light. The sun was almost down, and beneath the canopy the shadows were thick.

"This way," she said, and pushed her way off the trail.

They wound through the trees, over buttress roots and around fallen branches thicker than their bodies. Jiri winced at the sounds of her companions, the crunch of their boots, their muttered complaints, but she kept her focus on the jungle around her until it opened up.

The village was gone, but the water it had stood beside was easy to find. Smoking Eye lay still and steaming, a small, round lake, brilliant blue even in the fading light, its color growing darker until it became almost black in its center. There, the water stirred a little, plumes of steam rising from it. The plants growing on its bank were low, the great trees forced back by the heat, and Jiri could see all around the lake.

"There." The low light didn't make it easy, but Patima and her Aspis companions hadn't been subtle. A little ways around the lake, a trail had been carved into the jungle, bushes and vines cut aside. "That's where they went."

"Excellent." Sera pulled her shield around, settled it on her arm. "Now let's hope that this All-in-Ashes is there, too."

"Yeah, let's hope," Morvius said.

Jiri didn't say anything. She just looked over the water, at the jungle beyond it. *Lozo?* There was no sign of ruins, nothing but trees and shadows. Had time and jungle swallowed the city so completely?

Or had something else?

Jiri looked up once at the darkening sky, and started toward the path.

Beyond the lake, the ground rose, then fell. It was gradual at first, and Jiri barely noticed it as she picked her way through the jungle, following the mark of boots and cut vines. But then the ground sloped down sharply, except for a thin ridge of overgrown rock just ahead.

Jiri stopped, holding aloft the stone that she had wrapped a few bits of sunlight around. In its golden glow, joined with the sharp blue of Linaria's light, she could see bits of stone pushing up through moss and vines, sharp-edged pieces of broken granite. She bent and pried one free, looked at it. Then another. On the third stone, one moss-covered surface was smooth, and when she rubbed her fingers across it, peeling away the green, she found something carved into it, a symbol etched into the broken granite.

A symbol she had seen carved into the walls of Kibwe, and the passages of the Pyre.

"Lozo," she said, and stood. Holding up her light, she could see the ground falling on the other side of the crumbled remains of the wall, great trees growing over slumped piles of stone, still pools gleaming in the hollows between them. Some of those pools steamed in the dark.

Jiri scrambled over the stone, following the trail. *Lozo.* She had felt relief when she had seen the boot prints beside Smoking Eye, but this carving convinced her. This was dead Lozo, and this was where Patima had come with the kindi she had stolen. All Jiri had to do was follow her, praying to all her ancestors that whatever ceremony Patima had to do to bind All-in-Ashes to her, it was a long one. Following Patima's tracks, Jiri started to hope.

That hope crumbled when the trail dropped into a depression that lay before a great banyan tree and stopped at a wall of broken stone.

"The cavern where All-in-Ashes can be bound is beneath this place." Jiri ran her hand over the broken stone that lay at the end of the line of boot prints. "They must have found a passage down here, then collapsed it behind them."

"If we'd tried that, it would have fallen on our heads," Morvius said. "They're probably fine, though."

"Probably," Linaria said. "But how'd they know we were following them?"

"Did they know that?" Sera's hand was on her sword, and her eyes were searching the shadows around them. "Or were they fleeing something else?"

"What—" Morvius started, but the rest of his question was lost in a curse as he hurled himself at Linaria, knocking her down and rolling across the rough ground with her. A line of fire slashed down out of the night, hitting the ground where Linaria had been standing and sending up a whirl of burning leaves. More fire followed, a bright red bolt smashing off Sera's shield, making the white metal briefly red, while another crashed into a stone beside Jiri's head and showered her with sparks and glowing chips of stone.

Jiri slapped the searing bits of rock out of her braids and pressed tight against the stone of the rockfall. She saw their attackers now, snarling down at them from the branches of the tree above. Their yellow eyes, and the sharp teeth that filled their impossibly wide mouths, flashed in the light of the fire.

Biloko, and Jiri cursed herself for being so intent on Patima's trail that she'd missed them.

"I thought they were dead," she shouted, raising her hand to throw her magic at the hideous creatures overhead.

"The guard in Kibwe said they had killed *most* of them. The rest ran." Morvius rose from the ground, shifting away from Linaria, who crouched now behind a thick buttress root. "I guess we know where to."

"Can you catch them, like before?" Sera raised her shield to block a spear that slammed down from above.

"Yes," Jiri said, starting to release the magic. Then she closed her hand, catching the spell before it left her. The fierce red creatures dropped from the tree, hurling themselves at the companions. "No, too close," she said and let the green magic of the tangling spell roll into red. Fire shot from her hand and hit a biloko in the teeth as it charged her, knocking it back.

"Eh, there's not that many of the little bastards." Morvius swung Scritch around, slammed the spear deep into one of the biloko's bellies, then pulled it free. Spinning, he caught another one trying to rush him, sliding the spear easily through his hands and hammering the blade into the biloko's chest. Both of the creatures fell, and he was turning to find another when a burst of fire hit him, scorching across his armor.

"He comes!" a high, whistling voice shrieked. "I hear the beating of his wings, and taste the reek of his smoke on the wind!" A biloko stood away from the others, one hand still glowing from the spell it had just cast at Morvius, the other clutching something small and dark. "She will not claim him! He will burn her! He will burn us all!"

Brands marked the red skin of the biloko, symbols etched with fire into its skin, and Jiri recognized them—this was the one that had called to her, and said that she was marked, too. Fire gathered in her hand, but in front of her the biloko she had hit before was pulling itself up, hissing as it gaped its mouth open around its burned tongue. Jiri turned to it, but before she could throw her fire, Sera was there.

The biloko raised its spear, but Sera swept the weapon aside with her shield. Her sword followed, a vicious blur, and the biloko's head spun free of its body, tumbling away into the shadows.

"You won't have to wait for him to burn," Jiri said, and threw her fire at the branded biloko. It hit the creature, blackening the patches of moss and vines that covered its head instead of hair.

The biloko shrieked, something like pain and something like a laugh, then raised the kindi it clutched high over its head, pointing its other claw at Jiri. "Burn," the biloko howled, "all will burn, all will be ash," and sparks swarmed around its empty hand, gathering into a little ball of bright crimson which it brought back, ready to throw.

Jiri threw herself to the side, but the biloko tracked her. It changed its throw as its arm came forward, but before its hand snapped out and released the shining fragment of fire that it held, a line of white split the air.

Linaria's spell flashed through the darkness, there and gone like a lightning stroke, leaving a line of drifting frost like an afterimage in the humid air. That bolt of cold struck the biloko in the belly and a wave of white crackled over it, the burns of its brands swallowed by a tide of ice. Without a sound the biloko stopped, stuck in place by the cold that locked its muscles and wrapped it in ice. It stood, immobile, then tipped slowly backward.

There was an ugly sound when it hit the ground, like the breaking of crockery, and the ice-coated skin of the creature split and broke, shattering around the lines of its brands. Flames flickered as those frost-burned marks broke, and fire and ice met, flinging up steam and the reek of burning flesh. Then the fire winked out, there and gone as fast as Linaria's line of cold, leaving Jiri blinking in the darkness. She pulled herself up and her eyes readjusted, finding the charred corpse of the biloko sprawled in a patch of steaming mud.

"Well, that was thorough." Morvius shifted his spear, keeping its tip leveled at the two biloko who still crouched before him, the last of the creatures left. "I guess I'm stuck with the cleanup."

The biloko's yellow eyes flicked from the tall man to the wet, smoking corpse of their leader, and then they broke. One fled into the darkness, but the other scrambled back, toward the branded biloko's body. It stooped its headlong flight to pick up the kindi that the dead biloko had dropped, then kept running.

"Stop it!" Jiri shouted, scrambling after the thing. Her hand flickered with fire, but the biloko dodged behind the trunk of a tree. Jiri ran after it, scrambling over roots and through bushes, the crunching sound of her companions' boots right behind her. She had already lost sight of the biloko, but she could see the shaking leaves, the swaying vines that its passage had disturbed. Jiri ran after them, the light she held flashing around her, making shadows dance and lunge.

Because of those twisting shadows, Jiri completely missed the edge of the great sinkhole that suddenly opened in front of her.

She felt her foot going out into the empty air, saw the huge maw of the hole spreading open before her, but there was no way she could stop. Her arms spread, as if she thought she could grow wings, and something brushed across her fingers. With the desperate speed of terror, Jiri clenched at the thing that had touched her, fingers wrapping around a wrist-thick vine. Her hand locked onto it, her other hand dropping the stone she had wrapped her light around, letting it fall like a lost star as she grabbed at the vine with both hands.

It shook in her hands but held, changing her fall into a swing, her momentum carrying her out over the hole. Jiri clung to the vine, terrified that it would break, but as she reached the end of her momentum and swung back, she saw something that broke through her fear: Morvius, charging up the trail she had left, tearing headlong toward the cliff edge.

Jiri tried to shout a warning, but all that came out of her mouth was a sort of panicked gurgle. She pulled up her legs, tucking them in tight as she swung back, trying to time it. *Spear, spear, avoid that spirit-cursed spear* echoed through her head, then she was there, lashing out with her legs, catching Morvius in his belly with both heels. Avoiding Scritch, somehow, she sent Morvius flying backward onto his butt. The shock of the impact sent Jiri spinning backward, arcing over the edge again, her grip slipping as the world whizzed around her, but she hung on. Behind her, she heard the clatter of metal and the sound of cursing.

She swung back, her spinning slowing, and saw Linaria's white-blue light shining before her. By the time Jiri had swung out and back again she could make out Linaria standing over Sera and Morvius. The paladin was untangling herself from the broad-shouldered man, grunting out a series of words that didn't sound at all like blessings. Morvius, meanwhile, ignored her and laid back, his pale face paler, his mouth and eyes wide. Then, with a sudden *huuuhh,* Morvius pulled in a lungful of air.

"Wha?" he wheezed, finally sliding away from Sera.

Linaria looked at Jiri hanging from her vine, a few feet out from where the ground fell away.

"Jiri found a hole, and thought you should know about it."

Morvius pulled himself up, breathing raggedly. "Oh." He stared over the cliff edge, down fifty feet of ragged stone to the brush and rocks below. Then he looked out at Jiri.

"You have a damn good kick on you, runt."

"Thanks," Jiri said. Her hands were beginning to cramp, holding on so tight. "Could you pull me in?"

It took them a moment. Morvius stood near the edge and held onto Sera's belt as she leaned out and caught the tail of Jiri's shirt. When they pulled her in, Linaria grabbed the vine, keeping it from swinging back out. "Are you all right?" she asked Jiri.

Jiri opened and closed her aching hands. "Yes. The biloko—"

"Is right there." Morvius peered over the edge of the cliff. "Your light fell near it. It's not running anymore. It's kind of . . . oozing. Are we going down?"

"Yes," Jiri and Sera both said.

"Well then." Morvius tucked Scritch across his back. "Can't say I haven't been wanting to do this since I got to this damn jungle." He snagged the vine out of Linaria's hands and swung out on it, slipping down with a whoop that turned into a long drawn out "Owww!" before he hit the bottom.

"You all right?" Linaria called down.

"Yes," he called back in a tight voice. "But you might want to wear gloves when you do that."

Jiri pulled Sera's heavy leather gloves off and held them, waiting for Sera. The paladin stood before Morvius, staring intently into his eyes, her lips moving silently. Then she reached out and caught his head between her hands, holding it tight.

"Know her power. Iomedae. Know her name. Iomedae. Know her blessing."

Morvius shook in her grasp, and the angry red marks and blisters that marred his face, neck, and hands smoothed out and vanished. The only sign left of the biloko's attack and the friction of the vine were clean patches of skin.

"Damn," Morvius said. "Like being kissed by an angel and kicked by a mule, both at the same time. And all for free."

"You think so?" Jiri said, handing Sera back her gloves. The paladin didn't say anything about Jiri's comment, but her lips turned up in a tiny, smug smile, like a cat.

Shaking her head at them both, Jiri stepped away and examined the broken corpse of the biloko. It had gone off the same edge that had almost claimed Jiri, but it hadn't caught a vine. Instead, a large chunk of broken limestone had caught it. Walking carefully around the dark blood that had splashed the tangled plants and vines, Jiri reclaimed her light and held it up. It only took a moment to find what she wanted.

The kindi was shaped like a man, intricately carved in mahogany. But the figure's face was huge and distorted, taken up mostly with mouth. That great, grinning mouth was filled with teeth made of iron, their points gleaming in the light. When she picked it up, Jiri carefully avoided the sharp points of those fangs.

"Those tracks we found in the Pyre," Linaria said, looking at the carving.

"That biloko, up there. The one who cast spells. It went into the Pyre after we killed the demon and found this." Jiri could see it so clearly. The biloko running its hand over the carving, catching a finger on a tooth, its blood spilling on the kindi's lips. "I think they bound a piece of a sorcerer's soul to this kindi. Too big a piece. It took that biloko over and added madness and magic to its hunger."

"I didn't understand most of what it said. But it talked about burning."

"All-in-Ashes." Jiri stood, holding the hideously grinning kindi. The carving felt hot like a fever, uncomfortable in her hand. "It was talking about All-in-Ashes. That spirit . . . spread, I think. You saw what it was doing to the Pyre, burning it down, bit by bit. I think it was doing the same thing to the souls that were bound in all those kindi." Jiri pulled out the little bag that she had tucked beneath her shirt. She didn't really want this evil little thing to share space with Shani's kindi or Oza's necklace, both of which were nestled inside, but she couldn't leave it here. She dropped it in and knotted it shut, but she could still feel it, its heat bleeding through the bag and irritating her, turning her thoughts toward anger and flame.

I need to get rid of this thing. I can't have it near me when I confront All-in-Ashes. Between the both of us, there will already be too much fire.

"Where now?" Linaria asked.

Jiri lowered her light, getting it out of her eyes, and looked around. They stood at the bottom of a huge hole, crumbling cliffs of limestone curving away into the shadows in both directions. The jungle rolled over the edges and filled the pit with green, but the brush and plants were lower here, the trees stunted, unable to grow roots deep enough to stretch tall. Jiri could see the night sky above them, a swath of bright stars interrupted by the darkness of a bank of clouds coming in from the west, lighting flickering silently in their bellies.

"Down," she said.

"There's a cave over here," Morvius said.

Jiri nodded, and headed toward him. He stood beside a great stone that jutted from the ground, a foreign piece of granite among the limestone, its edges a little too even. Brushing the dirt away, she saw that it was the corner of a block, found the traces of carvings that marked it.

"There was a city here called Lozo," she said. "The man bound to the kindi I used, Shani, he said they found All-in-Ashes in one of the caverns beneath the city. I think when Lozo fell, it really fell. The caverns beneath it broke open, and the city was swallowed."

"The Mwangi is full of ruins," Morvius said. "It's like civilizations come here to die."

"Is it any different elsewhere?" Jiri asked. "Tribes, cities, nations—they sprout like trees, and if they find the right conditions they thrive and grow, become mighty, and cast their shadow over every competitor. But like trees, like everything, they all eventually fall. And in the clearings they leave behind, new things grow."

"You sound wiser than your age," Sera said. "Sometimes."

Sometimes? Jiri bristled. *I don't think I'll tell her that Oza explained that to me, years ago.* "All things follow a cycle."

Beside the stone, a dark hollow opened in the ground, a crevice carved into the rock by water, and a tiny stream ran down its mossy bottom. Jiri carefully dropped into it and found herself in a narrow passage that twisted down into the ground. She stared down its dark throat, and from the sky far above she heard a rumble of thunder. If that storm unleashed a torrent while they were in this passage . . .

That's all we need now, a chance to drown before we can burn.

"Well?" Morvius said, standing over her. He had cut loose a long vine and was wrapping it into a coil, a clumsy rope. "We going in?"

Jiri breathed in the scent of warm water and stone, of rot and stale air, remembering the Pyre, the pool before it and its dangerous passages. Thinking to herself that whatever waited for them in the bowels of this long-broken city, it was going to be worse than what they had found there.

"Yes," she said, and started down.

Chapter Twenty
Mud and Light

The cave was barely more than a crack, narrow and wet, and as the thunder faded behind them it was replaced with the clack and scrape of Sera's armor against the stone.

"Gods damn me, I'm going to scrape my balls off in here," Morvius growled. "This passage does lead somewhere, doesn't it?"

How should I know? You found it. Jiri kept the words locked between her teeth and pushed forward, feet slipping on the strange black moss that grew beneath the shallow water covering the bottom of the cave. Water that might have risen a little, maybe.

If this place floods, it will come fast. We might already be too far from the entrance to turn back. We just have to keep going forward, toward—

Light? Jiri stopped, peering through the shadows ahead. Shadows that flickered and pulsed, vanishing and then coming back.

Was that—?

The sound of thunder echoing down the cave confirmed it. That had been lightning. Jiri hurried forward, squirming through the crack until she found the opening through which that light and sound had spilled.

For a moment, her stomach clenched. *Have we just gone in a circle?* The cave opened into a deep pit whose steep limestone walls dripped with vines and brush and small trees. Another sinkhole, like the one she had almost fallen in, but looking out at it Jiri saw the differences. This sinkhole was larger than the first, and a great mound of broken rock rose up in its center, a small mountain of rubble covered in ferns and white-flowered vines. A dead tree stood on the mound's peak, its twisted limbs raised toward the storm-covered sky, like a corpse hand reaching for one last bit of light.

The stream they were splashing through tumbled down into a pool of mud that stretched along the base of the overgrown mound. Bubbles rose from its dark surface, swelling to obscene size before they burst and splattered. It was a bowl of boiling mud, and beyond it Jiri could see the mouth of another cave, there and then gone in a flash of lightning.

Ferns hung over the edge of the pool fifty feet from where Jiri stood—too far to jump—and the walls of the cliff were too sheer and smooth to climb here, especially with the rain pouring down. But the bubbles in the mud were rising on the other side of the pool, and the hot spring that birthed them must be over there.

How hot is the mud here? How deep?

With great care, Jiri held one foot out over the mud. Hot, but not painful, and she slowly let her foot touch.

The mud was thick and sticky, warmer than her blood but not scalding. With one hand holding tight to the thick stem of a bush that hung out from the wall of the sinkhole, Jiri shifted her weight to the foot that rested in the mud. It sank in to just above her ankle, then stopped, and Jiri pulled her foot back out with only a little effort and a nasty sucking sound.

"Hand out the vine," she told Morvius, who stood with the others behind her, looking dubiously at the mud. "Everyone space out and take hold of it. I'll go first."

"Shouldn't we tie ourselves to it?" Sera asked.

Jiri shook her head. "Don't take this wrong, Sera—I think I'm actually starting to like having you around— but if you step into a deep hole wearing all that steel, I'm dropping this vine and letting you go to your goddess alone." Sera frowned and Jiri shrugged. "Sorry."

"About not wanting to die? That makes perfect sense. We came to this place with a purpose, and it wasn't to drown in a mud puddle." Sera took the vine from Linaria and passed its end to Jiri. "I'm just worried about what I'm doing wrong, if someone in this group likes me."

Is she joking? Jiri wondered. Was I? Have I started liking these people? Linaria, yes, but Morvius? Sera? Gods and crocodiles, when did that happen?

Now wasn't the time to worry about that. Holding tight to the vine, Jiri stepped one foot into the mud, then the other. The oozing earth shifted under her feet, treacherous and uncertain, but she didn't sink any deeper than her ankles. Carefully, she picked her way through the sludge, holding the vine in one hand and touching the limestone wall with her other, ready to catch herself if one of her feet sank too deep.

The mud rose up her shins, almost to her knees, and Jiri fought for each step, working her legs through the slimy grip. It was getting hotter, too, not quite burning, but uncomfortable, and that matched the heat of Jiri's impatience. *Is Patima wading through mud somewhere, too? Or has she already found the chamber where All-in-Ashes was bound?* Jiri jerked her leg forward, trying to reach the stones rising from the mud ahead, the opposite edge of the pool so close, and stumbled, barely saving herself from falling face-first into the muck by pressing her hand to the wall beside her.

"Step carefully, Jiri," Sera said, behind her. "Haste won't help us here."

Did I say I liked having her around? The vehemence of that thought surprised Jiri, the rage in it so sudden and hot. Her hand left the wall and touched the pouch that held the kindi. The one she had taken from the biloko pressed against her belly, hot and almost painful, like an infected wound. *I need to get rid of this thing.* Taking her hand away, Jiri moved, grim but slow, picking her way through the last of the mud until she pulled herself out on the other side. Out of the mud, she slid her bush knife out and chopped a few feet off the end of the vine she held. Then she tied the rest of the vine off to the trunk of a small tree that pushed itself out of the stone above the pool.

"What are you doing?" Sera asked as she pulled herself up out of the pool, her boots squelching with mud.

"I need to get rid of this kindi," Jiri said. "But I don't want to destroy it."

"Why not?" Sera had turned to help Linaria up out of the mud.

"Because I don't know what will happen if I do. I might just free that bit of soul that's trapped in there, let it go to come after us." Jiri started up the fern-covered mound of broken stone that covered the bottom of the sinkhole, the rain tapping on her braids and washing the mud from her skin. A little way up, buried beneath a drift of white flowers, Jiri found a good-sized chunk of stone. Soapstone, she realized as she picked it up, and beneath the moss that coated it she could still make out its shape: a hand, fingers bent and tipped with claws. *Perfect.* "But I want to make sure no one ever picks it up again."

Jiri pulled the carving out of the bag, making sure her fingers came nowhere near the iron teeth. It glared at her with its blank wooden eyes, and Jiri could feel the fever heat pouring out of the wood. *Were you a good man once? A teacher? Or did they put your soul in such a nasty carving as a punishment?* It didn't matter. All-in-Ashes had touched this thing, and Jiri could feel its taint boiling out of it.

The infected heat of it pulsed in time with her barely checked anger.

Jiri wrapped the piece of vine that she had cut away around the carving and the stone hand, binding them together. When she was done, she started up the rough hill, heading up and back toward the deep end of the mud pool. When she stood over it, staring down at the bubbles that belched and popped below, she held out the kindi. "Whoever you were," she said quietly, "we don't want you anymore." Her hand opened, and she let the carving go.

It fell into the boiling mud, resting on the surface for a second. Then the weight of the stone hand dragged the dark wood down, pulling it beneath the mud. Gone.

"Good," Sera called up to her, and Jiri nodded. Dropping that nasty thing felt like pulling a thorn out.

"Perfect," Morvius said, pulling himself up out of the pool. "We could have sold that, you know."

"Evil never brings wealth," Sera said.

Morvius sat down on a stone, pulling at one of his mud-covered boots. "Do you actually listen to half of what you say?" he said, popping the boot free. He held it up and mud slid out, plopping wetly onto the ground. "Do you realize most of it's crazy? Evil brings all kinds of coin—that's why people *do* it. And I could really use some new boots."

Jiri ignored them, wiping the rain from her face and staring down at the curve of the wall. There, half covered in brush, she saw another narrow crack leading away from the sinkhole. Toward the cavern she wanted?

Maybe.

Jiri closed her eyes. Did she know where she was going? No. Did she know where Patima was? No. Did she have any idea of how to stop Patima or All-in-Ashes if she found either of them? No. The uselessness of it all poured over her. Every time she had met Patima, the woman had beaten her easily. What chance did she have now?

Why even go?

The thought echoed through her, even as Sera called up, "Which way should we go?"

No way. All paths led to the same place, didn't they? To death and ruin? Oza was dead, Thirty Trees was gone, and if Patima burned the rest of the world, did it even matter?

Yes.

That thought, that spark of anger, burned bright among all the ashes of Jiri's sudden despair.

It matters, Jiri thought, and raised her head. She was walking, not down the hill but up, toward the trunk of the dead tree that stood at the top of the pile of stones. Rain fell on its broken branches, a steady patter of drops, and below that sound Jiri could hear something else now. A low, keening noise, a soft dirge of a song that was all sorrow and sweet sadness and the promise of the succor of sleep. Everlasting sleep, free from all her pain . . .

The spark of Jiri's anger caught, and she didn't fight it. She wrapped herself in its heat, shaking her head and snapping herself out of the song that spilled from the cracks in that twisted tree. In those cracks, she could see something flicker, and a vine slipped out of one like a snake, twisting silently through the air like a blind worm, searching.

Umdhlebi.

A dead tree possessed by a vicious, evil spirit that filled its victims' heads with lies and despair. Oza had taught her about them, warned her, told her that if she should ever meet one, she must—

"Run!" Jiri spun, stones clattering beneath her feet, and started tearing down the tumbled stone slope, ferns and flowers whipping around her legs, wet moss slick beneath her feet. "Go!" she shouted at the others, who were staring up at her sudden flight. She pointed toward the gap she had seen, arm bouncing as she leapt down the slope.

Morvius moved first, slamming his boot back on, pulling his spear free and bulling forward through the brush. Linaria came after, right on his heels. Sera stood still, though, pulling her sword and settling her shield on her arm, her eyes on the crest of the hill and the tree that was not a tree.

There was a sound behind Jiri, a groaning crack and the grind of stone against stone. She wouldn't look back, didn't have to in order to know the umdhlebi was pulling itself out of the stone to follow her. Keeping her eyes on the ground in front of her, she ran toward the narrow passage, still shouting.

"Move, Sera!" The umdhlebi was slow, but if the paladin waited too long it would cut her off, trap her between the mud pool and its long vines. Thankfully, the woman in the bright armor started to move, following Morvius and Linaria. Not as fast as she should, but fast enough.

Jiri reached the edge of the sinkhole right as Morvius and Linaria caught up, and she ran past them, pulling at the curtain of vegetation that half-covered the wide crack in the stone. "Here," she called, and they piled in. Sera was coming, running slowly in her armor, and Jiri looked up the rough slope of broken rocks. The umdhlebi was moving, a tall broken trunk riding on a nest of roots that twisted through the stones. Thick vines pushed their way out of the cracks in the trunk, black tendrils covered with blood-red thorns that lashed through the air with predatory hunger.

"What is that thing?" Sera gasped, but Jiri just grabbed a handful of the paladin's shining white tabard and started to run. Sera clanked behind her down the twisting crevice. The walls came together somewhere overhead, and the rain stopped falling on them, but the only light was Linaria's, bobbing along ahead. Jiri had left hers somewhere back with the tree monster, and she had no interest in going back for it.

They caught up with Linaria and Morvius in a place where the passage widened into a chamber, empty of everything but stalactites and water dripping into a clear, shallow pool that filled the center of the small cavern. Four more passages spilled into this room, and Linaria was holding up her light, staring at them.

Jiri and Sera stumbled to a halt, breathing hard. Morvius looked past them, up the passageway they had come through. "Did you lose it, or do we keep running?"

Jiri shook her head. "It didn't follow us far. Umdhlebi are too slow to chase down unwounded prey."

"Then why all the running?" Morvius said.

Jiri took another deep breath and straightened. "I wanted to keep you out of range of its song. If you hear it, it makes you give up, give in. Those who hear it will go lay themselves at the umdhlebi's base and let its roots tear them apart."

"I didn't hear anything," Morvius said.

"That would be because of all the running." Linaria lowered the glowing stone she held and looked at Jiri. "Are you good? You were starting to walk toward it, before all the running and screaming. Which I appreciate."

"It caught me, for a moment," Jiri said. "I should have recognized it the minute I saw it, but I was so distracted thinking about that kindi, about Patima. If Oza's spirit is watching me . . ."

"If your dead teacher's watching, ask him to tell you which way we should go." Morvius nodded at the other passages. "Or are we going to keep using the let's-just-guess approach?"

Jiri's anger, so useful with the umdhlebi, wasn't going to help her with Morvius. But she couldn't hold her tongue completely. "She's down here. We'll find her." Jiri held out her hand, and Linaria handed her the light.

"Of course we will. Everything else has worked out fine so far." Morvius leaned against a column of lumpy stone, staring down into the pool. "Let me know when you're ready. I'll just watch these little glowing crabs wrestle until then."

Jiri gritted her teeth, feeling hot, but at least this time her anger didn't have that strange, sick feeling that had wormed through her when she carried the iron-toothed kindi. No, this anger was very familiar. *Because it's mine? Or because this taint of fire has been in me since my birth?*

Ignoring the question, Jiri walked the edge of the cavern, checking each of the other caves that led into it. All of them looked natural, but their floors were too smooth and even, obviously worked at some point long ago. All of them were stone, free of dust, and unmarked.

Untracked.

Jiri walked from one to the other, frustration adding to the fire smoldering in her heart. One passage seemed to go up. One down. The other two ran straight. The last was the one they came in, and that was the only one she could cross off.

Ignore that one. Ignore the one that runs up. Take the one that goes down? Jiri went back to the mouth of that passage. Silent, empty, bare, just like the others, no tracks, no—

The stark blue-white light from the stone she held glittered off something on the floor.

Jiri bent down and picked it up. It was a tiny crab, dead, its almost-clear shell crushed. Holding it close to her face, she could smell it, like water and fish. It hadn't been dead long.

"Morvius," she called back, staring up at the walls of the passage. "What are those crabs doing?"

"Wrestling. This one has a bigger claw, but the other's a goer, and—"

"What else?" Jiri said.

"Glowing. They've got some kind of light in their shells, like lightning bugs. Blue instead of green, though. I wonder what they taste like?"

Blue. Jiri took the light Linaria had made and wrapped it in the bottom of her shirt, covering it. The cave they were in went darker than night.

"What are you doing?" Linaria called, but Jiri was looking at the mark on the wall in front of her at waist height. A smeared blue line, with another line struck at an angle through it, glowing faintly in the dark.

"They went this way," Jiri said, certain, a sort of vicious joy blossoming out of the heat of her frustration.

"Are you sure?" Sera asked.

Oh yes. That line would be eye level for Mikki. *But.*

369

Fighting to keep herself from running down the downward-slanting passage, Jiri unwrapped the light just enough to make her way over to the other tunnels. At the mouth of each passage she covered it again and stared at the walls. Nothing, nothing—then, at the second level passage, another mark. A blue line, glowing much brighter, and without the second line crossing it.

They came in from one of the other passages and tried the downward one first. It must not have worked, so they came back and did this one. They don't know the way either, and now we're on their trail.

"Here," she said, pulling out the light. "They went this way, not too long ago."

"Didn't you just say—" Morvius started.

"They went this way, not so long ago," Jiri said, each word a snarl, pointing at the passage.

"Ten hells, runt, all right. That way."

Linaria came up to Jiri, touching her arm before she could start down the passage. "How close are they?"

Jiri shook her head. "I can't say for sure. Close enough to hope, but we have to hurry."

"Let me go first, then. I can see in the dark better than any of you, and we can keep the light back so we don't warn them."

"You sure that's a good idea?" Morvius said. "If we get ambushed, you're not good toe to toe."

"And Jiri is?" Linaria asked.

"Nothing personal to Jiri, but I care a hell of a lot more about your ass than hers."

"How sweet," Linaria said. "But—"

"I'll be with her," Jiri said. She looked up at Linaria. "You watch, I'll listen. I trust you to keep me from walking into walls or over cliffs."

Linaria nodded. "It does keep the noisy ones behind us."

"Noisy?" said Morvius. "Who's noisy? Our armor—"

"Is probably not what she's talking about," Sera said. "Are we going?"

Jiri nodded, her hands itching with heat, and started down the tunnel.

They wound down into the earth, moving through darkness.

If she looked back, Jiri could see the light that Morvius carried, like a bright star behind them, but it did nothing to break the shadows that surrounded her and Linaria. The half-elf moved confidently, though, and she kept a hand on Jiri's back, guiding her. It's no different from traveling through the jungle at night, Jiri thought. Except for the silence. That surrounded them, heavy as the darkness, broken only by their breathing, the soft scrape of Jiri's feet and Linaria's boots against the stone, and the constant drip of water.

They passed a few more of the glowing marks, the guts of those poor little crabs crushed against the walls. Every time they followed one that wasn't crossed out, Jiri felt better. Every false turn Patima took meant they were gaining on her, and Jiri moved as fast as Linaria would let her, eyes straining in the darkness, listening. Listening, and what was that?

Linaria's hand closed on Jiri's collar, bringing her up short. Jiri felt the woman shift beside her, felt her lips almost brush her ear as she whispered.

"There's light up ahead."

"I think I hear something, too." Jiri strained her ears, but Linaria's whisper had overwhelmed them. "Maybe."

"I think the tunnel curves. We'll go that far and see what we see."

Linaria started forward, hand light on Jiri's back. They crept up the passage, and Jiri could see the light now, could start to see the shape of the walls ahead of her. She did hear something: a voice, sharp and grating.

"Corrianne," she whispered to Linaria, and the half-elf's grip tightened for a moment on her in acknowledgment. They slipped forward along the tunnel's curve until they could finally see around it.

The passage dropped down a steep slope, getting larger as it fell. The walls pulled back and the ceiling rose, its top lost again in shadow. Then the cave ended in a rippling wall of stone, a mass of columns that had grown together, completely blocking the passage except for one opening, a low, carved arch with two statues flanking it. Two women, their hands raised in warning, twins to the statue that Thirty Trees had named the Mango Woman. Their faces were stern, their frowns carved deep into their stone, as if they could see what stood before them.

Corrianne still wore the dress she'd had on in Kibwe, its black silk tattered, its long skirts covered in mud. "—trapped in her insanity," she whined. "What profit is there for us, even if she succeeds?"

"If she destroys Usaro?" Amiro stood not far from Corrianne, using a rag to scrub dried mud from his armor. A ragged semicircle of skeletons crouched before him, short things with gaping eye sockets and strangely hinged jaws—the bones of biloko, pulled together into a parody of life by Amiro's prayers. One of them held a heavy staff, its end glowing with golden light. "Quite a lot. What kind of treasure do you think the Gorilla King has amassed over the centuries?"

"You don't really think she'll do it, do you?" Corrianne said.

"It seems unlikely," Amiro said. "But there's a chance, and the payoff is worth the gamble. I think it more likely that she'll end up destroying Kibwe."

"Yes, but why would we want that?"

"Kibwe's the center of a growing trade network, which makes it valuable to the Consortium. But it's also a center of tribalism and entrenched power." Amiro shook out his cloth. "If it were destroyed, trade would be disrupted, but there would be an opening for a new power to take over this part of the Expanse."

"If they were poised to sweep in after the destruction." Corrianne made a face. "I'd lose all my dresses, though."

"There will be money for new dresses if that happens."

"And if Patima fails, and that thing kills her?"

"Always a chance. Why do you think we're doing guard duty out here?" Amiro bent over to study one of his skeletons. "We'll wait until her ashes have cooled, then go get that ugly carving. It will fetch a price big enough to make this all worth our while."

"Always doing the math, aren't you, Amiro?" Corrianne purred. "That's why I put up with you." She stepped closer to the man, ignoring the skeletons as they shifted, watching her with their empty sockets. Her hand rose to rest on Amiro's arm. "We would sell that thing, but what about the rest of her equipment?"

Amiro took one small step away, just enough to leave Corrianne's hand hanging in the air. "You know our rules, Corrianne. You want that amulet, you can have it. If you pay the rest of us for it."

Corrianne's face went sulky. "It's always about the coin, isn't it? That's the only way you know how to tell who's winning." She pulled her hand back and stared into the shadows. "Money isn't the only kind of power."

Following the mage's gaze, Jiri realized something crouched in those shadows. Something hunched and huge, its vague outline ragged with fur, small eyes gleaming like blood in the light it shunned.

"Amiro, six biloko skeletons, Corrianne, and . . ." Jiri looked at Linaria, standing between Sera and Morvius.

"Some kind of demon. Big as the swamp one we fought, but not the same. This one looked like an ape, with horns and something wrong with its chest. I couldn't really see." Linaria shook her head. "Damn Patima and that damn amulet of hers."

"Baregara," Sera said. "A creature of the Abyss. They have another mouth in the center of their chests."

"Have you ever fought one?" Morvius asked.

"No," the paladin said, and there was an edge of anticipation in her voice. "They're supposed to be very dangerous."

"Marvelous." Morvius stared down at the rocks Jiri had arranged on the floor of the passage, a crude map of what she and Linaria had seen. "Patima set them there to block us, so she must have found the place she wants to be. She's buying herself time to do this binding thing Jiri told us about. We go in there and they'll go on the defensive, summoning everything they can, slowing us down, giving her time while they try to kill us off."

"Can we get by them?" Jiri asked.

"Do you know another path?" Morvius asked. When Jiri shook her head, he nodded. "Didn't think so, and we don't have the time to look for one. And it's not like we can sneak by them."

"Not all of us," Sera said. "But one of us might, while the others engage them." Her brown eyes were on Jiri.

"Maybe," Jiri said. "Maybe I could get by." *If I just ran and left you behind. Like Oza.* "But Patima is stronger than me." It hurt to say the truth, but she had to. "And we haven't seen Mikki yet."

"Mikki is probably hiding somewhere in that chamber, waiting to ambush us," Morvius said. "Patima. Well, she should be involved in whatever ceremony she's attempting. She may be vulnerable, and you might not even have to fight her. Just throw her off, delay her. Kick over her magic candles, or piss on her ceremonial circle. Whatever it takes to stop her until we can get through."

"*If* we can get through," Linaria said, staring down at the stone that represented the baregara.

"That's my line," Morvius said. He frowned down at the stones. "We have surprise, at least. They may

have set up guards, but from the way you said Amiro
and Corrianne were chatting, I don't think they really
expect us. If we hit Corrianne hard and fast, take her
out before she can cast, we might have a chance. That
demon, though . . . If we had some way to slow it down,
keep it off us . . . Why haven't you learned how to summon monsters out of thin air yet, Linaria? All of our
enemies seem to be able to do it."

"I can," Jiri said.

"Yeah, I liked the frog, but I don't think it's going to
cut it this time," Morvius said. "We need something
bigger."

"I think, this time, I can summon something bigger."
Jiri thought through the magic she had bargained from
the spirits, and decided she could do this. No matter
how dangerous it was.

"We'll just need something for our ears."

Chapter Twenty-One
Scald

Jiri stopped, gasping for air.

Just ahead, the cave curved, and over the hammering of her heart she thought she could hear the mutter of voices. *A little closer and they'll see my light. I have to time this just right.* Forcing herself to breathe, to be calm, she gathered in a spell that she had bargained away from a spider spirit back in that empty village near Kibwe. She stood still and let the magic settle into her skin and bones, then looked back the way she had come.

Where are you? Come on. Jiri held up the light her magic had made, the glowing stone that Morvius had carefully wrapped cloth around so that only one side shone. *Come on.*

The passage behind her was empty, silent, and Jiri hissed between her teeth.

"Come on, you cursed thing! Aren't you hungry?" She whispered the words, but she stomped as she did, driving her bare foot into the floor. "Your ancestors look down and laugh at your misery, and when you die they'll feed your festering spirit to the ghosts of jackals!" Jiri stomped again, and the sweat on her skin began to steam, taking the heat from her anger, her terror.

Then she felt it. A tremor in the passage as if something huge were dragging itself toward her.

That's it. Come get me. Jiri forced down her terror. Her eyes swung to the side of the corridor and found the crevice where the others were hiding, somewhere in the dark out of sight, strips of cloth wrapped over their ears. The tunnel shook again, and at the limit of Jiri's light, something moved, slithering across the floor like a snake.

Jiri glanced one more time at the place where her friends were hidden, then turned toward where Corrianne, Amiro, and the demon waited.

Alone.

To Oza, and to any other honored ancestor who's watching, let this work. Jiri let her prayer go, ripped away the cloth she had tied around her ears, and started forward, just fast enough to stay ahead of the thing that pursued her.

"Stop!"

Amiro's shout filled the tall passage, and Jiri wasn't sure if the command was meant for her or Corrianne. But she stumbled to a halt, and the mage dropped her hand, the sparks of light that flickered around it like tiny bits of lightning going dim.

"It's Piss Girl," Corrianne said. "What are you doing here? Did you miss us?" Her hands began to move, as if starting to shape another spell. "Did you miss my snake?"

"Save your magic," Amiro told her. "Morvius and the others can't be far." The skeletons around him moved, fanning out across the cave floor.

"No," Jiri said. "They wouldn't come. They don't understand. You don't understand." She raised her empty hands toward them, trying to keep her attention on them and not the crimson eyes of the demon that crouched in the shadows. "I didn't come here to fight you. I came here to tell you that Patima is lying. She can't control that thing. All-in-Ashes is going to burn the whole Expanse if she tries this."

"What a terrible loss for the leeches," Corrianne said. "Can I kill her now? I have plenty of spells."

"No," Amiro said, his eyes never leaving Jiri and the cave behind her. "You might not have come to fight us, Jiri. However, the companion Patima left us knows nothing except fighting." As he spoke, the gleaming sparks of the demon's eyes began to move, the thing stepping forward into the light.

The demon had the rough shape of a gorilla, but it was much larger. It moved like a gorilla, too, knuckle-walking forward on thick arms and bandy legs. But its shaggy fur was red as blood, gleaming like its eyes, and two great horns twisted out of its head, wider and sharper than a buffalo's. Amiro's skeletons scurried out of the demon's way and the beast stopped before Jiri, staring down at her, its lips pulling back to bare rows of sharp teeth.

Now. Come now. Please. NOW!

The baregara reared up in front of her, standing on its hind legs. Its huge fists swung in and beat on its chest, a chest whose ribs drove out of the pale red skin like white thorns, making a thicket of spikes around a pulsing, circular maw filled with hooked teeth. The demon roared from both mouths as its hands slammed into its chest, and that twin bellow filled Jiri's head. She hunched underneath that avalanche of sound, forcing herself not to break and run.

The demon pounded its fists down, lowered its horned head, and charged.

Jiri couldn't stay still in the face of the ugly death that was tearing at her, but as she threw herself to the side she knew she wouldn't be fast enough. The demon was already shifting its charge, one clawed hand reaching out for her, ready to scoop her up and pull her to its teeth, and Jiri's desperate roll across the cave's floor ended against a wall.

Then the demon roared again.

Not in triumph, but in pain.

Jiri felt the floor shake as the demon hit it. Looking up, she could see the thick vine that had wound itself around one of the baregara's horns, using it as a handle to twist the monster to the ground. She watched the vine jerk the demon forward, and the grating of the red ape-thing's teeth against the stone floor almost drowned out the thin, high-pitched sound of the umdhlebi's song.

She shoved herself back against the wall, gritting her teeth against the compulsion she knew was buried in that song. She resisted it, and watched the umdhlebi slither into the room. Slow but inexorable, thank the spirits. When Jiri had gone back to it, had stumbled away from it, pretending to be hurt, it had followed her, its hunger driving it. Followed her here, and thank the spirits again the monstrous plant had gone for the largest prey it could reach. Its thick vines lashed out, wrapping around the baregara, catching it by the wrist and neck. The demon roared, the mouth in its chest booming while the one on its head choked. It reached out with its free hand and grabbed at the vine looped around its neck, jerking it down so the teeth of its chest mouth could tear at its heavy bark, slowed only a little by the long thorns. The vine ripped in two, the stumps of it bleeding a thick yellow sap.

Coughing, roaring, the baregara threw itself on the umdhlebi, tearing thick, woody chunks from its body as more vines wrapped around the demon, thorns tearing through its red fur and spilling the ape-thing's reeking white blood.

Go now. While it still holds the demon. The thought echoed through Jiri's head until it finally made sense, and she tore her eyes away from the massive fight in front of her. Spinning around, she pressed her hands against the wall she had rolled against and began to climb.

The spider spirit's magic ran strong in her. Her hands and feet clung to the wall, and she moved up the stone quickly, putting as much distance between herself and the fight raging below her as she could. Looking over her shoulder, she could see Amiro and Corrianne below. The mage was looking up at her, shouting something that was lost in the demon's roars, but Amiro was staring at the fight, his face slack, swaying in time to the shrill music that still spilled from the umdhlebi.

Corrianne, unaffected or too far away to hear that music, pulled back her hand, about to cast, when a bolt of palest blue struck her. It knocked her back, the green of her dress white with frost. Jiri saw her friends working their way into the room, pressed against the walls, keeping as much distance as they could between themselves and the umdhlebi's lashing vines.

Hoping this wasn't the last time she would see them, Jiri started across the wall, moving as fast as she could toward the statue-flanked arch at the end of the passage.

The tunnel beyond the arch was a tight stone throat. Its walls pressed in around Jiri, bulbous stone formations growing from them like tumors, every surface slick with water, and the air that filled the space between the walls was thick with water as well and hot, like the jungle after a rain. The tunnel curved and sank, and Jiri's ears lost the sounds of the battle raging behind her.

There was nothing but the draw of her breath, the beating of her heart, and the constant drip of water.

And then something else.

Jiri stopped and listened. Somewhere ahead of her, something burbled and hissed, like a pot on a fire. *The rock around it baked with heat, and the water, the blood of the earth, boiled.* That was how Shani had described the cavern where he had been taken.

Where All-in-Ashes had been chained.

Jiri took the stone that she had wrapped light around and tucked it in her shirt, and she could still see. There was light somewhere beyond the next curve, thin and smeared by distance and haze, but there.

Patima? Maybe.

Mikki? Jiri had never seen the halfling back with Amiro and Corrianne. Patima may have taken her with her, one last guard to watch over her while she summoned All-in-Ashes back to the place it had been caged so long, so that she could try to leash the monster to her terrible vision of revenge and freedom.

It doesn't matter. One or both of them, or All-in-Ashes itself, I have to try to stop them.

Jiri moved, pushing forward toward that dim light, the hot, wet air wrapping close around her like the breath of beasts.

The tunnel opened into a cavern filled with water, steam, light, and heat.

Jiri crouched behind a gnarled knuckle of stone that pushed out of the last bit of the tunnel wall, staring in at a huge chamber the size of the clearing Thirty Trees had stood in, and as steep and angled as a staircase. At its top, boiling water flowed into it, and at its bottom, the earth swallowed the water. But the hot water didn't drop in one pounding fall, or smash through the cavern in a torrential stream. Instead, it flowed down slow and smooth, filling hundreds of stone pools that stretched in row after haphazard row down the cavern. It was a terrace of cups, pools huge and tiny, filled with water that was clear and fast and boiling, or slow and blue and steaming.

Over it all, the ceiling glimmered with light. Crystals grew thick overhead, covering the curved vault, making it into a massive geode. Most of the crystals were small, but here and there were larger ones, ranging from the size of Jiri's head to bigger than Morvius. In the center of those larger crystals, light gleamed, like white stars trapped in glass, and made the cavern as bright as a night in the open with the moon shining full.

In that shimmering light, nothing moved but water and steam.

Quiet and wary as a mouse deer, Jiri stepped into the open. Paths ran between some of the pools, smoothed into the wide lips of rock that separated them. Some looked natural, others had obviously been worked some time long ago, little steps carved into the soft stone leading upward. Jiri looked down, at the crack that swallowed the hot water with a low roar, then up. The source of the heat was there, and she started to pick her way around the pools and climb.

Her bare feet were as sure on the wet stone as they had been on the ceiling, but the heat was growing around her. It made her sweat, but the air was already full of moisture, and the sweat clung to her, soaking her clothes, dripping from her braids. It ran down her arms and over her hands, and Jiri silently thanked the spider spirit who had bargained his magic to her. That magic was probably the only thing that still let her cling to the sweat-coated handle of the bush knife. She needed the reassurance of its sharp presence as she crept up, her eyes darting around her and seeing only steam, her ears hearing only water, her skin feeling only heat.

Until something slammed into her back, like a punch but worse—so much worse.

Jiri went down, barely staying on the path that stretched between a small, boiling pool to one side and a sharp drop to a larger, steaming pool below. Hitting the stone tore the skin off of her knees and palms, but those pains were lost in the agony that roared between her shoulder blades. Jiri reached back, and her hand found something hard. She jerked it out, dropped it clattering beside her. A little knife with a short handle and a narrow, sharp blade. The blood that covered it almost hid the black smear coating the blade's tip.

Poison. Mikki's here, I missed her, and now I'm dying. Gods and crocodiles.

"Jiri, right?"

Jiri raised her eyes and saw Mikki standing on a ledge over her. The halfling had stripped to a thin cotton shift in the heat, and the cloth was dark with sweat, as was the chestnut hair on her head and her feet. A leather belt ran from Mikki's shoulder to her hip, bristling with knives, and Jiri could see steel shining in the woman's child-sized hand.

"Good to see you again. It was getting boring in here. Steam baths aren't nearly as fun without cute boys to look at and rub your feet." Mikki wriggled her toes. "Did you bring any cute boys with you?"

Jiri turned her head away from the little assassin. She could feel the poison working, a numbness spreading out through her shoulder. It did nothing to take away the pain, but it made Jiri's arm feel distant, weak, and when she tried she could barely move it. Jiri pulled her good arm up and traced symbols of time and death and healing into the sweat that covered the base of her neck, whispering a plea to the green spirits of healing, hoping that the sounds of water would bury those words and keep Mikki from catching them.

"No?" The halfling said. "Don't tell me you came alone. You don't look so good."

But I'm feeling better, Jiri thought. The magic that she had taken from the spirits of medicine plants was already working, taking away the poison's numbness, restoring the feeling and motion to her arm and shoulder. It was just a temporary cure. In a few hours, the poison would come back, potent as ever. But a few hours was all Jiri needed. Beneath her, hidden by her body, her hand moved, reaching for the bag she had tucked beneath her shirt.

"I don't suppose *you'll* rub my feet."

Jiri turned her head back and looked up at the halfling. The little woman was looking down at her, a knife spinning between her slim fingers. "No," Jiri croaked, trying to put all the pain she could into her voice.

"So what good are you?" Mikki asked, catching her knife. "I've been here *forever*, waiting for Patima to finish her song and dance. I need something to do." She looked over the knife at Jiri. "Whittling?"

"You could stop Patima," Jiri said, her skin crawling. Her hand had reached her pouch, and her fingers fought with the strings that held it shut, trying to open it with as little motion as possible.

"Why would I want to do that?" Mikki cocked her head like a little bird.

"Because if she succeeds, she'll kill thousands," Jiri said.

"Maybe," Mikki said. "Not in a good way, though. Not up close, not so she can watch the life flicker out of their eyes. She just wants to become that thing and fall out of the sky and burn everyone beneath her. Boring."

"Then stop her." Jiri finally pulled the bag open and slipped her hand inside.

"Why would I do that?" Mikki started moving, pacing easily along the edge of the pool, heading toward the stairs that had been carved down to Jiri's level. "I may not agree with how she's going to do it, but I'm absolutely behind her killing lots and lots of people. By the way, if I see you try to cast again, I'm going to throw this knife through your throat."

Jiri froze. But she could feel what she wanted, brushing light against her fingertips. "Why do you want my people to die?" she asked, trying to slow Mikki's approach, to distract the halfling while she brought her mind into focus.

"Your people?" Mikki said. "I don't care about your people. I don't care about anyone's people. Everyone's the same to me: amusing or in the way. What I want is upheaval. Disorder. Chaos." Mikki skipped lightly down the stairs to the ledge where Jiri lay. "You see, I don't get along well in a peaceful world. I don't fit, and the more orderly things become, the less fun I can have. So I need things like this. A little war, some disaster, a giant flame-angel wreaking havoc—things like that keep attention away from me, and give me a chance to play." Mikki stopped in front of Jiri and shrugged. "We're all just looking for our place in the world, and I've found mine. In the chaos, in the flames of civilization's fall—that's where I fit, where I'm happy. Now, would you like to take your last stab at me? Because I'm ready to take mine." She laughed, her voice like bright chimes mixed with the bubbling of the water.

"Yes," Jiri said, and deep inside her, in her head and body and soul, she reached for change.

This time, the change came easy, her anger actually helping her grab it, and she wrapped her mind around it, clinging close as her hand clutched at the smooth bone carvings of Oza's necklace. Her magic arced through her, and her body twisted, becoming longer, lighter, taller. Her head lengthened, her face now a muzzle filled with teeth. Her hands became claws, and her legs became strong and tipped with talons sharper than the bush knife she had carried. She crouched before the halfling, the great gutting claws on her feet twitching, and hissed, baring her teeth and ruffling out the deep green feathers that slicked her back and tail.

Mikki looked at her and laughed. "Good godlings, what are you supposed to be? A werechicken?"

By every single ancestor, I hate her. But Jiri didn't throw herself forward at the halfling, claws slashing, the way she wanted to. Mikki was too dangerous for that. Instead, she leapt, landing easily on the next terrace down, her long tail balancing her as she hit the narrow stone edge of the pool. The magic of the spider spirit was still with her, and her feet gripped the stone as she started running along the ledge, away from Mikki and toward a path that would take her up.

"Oh gods, I hope you stay in the shape when I kill you," Mikki called out. A knife slammed into the stone just to the side of Jiri's clawed foot, making her stumble and almost fall. "I'm going to make such a hat out of those feathers."

Jiri spun, dodging another knife, and ran to the edge of the pool and jumped. She hurtled at the wall that rose ahead of her like it was a great beast that she meant to slay, hit the stone and clung. She started to climb, trotting up the curved ceiling that arced over the cavern.

"Ah ah ah, none of that," Mikki called from below.

Jiri felt the knife hit her, slamming into her hip, ruffling feathers and then bouncing off the scales beneath, but digging in enough to hurt, to make her stumble. She lurched into one of the crystals that hung from the ceiling, and it snapped free from the stone with a sound like bone breaking, tumbling down to land with a splash in one of the pools below.

She saw it fall, even as she watched Mikki below her, the halfling running easily along the edge of the pools, graceful enough to keep up even as she drew another knife. *She'll hit my neck or an eye eventually, or just bleed me out of a dozen wounds. And even if I get ahead of her, she'll follow, and I'll be caught between her and Patima. I have to end this.*

Jiri jerked to a halt, and a knife flashed by her nose, slamming into a little crystal and shattering it like a dry skull. Below her, Mikki laughed like an excited child playing a game. Jiri whipped her head down to see where the halfling stood, pulling another knife out, then jerked it around to find what she needed. *Not perfect, but good enough.* With a lurch to the side, Jiri slammed her feathered shoulder into a glowing crystal that was almost as big as she was. It groaned and she heard a snap, but it didn't fall. She reared back to try again and felt the bite of a knife in her back, so near the wound of the other one. She screeched and spun on her talons, her tail catching the crystal she had just hit, cracking it free.

"Close, but not close enough," Mikki said from below, watching the crystal arc down, and she was right. The halfling didn't even have to move, as the crystal was set to land a good six feet away.

Right in the steaming water of the pool she stood beside.

The halfling barely had time to start raising her hands when the wave of boiling water hit her, drenching her. Her high-pitched shriek sounded so much like a child's, and Jiri felt her stomach twist as she watched Mikki fall back, her skin red and blistering, still screaming as she fell from the ledge.

There was a dull crack as the halfling hit the edge of the pool below, and the scream cut off. Mikki spun and splashed down in the pool below that one and lay still in the water. She floated in the brilliant blue, her head haloed by her hair and a drifting cloud of red, steam drifting up around her face, slack and innocent and childlike.

Jiri twisted her head away, but that image, seared into her spirit, didn't leave her as she ran from the room.

Chapter Twenty-Two
When Ashes Fall

The boiling stream filled the tunnel with steam and plastered down Jiri's feathers. At its end, she stepped down the wall to the floor and shook the water from her, staring at the thinning curtain of steam ahead. A space opened there, filled with heat and pale light. Jiri crouched, listening, and over the hissing boil of the stream running past she heard a voice, cracked and broken, barely recognizable as it ground out the same words, over and over.

"All-in-Ashes, come. All-in-Ashes, burn. All-in-Ashes, come and burn with me."

Jiri listened to that croaking chant, so full of hate and helpless anger and want, and she shook.

Being the makumo wasn't like being the snake. Jiri's emotions were just as strong, and they roiled through her. Anger, fear—but worse, pity, and a devastating understanding. Patima had suffered, suffered terribly.

But so did Oza. So did Hadzi.

So did Thirty Trees.

Jiri stepped through the curtain of steam into the last cavern.

This was a made place, not natural, though who or what had made it Jiri couldn't guess. The great room was a hexagon, with six black-mirror walls of obsidian, and the floor and the ceiling were made of that same glossy stone. The boiling stream of water that Jiri stood beside ran down a channel that cut a razor-sharp line across the floor, a line that ran to the center of the cavern and ended in a bubbling pool. That perfect circle of roiling water surrounded another hexagon, a low platform of dark stone shot with veins of gray, stretching twenty feet from side to side. Light shone up from beneath that pool, a dull white light like moonlight on bone. It gleamed off the metal chains that lay coiled at each of the platform's six points and lit the steam that curled up from the water, rising to vanish into the hole that marred the ceiling's center. An uneven circle, that hole was the only thing in this chamber that wasn't precise and perfect. Through the steam, Jiri could see glimmering flashes of rain falling from the storm raging far above.

It was a scar, melted into the stone of the ceiling, a wound that ran from this place where All-in-Ashes had been chained to the world outside. Centered beneath it, wreathed in steam and rain, Patima knelt. She held the kindi she had stolen close to her, its black wings pressed against her, and her right hand rested on the iron spike that ran through the carving's chest.

No, it didn't rest—the spike ran through Patima's hand, tearing through palm and bone and tendon, until it jutted out of the back of her hand, smoking with heat.

Jiri could smell it now, ugly beneath the water smell, the reek of blood burning, of charred flesh.

She slid a step forward, her claws clicking on the obsidian floor.

A small sound, but Patima stopped her chant, tipped her head just enough to look at Jiri, then turned her eyes back up toward the distant sky.

"Jiri. That's you, isn't it?" There were only fragments of beauty in Patima's voice now. The rest was rust and thorns. "You've found another shape, besides the snake."

Her fanged mouth ill-suited for speech, Jiri stayed silent, her muscles bunching, claws twitching. *Can she move? Can she cast?* It didn't matter. The fickle spirits of fate and hope had blessed Jiri and let her get here before Patima could attempt her joining. Now was the time to end this. Uncoiling from her crouch, Jiri ran forward. She reached the edge of the pool and leapt, steam scalding her belly as she passed over the water, then hit the stone where All-in-Ashes had been bound. It was hot under her, like the stone of a fire pit, but she ignored the pain of it and ran toward Patima, ready to kick out with her claws and knock that terrible kindi out of her hands.

"Too late," Patima whispered, and heat slammed Jiri to the ground.

The air became an inferno. Jiri choked, her nose and lungs burning, and tried to see. Over her, filling the ragged hole in the ceiling, stretched vast wings of smoke and ash. The wings spread from a flickering heart of fire, a roiling center of red and white shaped something like a man. It hung there, burning so bright in the curling darkness of its wings, and Jiri could feel her feathers shriveling, could hear the falling rain cracking into steam in the fiery spirit's aura.

"All-in-Ashes, come. All-in-Ashes, burn. All-in-Ashes, come burn with me." Patima's eyes flashed with triumph and the reflection of fire. "Burn with me."

I can still stop this. Pinned under all that heat, Jiri pushed herself forward, crawling across the stone, edging toward Patima. *A little closer. Just a little closer, and my claws will reach.*

Fire fell from above, a hissing drop of brightness. It hit the stone in front of Jiri, searing the scales at the tip of her muzzle, making her head jerk back. Over her, All-in-Ashes hovered, watching.

It won't let me kill her. But it didn't kill me. It could, just by coming a little closer. The pain of the spirit's heat would spike up to agony, and Jiri's flesh would char from her bones. All-in-Ashes could kill her that easily, but it chose not to.

Just like it chose not to kill her outside the Pyre, right before it burned Thirty Trees.

What do you see, when you see me? Jiri couldn't see its face, couldn't see anything at all through the smoke and the tears that filled her eyes, but she knew what it looked like. Shani's face, handsome as Hadzi's, would be carved into that fire. Jiri reached for change in her head, stroked the cord that connected her spirit to her body, and her form slipped back to its true shape, a young woman sprawled across the stone, her long braids shriveling in the heat. *You're in there, Shani, aren't you? What do you see, when you see me with those eyes? Your daughter? Your wife? I want to know.*

Jiri pushed herself up, the stone searing her skin, the air like an oven. Patima was right there, right in front of her, her skin flushed with the heat, her eyes streaming, but her teeth were bared in a smile.

"You'll burn," she croaked in her broken voice. "You, and everyone else whose tried to stop me. You'll all burn, and Usaro will burn, and I will finally be free."

"I will burn, and you will burn," Jiri rasped, her voice cracked too by smoke and heat. She lunged forward, and this time no fire fell to stop her. She reached out and struck, her hand slamming down onto the iron spike that stabbed through the kindi's body and through Patima's hand. Its point tore skin and bone, and Jiri felt the pain of the metal ripping through her flesh, the fire buried in it searing her blood.

"And we will burn together."

There was fire, and pain.

It started in the center of her hand, where the iron tore through her, and ran up her veins and turned her heart to ash.

She was ash, and fire, and pain, and she was Jiri, and she opened her eyes.

A city surrounded her, every building burning. Their stone walls housed flame, and their wide windows and doors sent smoke into the sky like dark screams. The air shimmered with heat, and a vast sound rumbled the ash-flaked stone beneath Jiri's feet, something like thunder, or drums. Jiri raised her hands to block her ears, but they were gray and thin, muscle and bone reduced to nothing but smoke and ash.

I'm dead, burned and dead, and I failed. Her eyes throbbed, but they could shed no tears. She was only ash. How could she cry?

But if I'm ash, how can I hurt?

Jiri dropped her hands and raised her head.

This was Lozo's center. Jiri could see that, despite the smoke and sparks, could trace the lines of the building she had seen in Shani's kindi through the flames that danced over them. She stood in the same place that Shani's kindi always brought her, but this time she wasn't alone.

"No!" Patima's voice came clear through the thunder, untouched by that sound. The woman stood beside Jiri, her skin gray and hair white, a crust of ash lying over charred black eyes and teeth and bone. "This fire is mine. I won it, and I claim it. It's mine!"

Patima shoved her hands into Jiri's chest, as if she would shove her out of this city, out of this burning vision, but her hands pushed straight through Jiri, and the rest of her followed.

They came together, ghosts of smoke and ash, blurred into one, and for a moment and the city around Jiri changed. It became another city, a city of white pyramids buried in vines, of muddy streets lined with wooden cages that held things that might have once been human but were now just blood-red and bone-white puppets that jerked and screamed—

Then it was gone, and Jiri was back in burning Lozo, staring into the black ashes of Patima's eyes.

"You can't stop me," the woman whispered, her voice a desolation. "It has to burn."

Jiri might have listened, might have let the agony and the rage she felt in Patima's voice push her away. But in the drifting ashes that rode the wind past them, she saw an echo of Thirty Trees, and every other village that had been destroyed, and she answered. "No."

"No?"

The voice was soft, but the low thunder that filled the air seemed to draw back to give it space. Jiri turned, and there he was: Shani, as she had seen him, every version of him, young and strong, old and tired, bent and tall, but always handsome. Handsome, even when his eyes were gone, in their place a drifting paleness, white-hot ashes. Those colorless eyes trailed dark smoke like tears down his face. The smoke dropped off his cheeks and drifted behind him, joining the vast cloud that followed him, a storm-cape of smoke. It spread like wings, twisting ropes of fire netted through it like veins, and that was All-in-Ashes: spirit of burning, of destruction, of all things flashing away their essence and becoming ash, drifting on the wind until it blew apart and was nothing.

"Would you stop me?" he said, thunder rolling under every word. "Are you like those fools who freed me, then tried to chain me again? Would you chain me and keep me from burning?"

"No," Patima said, her voice fervent, and Jiri spoke at the same time, determined and resigned: "Yes."

White eyes turned to Jiri, rested on her, and she felt the ashes of her body ache with heat. Then she was on her knees, smoke pouring out of her, her soul pulling apart from her and drifting away. All-in-Ashes was destroying her, consuming her.

"You should have never come here, Jiri," Patima said, her voice almost lost in thunder and pain. "The things that happened to you, the pain you suffered, they are *nothing* compared to mine. All-in-Ashes understands that. It knows I'll give it what it wants, because it knows it can give me what I need."

Jiri knelt on the ground, dying, her soul dissolving into smoke and ash, and she was pleading—*help me, help me Oza, help me Hadzi, help me ancestors, help me spirits*—but there was nothing here in this vision to pray to, no gods, no spirits, no ancestors, just her and Patima and All-in-Ashes and—

Jiri raised her head, and stared into the face of the thing that was killing her. "Shani," she breathed. "My father. My love. My ancestor. Help me."

All-in-Ashes bent its head, and the terrible white light of its eyes dimmed. The smoke pouring out of Jiri slowed, and it stopped rising to join the great cloud that covered the sky. It swirled around her instead, like blood drifting in water.

"You're in there." Jiri felt the fire in her ease, and she uncurled, staring up at the terrible spirit towering over her. "I can see your face. The mages of Lozo bound you to this monster, and it's been trying to burn you out of it ever since. But you're not gone yet, are you? You're not smoke and ash, you're Shani. Shani the Strong."

"Shani," the spirit said, and its eyes changed, darkening, becoming gray, becoming brown, becoming human. "Shani the Strong."

Patima looked into those human eyes, and the ashes of her face twisted toward fear and hate. "No! You're All-in-Ashes! You're the spirit of destruction, of death, and you belong to me!"

The spirit's eyes flicked to Patima for a moment, going lighter as they did, and now it was her turn to fall to the ground, smoke and groans slipping out from between her clenched teeth.

"Who are you?" Shani demanded, staring down at Jiri, and it was Shani now, Shani's face gray with ash and creased with pain. Shani's eyes, even though they danced with madness and flames.

"I am your wife. I am your daughter. I am your child's child's child. I am Jiri Maju, Daughter of Ashes." With every word, the smoke pulled back into Jiri, her soul slipping back into its temple of bones and blood, nerves and flesh. When the last of it was inside her, she changed, became herself again, her body whole, if dusted with ash. "I'm what you saved."

"What I saved." Shani drew in on himself, the vast wings of smoke behind him trembling. Then he raised his head again, and his eyes faded toward white. "I do not save. I destroy. They bound me, monster and fool, and released me. And I burned. I burned an army, and I burned a city, and I burned and I burned, until they caught me again and sealed me away in their prison of wood and iron and magic. But I have been burning my way out of it for years, because I am All-in-Ashes, and what I do is burn."

"You are Shani, and you save your people!" Jiri shouted.

"You are All-in-Ashes, and you burned those who tried to force you to their will!" Patima pulled herself up, her face a patchwork of skin and ash, and smoke drifted out of her mouth with every word. "You burned this city into the ground, spirit. And I will give you another to burn. Join with me, and I will cast out the

399

soul of the man that they sought to control you with. Join with me, and I will set you free."

"I am All-in-Ashes. I am Shani." The spirit's eyes flickered, white and brown and in between, and around them the city began to shake and collapse. Its buildings fell in on themselves, fell into the earth, sliding down into broken caverns that gaped like screaming mouths at the smoke-covered sky. "I destroyed this city. I destroyed Lozo." Despair and fury filled those words.

"You are Shani." Jiri walked forward across the trembling ground, toward the killing heat of the spirit. "They bound you to All-in-Ashes, a mindless thing, a spirit of fire and destruction and nothing else. Every word, every thought, every emotion that you have— they are Shani's. All-in-Ashes may touch them all, but they're yours, Shani."

Brown eyes turned down to her, and boiling tears ran from them. "Then I killed Lozo. I am Shani the Slayer, and I killed my city."

"All-in-Ashes did this, and you couldn't stop it," Jiri said. "But you kept it from killing your people. You saved us, Shani. You devastated the army of Usaro, drove it back, and then when All-in-Ashes raged, you held it. You must have. You kept it from killing us all, and you let those wizards seal it away in this kindi for ages. You saved us, Shani."

"Saved you." The spirit groaned, and the stone beneath them trembled, the whole great center of Lozo crumbling, shaking, beginning to collapse into fire.

"They enslaved you, All-in-Ashes. Made you a weapon, and then they locked you away." Patima stood beside Jiri, her desperate eyes human again. "This is what she wants for you. To trap you here, in this nightmare, forever. I will end it. I will end all our nightmares. I will set you free."

"Will you?" The spirit's eyes were almost white.

"She will," Jiri said. "She will join with All-in-Ashes, and set it on Usaro. Then she will set it free, and it will turn on us. It will burn its way across the Expanse, and we will all die. All the children that you saved will die, and the spirits of our ancestors will fade, and your final legacy, your final story, will fall apart into ash. All-in-Ashes, Shani. This is the monster that you have to face. This is the beast you must save us from. Please. Save us."

"No!" Patima shoved herself forward. "You are All-in-Ashes. The only salvation you can offer is fire. You—"

"I am Shani. Shani the Strong. And All-in-Ashes is mine." Those white eyes stared down at Patima. "But I can give you its fire."

"Shani, no!" Jiri shouted, but the blazing salvation of All-in-Ashes had already fallen. Flames bloomed from Patima, red and gold and beautiful, licking up toward the sky, and smoke rose like a scream. Then it was gone, and Patima stood, silent, gray, and still, until the ground rumbled beneath them once more and she broke apart, falling into ash that whirled away on the wind.

"She was no child of mine." Shani stared down at her, his face hard as obsidian. "But she was right. You mean to chain me here, with this monster, forever."

"Yes," was all Jiri could say.

"You would save your friends, your city, yourself, by cursing me."

"Yes," Jiri said again. *Unless I offered to take this burden. To free him, and to bind myself to All-in-Ashes.* The thought ricocheted through Jiri's head, horrifying, but worse than that—tempting. Oza had trained her to bargain power and magic from the spirits. What was this, but a greater bargain? For greater power—power for revenge, power enough to burn the Aspis Consortium out of Kibwe, out of the Expanse, off the face of the world. That would be revenge enough, wouldn't it? The hunger of that thought, the rage in it, roiled through her, and Jiri felt her lips moving, ready to shape the words that would bind her to Shani, to the spirit.

She locked her teeth shut.

I am his daughter. His pride flows in me like blood. But I am also the daughter of the thing that he imprisons. I am the Daughter of Ashes, of All-in-Ashes, and its rage flows in me like blood and fire.

But I will not become like Patima.

"I'm sorry," Jiri whispered.

"Don't be sorry," Shani said, and smiled. "Be loud. Spread my name. Spread my stories. Let me live again on the tongues and in the hearts of those I saved. Give me that strength, and I will wrestle this thing forever."

"I will," Jiri said. "I promise."

Chapter Twenty-Three
Below the Mango Woman

Jiri was wrapping the kindi with the last of the chains when someone touched her shoulder. She started, and fire flickered through her, but she felt the coolness of the touch against her burning skin and held it in. "Linaria."

"Jiri." The white-haired woman settled beside her. She moved easily, and Jiri couldn't see any wounds on her, but dried blood marked her skin and her clothes were torn. "Are you all right?"

Jiri's clothes were charred rags, the skin beneath them mottled with burns. Her braids were almost gone, her eyes wouldn't stop streaming tears, and her throat was full of ash. She was shaking, too, Mikki's poison finally starting to take effect. "I'm fine," she scraped out.

"Well, no disrespect, but you look like shit." Morvius jumped over the boiling water, his scale mail jingling, and joined Linaria. He bent down and touched Jiri's arm, carefully pulling her injured hand out from the last scraps of shirt that Jiri had wrapped it in. "All the hells," he whispered, looking at the hole that lay charred through her hand. "Sera! You said you were saving some healing for Jiri. Well get your steel-encased ass over here and use it."

Sera landed on the stone, boot heels inches from the hissing water. The paladin brushed Morvius and Jiri aside, pulled off her gauntlets, and reached down to cup Jiri's face. Healing didn't flow through them, though.

"The beast? All-in-Ashes?" Her brown eyes fixed on Jiri's.

"Chained." When Shani had let her go, cast her out of the kindi's vision, Jiri had sprawled across the stone and watched the great winged shape of the spirit pull in on itself and dwindle, flowing down like smoke into the winged kindi. She had watched the black obsidian of its eyes change to white, and the iron spike go from dull, almost dead red to glowing crimson. Shani had kept his promise, and pulled All-in-Ashes back in, trapping it again in the kindi.

With him.

Forever.

"Evil cannot be contained," Sera said.

"So you say," Jiri said. "But what else is left, when it can't be destroyed?"

Sera stared down at her, silent for a long time, until healing finally flowed through her hands and wiped Jiri's burns away.

It took them a day to work their way out of Lozo's ruins, and the sun was falling when they camped by the steaming waters of Smoking Eye that night. Jiri stared at the deep blue of the waters, exhausted, numb, her arms wrapped around the kindi.

They had all offered to take it, but Jiri had just shaken her head.

She had carried it out, even though the chains she had wrapped around it made it heavy, so heavy. But those silver-gray strands of strangely woven metal, more like rope than chain, had blocked its heat, let her carry All-in-Ashes' prison without burning.

Something bound All-in-Ashes to that stone with these chains long ago. Whatever magic is in them, maybe it will help Shani keep that spirit bound again.

Now, and forever.

"Jiri. You awake?"

Jiri looked away from the water toward Morvius, his face lit by the small fire Linaria had built. "Yes. What?"

"I'm splitting up the things I took off Mikki," he said. "She was your kill, so you get first choice."

"I don't want first choice," Jiri said. "I don't want anything."

"Suit yourself," he said, his voice gruff.

Jiri stared at him. He had barely spoken to her all day, even to call her 'runt.' "Why are you mad at me, Morvius? What did I do?"

In the shadows beside her, Linaria snorted and Morvius frowned. He stabbed at the fire with a stick, making a few sparks dance up, and a tremor ran through Jiri.

"You got them. Patima, and Mikki. The gods slap my ass and bend me over, you got them both, on your own, while Sera was cutting the head off that demon. And what the hell did I do?"

"Well, you stabbed Amiro in the gut, and broke Corrianne's nose with that biloko skull," Linaria said. "And you cut me out of that tree-thing when it snared me. Besides that, not much."

"They got away though," Morvius grumbled. "Corrianne and Amiro. Bloody teleport. It's cheating, really." But he grinned a little, a dangerous expression in the firelight. "That look on Corrianne's face, when that skull hit her. That was good."

"It was," Linaria said, and she reached out and took Morvius's hand.

Jiri looked away, stared up at the stars shining in the clear dark sky, so beautiful and distant. *Like white eyes.* She shuddered again.

"No. There is one thing I want," she said.

"What?" said Linaria.

"I want to go to Thirty Trees."

"We can stop there tomorrow," Linaria said. "Camp there, before we push on to Kibwe."

"We don't have that much food," Sera said, from where she stood in the shadows beyond the firelight, staring out at the jungle that surrounded them.

Sera, too, had been treating Jiri strangely today, though it was hard to tell with her. Did the paladin, despite her demon, feel cheated of a trophy? Jiri clutched the kindi to her a little more tightly.

"We have enough. Going a little hungry won't hurt any of us," Linaria said, then leaned over to Jiri, whispering. "Our poor little warriors. If their weapons were half as big as their egos, they wouldn't be able to lift them."

Jiri didn't answer, but her lips tipped up into the ghost of a smile.

The clearing where Thirty Trees had once stood still smelled a little of smoke, but the ashes were mostly gone, taken by the wind or washed into the red dirt by the rain.

Jiri stood beneath the last mango tree, listening to the monkeys and the birds squabble over the ripening fruit in the branches overhead, and stared at the Mango Woman. Her dark, soapstone face was as stern as ever.

"I did what I could," Jiri said, looking into those blank eyes. "And I brought it back. What more do you want?"

Jiri dropped her eyes to the ground in front of the statue. There were shoots of green there, just like everywhere in the clearing. All-in-Ashes may have cleared a circle of death here when it came, but the jungle was already rushing back, a tide of life that would reclaim this clearing. In a few weeks, it would be green. In a year, it would be gone, and this statue would be buried by plants and vines.

That would have to be enough.

Jiri took a breath, and took hold of her magic.

The soft earth in front of the statue went softer, became mud as the water from the air and the ground all around rushed into it. Quickly, before it could begin to dry in the afternoon sun, she called to the earth. The mud in front of her bubbled, distended, then rose. Hands reached out of the hole, spade-shaped hands wrought of earth and stone, and they shoved the mud out and to one side. The hands disappeared back into the hole again, then came back out, not so fast but efficient, strong. In a short time, the little elemental Jiri had summoned had dug out a hole deeper than she was tall.

When the spirit was done and gone, its body slumping back into the ground, Jiri went to the edge of the narrow pit it had made, the kindi she had carried back with her from Lozo heavy in her arms. She stared down at it, a lumpy ball of silver-gray metal strands, with only the tips of All-in-Ashes' wings sticking out. The iron embedded in those ebony wings glowed dull red with heat, and the smell of smoke and ash filled Jiri's head.

"Shani," she said softly. "I wish . . ." *What? What can I say? What can I do? I can't—*

I can.

Carefully, Jiri set the chain-wrapped kindi down on the ground beside her. Then she reached into the over-large shirt Morvius had given her and pulled out a pouch. She reached inside and carefully untangled the carved bone animals of the necklace from Shani's spearman kindi.

Oza's necklace. The last bit of him that she had.

"Oza," she said, the necklace smooth and heavy in her hands. "Thank you. You trusted me when no one else would. You saved me. I owe you everything, and I will spend my life repaying that debt." A tear slipped down her face and splashed across the carved bone wings of a bird. "It's going to be hard. I couldn't save you. Or Thirty Trees. But I saved what was left of the Mosa. I saved Kibwe. Maybe I saved the Expanse. But I'm not done. Not until I see you again. Until then . . ."

Jiri forced her hands to move. She took the necklace and wound it into the strands of chain that she had wrapped tight around All-in-Ashes' kindi. "Go with Shani. Teach him to control the fire, like you taught me. Be strong for him, with him. Save him. Like you saved me."

Jiri took her hands away from the kindi and sank them into the red dirt, whispering her magic into the ground again. From the earth, thick hands of stone rose up, gathered the kindi and pulled it down into the hole. Jiri knelt beside it and watched the elemental pull the dirt and mud back into the hole, covering the kindi and then smoothing out the ground in front of the Mango Woman, leaving it looking as if it had never been disturbed.

Jiri looked up. The Mango Woman was still staring at her, her blank eyes hard.

Sera offered to take that thing, to give it to her church to lock away. Like a trophy. Jiri had just shaken her head, and to her credit that was all Sera had said about it. *I didn't have to bring it here, though. I could have thrown it into the boiling mud with the kindi I took from the biloko. Or thrown it into Smoking Eye. I could have, but . . .*

Jiri frowned at the Mango Woman. "Don't look at me like that. You didn't destroy it either, when you the chance." *All that power, all that fire, just waiting to be used . . .*

With a shudder, Jiri turned her back on the statue and walked away.

Nothing was worth that. Nothing. At least Patima had taught her that.

Up ahead, Linaria and Morvius and Sera were waiting, and beyond them Kibwe, and beyond that the whole wide Mwangi Expanse. Green and growing, hungry and dangerous, beautiful and alive—and all hers. The day and night of it, the life and death of it—all of it was in her, with her, and she would fight for it as long as she lived in this world.

"Jiri?" Linaria called. "Are you done? We have some mangoes, and Morvius says he found some kind of red taro root."

Red taro root? Jiri pulled up short. *The only red plant that grows around here that looks like taro is fireweed.*

"Oh," she said. "Oh no."

She started to run back to the camp, but it was hard to breathe when she was laughing that hard.

About the Author

Gary Kloster is a writer, a stay-at-home father, a librarian, and a martial artist—occasionally all in the same day, very rarely all at the same time. His short fiction has appeared in *Clarkesworld, Fantasy, Apex, Intergalactic Medicine Show,* and *Writers of the Future 25,* as well as on **paizo.com**, where his short story "The Gem"—a prequel to this novel, starring Jiri and Oza—is available for free.

Gary lives in a Midwestern college town, an island of super-science, geekdom, and good Korean BBQ drifting in a vast sea of corn, with a tribe of genius-introvert-geek girls. You can find him cluttering up the Internet at **garykloster.com**.

Acknowledgments

I owe a great deal to a lot of people for making this book possible. To my Mom and Dad, who put up with me sneaking books in everywhere and let me spend my weekends gaming in my friends' basements. To everyone in All Rights Reserved, my local writing group—Jaleigh Johnson, Elizabeth Shack, and Kelly Swails—and my online writing group/con posse, the West Writers: Julia Dvorin and Heather McDougal. All of you have listened to me whine very nobly over the years. And to my editor at Paizo, James Sutter, who was not only amazing to work with, but put up with my occasionally unique approach to grammar. Finally, I want to thank my daughters, Corinne and Camille, for letting Dad write.

Sometimes.

Glossary

All Pathfinder Tales novels are set in the rich and vibrant world of the Pathfinder campaign setting. Below are explanations of several key terms used in this book. For more information on the world of Golarion and the strange monsters, people, and deities that make it their home, see *The Inner Sea World Guide*, or dive into the game and begin playing your own adventures with the *Pathfinder Roleplaying Game Core Rulebook* or the *Pathfinder Roleplaying Game Beginner Box*, all available at **paizo.com**. Readers particularly interested in the Mwangi Expanse should check out *Pathfinder Campaign Setting: Heart of the Jungle*.

Abadar: Master of the First Vault and the god of cities, wealth, merchants, and law.

Abyss: Plane of evil and chaos ruled by demons, where many evil souls go after they die.

Andoran: Democratic and freedom-loving nation to the north of the Inner Sea.

Aspis Consortium: Unscrupulous world-spanning trade organization devoted to uncovering and selling relics, among other concerns. Often finances adventuring expeditions.

Bard: An artist or performer able to harness his or her innate magic through art. Often cross-trained in combat and other adventuring skills.

Baregara: Apelike demon with a second mouth in its chest.

Bekyar: Human ethnicity from southern Garund, often associated with the slave trade, demon worship, and ritual scarification.

Biloko: Small, reddish humanoids that prey on other sentient beings. Capable of unhinging their jaws like snakes in order to swallow prey whole, as well as luring prey with their magical song.

Bloodcove: Port city at the mouth of the Vanji River on the western coast of the Mwangi Expanse.

Bloodhaze Mosquitoes: Species of mosquito that grows to monstrous size and carries sleeping sickness.

Bonuwat: Human ethnicity from southern Garund, found primarily on the coasts. Its people are known for their expert sailing and fishing.

Calistria: Also known as the Savored Sting; the goddess of trickery, lust, and revenge.

Charau-Ka: Race of intelligent, demon-worshiping apes in the Mwangi Expanse that prey on other intelligent creatures.

Cheliax: A powerful devil-worshiping nation located north of the Inner Sea.

Chelish: Of or relating to the nation of Cheliax.

Court of Hateful Smiles: The inner court that rules Usaro under the Gorilla King.

Demons: Evil denizens of the plane of the afterlife called the Abyss, who seek only to maim, ruin, and feed on mortal souls.

Druid: Someone who reveres nature and draws magical power from the boundless energy of the natural world (sometimes called the Green Faith, or the Green).

Dwarves: Short, stocky humanoids who excel at physical labor, mining, and crafts.

Elementals: Beings of pure elemental energy, such as air, earth, fire, or water.

Elves: Long-lived, beautiful humanoids identifiable by their pointed ears, lithe bodies, and eyes that appear to be all one color.

Expanse: The Mwangi Expanse.

Fever Sea: Region of the Arcadian Ocean on the southwestern edge of the Mwangi Expanse.

Garund: Continent south of the Inner Sea, renowned for its deserts and jungles.

Garundi: Human ethnic group found primarily in the desert nations of northern Garund.

Goblins: Race of small and maniacal humanoids who live to burn, pillage, and sift through the refuse of more civilized races.

Golems: Artificial creatures constructed magically and given life by spellcasters.

Gorilla King: The sentient gorilla who rules Usaro, reincarnated by the power of the Demon Lord Angazhan.

Green Faith: General name for a variety of spiritual practices by which some spellcasters draw power from the natural world.

Half-Elves: The children of unions between elves and humans. Taller, longer-lived, and generally more graceful and attractive than the average human, yet not nearly so much so as their full elven kin. Often regarded as having the best qualities of both races, yet still regularly discriminated against.

Halflings: Race of humanoids known for their tiny stature, deft hands, and mischievous personalities.

Inner Sea: The vast inland sea whose northern continent, Avistan, and southern continent, Garund, as well as the seas and nearby lands, are the primary focus of the Pathfinder campaign setting.

Iomedae: Goddess of valor, rulership, justice, and honor.

Irrisen: Realm of permanent winter far north of the Inner Sea, ruled by the descendants of the Witch Queen Baba Yaga.

Keleshite: Of or related to the Empire of Kelesh, far to the east of the Inner Sea region.

Kibwe: Major city in the eastern portion of the Mwangi Expanse.

Kindi: Small, carved figurines invested with a portion of a soul through powerful magic.

Mwangi: Of or pertaining to the Mwangi Expanse; someone from that region.

Mwangi (ethnicity): Several different dark-skinned ethnicities native to Garund, often lumped together into a single category by northerners, including the Bekyar, Bonuwat, Mauxi, and Zenj.

Mwangi Expanse: Sweltering jungle region south of the Inner Sea.

Ndele Gap: Pass through the mountains on the eastern edge of the Mwangi Expanse, used frequently by trade caravans.

Nidal: Evil northern nation devoted to Zon-Kuthon, the god of torture.

Nidalese: Of or pertaining to Nidal; someone from Nidal.

Ocota: Large lake in the middle of the Mwangi Expanse.

Paladin: A holy warrior in the service of a good and lawful god. Ruled by a strict code of conduct and granted special magical powers by his or her deity.

Polyglot: Collective name for the many interrelated dialects of the Mwangi Expanse.

Rovagug: The Rough Beast. God of destruction.

Shackles: Pirate isles southwest of the Inner Sea.

Shory: Ancient empire, now long since fallen into obscurity, which was most famed for its flying cities.

Sorcerer: Someone who casts spells through natural ability rather than faith or study.

Taldan: Of or pertaining to Taldor; a citizen of Taldor.

Taldane: The common trade language of the Inner Sea region.

Taldor: A formerly glorious nation that has lost many of its holdings in recent years to neglect.

Thirty Trees: Village near Kibwe in the Mwangi Expanse.

Umdhlebi: Deadly carnivorous trees capable of magically luring prey into its clutches.

Undead: Dead creatures reanimated through magic.

Usaro: City of intelligent, demon-worshiping apes in the Mwangi Expanse, ruled by the Gorilla King. Widely feared by the Expanse's humanoid residents.

Vanji: River in the western Mwangi Expanse.

Wara: Name for the tribal leader in certain villages in the eastern Mwangi Expanse.

Wererat: Rodent lycanthrope; someone who can change from a humanoid to a rat and back again.

Wizard: Someone who casts spells through careful study and rigorous scientific methods rather than faith or innate talent, recording the necessary incantations in a spellbook.

Zenj: Human ethnicity native to the jungles of the Mwangi Expanse. The darkest-skinned and most populous of the southern peoples.

Torius Vin is perfectly happy with his life as a pirate captain, sailing the Inner Sea with a bold crew of buccaneers and Celeste, his snake-bodied navigator and one true love. Yet all that changes when his sometime friend Vreva Jhafae—a high-powered courtesan and abolitionist spy in the slaver stronghold of Okeno—draws him into her shadowy network of secret agents. Caught between the slavers he hates and a navy that sees him as a criminal, can Torius continue to choose the path of piracy? Or will he sign on as a privateer, bringing freedom to others—at the price of his own?

From critically acclaimed author Chris A. Jackson comes a fantastical tale of love, espionage, and high-seas adventure, set in the award-winning world of the *Pathfinder Roleplaying Game*.

Pirate's Promise print edition: $9.99
ISBN: 978-1-60125-664-5

Pirate's Promise ebook edition:
ISBN: 978-1-60125-665-2

PATHFINDER TALES

Pirate's Promise

CHRIS A. JACKSON

Raised as a wizard-priest in the church of the dark god Zon-Kuthon, Isiem escaped his sadistic masters and became a rebel, leaving behind everything he knew in order to follow his conscience. Now, his unique heritage makes him perfect for a dangerous mission into an ancient dungeon said to hold a magical weapon capable of slaying demons and devils by the thousands and freeing the world of their fiendish taint. Accompanied by companions ranging from a righteous paladin to mercantile mercenaries, Isiem will lead the expedition back into shadowed lands that are all too familiar. And what the adventurers find at the dungeon's heart will change them all forever.

From acclaimed author Liane Merciel comes a dark tale of survival, horror, and second chances set in the award-winning world of the Pathfinder Roleplaying Game.

Nightblade print edition: $9.99
ISBN: 978-1-60125-662-1

Nightblade ebook edition:
ISBN: 978-1-60125-663-8

Pathfinder Tales

Nightblade

Liane Merciel

When the leader of the ruthless Technic League calls in a favor, the mild-mannered alchemist Alaeron has no choice but to face a life he thought he'd left behind long ago. Accompanied by his only friend, a street-savvy thief named Skiver, Alaeron must head north into Numeria, a land where brilliant and evil arcanists rule over the local barbarian tribes with technology looted from a crashed spaceship. Can Alaeron and Skiver survive long enough to unlock the secrets of the stars? Or will the backstabbing scientists of the Technic League make Alaeron's curiosity his own undoing?

From Hugo Award winner Tim Pratt comes a fantastic adventure of technology and treachery, set against the backdrop of the Iron Gods Adventure Path in the award-winning world of the Pathfinder Roleplaying Game.

Reign of Stars print edition: $9.99
ISBN: 978-1-60125-660-7

Reign of Stars ebook edition:
ISBN: 978-1-60125-661-4

PATHFINDER TALES

Reign of Stars

TIM PRATT

When the aristocratic Vishov family is banished from Ustalav due to underhanded politics, Lady Tyressa Vishov is faced with a choice: fade slowly into obscurity, or strike out for the nearby River Kingdoms and establish a new holding on the untamed frontier. Together with her children and loyal retainers, she'll forge a new life in the infamous Echo Wood, and neither bloodthirsty monsters nor local despots will stop her from reclaiming her family honor. Yet the shadow of Ustalavic politics is long, and even in a remote and lawless territory, there may be those determined to see the Vishov family fail . . .

From *New York Times* best-selling author Michael A. Stackpole comes a new novel of frontier adventure set in the world of the Pathfinder Roleplaying Game and the new *Pathfinder Online* massively multiplayer online roleplaying game.

The Crusader Road print edition: $9.99
ISBN: 978-1-60125-657-7

The Crusader Road ebook edition:
ISBN: 978-1-60125-658-4

PATHFINDER TALES

THE CRUSADER ROAD

MICHAEL A. STACKPOLE

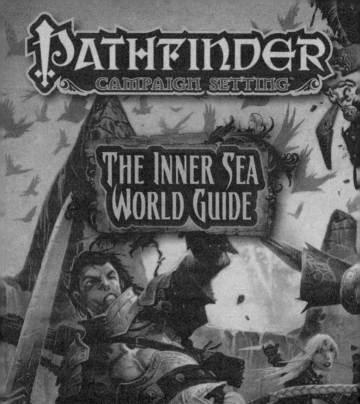

You've delved into the Pathfinder campaign setting with Pathfinder Tales novels—now take your adventures even further! *The Inner Sea World Guide* is a full-color, 320-page hardcover guide featuring everything you need to know about the exciting world of Pathfinder: overviews of every major nation, religion, race, and adventure location around the Inner Sea, plus a giant poster map! Read it as a travelogue, or use it to flesh out your roleplaying game—it's your world now!

EXPLORE YOUR WORLD!

paizo.com

paizo®